Katalyst

Harriet Redfern

Published in 2019 by Ambessa Publishing

First Edition

A CIP catalogue record for this title is available from the British Library.

By the same author

Tabikat 2016

Katseye 2018

ISBN-13: 978-1-9996348-2-7

Prologue

7.00am

"Ambulance Service."

"There's two people that looks really bad on a bench in Pittville Park in Cheltenham," said the girl, her voice trembling, "I think they're dying. Can you send an ambulance?"

"Whereabouts in Pittville Park, caller?" the call handler in the Ambulance Service Control Room in Bristol responded, typing on her keyboard. A map popped up on the screen.

"Near the little caff, where a road goes across the middle," the caller replied, "They're maybe even dead already."

"Are the people breathing?" asked the call handler, ignoring the caller's diagnosis.

"I dunno," the girl replied, "They look to be out of it on drugs. They've been sick an' everything. There's all sorts on the ground by the bench. I don't want to touch nothing. There's a lady trying to help them. She made me call the ambulance."

"Can I speak to the lady?" asked the call handler, patiently.

There was a pause, whilst the call handler heard the girl's voice, more distant now, saying, "He wants to speak to you."

A new female voice, that of a more well-spoken woman, came on the line.

"There are two casualties, a man and a woman," the new voice said, "Both in their twenties, I should say. I think they've probably had a bad batch of drugs, or something very strong, one or the other. Both unconscious, shallow breathing, slow pulses, clammy skin, unresponsive. They'll need to go to hospital."

3

"My dispatcher is sending an ambulance to you now," the call handler replied quickly, looking again at her computer screen, "Are you medically trained?"

"I'm a vet," replied the new speaker, "So, yes."

"Are their airways clear?" asked the call handler, continuing to type, "Are they breathing unassisted? Are they in a safe location?"

"Yes to all those, but they're very weak," came the reply, "They've taken something and the quicker someone can find out what it is, the better. There's nothing I can do for them other than stay here until you send the ambulance."

"The ambulance is on its way," the call handler confirmed, "I'll stay on the line until they get there. Let me know if anything changes. Do you know the names of the casualties or how they came to be there?"

"Never seen them before," the vet's voice replied, "I don't live here. I was working at the racecourse on Gold Cup day yesterday. Just out for a run before going home. I should say they've had a night out after the races and overdone it on some party drugs here in the park. There's plenty of stuff lying around. I've had to run past a lot of it."

"Any idea what?" asked the call handler, anxious to glean anything which might help the ambulance crew, who were now two minutes out from the Ambulance Station at Staverton on the West side of Cheltenham. The two paramedics had already passed behind the North side of Gloucestershire Airport, blue lights flashing and siren blaring, and were turning the ambulance left through a red traffic light onto the Old Gloucester Road.

"Stuff that's been smoked, snorted or swallowed," replied her interlocutor, "Ends of spliffs, empty plastic packets, lager cans, booze bottles, the works. No needles, not that that's to say there aren't any."

There was a shuffling sound and a movement at the caller's end of the line.

"Yes, OK, you can have your phone back," the vet's voice said, and then to the call handler, "The girl who lent me the phone wants to go. She's scared of getting brought into this. Are you sure you don't know them?"

This last remark was clearly addressed to the phone's owner.

The line went dead.

7.05am

Oscar and Lisa had just signed on for their Saturday shift when the call came through.

"Central Cross Drive, Pittville Park," Lisa told her fellow paramedic crew member, "Two people collapsed. What do you bet that's from a night out after Gold Cup day?"

"Too much celebrating," replied Oscar, glumly.

Oscar had lived in Cheltenham all his life, and was well aware of the unbridled chaos which followed the end of the racing on Gold Cup day. Local residents either loved the Festival or hated it.

Some people simply left town, renting out their properties to trusted guests, not wanting to see their normally respectable and quiet environment turned into something resembling a downmarket Spanish holiday resort, but with worse weather. Pubs and bars overflowed with inebriated customers, who spilled out onto the cold and often wet pavements, all talking at the tops of their voices. Young men in tight suits urinated in the hedges whilst their girlfriends shivered in unsuitable clothes and fell off their high heels. A range of accents, many of them Irish, supplemented the local Gloucestershire ones.

Other Cheltenham residents stayed put, either because they were going to the races themselves or were making money from them.

Cheltenham racecourse offered plenty of casual work during the races in its efforts to feed, water and supply alcohol and betting facilities to the tens of thousands of enthusiastic humans who passed through its gates over the four days of the world-famous Cheltenham Festival. Pubs, bars and restaurants around the Regency town took on extra staff and applied for temporary extended licences, some of them quickly metamorphosing into seedy nightclubs. Strippers and pole dancers were hired and pop-up brothels popped up. All hotels and B&B establishments, respectable or otherwise, were fully booked weeks in advance for miles around.

"Magaluf on steroids," Lisa opined, equally glumly, steering the ambulance towards the junction with the Tewkesbury Road, "It's two years ago today that I went to some bloke who'd been in a hit and run near GCHQ. Drug dealer I reckon he was. Someone had bashed his head in. Been out there all night, he had. Dead before they even found him."

"I got one like that last year just after the races," Oscar told her, "Fallen off the top of Cleeve Cloud. He was dead too. It was a real problem moving him. He was in a lot of brambles and grass and bits of broken rocks. There was some gypsy bloke came along and threatened us with a metal bar when we arrived on scene. I'd say the gyppos were camping somewhere around there. He ran off quick enough with it when the police came."

At that moment, the voice of the dispatcher in the Control Room in Bristol came onto the radio.

"Just to let you know, we've lost contact with the caller," she said, "I've tried to call back, but no joy."

"No worries," replied Lisa, as they turned onto Tewkesbury Road, "We're going to the café in the middle of Pittville Park. We should be able to find them easily enough."

7.20am

"Can you send a second truck?" Oscar asked the Control Room, "There are three casualties. I think one of them is the member of the public who you spoke to."

"What's happened?" asked the dispatcher in Bristol, who had taken over the co-ordination of the incident, leaving the call handler free to take other incoming calls.

"The third person, she's got some of the same symptoms as the other two. She's on the ground. Slow pulse, barely conscious, shallow breathing, and I reckon she's hit her head when she went down," Oscar replied, "Thought at first the other two could have had Black Mamba or Spice. But it might not be that, if this third casualty went down after contact with them. There's no-one much around so we can't ask what's happened."

"Second truck is on the road. Is it a job for the HART?" asked the dispatcher.

"Think you're right," Oscar told her, looking at the scene before him. "We've got two on the bench and one on the ground. Something's not right."

"Hazardous Area Response Team being called now," his colleague confirmed, "And the police."

8.00am
Cheltenian News Radio, Traffic News

Cheltenham drivers are advised to avoid the area of Pittville Park between Evesham Road and Albert Road. These roads and also Central Cross Drive are closed because of a police incident. If you are thinking of going to Pittville Park or joining this morning's Park Run on the West side of the park by Tommy Taylor's Lane, please plan your route accordingly.

9.00am
BBC News, South West

Sophie Wilde, Newsreader

In Breaking News just in, we are hearing reports of a Hazardous Area Response Team from the Ambulance Service attending an incident in Pittville Park in Cheltenham. The police are in attendance and have cordoned off the area. Max Bennett has gone to the scene. What can you tell us, Max?

Max Bennett, Reporter

Not a lot at the moment, Sophie.

I'm standing at the bottom end of Pittville Park in Cheltenham. The park is just North of the town centre. It's quite a large park which stretches uphill nearly as far as the racecourse, where the Cheltenham Festival finished yesterday. It's a typical town park, with a children's play area, boating lake, duck pond, and a lot of trees and lawns where families come with picnics. It's popular with joggers and people attending events in the picturesque Pittville Pump Room at the top of the hill.

Last night the park will have seen thousands of people exiting the racecourse after the Festival ended. There was a temporary bar outside the Pump Room, so some of them would probably have stayed around in the park during the evening before going on into the town. It was quite cold yesterday evening and night – it is only March after all – but there was no rain.

The police have cordoned off an area of the park which is by a cafeteria in the centre. From what I can see, there is more than one ambulance in attendance and other vehicles, including a number of police cars. People are being warned to stay well back.

Sophie

The presence of a Hazardous Area Response Team suggests that there is some kind of danger to the public associated with this incident. Do we know anything about what this might be? A gas escape or something like a chemical spillage, for instance?

Max

All I have to go on at the moment is a report given to me by a couple who were out running and were turned away from their usual route by the police. They said they saw some people slumped on a bench and possibly another person on the ground.

Sophie

So, there are three casualties, Max?

Max

That is what the runners told me they saw. Hold on, one of the ambulances seems to be leaving the scene as we speak. It's passing alongside me now down the Evesham Road, presumably taking one or more of the casualties to the local hospital in Gloucester.

Sophie

Thanks, Max. We'll come back to you later.

11.00am
BBC News

Natalie Holmes
Newsreader

It's been reported that three people from Cheltenham were taken to hospital in Gloucester this morning. The people were members of the public who were found in a collapsed state in Pittville Park near Cheltenham racecourse, where the annual Cheltenham Gold Cup race took place yesterday afternoon.

Inspector Christopher Briggs of Gloucestershire Police gave this interview a few moments ago.

Inspector Briggs

Three people have been taken to the Gloucestershire Royal Hospital earlier this morning after been found unconscious in Pittville Park in Cheltenham. We are working to identify the three persons now. They are a young male and female who were found together on a bench near the café at Central Cross Drive in the park. The third individual is a female, who we believe was out running, and who came into contact with the other two persons at around seven o'clock this morning.

Questioner (off screen)

Can you tell us anything about their condition, Inspector?

Inspector Briggs

The young male and female are in very poor condition. We believe them to have been in the park for several hours, possibly all night. I would ask anyone who believes they know these two people to contact the police straightway. I have no information on the third individual at the present time. She is a young woman, probably in her thirties. If anyone in your family has failed to return from their regular morning run, please contact us immediately.

Another questioner (off screen)

Why was a hazard response team sent to the scene, Inspector?

Inspector Briggs

It was requested by the ambulance crew attending the casualties. I am not able to say more at the moment. The area will remain sealed off until we are satisfied that the hazard has been fully dealt with.

First Questioner (off screen)

Are you able to tell us nothing about the nature of the hazard, Inspector? Is it a noxious gas, a chemical spillage, contaminated needles, for instance?

Inspector Briggs

As I said, I am not able to say more at the moment. Our first priority remains to establish the identity of the individuals involved in this incident and to ensure that they are given the best possible medical treatment and ongoing care. That's all for now, thank you.

12.00pm
BBC News

Natalie Holmes
Newsreader

Speculation has been growing about an incident in Cheltenham this morning which resulted in three people being taken to hospital and an area of Pittville Park in the town being cordoned off by the police.

We understand that the cause of the incident to two of the people was initially assumed to be a bad batch of some kind of illegal drugs. But the collapse of a third person who apparently tried to give assistance to the other two has now led to suggestions that something more sinister, such as a nerve agent, may have been involved.

Local BBC News reporter Max Bennett, outside the Gloucestershire Royal Hospital, do we know any more?

Max

This is certainly the rumour which has begun to take hold now, Natalie. The police have released nothing more in the way of information on the incident since the interview earlier this morning with Inspector Briggs of the Gloucestershire Constabulary. The hospital itself has released no statement as yet, but staff coming in and out of this busy place have mentioned hearing that the ambulance crew were initially concerned about contaminated drug paraphernalia but that the decision to call the Hazardous Incident Response Team, the HART, was made in the light of the collapse of the third, unrelated, casualty. The precautions apparently being taken in the hospital have been interpreted by some as those appropriate to a chemical attack, such as a nerve agent or poisonous gas. We are hoping that the hospital will make a further statement soon.

12.30pm
Gloucestershire NHS Trust Statement

Three people were admitted to Gloucestershire Royal Hospital at about 9.30 this morning suffering from the effects of an as yet unknown contaminant. Two of them remain in a critical condition. All necessary precautions are being taken whilst the substance concerned is identified and there is no reason to believe there is any risk to members of the public in Cheltenham.

One Year Earlier

1

If Merlin ap Rhys had hoped to pass unnoticed at the unexpectedly sunny March point to point meeting at Cuffborough, he was destined to be disappointed. Two days after winning the Cheltenham Gold Cup with the talented Irish chaser Tabikat, the equally talented jockey was instantly recognisable to anyone with the least interest in National Hunt racing.

Normally, Merlin would have lapped up the admiring attention. Ever since he had driven his flashy black BMW sports car into the muddy car park, he had been surrounded by waterproof jacketed and green booted people of all ages, some asking for his autograph, others asking after the welfare of the horse on which he had triumphed, but most just wanting to give him their congratulations and wish him well in whatever race he was next due to compete in with his successful equine partner.

Merlin was sure that James Sampfield Peveril, Tabikat's trainer, out and about somewhere on the crowded rural point to point course, would be receiving the same good wishes and responding to the same questions about the famous horse. Tabikat himself was safe at home in the Sampfield Grange yard, alongside his handsome half brother, Katseye, also a recent Festival runner. The yard had had its fair share of eager visitors and well-wishers over the last forty eight hours and the Sampfield Grange staff had been happy to bask in the reflected glory of their stable stars. The earlier victory of the Sampfield Grange hurdler, Curlew Landings, in the Champion Hurdle on the first day of the Cheltenham Festival, had hardly had a chance to sink in before Tabikat's even more spectacular triumph had been added to the week's scarcely believable events.

A large and enthusiastic crowd of local residents had formed outside The Charlton Arms to applaud Tabikat as Sadie Shinkins, yard manager and head lass at Sampfield Grange, had paraded the triumphant steeplechaser along the village street on the morning of the previous day, his Cheltenham Gold Cup Winner rug fastened over his broad back. Behind Tabikat walked a chippy Curlew Landings, sporting his Champion Hurdle Winner rug, and requiring the combined efforts of stable staff Travis Byrne and Kye McMahon to keep him walking in a straight line.

A long coloured banner bearing Tabikat's name had been strung across the front of the half timbered rural coaching inn and the small local brewery which supplied the establishment had already announced that it was to name one of its newest beers after the horse. Sadie had been bursting with pride at the achievement of her magnificent mahogany-coloured charge, who had taken the whole experience in his imperious stride, walking calmly alongside the noisy throng of admirers, with his customary air of a monarch accepting the due adulation of loyal subjects.

A benign early Spring sun had beamed favourably down upon the celebratory proceedings and a light breeze had quietly ruffled Tabikat's dark mane. Curlew Landings, playing second fiddle to his older companion, had been less dignified, but had nevertheless cut an impressive figure in the crowded village street. The stable staff had found themselves pressed by the eager spectators to accept gifts of mints, apples, carrots, and other less suitable offerings for the horses, all of which they had hastily stuffed into bags and jacket pockets to be sorted through later. Tabikat would not be consuming the packet of chocolate buttons given to him by a young well-wisher, but Sadie had accepted them gracefully in the certain knowledge that someone at Sampfield Grange would be glad to eat them on the horse's behalf when the parade party returned to the stable yard.

On Sunday, James Sampfield Peveril, known to his friends in the racing world simply as Sam, was now back to business as usual. His promising young pointer Indian Rocks was due to be ridden that afternoon at Cuffborough races by Sadie Shinkins, who, in addition to her duties at Sampfield Grange, also held an amateur jockey's licence. It was Sadie whom Merlin had really come to see on that bright and chilly afternoon.

Merlin's torrid and mutually satisfying relationship with Sadie had lasted for a little less than four months before being brought to an abrupt end by Sadie's discovery on Merlin's phone of compromising images secretly filmed in a hotel bedroom, and subsequently edited by an employee of an escort agency in Liverpool, following the previous year's Grand National. Sadie and Merlin had been apart for almost eleven months now, during which time a frustrated Merlin had looked in vain for an opportunity to explain to the elusive Sadie the truth of what had happened to him, insofar as he had understood it himself. But now, the story of the production of these and other faked images had become public news, and, on Gold Cup Day, Merlin had extracted a hurried promise from Sadie that she would make time to talk to Merlin following the conclusion of her race at Cuffborough that Sunday.

At one time, Merlin would have sought out James Sampfield Peveril and his staff and offered help in the preparation of the inexperienced Indian Rocks for his race. But he did not wish to do anything which might upset Sadie before she went out to compete. Although Sadie had been riding as an amateur jockey, something which Merlin himself had originally encouraged, for several months now, Merlin had never watched any of her races. He found, quite unexpectedly, that he felt slightly nervous at the prospect of watching her negotiate the Cuffborough fences at racing speed on the young horse. Merlin never gave a moment's thought to his own safety when he was race riding, but Sadie's was a different matter. The thought of her lithe and strong body, which had frequently been pressed naked against his own, lying damaged in the mud of Cuffborough racecourse did not appeal to him at all.

"I mus' be goin' soft," Merlin said to himself, shaking his head, as he approached the parade ring, from which horses had already departed for the start of the race immediately before the one in which Indian Rocks was entered. The earlier race would go off within minutes, but Merlin was not interested in watching an event in which he had no personal stake.

Instead, Merlin stationed himself at the far side of the small parade ring, into which the horses entered in the race in which Sadie was to compete would soon be brought. In the horsebox park, some distance away on a slope to his right, Merlin could see the tough

16

little figure of groom Jackie Taylor, who had led up Katseye for his race at Cheltenham, preparing Indian Rocks, a bright looking chestnut gelding. Sadie, dressed in the green and red silks of Sampfield Grange, was standing nearby. She was talking to Mr Sampfield, the name by which the owner and trainer of the horse was known by his staff, and his stockily built red haired cousin, Gilbert Peveril, an amateur jockey who would be riding one of the older Sampfield Grange horses, Rooker Sunset, in a later race. Sitting expectantly in the back seat of Mr Sampfield's green Range Rover, Merlin could see Teddy and Tessa Urquhart, relatives of Mr Sampfield's mother from Australia. The tailgate of the Range Rover was folded down horizontally to provide a table for a large wicker hamper which contained the remains of the sociable party's earlier lunch.

As Merlin, leaning on the parade ring's white railing, stared idly towards the assembled Sampfield Grange group, he realised that someone had come to stand by his side. Assuming it was another racegoer keen to congratulate him on Tabikat's Gold Cup win, Merlin turned towards the newcomer. He found himself looking into the eager face of Luke Cunningham.

Merlin had met Luke Cunningham once before. Luke, an amateur jockey, and the son of Sir Andrew Cunningham, whose estate was situated close to the Cuffborough course, had been standing with a proprietorial arm around Sadie at Cheltenham racecourse at the November meeting earlier in the season. Merlin had made a point of approaching them, principally to ensure he got a good look at the red-trousered interloper and found out his name. Sadie had effected the introductions, but had then remained silent, looking uncomfortable. For his part, Merlin had adopted the professional demeanour which he affected when meeting racehorse owners in the parade ring, and had interacted with them courteously and with apparent pleasure throughout the introduction and subsequent short chat. Merlin had been quite sure that neither Sadie nor the smiling and flop-haired Luke had had any suspicion of the fury which had been seething in his chest during the brief encounter.

"Good afternoon to you, Mr ap Rhys .. Merlin..," Luke now began, politely, "Luke Cunningham. You will remember, I'm sure, that we were introduced by Sadie Shinkins at Cheltenham last year. Congratulations on your win in the Gold Cup. Terrific animal, that Sampfield horse."

"Thanks, Luke. Yes, I do remember meetin' you," Merlin replied, his annoyance at the appearance of his rival, as he viewed Luke, not showing in his tone, "You come to support Sadie today, 'ave you?"

"Well, not exactly," Luke informed him, with a laugh, "I'm riding against her in the same race, so I shall be trying to get the better of her today."

"Is that so?" Merlin replied, smoothly, gritting his teeth, "'oo shall I put my money on, then? You or Sadie?"

"Well, I think that Sadie is riding the better horse," replied Luke, taking the question seriously, "But she's had less experience than I have at race riding. I was hoping to get a spin in the Foxhunters last week, but unfortunately neither of our good horses managed to qualify."

As Merlin opened his mouth to express manufactured condolences, Luke's well articulated tones suddenly became lower, sounding almost conspiratorial.

"The fact is, Merlin," Luke said, quietly, "I wondered if you might be able to help me out with a bit of inside information."

"What sort of information?" asked Merlin, warily, wondering what was coming next.

"It's about Katalyst," Luke stated, quickly, "What do you know about him?"

"Well, as we speak, nothin'," responded Merlin, taken by surprise, "I assume it's a 'orse you're talkin' about, is it?"

"Yes, that's right," Luke responded, sounding disappointed, "I thought you just might have some news of him."

"Why would you think that?" asked Merlin, his mind moving quickly, "Is it because of the name? Sounds like the 'orse might be from the same line as Tabikat and Katseye, is that it? Wouldn' Mr Sampfield be the man to ask?"

"Of course, yes, my father will be having a word with him as soon as he can," replied Luke, "But seeing you standing here, I thought I'd take the chance of asking you."

"'ow did you come to 'ear of the 'orse, then?" asked Merlin, interested, despite his continuing hostility towards the apparently guileless Luke.

"We were given a whisper that he would be included in the lots for the Cheltenham sale after racing last Thursday," Luke told him, "When we heard the name, especially as we were told that it was spelt with a K, like Katseye, we wondered if the horses were related. My father and I should certainly be interested in acquiring a horse from that family."

Merlin considered for a moment what he knew about the bloodline of Tabikat and Katseye.

"As I recall," he said, slowly, "The Kat part of their names comes from the dam's side. The breeder is a Mr Eoghan Foley in Ireland. Did he put up this 'orse, Katalyst, in the sale, then?"

"Katalyst never came up for sale," Luke replied hurriedly, "The horse was withdrawn before the catalogue went to print. As I say, it was just a whisper. We didn't receive any details."

"I'll keep my ears open," Merlin said, apparently helpfully, although privately not intending that Luke should be the beneficiary of any information which he might acquire, "But your dad is goin' to be up against a lot of other bidders if this one really is from the same family as Tabikat and Katseye."

Luke, it seemed, was now in a hurry to prepare for his race, so the two young men parted company with a quick goodbye. Merlin could see that a lively Indian Rocks and his attendants were now approaching the parade ring, and that Jackie had spotted Merlin by the railing, and was waving enthusiastically.

A few puffy and grey-edged clouds were now decorating the sky, intermittently obscuring the still weak sun, and casting slowly moving dark shadows over the small and rapidly filling parade area. As Jackie established Indian Rocks in a brisk walk around the inside perimeter of the ring, Merlin could see that the youngster was on his toes. The horse's alert head flicked from side to side and his ginger ears moved back and forth as he took in the interesting sights which popped into his ever moving field of vision. Now that more horses were arriving ready for the start of the race, many spectators were drifting across towards the parade ring.

Sadie and Mr Sampfield formed part of Indian Rocks' retinue and duly positioned themselves in the centre of the ring, ready for Sadie to mount. Merlin knew they had recognised him standing by the fence, and gave a thumbs up sign directed at both jockey and trainer. Within seconds, Sam had legged Sadie up onto her excited young runner, and Jackie had led them out onto the nearby course, along which Sadie cantered away to the left, the horse still full of bounce and flinging his head about.

Once the ring had emptied, Sam walked immediately over towards Merlin.

"Indian Rocks is lookin' keen," Merlin commented, "I 'ope 'e's listenin' to 'is jockey."

"Sadie's very good with him," Sam responded, sounding confident, "But he's not had much experience of racing as yet. There are seven horses in this field, and I have told her to make sure she keeps him out of trouble. We don't want the horse panicking."

As Merlin and Sam trudged over towards the muddy earth bank on which many of the day's attendees had situated themselves, along with numerous milling children and accompanying dogs of varying shapes and sizes, Merlin could see the seven runners congregating at the start line, which was situated over to their left. Sadie appeared to be following her employer's instructions and was keeping Indian Rocks slightly apart from the other six horses. Luke Cunningham, mounted on a strong looking bay horse called Merriott Marsh, was already moving into the best position for an advantageous start.

"And they're off!" called out the crackling voice of the amplified commentator, as the horses thundered enthusiastically towards the spectators, passing in front of them to follow the line of the course to the right of the bank. An encouraging cheer arose from the crowd as the field, still closely packed at this early stage, swept past and started to descend the shallow curve which took the course down the steep gradient. Soon the horses would be out of sight behind a row of tall trees, their bare branches newly touched by the first green signs of Spring, which lined the lowest, and largely invisible, section of the slanting course.

"The whole field has cleared the first two obstacles," announced the voice from the nearby loudspeaker, "They're well spread out across the course, with Merriott Marsh and Luke Cunningham in the lead. Property Man and Gracie Samways are hard on their heels. Sampfield Grange's youngster Indian Rocks is running about a bit on the inside of Property Man. Jockey Sadie Shinkins is doing a good job of keeping him focused."

After a short interval, during which not even the commentator appeared to have a good view of the runners, Merlin could make out the horses galloping up towards the brow of the rising ground to the spectators' left, as the field returned to pass its starting point. The race comprised just over two laps of the hillside track, the finishing line being just in front of the point at which Merlin and Sam were standing.

Merlin could tell that the over-enthusiastic Indian Rocks was making Sadie's life very difficult.

"Good girl, *cariad*, you're doin' a great job," Merlin muttered to himself, as the horses swept past the spectators once again, Indian Rocks still tugging at the bit and trying to push his way alongside the dark bulk of the steadier Property Man, "Jus' don't let 'im get squeezed out on the inside at the nex' jump."

According to the disembodied voice of the commentator, however, Merlin's fear on this score soon proved to be well founded.

"And Indian Rocks has run out at the fence on the downhill section!" exclaimed the commentator, "Jockey Sadie Shinkins had no chance and has been dumped straight out of the side door. The horse is now running loose on the course. Take care please, people standing down at the far end. Merriott Marsh continues to lead the remaining runners."

Merlin and Sam could see Sadie in the distance, getting to her feet as Indian Rocks shot away, chasing futilely after the other horses. Luckily, Sadie seemed to be uninjured and was visibly refusing the attentions of a first aider in a hi-viz jacket who had run forward to assist her.

With a quick apology, Sam hurriedly parted company with Merlin, planning to seek out Jackie and Gilbert. The chances were that Indian Rocks, unencumbered by a jockey, would simply follow his fellow competitors back towards the finishing line, where he could be caught. The Sampfield Grange staff needed to be ready to do the catching.

Taking advantage of being unexpectedly left to his own devices, Merlin set off at a brisk jog along the course, aiming to meet Sadie as she trudged disconsolately back up the hill towards the spectators. Sadie had removed her hat and was pushing her dishevelled blonde hair back off her forehead with a brown gloved hand. She looked fed up and disappointed, Merlin thought, with a stab of professional sympathy.

"You OK, *cariad?*" Merlin asked, resisting the temptation to put his arm around his former lover, although his old term of endearment for her had come unprompted to his lips.

"Yes, I'm fine, Merlin," replied Sadie, irritably, clearly more annoyed than hurt, "Indy's gorgeous but he's a real handful sometimes. I thought I'd got him under control, but he just saw his chance to run out and took it before I could stop him."

"'e's green yet," Merlin told her, reassuringly, "'e'll learn better once 'e's 'ad a bit more experience."

Sadie's face creased into a small and rueful smile as she nodded in agreement.

"I know this isn't really the time, *cariad*," Merlin blurted out, deciding to take his chance whilst he had it, "But – that video on my phone last year – I wanted to explain. It was sen' to me out of the blue. I thought someone was tryin' to blackmail me."

"Yes, I heard about it on the radio last week," Sadie responded, as they walked up the slope together, whilst the disembodied commentator continued to inform the spectators of the progress of the race, which was just coming towards its end ahead of them, "Something about that footballer faking videos to make it look like other men were sleeping with his wife. Was that what happened to you, Merlin?"

"Well, sort of," Merlin said, carefully, determined not to say anything untruthful, "It was a bit more complicated than that. I wanted to tell you, Sadie, but you didn' give me a chance. Tell you what, let me drive you back to Sampfield Grange, an' we can 'ave a proper talk in the car. An' I can say 'ello to my three Cheltenham rides when we get there."

Sadie bowed her head and appeared to consider for a moment, finally saying,

"All right, Merlin. I've got something I want to talk to you about too. I thought you might be able to help."

"What's that, then?" Merlin asked, quickly, the recent conversation with Luke Cunningham coming back into his mind.

"Someone's been threatening Tabikat," Sadie replied, starkly.

2

Tegan Colvin was a criminal. She hadn't meant to be, she kept telling herself. It had just been an accident. Now it was too late to put things right. The guilt was keeping her awake at night.

The problem had started when she had been asked to prepare a bedroom previously occupied by an American visitor to The Charlton Arms last Saturday morning. Tegan, quiet, timid and slightly in awe of her employer, worked at the picturesque former coaching inn and pub at the weekends, and, on that fateful day, the flustered manager and regular staff had been trying to deal with a large influx of thirsty strangers into the bar of the usually quiet establishment. A racehorse trained by Mr Sampfield Peveril at nearby Sampfield Grange had won the Cheltenham Gold Cup and been paraded along the road outside the inn. People had come from far and wide to see and take pictures of the victorious creature. Tegan had not joined them. She was scared of horses.

The quiet American guest who had been staying in the large room which overlooked the historic Charlton crossroads had left the previous morning. On Saturday morning, his room had remained as he had left it, owing to the fact that the regular chambermaid had been ill on the previous day and had not come in to work. As this particular room had not been needed again until Saturday afternoon, the manager had concentrated on ensuring that those rooms booked for Friday night had been cleaned and prepared first. She had hoped that the missing chambermaid would be well enough to return to work on Saturday morning, but this had not been the case. So, Tegan had been asked to prepare the room instead.

Mr Casey had left the room in a tidy state. The bed had hardly appeared to have been slept in and the wastepaper basket and bathroom pedal bin had both been entirely empty of litter or discarded bathroom items. The upright chair, pushed slightly back from the writing table which overlooked the crumbling stone cross marking the centre of the intersecting roads outside the window, was the only evidence that the guest had spent any time at all in the room.

Dragging behind her the housekeeping trolley which she had brought, Tegan had carefully stripped the bed, heaping the white sheets and pillow cases in a pile just outside the door. Replacing these with clean bedding had taken a little longer, but Tegan had been satisfied with the neat result. It was a pity, she had thought, that new guests would soon disrupt and spoil her careful handiwork. Quickly, she had cleaned the barely used bathroom, replaced the small flower-decorated containers of complimentary shampoo and bodywash, pocketing a couple for her own use at home, and had run the ancient and heavy vacuum cleaner over the patterned carpet.

Struggling a little with the weight of the housekeeping trolley, Tegan had quickly manoeuvred it outside into the corridor and had locked the bedroom door. As she had started to push the trolley back along the landing, she had heard a metallic clattering sound. Something had dropped from the bottom of the trolley, something which had evidently fallen from the heap of sheets as she had stuffed them into the laundry bag attached to the end. Tegan had bent down to pick the item up. It had been a small gold ingot on a silver chain.

Scarcely stopping to think, Tegan, like a magpie, had slipped the shiny item into the pocket of her green cotton overall. She could hand it in at the reception desk later, she had told herself. But she hadn't. Now it was too late, because the police had attended the hotel on the following Monday, when Tegan had not been working, and had asked questions about Mr Casey, who, the manager had been shocked to learn, had met with a fatal accident somewhere near Cheltenham.

The bright gold ingot on its silver chain had not been missed, or at least no-one had asked about it, so perhaps no-one knew of its existence. Tegan now had her lucky find hidden under the pillow in her tiny bedroom in the poky flat above the local garage, the home which she shared with her brother Graham, a car mechanic, and their infirm mother. Graham and Tegan's father had left his family to its own devices long ago, and it was generally assumed that he was now in prison somewhere. If he wasn't, he certainly deserved to be, Tegan had often heard her mother say.

Tegan knew that she should be in the kitchen making something for the household to eat that evening. But the lure of the little gold ingot was too great. She pulled it out from under the blue cover of the pillow. She draped the silver chain over her hand and held the pendant up to the light slanting in through the dirty window, where a little of the dull sun reflected from its bright surface. There were odd markings imprinted on the side of the ingot, which Tegan decided must be hallmarks, which indicated that the gold was genuine.

Perhaps her bed was too unsafe a hiding place for such a valuable item, thought Tegan. Her mother was unlikely to find it, as she was scarcely able to move from her, once temporary, bed in the living room without assistance, but Tegan was fearful that Gray might come across it. Tegan knew that her brother was often short of money for the pub, and for the weed and Es that he liked to buy. Gray just might think he could find some loose change in her room. If he found the gold ingot, she would never see it again.

Scrambling off the bed, Tegan went to the corner of the dark little room and lifted the threadbare brown carpet. It came away easily from the skirting board, from which it had been lifted many times. Beneath it was a loose floorboard. Pulling a screwed up tissue from her pocket, Tegan quickly wrapped the precious item in the creased paper, and levered up the edge of the old wooden board. Beneath it was a dark cavity, which probably contained black spiders and other unseen horrors, but Tegan tried hard not to think of those. Reaching in her hand as far as she dared, she gently placed the makeshift little parcel onto the decaying plasterboard between the wooden joists. Quickly replacing the floorboard and smoothing the carpet down over it, Tegan stood up and wiped the dust from her hands. The ingot would be safe there, she thought. No-one would find it now. She went into the kitchen.

At about the same time that Tegan Colvin was attempting to protect her stolen goods from discovery, James Sampfield Peveril and his Australian cousins, Teddy and Tessa Urquhart, were sitting in the spacious Sampfield Grange drawing room. The wide leaded window overlooked the neatly tended garden, which was copiously decorated with clumps of purple and yellow crocuses, still in healthy bloom, having eclipsed the smaller and earlier waking snowdrops, the first flowers which had dared to show their white heads to the potentially hostile early Spring air. The grassy bank below the hedge was studded with companionable groups of nodding daffodils, behind which could be seen the quietly sunlit slopes on which the horses were exercised. The trackside trees, reaching upwards along the slope which ran from the yard behind the back wall of the garage, glowed green with the beginnings of new leaves, whilst thick clusters of bluebells were starting to push skyward alongside their trunks. The cheerful sound of hidden songbirds could be heard as they called cautiously to each other across the brightening lawn.

A darkly carved Italian writing desk and chair stood by the wide and leaded window, so as to allow anyone seated there to take advantage of the peaceful view. Beside the desk stood a tall lamp with a recently repaired decorated parchment shade. A large and infrequently used television screen occupied a convenient gap in the run of deep bookshelves, providing a strange contrast to the old fashioned decadence of its surroundings.

A neatly sliced Victoria sponge and a stack of newly baked fruit scones were arranged on a cake stand alongside the low and well-polished mahogany coffee table in the centre of the room. Gold rimmed white teacups and matching saucers and plates were laid out close by, together with a large silver teapot, resting on a wrought metal trivet. Lewis, the male half of the couple responsible for the housekeeping at Sampfield Grange, had carefully carried the bone china teaset and the accompanying food into the drawing room half an hour earlier, returning at intervals, ostensibly to replenish the contents of the teapot, but also in the hope of picking up any family gossip which he could relay to his wife, Kelly, in the kitchen.

"I believe we have our way forward at last," Sam said, as Lewis reluctantly closed the door, "I spoke to the Foleys this morning, and also to Merlin. Tabikat goes to Aintree in three weeks."

"Is that to the biggie?" asked Tessa, reaching forward to take a slice of Kelly's excellent cake.

"The biggie? Oh, you mean the Grand National," responded Sam, initially confused by Tessa's expression, "No, Mrs Niamh Foley, who represents the owners, apparently didn't want him to be risked in that, but Genie Foley, her brother in law, who bred the horse, told me that they would like to get another run into him before the end of the season. Aintree is a bit soon after Cheltenham and we'll have to hope that he's ready. The only other options are to go to the final big Chase at Sandown Park at the end of April, although that's a handicap, so not the same sort of race as at Cheltenham and Aintree, or else to the Punchestown Festival to defend Tabikat's title in the Gold Cup there. So, I've told Bethany to put Tabikat in for the Bowl Chase on the first day, the Thursday, at Aintree. If that doesn't come off, then we will have to think again. I know Ranulph Dicks is sending his Fan Court to run in a two mile Chase on the same day, so the horses can travel there together."

"Sounds like a plan, James," Tessa Urquhart responded, not quite following all the technical details of Sam's careful explanation, "We'd love to see Aintree. And it'll be a great few days out if we stay there for the whole meeting. But what's stopping you going for the Irish race you said Tabikat aced last year? That's another great event too, if the people we spoke to in Helen's crowd are to be believed."

Teddy and Tessa had been guests in the box of Sir John Garratt and his wife Helen during the opening and final days of the Cheltenham Festival and had been able to bask in the reflected glory of the respective victories of Curlew Landings and Tabikat. Even Katseye's second place in his three mile hurdles race had been an occasion for a consolatory glass of champagne.

"The Foleys don't want Tabikat back in Ireland," Sam told her, firmly, "Declan Meaghan said there was some problem at their yard with threats so they want the horse to stay in England at the moment. That's why he has been here with us since January."

"Yeah, you told us about that before," put in Teddy, standing up to help himself to a warm scone, "Shonky business, this horseracing, if you ask me. All that jiggery-pokery that happened with Ryan and Travis in Vic, and now we're having it here too."

Such was Teddy's reference to the threats which the Urquharts' son Ryan, and his young friend, jockey Travis Byrne, had received from Australian trainer Jack Tytherleigh. The threats had resulted in a stitch up, as Travis had explained to Sam and the Urquharts, to ensure the suspension of Travis's jockey's licence. The two young men had uncovered evidence of horse doping in the Tytherleigh racing yard, where Travis had worked, but action to prevent them from revealing what they knew had been swift and brutal. Travis was now working at Sampfield Grange on an informal basis until something could be done to ensure that the suspicious findings could be investigated through the proper channels.

"As far as Travis is concerned," replied Sam, "We'll be getting some advice back from my contact at the British Horseracing Authority soon, I'm sure. He's been making some off the record enquiries with Racing Victoria about Travis's case. In the meantime, Travis can carry on looking after Curlew Landings as long as he needs to stay here. He's already done an excellent job with the horse, and deserves a lot of the credit for preparing him for his big wins at Wincanton and Cheltenham."

"What's next for Curlew, then?" asked Tessa, "Is there a race for him too at Aintree?"

"Regrettably, no," Sam told her, "This is a more difficult one. I'd like to see Curlew Landings run again before we put him away for the summer, but all the races at Aintree are a longer distance than he's been running over this season. Aintree is a flat course, and he's done well at the longer distance on flat courses in the past, but both Merlin and I would like him to stay with the two miles which he's been used to."

"So, what are you thinking, then?" asked Teddy, in a voice which Lewis could probably have heard in the kitchen without the bother of lurking in the hallway outside the drawing room door, "Ryan will be stoked if he can keep Curlew in training a bit longer. He was bending my ear again this morning, telling me what a little ripper of a horse Curlew is."

"Well," began Sam, "Before I answer that, let me tell you about the rest of my plans for the other horses at Aintree. And then I want to ask you both a favour."

"'Course, James, you just name it," Teddy replied, immediately, as Tessa nodded in agreement, "After what you've done for Travis and Ryan, we owe you."

"I'm planning to enter both Katseye and Highlander Park in races on the final day of the Aintree Festival. There's a three mile hurdle race for Katseye, which the Foleys agree with me would suit him. I've sent a message to the owner, Mr Ardizzone, to ask for his approval for the entry. And there's a conditional jockeys' race over two miles at the end of the meeting, in which I thought Kye and Highlander Park might take their chance, given that we're already there that day. So, Sampfield Grange will have a double presence on the day of the Grand National, even though we don't have a runner in the big race itself."

"Helen told us that they'll be running their Alto Clef in the National," Tessa put in, "She said the horses have to qualify but they were sure Alto Clef would get in."

"Yes, I'm confident he will," Sam told her, "Which means that you get to be Helen's guests on Grand National day."

"Strewth, James, I can't see how we'd be doing you any favours," Teddy pointed out, "Sounds like we're the ones being well looked after here. What's it like at Aintree, then?"

"I have to admit that I have never been there," Sam told his cousin, "It's only in this last season that I have had horses of sufficient calibre to need to look that far afield for races. I didn't expect to have either Tabikat or Katseye in my string at all. I thought Tabikat would be back with the Meaghan yard, and Katseye was sent to me out of the blue by his previous owner, Mrs Crosland. If it weren't for those two horses, I would have found something more local for Kye and Highlander Park, and, as I say, there's nothing for Curlew Landings at Aintree anyway."

"OK, so what's the deal with Curlew Landings?" asked Tessa, sensing that this was the source of the forthcoming request for a favour.

"I want him to run at the Punchestown Festival in their Champion Hurdle," Sam told his expectant audience, "Some of the Irish contenders in the Champion Hurdle at Cheltenham are likely to be running and Merlin is keen to put Curlew up against them again."

"Trav'll be well in with that idea," commented Teddy, as he and Tessa waited to learn what Sam was intending to ask of them.

"I wondered," Sam said, his words coming out in a rush, "Whether you would be willing to extend your visit and come with me to Punchestown? I'd like to take Travis to look after Curlew Landings, as usual. But Sadie told me last week that Ranulph Dicks's daughter, Amelia, who has just come back from a visit to Australia, thought she recognised Travis at Cheltenham. I can't think there will be many people from Australia at Punchestown, but it is an international event, and I would appreciate some back up if Travis should be recognised. As you know, up until last week, everyone thought Travis was Ryan Urquhart, and a member of my family. Your presence at the races might just allow that assumption to remain in place. I'm not asking you to deceive anyone deliberately, of course. If anyone asks directly, I will say that he is the son of a former employee of yours, and a family friend, which I understand to be nothing less than the truth."

As Teddy and Tessa stared at him in surprise, Sam added, hurriedly,

"But I quite understand, if you would rather not do this. I know that it is an imposition on you."

"You having a laugh, James?" asked Teddy, eventually, "You invite us to join you at a top race meeting in Ireland, and you think we're doing you a favour by agreeing? 'Course we'll come with you. Leo'll be right looking after things at home for a bit longer. As for Travis, as far as I see it, he's our responsibility, not yours. You've done plenty for him already, James."

"That's very kind of you," Sam said, relief sounding in his voice, "I have never been to Punchestown races, either, so this will a new departure for all three of us."

As Sam spoke, there was a knock at the drawing room door, and Lewis appeared in the open doorway, looking flustered.

"Mr Sampfield," he said, "I'm sorry to interrupt, but Sadie would like a word with you in the yard. She says that Curlew's gone down in his box. There's something wrong with him."

3

Sadie Shinkins' carefully ordered world had been thoroughly shaken up. The apparent threat directed at Tabikat a few days ago had been bad enough, then Indy's run out at the downhill jump at the Cuffborough point to point course had put paid to their chances in his race, and now something had gone wrong with Curlew Landings too. On top of that, there was the nagging regret over her erstwhile lover, Merlin ap Rhys.

Merlin's willingness to listen to Sadie's concerns about Tabikat had been the overriding factor in her decision to accept the offered lift home from Cuffborough to Sampfield Grange in Merlin's black sports car. Merlin and Sadie had enjoyed much indecorous fun in the leather seats of the car during their brief relationship over a year before, but Sadie was not keen to revisit those memories just at the moment. Her self-imposed eleven months apart from Merlin, who had tried hard, at least at first, to communicate with her, had initially come at some cost to her emotional well-being. Neverthless, she had tenaciously stuck to her decision to put aside what she knew to have been a largely sexually driven relationship and one which had appeared to involve more commitment on her part than on her lover's. As a result, she had gradually developed a hard won measure of self-respect, together with a determination that she would in future hold her own in any relationship, rather than put herself again at the beck and call of a selfish partner.

Sadie's more recent liaison with the pleasant and well-mannered Luke Cunningham had been, as a result, a much calmer affair than the torrid period which she had spent with Merlin. But therein had lain the problem. Sadie had truly enjoyed herself with the arrogant and self-centred young Welshman, whereas the relationship with Luke had felt more akin to that which Sadie observed between her sister Kelly and Kelly's husband Lewis. Sadie and Luke shared much in common, with their respective equestrian activities and local Somerset background, but Luke's attentions had lacked the overt sexual drive which Sadie had experienced from Merlin, and which, she had to admit, she had felt for Merlin in return. Even almost a year apart had hardly diminished her desire for Merlin, although Sadie had now become well practised in disguising this from everyone, including Merlin himself.

Having checked that the disobedient Indian Rocks was safe and that Mr Sampfield was happy for Jackie to drive the horsebox home with Mrs Urquhart for company in the cab, Sadie had congratulated Luke Cunningham on Merriott Marsh's win in the recently concluded race, and had told him that Merlin wanted to visit Tabikat but had no time to wait around for the arrival of the rest of the Sampfield Grange party. Luke had been too pleased with his victory to raise any objections.

"So, what's been goin' on with Tabikat then?" Merlin had asked, as his unsuitable car had slipped and swerved over the churned up mud which lay in between the car park and the exit gate from the Cuffborough point to point course, "You said someone 'ad been threatening 'im? What with?"

Sadie had pulled a folded piece of paper from her jacket pocket.

"With this," she had said, smoothing it out flat and holding it towards Merlin.

Merlin had given the paper a brief glance as he had waited to turn out into the stream of Sunday afternoon traffic on the main road at the end of the short lane leading from the gate. It had shown a childishly drawn picture of a stick-legged brown horse with a cylindrical body and outstretched head galloping up a scribbled green slope, its black tail streaming behind. On its back was the figure of a rider in a blue shirt decorated with a yellow star. One of the rider's arms was lifted up and holding what looked like a whip. Lines of roughly drawn people, with a variety of hairstyles and wearing a range of strangely coloured outfits and hats, were standing in a ragged group near the horse. The sun, with the benefit of a smiling face, overlooked the scene. A few pencilled clouds with m-shaped birds in front of them punctuated a sketchily drawn sky. Underneath the drawing was the single word Tabikat.

Merlin had been expecting some type of abusive social media trolling message, complete with foul language, to be shown to him on the screen of a mobile phone. He had been on the receiving end of plenty of those in the past, when his riding had not been to the liking of those who had bet their money on his rides but had not obtained the financial outcome which they had wanted. He had certainly not expected Sadie to show him a child's sketch, and for a moment was unsure what to say, eventually resorting to a statement of the obvious.

"Looks like a kid's drawin' to me," he had said, carefully, "What's up with that? Where did it come from?"

"Someone gave it to us when we paraded Tabsi and Curlew outside The Charlton Arms yesterday," Sadie had told him, "There were a lot of children there handing us sweets and presents for the horses."

"So what's the problem then?" had asked Merlin, mystified, "Some little kid just wanted to give you a picture of me an' Tabikat winnin' the Gold Cup."

"It's what's on the back, Merlin," Sadie had gone on, firmly, "I'd better read it out loud, or you'll drive into something. It's in text language as if it was supposed to be a message on a phone. It says **I cu at Chelts agen I brak ur legs.**"

"OK, I see the problem now," had commented Merlin, after a pause, "'oo's legs are they after breaking then, mine or the 'orse's?"

"I assume it's Tabsi they mean," Sadie had told him, crossly, "His name's on the front, not yours. It isn't always about you, Merlin."

"Sorry," Merlin had replied hastily, realising that he was in danger of shattering the fragile truce which had been so carefully struck up with Sadie, "It's just that I get a lot of this type of abusive crap. It's not usually directed at the 'orses, that's all. 'Ave you shown it to Mr Sampfield?"

"No, not yet, he's been so busy since Friday with people calling him and having Travis's problems to deal with too," Sadie had responded.

Merlin had thought for a moment.

"Did you see 'oo gave it to you?" he had asked, "Was it a kid or someone older?"

"That's just the problem, I don't know," Sadie had admitted, ruefully, "There were three of us there, me with Tabsi, and Kye and Travis leading Curlew. It was chaos with all the people swarming around, and we were trying to keep the horses calm, especially Curlew, who got a bit excited. Tabsi was as good as gold, as usual. So we just stuffed everything we were given into our pockets and into a bag which someone gave Kye with carrots in it. I don't even know if it was me who took the drawing, let alone who gave it to us. We emptied everything out when we got back to the yard and I took the picture to put on Tabsi's door. Then I saw the message on the back. You said you're used to getting nasty messages from horrible people. What should we do about this one, then?"

"It's weird it should be written like it was a text," Merlin had said, slowly, "Why write it like that if it's on a piece of paper?"

"Maybe the person couldn't spell properly," Sadie had suggested, "Perhaps they write things down like that all the time."

"Per'aps they tol' the kid 'oo did the drawin' to write it down for 'em, and it was the kid that couldn' spell," Merlin had initially guessed, but, then, with a sudden flash of insight, had added, "Or maybe it was a text message to start with and someone copied it down onto the paper from the screen on the phone."

"Why would they do that?" Sadie had asked.

"What if it was the only way of getting the message across?" Merlin had said, "Maybe they didn' 'ave the number of the phone they wanted to send it to."

"Tabsi doesn't have a phone," Sadie said, with a sudden giggle.

"An' 'e can't read either!" added Merlin, laughing too.

There had been a short silence, as Merlin had slowed the car to make the turn into the road which led past The Charlton Arms. For a second, things had felt almost friendly again between the two of them.

"Look, *cariad,*" had said Merlin, the old endearment slipping out unintended once again, "The message says Cheltenham, isn' it? Tabikat's goin' nowhere near Cheltenham for months now. If he runs at all again this season, it'll be either Aintree or Punchestown, or maybe Sandown, but definitely not Cheltenham. So my suggestion is that we do nothin' at the momen' an' I'll ask around a bit to see if any of the other jocks in the Gold Cup 'ave 'ad anythin' similar. It's probably just some shitty punter 'oo lost a lot of money on one of the other 'orses, and doesn' want Tabikat runnin' in the Gold Cup again."

"OK," Sadie had responded, as Merlin drove the car in through the gates of Sampfield Grange, "That makes sense. And Merlin, about those pictures on your phone last year...."

Merlin had stopped the car engine and waited, wondering what Sadie was about to say.

"I've been thinking about it a lot," Sadie had said carefully, "I was angry with you last year because I found out that you were cheating on me and it looked like you were watching recordings of it, like it was porn, on your phone too. I know now that you somehow got dragged into a weird mess with that footballer and the sex worker who was killed in Liverpool, so maybe it was different to what it seemed to me then. You said something about blackmail, so it must have been something nasty. But it's not my business, Merlin, and you don't need to explain. I'm not your wife and we weren't even living together, so you hadn't promised me anything. What you do with your life is up to you."

This was a long speech for Sadie to make, but it was one which she had planned the previous day. It had made her feel better to get the words off her chest and to give herself an appearance of authority. Like the horses, Merlin needed to think Sadie was in control, even if she herself knew that they, and Merlin, were capable of getting the better of her if they saw their chance, just as Indy had done this afternoon.

Merlin had taken a deep breath.

"Fair enough," he had said, after a pause, "I'm 'appy with that, just so long as we can talk to each other again without all this bad feelin' 'anging over us."

So the two of them had got out of the jockey's flashy car and had spent half an hour with Tabikat, Katseye, and Curlew Landings, and had listened to Travis's enthusiastic plans for the future of his talented charge, who was now standing in his box looking like a drunk.

Contrary to Lewis's agitated announcement to Mr Sampfield, Curlew had not gone down in his box, but certainly looked as if he was thinking about it. Whatever had happened to the horse had happened very suddenly, a white faced Sadie told her employer, when he arrived in shirtsleeves outside Curlew's stable, not having paused even to put on his customary hacking jacket. Travis stood in the box with the unsteady Curlew, stroking his brown neck and talking soothingly to him. Curlew's head was dropped towards the floor of the box and his breath blew from his nostrils in gentle snorts as though he were snoring. Teddy and Tessa Urquhart had followed Sam down the path from the boot room with Lewis, and stood nearby, ready to offer any help, but in reality having no idea what they could do.

"I just found him like this, Mr Sampfield," Travis stammered, as Sam looked at him with inquisitorially raised eyebrows, "He was right as Larry this morning. Did a bonzer workout, just like normal. Left him with a haynet and some carrots over lunchtime. Couple of hours later, I find him like this, as if he's been on the grog or something."

"Have you called Rachel?" Sam asked Sadie, referring to Rachel Horwood, the equine vet who looked after the Sampfield Grange horses. Sadie nodded wordlessly.

Sam quickly turned to Travis, asking hurriedly, "What's he eaten today? Has he had plenty of water? Did he pick anything up out on the gallops? Ragwort, foxgloves – it's bit early for those outside, though - privet cuttings, nightshade, old acorns? Something poisonous infecting his foot? Have you checked the hay? What about the other horses?"

"Jackie's checked everything in the feed room," Sadie told Sam, before Travis could speak, "It's all clean. And we've checked the other horses too. It's just Curlew who's like this. Kye's gone up on the gallops to see if we can see anything Curlew might have eaten or trodden on without Travis noticing."

"He didn't eat anything outdoors," Travis put in, firmly, "I would've seen."

"Kye's right to check, though, Travis," Sam put in, keenly aware of how upset Travis was, "We have to look at everything, likely or unlikely. The vet will ask us the same questions. No-one's blaming you."

Travis nevertheless looked miserable, as he ran one hand through his rumpled fair hair and patted Curlew's neck with the other. The horse seemed oblivious to his carer's presence, and continued to sway gently, his nose almost touching the floor.

"You'll be right, Curlew, mate," Travis said softly, "The vet's coming to look after you."

After an anxious twenty minutes, during which Sadie and the other yard staff assembled as much information as they could about Curlew's activities and demeanour during the earlier part of the day, the sound of Rachel Horwood's mud spattered black four by four vehicle could be heard entering the gates, shortly followed by the slam of the vehicle door.

"Good afternoon Mr Sampfield and everyone. So, what's been going on here?" asked the forthright young red haired vet, as she entered Curlew's box and stood looking at him, her every action followed by the watchful eyes of Sam, Sadie and Travis. The Urquharts and Lewis had by now returned to the house, and Kye and Jackie were attending to the other horses, who had been observing the unexpected human activity with interest.

"Have you been giving young Curlew sedatives?" Rachel went on, stroking the horse's neck, "He looks like he's waiting to have his teeth done. You've overdone it a bit, though."

"No, not at all," Sadie assured her, "All he's had is his usual feed and water. As far as anyone can remember, his poo and wee were normal this morning. Travis said he did all his usual exercise work and seemed just the same as he always does. Then, we found him like this about an hour ago."

"So what checks have you already done on him, Sadie?" asked Rachel, setting down her large canvas bag and pulling open the zip.

"Skin pinch shows good hydration, his coat's fine, both eyes look normal although he has them half closed, his mouth and gums look the same as usual, no injuries I can see. His gut seems to be working properly, as far as I can hear by putting my ear against his sides and belly. There's no heat or signs of pain in his legs. He isn't in any sort of distress, just wobbly and half asleep."

As Sadie stopped for breath, Rachel interjected, "Good work, Sadie. Let's see if I can find out anything more."

With the help of a stethoscope, Rachel also listened to Curlew Landings' internal workings and then, lifting Curlew's tail, she stuck a thermometer up the unprotesting animal's rear end.

"Heartbeat's a bit slow, but nothing out of the ordinary for a fit horse at rest. Temperature's normal. Nothing poisonous stuck in him anywhere that I can see, at least. He's a bit too unsteady for me to pick up his feet just here. I don't want him going down and getting injured or cast. I can't hear anything to suggest colic and he's not presenting with anything which looks like colic, anyhow. Best thing I can do is to take some bloods for now and you keep him under observation until we have more information. If he does a pee, try to get some of that for testing too. I'll have to take the bloods back to the surgery, as you don't have the facilities I need here, Mr Sampfield. It won't take me long. No food or water for him, either, please."

Fifteen minutes later, the phone shrilled in Bethany Morgan's little office in the yard. Bethany herself was no longer there, as the previous day had been her last at Sampfield Grange before she had left to join her husband and baby in their new home in Devon. Sadie had been waiting anxiously by the phone, having left Curlew Landings under Travis's vigilant supervision, and snatched up the handset from its cradle.

"It's Rachel," announced the disembodied female voice from the other end of the line, "Looks like your lad Curlew's been hitting the club scene."

"What do you mean?" asked Sadie, as Sam, alerted by the sound of the telephone, came to stand beside her. Sadie pressed the button to turn on the phone's loudspeaker, so that they could both hear what Rachel had to say.

"Your horse has been doing K-bombs," Rachel told her, baldly, "He's drugged up like a Ket-head at a student party. It should wear off in an hour or two, but you'll need to keep a close eye on him for the rest of the day."

"K-bombs? Ket-head?" exclaimed Sam, slowly grasping the meaning of Rachel's explanation, "You mean Curlew's had ketamine? We don't have any of that here."

"Well, somebody does," Rachel told him.

4

Tabikat had become a superstar. Watching the stately progress of the Gold Cup winner as he was led by Sadie around the centre path of the Aintree parade ring before the Bowl Chase, Sam could see that Tabikat was the centre of everyone's attention.

"Look, thair's Tabikat," Sam heard spectators telling each other, "Yez know, the one that's won the Gold Cup at Cheltnem."

"'E's luvlee," enthused a female voice, "An' that jockey that rides 'im isn' 'alf bad either."

This latter comment, spoken at a volume designed to carry some distance, had been made especially for the benefit of Merlin, who was at that moment descending the steps which led down from the weighing room, and whose appearance had been noted by the small group of sharply dressed young women who had placed themselves as close as possible to the route to be taken by the emerging jockeys. Noting that Sadie and Tabikat were now at the far end of the parade ring, being pointed at and commented upon by those racegoers who had congregated there, Merlin flashed his three female admirers a quick smile and a wink as he passed them.

"Ooh, look, 'e fancies yez," shrieked one of them, as the three women collapsed in a fit of giggles, "Come ou' with me ternigh', wil' yez, luv?"

Although Merlin heard the invitation, he was careful to show no sign of having done so. The last thing he wanted, he thought to himself as he approached the assembled group of Tabikat's connections in the neatly mown grassy centre of the parade ring, was another unplanned night out in the treacherous territory of the city of Liverpool.

Tabikat's supporters today, Merlin could see, consisted of trainer James Sampfield Peveril and his Australian cousins, Teddy and Tessa Urquhart. With them, Merlin recognised Eoghan Foley, the former Irish jockey who had bred Tabikat. There was no sign of the two female members of the Foley family, one of whom, Niamh Foley, usually represented Levy Brothers International, the bank which owned Tabikat, at his races, and her sister Caitlin. With Eoghan Foley instead was someone Merlin recognised from Gold Cup day. She was a small and strong-looking young woman, dark haired and dark eyed, who looked uncomfortable in her red floral dress and shiny black stiletto heeled shoes. She wore large sunglasses, currently pushed back and upward over her thick hair, and was listening without comment to the discussion between the others in the group whilst her gaze followed Tabikat's circular progress around the parade ring path.

Crossing between two of the parading horses, Merlin spotted someone else he knew to have a connection to Tabikat. Racing tipster to the Smart Girls, Stevie Stone was the daughter of Tabikat's former owner, the now deceased Mrs Susan Stonehouse. Merlin had raced in Susan Stonehouse's purple and gold colours on the first occasion on which Tabikat had attempted to win the Cheltenham Gold Cup. Now Tabikat raced in the gold stars on a blue background of Levy Brothers International, who seemed to have decided to send the horse to be trained permanently at Sampfield Grange, moving him earlier in the year from his previous base with County Meath trainer Brendan Meaghan. Merlin had been surprised to learn of this decision, particularly since it also appeared to preclude Tabikat defending his title as the Gold Cup winner at last year's Punchestown Festival. Instead, the horse would contest today's Bowl Chase at Aintree.

Merlin had no doubt that he and Tabikat would win their shortly upcoming race. Tabikat, he had learned, had not raced at Aintree before, but this particular race, slightly shorter in distance than the Cheltenham Gold Cup, was over the conventional fences of the sharp Mildmay course, rather than the extended route with the distinctively large fences, some individually named, so well known to the general public from the televised extravaganza of the famous Grand National Handicap Chase. Most of this occasional racing public were probably unaware that the Grand National Festival at Aintree racecourse was an event lasting three days, commencing on the Thursday prior to the great spectacular itself, and that two other races had already been run over the same challenging fences, albeit over a shorter distance. The first of these races was due to be run that same afternoon, an Open Hunters' Chase for amateur riders.

Stevie Stone, with the help of her talking kitten, Tabby Cat, whose racing knowledge was supplied by an invisible and apparently permanently hungover Essex lad called Jayce, had tipped Tabikat to win the Bowl Chase. It was not a difficult tip, thought Merlin, watching the popular female internet tipster, her long multi coloured hair snaking down her back, moving towards a group of eager girls by the parade ring, making ready to ask them their opinions about the horses in the race. Tabikat, notwithstanding the strange gaps in his pedigree, was by far the classiest horse there, and only one of his rivals today had competed against him in the Cheltenham Gold Cup less than a month ago. Admittedly, two of the runners had been placed in the King George VI Chase at Kempton Park on Boxing Day, one of whom had also been the winner of this same race last year. But neither of the main rivals, The Page of Cups and Macalantern, who had followed Tabikat up the hill at Cheltenham, were here today. The result was that Tabikat had become a short odds-on favourite, and Tabby Cat's and Jayce's main challenge had been to suggest which of the remainder of the nine strong field would be likely to be placed second.

The first day of the Aintree meeting had been favoured by bright Spring sunshine and unexpectedly warm temperatures. A timorous breeze from the East carefully lifted the hems of the numerous flags which fluttered weakly from the roofs of the extensive white temporary buildings erected alongside the Grand National course, ready for Saturday's climax to the season's final meeting. The parade ring itself was orderly and calm, the expertly managed procession of experienced Grade 1 chasers circling the tidy groups of connections standing quietly in the centre of the equine arena.

The familiar routine of the preparations for the race had helped to calm Sam's jangled nerves. The drive to Aintree, made in the company of Ranulph Dicks, the trainer of the haughty Fan Court who was to run in the first race of the day, a two mile Novices' Chase, had been accomplished by navigating an interminable tangle of crawling road works and interlinked motorways. Sam had rarely ventured further North than Warwick, and so was unfamiliar with the network of major routes in the area between Birmingham and Liverpool. Overhead blue signposts referring to The Lakes invoked half-forgotten memories of summer holidays with the family of his old schoolfriend Frank Stanley, during which Sam had learned to sail, kayak and rock climb, skills for which he had nowadays no further use.

Sam, having never visited Aintree racecourse before, had been taken by surprise by the busy urban environment in which the famous facility was situated. The Range Rover containing the two Somerset trainers had edged past retail parks and traffic lights, before arriving at the congested junction with the Melling Road, in which the Owners' and Trainers' entrance was to be found. Fortunately, Ranulph Dicks had been more familiar with the area and had been able to direct Sam, the driver, with reasonable confidence.

Standing in the parade ring, where the Liverpool traffic could be heard buzzing busily on the other side of the Red Rum garden, Sam had been relieved to find that Sadie, together with Ranulph's travelling head lad, had already settled Tabikat and Fan Court into their Aintree accommodation. The two horses had travelled together from North Somerset earlier in the day and their shared box had negotiated the tortuous route without serious delay. Notwithstanding the unfamiliar nature of the surrounding environment, the stable yard and its raceday routines had been reassuringly normal, and Sam's strange feeling of agitation had abated a little as he had watched the methodical activities which had for so long been part of his life.

The unexpected elements of the day's experiences had been compounded by the appearance in the Owners and Trainers facility of Eoghan Foley with his niece Feanna Foley by his side. Eoghan was a wiry and fit looking man, with dark hair turning grey, and an open and friendly smile. Slightly shorter than Sam, he walked quickly, but with a stiff-legged limp, a legacy of the smashed knee which had ended his career as a jockey over thirty years earlier.

Whilst Sam had expected to meet representatives of the Foley family at Aintree, it had been Niamh Foley, the mother in law of the owner, who had recently been in attendance when the horse ran. Sam had first met Feanna, the jockey who had steered Tabikat's half-brother Katseye to his Irish point to point victories, on Gold Cup Day at the Cheltenham Festival. She seemed a serious sort, Sam had once again surmised, as he had shaken hands with the raven haired young woman, whom he had judged to be in her early thirties.

"I am very pleased to see you again, Miss Foley," Sam had told Eoghan's niece, "I imagine you are looking forward to seeing Katseye run on Saturday?"

"Indeed I am," Feanna Foley had responded, in a warm Kerry accent similar to that of her uncle, "But today I am here to represent my mother and my sister. I am happy to be seeing Tabikat again. His dam was the first of the horses which we bred at Enda's Farm and we are very proud of him, to be sure."

"With every justification," Sam had agreed, "And I feel very fortunate that your sister's family has shown their confidence in Sampfield Grange and allowed us to continue to train the horse."

Feanna had made no reply to this comment, simply smiling and allowing her uncle, Eoghan Foley, to continue a polite and, Sam felt, rather guarded conversation with Sam.

"Will you be attending the sale today, Sam?" Eoghan had asked, as the party had made ready to go towards the parade ring, now that the nine horses competing in the Bowl Chase had been brought into the pre-parade area behind the weighing room.

"Yes, my neighbour Ranulph Dicks and I thought we would stay for it," Sam had replied, "Although neither of us is in the market for new horses at the moment. But it's always of interest to see what

47

is around, particularly as I never come to the Northern sales as a rule."

The sale which had been the subject of their conversation was an auction of horses due to take place at the racecourse following the conclusion of the day's racing.

"And you have viewed the catalogue showing the lots?" Eoghan had persisted.

Eoghan was unaware that Sam's dyslexia prevented him from comfortably reading any written document, whether in print form or on a computer screen. A closely printed catalogue, with its complex and detailed entry for each horse in the sale, would have presented Sam with a major challenge. Normally his cousin Gilbert, who was aware of Sam's difficulty, accompanied Sam to auctions to describe the catalogue lots to him. Sam had simply replied to Eoghan in the negative and had turned the question back onto the other man by asking, "Do you have an interest in any of the lots yourself?"

"Well, now, our lot has been withdrawn," had replied Eoghan, the statement taking Sam by surprise, "But I believe that Ronan Brody from Mallows has a few horses still in the sale."

"Your lot?" had asked Sam, as the two men entered the parade ring, Feanna Foley following silently behind them.

"We have for sale a three year old colt," Eoghan told him, "But we have taken him out. His details were already entered in the catalogue but as the auctioneer will inform the buyers, he will not be here for sale today. We were not able to get together in time the paperwork required for a sale in England."

Sam, genuinely interested in the unexpected information, had been about to ask for more details on the young horse when a familiar voice had hailed him from the parade ring rails.

"Tracked you down at last, James," had boomed the Australian tones of Teddy Urquhart. Sam had become involved in greetings and small talk between the various connections, and the opportunity to pursue the recent statement by Eoghan Foley had been temporarily lost.

Now Merlin was walking towards the group in his blue and gold silks, the bell to tell the jockeys to mount was about to be rung, and Sadie was leading Tabikat towards them with a bright smile on her face.

"It will be interesting to see how Tabikat takes to this track," Sam said to Merlin as he quickly legged the jockey up into the tiny saddle, "He was fine on the flat, left handed track at Newbury as you know, but this one has some sharp turns in it."

"I can't see Tabikat bein' bothered by this track," Merlin responded without hesitation, "We'll see you in the winner's enclosure, Mr Sampfield."

Sam wished he was as breezily confident as Merlin. Not that Sam doubted Tabikat's ability to win, but he was always aware that nothing could be taken for granted in any race, let alone one of this calibre. There were eight other top quality horses on their way to the start with Tabikat and any one of them had a chance of snatching the prize from Tabikat's grasp.

As Sadie led the regal Tabikat back past his many admirers by the pre-parade area and along the horsewalk onto the near corner of the famous course, Sam looked carefully at the other runners. The main threat seemed to Sam to be the iron grey, Inkspot, who had won the race last year, and had been placed third in the King George VI Chase, although finishing well down in the field in the recent Cheltenham Gold Cup race. Bees and Mist, a light grey, had also competed in the King George, but had not been placed in what had been a very high quality field of runners. A third potential threat, Sam thought, was a bay horse called Poseidon's Gold, trained by Dorset trainer Justin Venn, which had run at Cheltenham on Festival Trials Day in January.

The large screen in the parade ring showed Sadie releasing the rein to allow Merlin to canter Tabikat down the course towards the starting line located at the far left hand end of the track. Sadie stood still for a while, watching the combination moving away from her past the massed spectators, who were pressing themselves several deep along the rails.

One of the television presenters was roaming the parade ring and managed to position himself at Sam's side, followed quickly by his cameraman.

"Are you feeling confident today, Mr Sampfield Peveril?" asked the young man in a silken voice which matched his slicked back and carefully streaked blond hair, "You clearly think that Tabikat has come out of the Gold Cup well if he is to be running again so soon. I imagine this means he won't be at Punchestown this year, then?"

"You are correct on all counts," Sam stated quickly, trying to cut the conversation as short as possible, "We have been very pleased with him at home and he is good and ready for this race."

"Does that mean we might be seeing Tabikat in the King George this year?" went on the interviewer.

"I have not made any plans at all for next season," Sam told him, firmly, "I will need to talk to the owners first. Speaking of which, I must rejoin them now, if you will excuse me."

Returning to his party, Sam was conscious of the interviewer's eyes following him and conducting a quick appraisal of his parade ring companions. It would not have been obvious to anyone which of the group was the owner of Tabikat, given the variations in his recent ownership. No doubt the interviewer would take a keen interest in which of the party went up to receive the prize, should Tabikat win the race.

As Tabikat's connections walked towards the owners' viewing area, Eoghan Foley chatting amiably with Teddy and Tessa Urquhart, some people by the nearby parade ring rails caught Sam's attention. Stevie Stone had finished her interviews with her carefully targeted little knots of enthusiastic female racegoers, and had wound up her long hair under her signature burgundy hat and moved back into the centre of the parade ring, reading her iPad in preparation for the next race. The place where she had previously been standing had been filled by a group of three men. One, wearing a navy blazer, was standing with his back slightly towards the parade ring, whilst the other two men faced him, their gazes directed upwards at the large viewing screen. All three were wearing similar well cut blazers, and, in deference to the sunshine bathing the area in the warmth of its rays, straw fedora style hats. They looked like members of a veteran sports team on a day off.

As the group moved away towards the course, the man who had had his back to the parade ring turned to his left and put his arm across the shoulders of one of the other two men. As he did so, his full profile came into view.

Sam knew that profile as well as he knew his own. It was that of his old schoolfriend and teenage lover, Frank Stanley.

5

The Bowl Chase went off far too fast. Standing in the Owners and Trainers viewing area, Sam did not need his well-used field glasses to see that the pace set by the two front runners was a hot one. The horses were swiftly approaching the crammed viewing stands, racing along the finishing straight from Sam's left, the light grey Bees and Mist in the lead, closely shadowed by the iron grey Inkspot.

Sam had watched the starting preliminaries on the large viewing screen located on the opposite side of the track. It had been quite evident even then that the two current leaders had been vying to go off in front and to tow the field along behind them. Their respective jockeys had edged their well-primed charges firmly towards the starting line and had done their best to keep them there until the starter had at last climbed the mobile steps placed by the three mile and one furlong start and had brought down his yellow flag. As the orange tape had sprung back, the two horses had immediately set off at a rattling pace, so the field was already well strung out as it passed what would be the finishing line in two circuits' time. The horses swung to the left around the bend by the Earl of Derby Stand, spurred on by the enthusiastic cheers of the large and excited crowd.

Sam could see that Tabikat and Merlin were up with the pace in the middle of the field. Two of the runners at the back were already struggling to maintain the speed of the early gallop, but Tabikat was well in touch with the iron grey Inkspot who in turn remained hot on the heels of the lighter Bees and Mist.

"Bees and Mist continues to lead the field as they leave the stands and approach the turn into the back straight by the Melling Road," the commentator stated, "The two greys remain at the front, followed by Tabikat and Poseidon's Gold still in close attendance behind them. These four have already opened up a gap ahead of the others."

All nine of the horses successfully negotiated the tight turn into the far side of the course and approached the fourth fence at the same quick pace. As the classy field poured over the jump, Poseidon's Gold, on the outside of Tabikat, stumbled slightly on landing and knuckled forward over his off foreleg. The combination of the overbalancing and the speed of the landing was enough to unseat his unlucky jockey, who clung on for a few heroic seconds before tumbling inexorably downward onto the grass.

"Poseidon's Gold has unseated at the fourth!" exclaimed the commentator, as a collective groan rose from the stands, "The horse is continuing with the field, although the favourite Tabikat has had to switch smartly towards the rail to avoid him. The jockey is sitting up and appears uninjured."

"Is that loose one going to cause us gyp, Genie?" Teddy Urquhart asked Eoghan Foley, who was standing alongside him, following the progress of the race intently.

"Our jockey knows his trade," Eoghan replied, calmly, "And the riderless runner has probably no need of a pilot. I can see the horse enjoys his job and it will be all the easier with no weight on his back. I would say he will stay with the field. The only danger is that he might run out at this corner down here, back to the stables. But Merlin will keep Tabikat well out of the way of that danger, I am sure."

In truth there was little opportunity for any of the horses to deviate from the running line over the next four jumps, which were positioned in a straight line, after which the course angled round to the left again back to the starting point. In line with Eoghan's prediction, Poseidon's Gold continued to run determinedly with his fellow competitors, clearing the jumps with aplomb, reins flying, not knowing or caring that he was out of contention for the valuable prize. As the field approached what would in two days' time become the Elbow in the forthcoming Grand National Chase, there was no change in the order, although the pace had begun to steady slightly, with the result that the chasing group had begun to close up on the leaders. Tabikat remained in third place, running alongside the riderless Poseidon's Gold.

Poseidon's Gold did not, in the event, take the opportunity to run out by the Lord Sefton Stand, and continued onwards alongside the other horses up the short side of the track and back around the tight turn into the back straight.

"I think that loose horse knows his way round here," commented Tessa to Sam, laughing, "He's having a blast out there with no rider."

Sam was not much bothered as to whether Poseidon's Gold was enjoying life. As far as he was concerned, there was now one fewer opponent to defeat, and his main worry was how much the early pace had taken out of Tabikat. Notwithstanding his earlier comment to the TV interviewer, Sam was acutely conscious that it was less than a month since Tabikat had won the Cheltenham Gold Cup, and a less frenetic pace would certainly have been preferable. Clearly, his rival trainers had been well aware of that issue and had crafted their racing tactics accordingly.

As the beautifully bred animals arrived at the far end of the finishing straight, it was clear that, barring accidents, the first three places would be taken by the dark Tabikat and the two grey horses, the remainder of the field having been well beaten off with two of them pulled up before three out.

The watching crowd soon became noisier and more animated as the trio of front runners, accompanied by the jockeyless Poseidon's Gold, cleared the second last and began the long run past the Grand National fences towards the final fence before the finish. The three leaders flashed across the chequerboard mown grass almost in a line. Sam could see that Merlin was working hard, encouraging Tabikat to keep going, no doubt telling him that the finish was in sight, that he could beat these inferior rivals and emerge triumphant.

It was probably the flatness of the course and an excellent final leap which saved Tabikat from defeat that day. All three horses cleared the nineteenth and last obstacle with an effort, their jockeys appearing to lift them over the fence by sheer willpower.

"And Tabikat lands just ahead!" shrieked the commentator, "The Gold Cup winner shows his class. But the others aren't giving up, they're trying to come back at him."

In the event, the loose Poseidon's Gold crossed the line first, with Tabikat just behind. Poseidon's Gold quickly slowed to a trot soon after passing the finish, and circled about, tossing his head, bearing out Tessa's assessment of his enjoyment of the day's action as well as Eoghan's comment that the horse knew very well what he was doing.

"Tabikat has just added the Bowl Chase to his list of successes," the commentator announced to everyone who had been watching the hard-fought victory, whether at Aintree racecourse or on TVs and computer screens in homes and betting shops throughout the country, "Second and third go to the judge in a photo between Bees and Mist and last year's winner Inkspot."

Two hundred miles to the South, in the Sampfield Grange kitchen, Lewis and Kelly clapped and cheered, whilst Travis, Kye and Jackie, who had shouted themselves hoarse during the close finish, sighed with relief, knowing that Sadie's and Mr Sampfield's efforts to get Tabikat fit for the race had paid off. The partisan little audience watched with close attention as Merlin was congratulated by some of the defeated jockeys and then asked for his comments by a TV interviewer who had made her way out onto the course.

"Well done, Merlin," said the smartly dressed young woman, who was holding a microphone up to Merlin's face, as Tabikat walked around her, snorting and blowing after his exertions. Sadie had come running forward to seize Tabikat's bridle and to kiss the tired horse on the nose.

"You can have a good rest now, Tabsi," she told her beloved charge, "You deserve it."

Tabikat soon resumed his customary stately demeanour, but Sadie fancied it took him just a little longer than normal to settle into himself. She patted his neck reassuringly as the interviewer spoke to Merlin, pricking up her ears, as Tabikat would no doubt have done had he understood what they were saying, when she heard the young woman's question.

"So, Merlin, is this horse a King George prospect now, would you say?"

"I 'ave no idea," Merlin replied, shaking his head, "E's always raced in Ireland over Christmas, so it's anybody's guess what they 'ave in mind for 'im this year."

"But you think he could be a contender?" insisted the woman.

"'E's certainly capable of it," Merlin stated, sounding confident, but secretly rather relieved following his narrow victory, "But it's a long way off yet, and not my decision."

As Sadie led Tabikat and Merlin along the long horsewalk to the famous Aintree winner's enclosure, numerous admiring spectators shouted their congratulations to all three of them. Their party of connections was awaiting them excitedly and the arrival of the triumphant horse was greeted with a huge cheer from all those assembled nearby. Feanna Foley, in spite of being dressed for her day out, was quick to help Sadie drench Tabikat with water from one of the numerous nearby buckets, as soon as Merlin had pulled the lightweight saddle and damp number cloth from the sweating horse's back.

"Do you remember me from Gold Cup day? I am Feanna Foley from *Feirm Enda*," Feanna said by way of explanation, when Sadie looked at her, questioningly, "I have known Tabikat since the day he was foaled. I am representing my mother and my sister here today."

"It's nice to have you here with Tabsi again, Feanna," Sadie told her, as the two women pulled the winner's rug over Tabikat's broad back, whilst Merlin stood talking to Sam and Eoghan about

Tabikat's winning performance, "I work for Mr Sampfield. Tabsi is my favourite horse. I should love to come to Enda's Farm one day to see where he and Katseye came from."

"You and Merlin are welcome to visit at any time, of course," Feanna told her.

"Oh, well.... It would be just me," Sadie stammered awkwardly, "Merlin and I aren't together anymore."

"I'm sorry, I thought .... Caitlin, my aunt, told me ....," Feanna replied, sounding embarrassed and attempting to move the conversation quickly forward, "Then you would be most welcome on your own, to be sure. There is lots of riding to be done at *Feirm Enda*. And you could meet Tabikat's dam, Little Kitty Cat. We call her Kitty. She was a great success in her racing days. And her own dam, Kat's Gift, is still alive too, although she is very old now."

The presentation of the prizes to Tabikat's connections involved most of the party going up onto the podium whilst Tessa Urquhart took numerous photographs of them all. Unexpectedly, Eoghan Foley himself accompanied Feanna onto the rostrum to receive the owner's prize, the two of them being introduced by name as well as being described as the representatives of Levy Brothers International. Sam, Merlin and Sadie all accepted their own prizes, as Tabikat had won the best turned out prize as well as the prestigious race itself. As she stood alongside Merlin, a smile on her face for the snapping cameras, Sadie hoped that he had not overheard her conversation with Feanna Foley.

Much to Sam's surprise, Eoghan Foley agreed to be interviewed by the racecourse presenter after the prizegiving had taken place. Eoghan had always struck Sam as a reserved man, happy to allow others to occupy the limelight when it came to taking credit for Tabikat's achievements.

There was no sign of any reserve on the part of Eoghan now.

"I understand, Mr Foley, that you are the breeder as well as part of the family which owns Tabikat," the stout, grey-haired presenter started, importantly, "Not to mention a successful former jockey yourself. You must be very proud of the horse's achievements. Not just today's triumph, of course, but the Cheltenham Gold Cup last month, the Hennessy, and the Punchestown Gold Cup last year. Did you ever imagine your horse would become so successful?"

"It was always a possibility," Eoghan replied, without preamble, "His dam, Little Kitty Cat, was a three times winner in Ireland and he himself is by the great chaser Tabloid News. We have had him marked out as a potential Grade 1 contender since the day he was foaled."

"Will the horse be staying in England now?" the well-practised presenter asked, "He was moved from Brendan Meaghan in Ireland earlier in the season, was he not? What was the thinking behind that?"

"Brendan Meaghan is one of my oldest friends, and we both agreed that the horse's future lay in England," Eoghan answered, not really providing the explanation which the questioner was seeking, "Tabikat has been very successful since he went to Sampfield Grange. We shall be looking for opportunities for him in England next season. He will have the summer off now."

"Will you be aiming to produce more future champions at home?" the questioner went on, "I understand Katseye, with the same dam, is racing here later in the week and was also a Cheltenham Festival contender. Forgive me, but I believe your set up at Enda's Farm is quite small, so to produce two horses of this calibre is quite an achievement."

"We have indeed been very fortunate," Eoghan conceded, "Katseye and Tabikat have indeed the same dam, and she herself is a daughter of Alakazam, so there is top quality in the bloodline. Both my horses are geldings, but we have an entire colt from the same line, who is a sure prospect for the future."

"We shall look forward to seeing him. Well done, Mr Foley," said the presenter, quickly wrapping up the interview as the horses for the next race began to occupy the parade ring.

Sam had only half listened to Eoghan's conversation with the racecourse presenter, which had been met with a round of polite applause from those members of the crowd who had not already drifted off to the bars and betting shops around the grounds. Tabikat had been taken quickly back to the horsebox park where he was awaited by his travelling companion, the showy Fan Court, who had been a close second when also ridden by Merlin ap Rhys in a Novices' Chase earlier in the afternoon. The younger horse looked fresh and lively beside the tired Tabikat, and Sadie had made a great fuss of her weary champion as she had prepared him for the journey. After ensuring that Sadie and her travelling companion from the Dicks yard had everything in order in the horsebox, Sam had walked back into the spectator areas in the hope of seeing Frank Stanley once again.

Sam had not spoken to his former teenage lover Frank since the final day of the Cheltenham Festival, when Frank had arrived unexpectedly in the parade ring alongside Katseye's owner, Arturo Ardizzone, and his companion, a mysterious woman who had been introduced as Dr Lara Katz. All three of them had left the racecourse abruptly at the end of Katseye's race, Dr Katz having been alerted by some apparently urgent message on her mobile phone.

Frank had only in the last eighteen months resumed the beginnings of a new friendship with Sam, in the course of which he had drawn an initially unwitting Sam into his work for the security services, as Frank had described his present occupation. Frank's original career had been in the Army. He had graduated from Sandhurst after leaving the school which the boys had attended together and Sam had not subsequently heard from him for many years. Sam's mother, now suffering from dementia and living again on Teddy and Tessa Urquhart's Australian cattle station, where she had been brought up, had made it clear to the two teenage boys that she wanted her only son to marry and continue the Sampfield Peveril family line. The existence of a relationship with a male lover had therefore been out of the question. The unhappy consequence of this decision on old Mrs Sampfield's part, Sam's now deceased father having had no idea of the true nature of the relationship between the boyhood friends, was that Sam had never married, and there was still no heir to the Sampfield Grange estate.

Ranulph Dicks soon came to join Sam in the Owners and Trainers bar, Sam having eventually concluded that Frank Stanley and his two companions must have left the racecourse. Ranulph Dicks was a well-established trainer, a little older than Sam, who had given up an ambition to be a jockey, when he grew too tall. Still lean and spare, he had a thick head of greying brown hair, sharp blue eyes, and very little tact. Sadie had spent some time working at his yard in recent months, and Sam could see that his talented yard manager had grown in confidence as a result of the experience of working in the larger and busier Dicks establishment.

Eoghan and Feanna had left to meet Ronan Brody from Mallows Stud prior to the forthcoming horse auction, whilst Teddy and Tessa had arranged an evening out in Liverpool, so the two trainers had an hour or more to kill before the start of the sale. Having discussed their respective horses' performances that afternoon, Ranulph moved the conversation onto the forthcoming equine auction.

"What do you know about this lot from Enda's Farm, Sam?" he asked, setting his empty glass down onto the round table at which they were seated, the conversation of other trainers and their owners, most of whom were from the North and Scotland, loud around them.

"I believe the lot has been withdrawn," Sam replied, "But Genie said that it was a three year old colt."

"A colt out of the same dam as Tabikat and Katseye, he said in the post race interview," Ranulph added, significantly, holding out the auction catalogue, "That's something which is going to attract a lot of interest, Sam. Shame we shan't been seeing it today. Did he say whether it would be entered in the next sale at Cheltenham?"

"I haven't brought my reading glasses," Sam hastily told him, using his customary excuse for not looking at printed materials in public, "Just tell me what it says, if you'd be so kind, Ran."

"It says here that the colt is the third produce of Little Kitty Cat," Ranulph read aloud from the glossy printed brochure, "The sire is Doctor Lyster from Mallows Stud. And Little Kitty Cat is shown here as being by Alakazam out of Kat's Gift."

Sam's mind suddenly processed something which he had only partly taken in earlier in the afternoon. Eoghan Foley had mentioned in his interview that Little Kitty Cat was a daughter of Alakazam. But if he had understood Brendan Meaghan correctly when he and Brendan had first met over fifteen months ago in the Queens Hotel in Cheltenham, the presence of Alakazam in the bloodline had never before been acknowledged. Yet Eoghan had now spoken openly of Alakazam's involvement in creating the talented equine brothers which Sam now had the privilege to train. What had changed, he wondered. Had someone done a DNA test? Had Mallows Stud now been keen to benefit from Tabikat's recently acquired superstar status? Had the covering by Alakazam been paid for, and thereby made official, after all?

"Does the colt have a name?" Sam asked, his thoughts running fruitlessly over the sudden conundrum.

"He does," replied Ranulph, "His name is Katalyst."

6

Whilst Sadie and Tabikat made their disrupted and tedious way back through the crowded motorway system towards Sampfield Grange, Kye and Jackie were carrying out their usual late afternoon chores in the picturesque stone-built racing yard.

Sam's proposal to run Katseye in the Liverpool Hurdle on the final day of the Aintree meeting had been accepted by Arturo Ardizzone, who had regretted that other commitments meant that he could not be present to watch the race himself. He had suggested that Meredith Crosland, the horse's previous owner, be invited instead. Jackie had been jubilant when she had heard the news, knowing that it would give her imperious black charge an opportunity to show that he too could win another of the big races. His last win had been at Cheltenham in January, the single victory under Rules having been amongst three second and one third places, albeit in highly competitive events. Jackie had been sad that Katseye had not been included in the Sampfield Grange victory parade which had thrilled the crowds assembled by The Charlton Arms almost four weeks ago.

"You'll show them, won't you, Big Kat?" she told the silent horse, as she approached the door of his box to pat his black nose, "If Tabikat can win his race this afternoon, then you can win yours on Saturday too. And you'll have Highlander for company in the box. You can both have a good talk about it on the way there, can't you?"

Katseye's head was well above the eyeline of the diminutive Jackie, and he seemed to be looking at something in the distance which Jackie could not see. As his young groom spoke, Katseye gently dipped his handsome head downwards, so that the side of his velvet nose brushed Jackie's cheek. It was a slow and soft motion, like a kiss from a child.

"You're my best friend, Big Kat," Jackie told him, running her hand up the side of the horse's dark face, "I'll turn you out like an emperor on Saturday. Highlander will be right jealous, you'll see."

As she talked to Katseye, Jackie could see her work colleague and bedfellow, Kye, moving about in the nearby feedroom, starting the regular preparation of the evening feeds for the horses. The heavy wooden door stood open, and the last rays of the sun spread palely onto the dull stone floor, ingrained as it was with the minute debris of decades of equine foodstuffs. The dust seemed to have entered into the very fibre of the soft stone and had formed a laminated crust over the once porous surface.

Jackie had been at Sampfield Grange for almost eleven months now and it had been one of the happiest periods of her short life. Brought up by a foster family from the age of two, she had subsequently been adopted by her murdered mother's kindly brother and his sweet-natured wife. Jackie remembered nothing of her mother, with whom she had lived a squalid life as a toddler in a Manchester squat, until one day her drug addicted parent had not woken up. An assumption by a fellow squatter that Ally had overdosed on something had quickly been replaced by a befuddled realisation that the young mother had blood soaking through her dirty clothes and that her purse containing the little money she possessed had been taken. An occasional visitor to the squat had later been arrested and charged with Ally's murder, all for the theft of the grand sum of £4.62. Jackie's natural father had been lost in the mists of her mother's chaotic history, and so the bewildered little girl had been sent into the care of a foster family, where she had been clothed and fed properly for the first time in her unfortunate life.

The offer by Ally's brother, a postman who had little in common with his dead sister, to adopt the child had been unexpected, but welcome. Notwithstanding his blood relation to the child, the adoption process had been slow and painstaking, during which time Jackie's foster parents had come to love her dearly. A second unwanted parting had soon again disrupted Jackie's life, although her uncle and his wife, who gave up her job in a department store to become a full time mother, had promised to make sure that

Jackie could keep in touch with her previous carers. It was years before Jackie realised that her adoptive parents had been unable to have children of her own and that she would always be an only child.

Jackie's new parents had not been able to believe their luck at being able to adopt their young niece, and soon the little family had settled into a quiet and unambitious lifestyle on the western outskirts of Greater Manchester. There had been plenty of green fields within a short distance of their home and in those fields had been horses and ponies. Jackie had seen them every day as she had walked to the local school hand in hand with her adoptive mother. Sometimes the two of them had stopped to talk to the animals when they had come up to the fence looking for treats.

Jackie's mother had known nothing about horses, but the family of one of Jackie's friends from her primary school had owned two of the ponies in the nearby field, and it was through that connection that Jackie had learned to ride. Like many a pony mad teenager, she had later helped out at a local stableyard in return for the opportunity to ride and exercise their horses and had taken numerous holiday jobs there as a stable hand. Jackie had wanted nothing more than to work with horses. She had not been able to wait until the day she could leave school.

Around the time of Jackie's sixteenth birthday, her plans had been unexpectedly changed. Watching the Trooping of the Colour one June Saturday on the living room television, she had been dazzled by the rows of uniformed soldiers riding large bay hunters to create a magnificent spectacle in faraway London. Surely, the Army must need people to look after these beautiful creatures, she had thought, and maybe even to ride them, although the soldiers whose faces she could see appeared all to be men. From that moment onwards, Jackie had formed an ambition to join the Army and had soon been enrolled in a local cadet corps near to her home.

Jackie's quiet parents had not been at all keen on the idea of her joining the Army and had opposed the plan. But they were far from being authoritarian people and had gradually allowed themselves to be talked round by the highly determined Jackie. Neither they nor Jackie were to know that her chances of being able to work with horses in the Army would be very limited, as there were now only two mounted divisions, both based in London, and only one of them open to female soldiers.

As it had turned out, once she had completed her basic training, Jackie had been assigned to the Royal Regiment of Electrical and Mechanical Engineers and her horse-related ambitions had appeared to be at an end. She had become a competent mechanic and had learned to service a wide range of ground vehicles and weapons-equipped aircraft. She had driven everything from armoured cars to fuel tankers. But the ambition to work with horses had remained with her like a nagging tooth, and, so, after a few years, during which she had been quickly promoted to the initial rank of Lance Corporal, she had decided to resign from the Army and to look once again for an opportunity to pursue her originally chosen career.

Hearing Jackie's story from her Colour Sergeant, who had been lamenting the competent young woman's decision to leave the Army, a young Captain who had overseen the unit of which Jackie had been part had suggested another plan for Jackie, with the result that she had been introduced one day to a Colonel F E Stanley. Colonel Stanley had asked Jackie if she would be interested in working for him, as her particular combination of training and abilities were exactly what he was seeking for the unit whose work he currently oversaw. Jackie would be involved with horses, he said, and would need to be able to drive large vehicles, to have some familiarity with aircraft, and would play a role in personal protection and security. The work was confidential and would take the form of a secondment from the Army to Colonel Stanley's unit for an indefinite period. Jackie had accepted at once.

Jackie's initial assignment had been strange. Following a short period of training in which she had learned about unarmed combat, close personal protection, and observational and communication skills, she had been sent as a stable groom to the establishment of a Sir Andrew Cunningham, located in a place called Cuffborough in Somerset. There she had been required to care for point to point horses and hunters, including driving them to competitions. The other part of her role, which was not to be mentioned to anyone else, was to act as a contact point for a mysterious woman called Isabella Hall, who had worked at another point to point establishment, Sampfield Grange, about fifteen miles away.

Mrs Hall, Colonel Stanley had explained, was currently under the protection of his unit and Jackie's job had simply been to meet her at pre-arranged dates and times and to convey any messages which Mrs Hall wished to send to Colonel Stanley. If Mrs Hall did not appear for the meetings, then Jackie was to report the fact immediately by sending a coded text to a specified mobile phone number. Mrs Hall had turned out to be a small middle-aged woman, who had arrived at the meeting places on a bicycle, a rather smarter one than Jackie's own, and who had usually had little to say. Jackie had not needed to use the mobile phone number.

Then, one day, a cryptically expressed text message had arrived for Jackie from the mobile phone contact number, indicating that Colonel Stanley required a face to face meeting with her during her next afternoon off, which had been the following day. This meeting had taken place in a little whitewashed cottage some miles from the Cunningham establishment. It was at this meeting that Jackie had been told the story of Kye McMahon.

Kye, it had seemed, worked as a stable hand at Sampfield Grange and was a small-time drug dealer. This of itself had not been an issue of concern to Colonel Stanley, but it had appeared that Kye had recently escaped the vicious clutches of his two brothers and their associates in gangland Liverpool, whose involvement in drug dealing had been on a much larger and more criminally serious scale. Jackie's instructions were simply that she should make friends with Kye, which could include buying weed and Es from him, if necessary. If Jackie were to see Kye with anyone who looked out of place at a country point to point meeting, she was to send a text to the usual mobile number straightaway.

Last year's Cheltenham Festival had quickly come and gone. In the three weeks leading up to the famous event, Jackie's meetings with Isabella Hall had been discontinued and she had seen nothing of Kye at the two point to point meetings which she had attended with the Cunningham horses. She had learned from the Cunningham yard gossip that Sampfield Grange had fielded a horse called Tabikat in the Gold Cup, and that he had run into third place. Jackie had wondered if Kye had been lucky enough to accompany the horse to the celebrated race.

After the Festival was over, Jackie's instructions had been changed. Kye, it had appeared, was now to be training at Sampfield Grange as a conditional jockey, his drug dealing activities having evidently been put behind him. Until his new licence came through, he would be gaining experience as an amateur jockey, riding one of the Sampfield Grange pointers, Highlander Park. Clearly, though, Kye's life was not henceforth to be straightforward. A role he had played for Colonel Stanley had put him at risk of reprisals and his safety had needed to be ensured as far as possible. So, Jackie had been instructed to ask Kye if he could help her to get a job at Sampfield Grange where it would be possible for Jackie to keep a watchful eye on him. It had been important that Kye should not be aware of Jackie's role as a protector of his wellbeing.

With the assistance of some influence from behind the scenes, the installation of Jackie as a groom at Sampfield Grange had been effected shortly afterwards and Jackie had eventually found herself responsible for looking after the fabulous Katseye. Her befriending of Kye, whom she had genuinely come to like, had been sufficiently successful for her to have become his girlfriend and they had shared a bed in the Sampfield Grange staff cottage for many months now. Even Kye's discovery of an element of Jackie's role in relation to his safety had only temporarily dented the genuine but shaky affection which had arisen between them.

So, Jackie was now very happy. She had a magnificent and beautiful racehorse to care for, a boyfriend who was training to become a professional jockey, and a special role as a secondee to the security services from the Army. Furthermore, in the year which had passed since the previous Cheltenham Festival, there had been no suggestion of any criminal threat to Kye's present quiet existence. This was a better life than Jackie had ever expected when she had left the safety of her family home to join the Army.

Absently rubbing the side of Katseye's black neck, Jackie noticed that Travis was sitting at the desk in the yard office, typing slowly and deliberately on the desktop computer. The office had been unstaffed since the departure of Bethany shortly after the Cheltenham Festival. No replacement for her had as yet been recruited. The office phone had been diverted to the house and a bookkeeper from the local accountancy firm, Purefoy and Associates, had called in twice a week to attend to the yard related paperwork. The office had therefore been left unattended and had been available for the yard staff to use.

Mr Sampfield had asked Travis to prepare a written statement of the unhappy events which had led to the suspension of his jockey's licence in Australia. This statement was to be sent to Mr Sampfield's contact at the British Horseracing Authority, who had agreed to try to make informal enquiries into the matter on Travis's behalf. This activity had entailed much email correspondence between Travis and Ryan Urquhart, who was currently travelling in the Far East, in order to get the facts of the unedifying story correct and the statement sufficiently succinct that it could be quickly understood.

Travis had been uncharacteristically nervous since the ketamine incident which had affected his charge, Curlew Landings. The ketamine, according to vet Rachel Horwood, had probably been ingested, after having been either crushed into hard feed or dissolved in water. Ketamine was a drug regularly used by vets to anaesthetise horses, but in those cases, the amount involved was significantly larger and was injected with a hypodermic needle into a muscle. The dose eaten or drunk by Curlew had been enough to make him dozy, but nothing more serious than that.

The event had created a number of as yet unsolved mysteries. The first of these was how the ketamine had been administered to Curlew without anyone knowing. The horse had been in the yard since he had come back from his morning exercise and Rachel had been fairly sure that the drug had been administered after his return to his box.

Rachel's analysis had therefore suggested that someone in the yard had been responsible, a deduction which in itself had led to other mysteries. Who had done it and why? The casual staff working that morning had all stoutly denied possessing ketamine for recreational drug use, and it was difficult in any case to see why any of them would have risked bringing the drug to the yard, an action which would have resulted in instant dismissal had it been discovered.

These enquiries by Sadie of her work riders had left the permanent staff and the household members as the only remaining suspects. But all of them had been together in the yard and afterwards in the kitchen when the incident had happened. The yard office had been empty, as Bethany had departed for Devon the previous day. Mr Sampfield and the Urquharts had been in the breakfast room and then the drawing room following the horses' return from exercise.

In the light of all this investigation, the only remaining option appeared to be that someone had crept into the yard unseen and had slipped the drug into Curlew's feed or water bucket and then crept out again. But who could have done this and what purpose they had in mind could not be fathomed. Travis's paranoid supposition that this was part of the ongoing campaign to discredit him by his former employer Jack Tytherleigh had been quickly dismissed on the grounds that Jack could have no idea of Travis's current whereabouts.

So, the mysteries had remained mysteries, despite much speculation and raking over the facts by Lewis and Kelly in particular. Vigilance and security in the yard had been improved, insofar as it was possible, and all feeds and water buckets scrupulously checked for any sign of interference.

"How's it going, Travis?" Jackie asked her colleague, leaving Katseye to his own devices at last.

"Not my bag, writing stuff down," Travis responded glumly, "It makes me remember how mad I am about what happened. That Jack Tytherleigh is a grade A bastard."

"Mr Sampfield will get it sorted, I'm sure he will," Jackie tried to reassure him, although she really had no idea how her mild-mannered rural employer could influence events in faraway Australia. Mr Sampfield was a friend of Colonel Stanley, though, and Jackie had the utmost faith in Colonel Stanley's ability to solve any problem he chose to tackle.

Kye, measuring out the evening feeds in the storeroom, could easily hear the short conversation taking place between his colleagues. Kye had two things on his increasingly unquiet mind.

The first of these was his coming ride in two days' time on Highlander Park in the final race at Aintree, an event for amateur and conditional jockeys. The decision to run Katseye in the Liverpool Hurdle had meant that the Sampfield Grange team would be taking a horsebox up to Aintree that day, and it had made sense, at least to Mr Sampfield and the equally keen Travis, to take the opportunity to put Highlander and Kye into another race in the same card. Kye knew well that his future career depended on his willingness to take as many opportunities as possible and that a good performance by him in this event might well secure him rides with other trainers. But Kye did not want to go to Liverpool on Saturday. This was because of the second problem which was bothering him.

Kye knew very well who had K-bombed Curlew Landings. It had been his brother Bronz's girlfriend, Sheryl.

7

The Saturday of the Grand National Chase started early at Sampfield Grange. Katseye and Highlander Park had been ready and loaded before it got light and were passing Birmingham by the time a crimson sun had shown itself above the eastern horizon shortly after six o'clock.

Security was tight at Aintree Racecourse's Seeds Lane entrance, but, although Sampfield Grange was still operating without an office manager, the joint efforts of Sadie and Kelly had ensured that all the necessary identifications for the three travelling staff and their two horses were quickly checked and found to be in order. Even though it was as yet early, the horsebox park was filling up quickly, and numerous bleary eyed stable staff were busy unloading their respective charges.

"Well, hello there, the lovely Sadie!" called a familiar male voice, as Kye switched off the engine of the Sampfield Grange vehicle and Sadie jumped down from her seat in the cab.

"Oh, hi there, Luke," Sadie responded, forcing a bright smile onto her face, "That's a coincidence, your box being parked right next to ours. Is it Merry you have in there?"

"It certainly is," Luke responded, "Merriott Marsh and I are up against your Highlander Park in the final race. I see your lad Kye is riding him again today. Still some way to go for him with riding out the claim, I see?"

"Kye's doing very well," Sadie told Luke, feeling that she needed to offer some support to her colleague, "If things go his way today, then he may get some more chances with other trainers."

Kye had by this time walked around to the passenger side of the vehicle, and chipped into the conversation, trying to give the impression of having more confidence than he really felt.

"Landy's fit and ready for you and Merriott Marsh, Mr Cunningham," he stated, firmly.

Luke laughed, rather dismissively, Kye thought, and wandered back to his own smartly appointed lorry, saying a quick hello to Jackie, who was lowering the ramp of the Sampfield Grange box.

"If only it was just Merry we had to beat," Sadie said, as she watched the well-spoken young man, who had taken her for granted as his girlfriend over the last few months, giving instructions to Merriott Marsh's groom, "There are fourteen horses declared for your race, Kye."

Kye did not need to be reminded. He had been studying the list of horses all yesterday evening. Many of them seemed to be from northern stables and he had little information other than what could be seen in their published form. He recognised the name of Josh Parry, the Cheshire trainer for whom he had used to work before moving to Sampfield Grange, but his horse and the jockey were unfamiliar to him. Already the nagging nerves were making themselves felt in his stomach and his throat felt rasping and dry. Being in Liverpool again did nothing to reduce Kye's worries, although it was difficult to see how any of Bronz's associates could get at either Kye, or the horses, given the level of security which surrounded them in the horsebox park and stable area.

"We have to get Katseye through his race first," Jackie butted in, pointedly, "That's right before the Grand National. Yours isn't until afterwards, Kye."

The feverish excitement associated with Grand National Day was already beginning to permeate throughout the entire course and its environs. The noise and excitement of the arriving spectators could be heard gradually increasing as the morning progressed. Car parks on the further side of the famous course were quickly filling with a stream of vehicles disgorged from the nearby motorway system, their noisy and excited occupants being ferried over the centre of the course by a succession of buses. Once in the area behind the viewing stands, the racegoers were assembling in large and animated groups, the continuing warm weather having encouraged many of them to adopt the sort of summer clothing more usually worn at flat racing. The colourful multitude milled and shifted about, an ever changing and increasingly voluble mass of humanity, all with the determined purpose of watching one of the most famous horse races in the world.

As Jackie had indicated, there were five races on the card to be run before the Grand National Chase. Katseye's was the fifth of these, so the team faced a long wait before their handsome charge could enter the parade ring. Although this left them plenty of time to prepare Katseye for his run, it gave them little to do other than to watch the preceding four races, the first of which did not go off until a quarter to two. The early start from Sampfield Grange seemed, though, to have been worth the effort, as it was clear that anyone attempting to reach the course later in the morning risked being stuck in the accumulating local traffic.

The racing TV channels were showing all the races, although the principal free-to-air network was not showing either the first or the final race, the latter being the one in which Highlander Park was entered. Much of the attention of the broadcasters was, though, on the Grand National Chase itself, with profiles of the forty runners and their owners and trainers having been featured throughout the three televised days of the meeting. Sir John Garratt's grey Alto Clef was amongst the more fancied runners, and he and his wife Helen had been interviewed about the horse's chances. Alto Clef had the additional distinction of being ridden by one of only three female jockeys in the race, so she had been interviewed alongside the owners, expressing her confidence that she would ride the horse to finish successfully.

Sadie knew that Merlin was booked for two of the races preceding Katseye's event, riding for Justin Venn and another trainer from his local area in Chepstow. Luke Cunningham had by now gone off to join his father, Sir Andrew Cunningham, in the Owners and Trainers area, having invited Sadie to join him. But Sadie had declined, saying that she would see Luke back in the horsebox park after his race. She had decided instead to remain with Jackie and an increasingly jittery Kye. Jackie and Kye had taken the opportunity to jog around the Hurdles course during the morning, but obtaining this slight familiarity with the terrain had not served to calm Kye's nerves.

"What're you worrying about, Kye?" Jackie had asked him, as they had eventually walked back towards the busy horsebox park, "All you have to do is keep Highlander focused, like always, and he'll take you round, no problem. You've been in enough races together to understand one other."

"It's not that, Jackie," Kye had replied, impatiently, "This is Liverpool. People know me here. People like Bronz and that Sheryl."

"What can they do to you when you are out on the course?" had asked Jackie, reasonably, "Neither of them's going to be riding in the race and they can't get into the parade ring. Anyway, what do you think they're going to do with millions of people watching on TV?"

"I don't know," Kye had responded, but the tight feeling of dread encircling his abdomen would not go away.

Kye had told no-one that, whilst he had been helping Travis to keep Curlew Landings in order during the victory parade outside The Charlton Arms, he had seen the hard face of his brother Bronz's girlfriend, Sheryl, amongst the pressing crowd. Sheryl had fixed him with an unblinking gaze and had quickly drawn a finger across her throat after which she had pointed the same finger straight at him. Then Curlew had bounced sideways in front of them, and when Kye had looked again, Sheryl had been gone.

It was as a result of this unwelcome sighting that Kye had become convinced that it was Sheryl who had been responsible for drugging Curlew Landings, although he had been at a loss to explain to himself how she could have done it. He knew, though, that he could say nothing of his suspicions, even to Jackie. If he had said anything, Kye reasoned, whatever information Jackie or Mr Stanley might put forward in his defence, Mr Sampfield would find out about Kye's past, and would never trust him to ride or care for his horses ever again.

The noise, crowding and bustle around the parade ring seemed to be reaching bursting point as Jackie led Katseye around the track in readiness for the Liverpool Hurdle. Katseye's lordly appearance made him a target for favourable comment from those racegoers who were choosing a horse on the basis of its appearance. Jackie's and Sadie's joint efforts to turn him out as beautifully as they could had enhanced the already gorgeous picture, and Katseye attracted many complimentary exclamations as he strode grandly alongside the parade ring rails.

Katseye's form had made him one of the favourites with the bookmakers too, and he was currently shown as second favourite behind the horse which had beaten him at Cheltenham a little less than a month ago. Many of the Smart Girls would probably have their money on him, Jackie thought, as he had been tipped as the potential winner by Tabby Cat and Jayce since the beginning of the meeting.

Jackie could see Mr Sampfield standing on the grass in the centre of the parade ring, accompanied once again by Eoghan and Feanna Foley. With them stood Mrs Crosland, wearing a smart green and white jacket together with a wide brimmed hat decorated with matching green and white ribbon. Stevie Stone, who had been working alongside the parade ring and interviewing racegoers for much of the day, stood next to her. She had stowed her iPad in a leather bag and had hidden her brightly coloured long hair under her usual burgundy coloured hat. Stevie would be busy soon interviewing more Smart Girls, Jackie was sure, once the Grand National preliminaries began.

Watching Jackie lead Katseye on his circular tour, Sam had scanned the racegoers clustered along the white rails for any sign of Frank Stanley and the men with whom he had been seen at the racecourse two days earlier. But, as he legged Merlin up into the saddle, Sam had seen no-one he recognised amongst the sea of faces.

Sam had tried to call Frank Stanley from the Audi on his way to the races that morning, but, for the first time ever, the number had remained unanswered and there had appeared to be no facility to leave a message for his elusive friend. Now, as Merlin walked towards them, clad in the green and white colours of Arturo Ardizzone, Sam could not help but remember that the last time he had seen or spoken to Frank Stanley was on the day that Merlin first had worn these newly issued silks. But Frank had not joined them today.

The Grade 1 Liverpool Hurdle started to the left of the viewing stands and featured nine highly classy horses. The unexpected sultriness of the air had led the racecourse authorities to instruct that water buckets be brought down onto the course in the event that the horses, more used to cold and wet weather conditions, became overheated during the race. This concern applied particularly in relation to the challenging Grand National Chase, due to be run over a distance of well over four miles in less than an hour's time.

Katseye's race went off steadily enough, the nine big horses closely grouped and hunting companionably around the first circuit of the course with little apparent effort. An injection of pace in the back straight on second time around saw three of the runners begin to detach from the rest of the field with five hurdles still to cross. The remaining six runners continued to press forward together with little to choose between them until they had completed their final turn into the finishing straight in front of the stands. Taking the last hurdle just behind the leader, Merlin sent Katseye to the front, trying to pass the same horse which had beaten him last time out at Cheltenham. Jackie, jumping frantically about by the end of the horsewalk, could see Merlin on the screen, kicking and urging Katseye forward as the horse gradually overhauled his rival, whose jockey, equally tenacious, forced his own mount to fight back.

"Come on, Big Kat!" screamed Jackie, her voice shrieking and cracking, to the amusement of those standing nearby, "Keep going! Don't let him get you now. You're going to win this time!"

Jackie was right, as her ecstatic face, when she went forward to take Katseye's rein and lead him off the course, with Merlin grinning down at her from the horse's back, clearly showed on the big screen. The result had been, though, too close for the comfort of Sam and the other connections assembled in the parade ring, who had cheered and shouted almost as loudly as Jackie and were now heaving heartfelt sighs of relief after the close finish. Watching Eoghan Foley hugging his niece Feanna, who was punching the air with a clenched fist as if she had ridden the race herself, Sam was heartily relieved to know that Katseye's last race of the season had produced the result which the Irish family who had bred the impressive black horse had truly deserved.

Sadie had remained in the horsebox park throughout all the afternoon's races. Although she had helped Jackie to prepare Katseye for his run, she had left it to her colleague to accompany the horse into the parade ring. Jackie, Sadie judged correctly, did not need her help. Katseye was as well behaved as Tabikat when he was at the races, unlike the more unpredictable Highlander Park, who Sadie would take into the parade ring for Kye later. Kye himself had been resting in the front seat of the horsebox until the excitement of Katseye's race had brought him out and the result had restored his mood to something approaching its usual positivity.

The presentation of the prizes to Katseye's connections was almost overshadowed by the preparations for the main feature race of the afternoon. Nonetheless, Sadie noticed, Mr Sampfield had used his brief post-race interview to confirm that he was considering sending Katseye chasing next season. Then the jubilant Jackie's return with the weary Katseye claimed her and Kye's attention.

Both Alto Clef and Merlin's ride, The King's Sorcerer, which he had ridden into fourth place last year, successfully survived the mad cavalry charge which always characterised the first circuit of the Grand National Chase. Alto Clef was unlucky to be brought down on the second time round the course at the Canal Turn, the fence just before the ninety-degree bend at the far end of the temporarily elongated course. Alto Clef, much to the relief of the Garratts, the Urquharts and everyone else connected with them in the parade ring, scrambled quickly to his feet and galloped away towards a nearby catching pen. His disappointed jockey also stood up promptly and walked resignedly to the side of the track, taking care to avoid a pair of loose horses who had evaded capture and were still careering enthusiastically along the now half demolished course.

The King's Sorcerer was amongst fifteen successful finishers, and once again achieved fourth place, the tough, experienced horse not having the turn of foot needed to produce a late spurt of speed against more energetic rivals in the final stages. Fortunately, the concerns about the runners becoming overheated in the lengthy and arduous race, and possibly collapsing as a result, proved unfounded, although all of the finishers were well doused in water from the numerous buckets set out in front of the stands as a precaution.

During the ecstasy and celebrations following the culmination of the lengthy race, Sadie quietly led an excited Highlander Park towards the pre-parade area, Kye having already gone to find his place and his red and green silks in the jockey's changing room. Highlander seemed highly interested by his novel surroundings, and his brown ears pricked and swivelled towards the noise of the celebrating racegoers. Even those racegoers who had lost their bets did not seem to be too upset and had happily joined in with the general party atmosphere which was enveloping the course.

Sadie could see Merlin standing by the weighing room talking to a large man in a baggy blue suit, the owner of his recent ride, she assumed, who seemed to be asking Merlin a question. Merlin appeared to be declining, shaking his head regretfully and holding up his right hand in a negative gesture. The older man shrugged and clapped Merlin on the back before walking off. Merlin turned towards the horsewalk and stopped when he saw Sadie approaching.

"Well done, Merlin, shame you didn't win," called out Sadie, "We'll see if Landy and Kye can do better in the last."

"Let Mr Sampfield know that I'll be roun' to see Curlew tomorrow," Merlin called back, "And tell Kye to keep Landy balanced on the turns and to 'ave a great ride. See you all in the mornin'."

Had Merlin known that this was the last time he would speak to Sadie in several months, he might have said more.

The Conditional Jockeys' and Amateur Riders' Handicap Hurdle had a much smaller viewing public than the Grand National Chase. The main television coverage had ended, although the subscription and betting shop channels were still showing the action, and many spectators had decided to leave the course once the main event was over. Two expensive looking helicopters took off from the centre of the racecourse whilst the remaining fourteen runners made their way around the parade ring. Highlander Park continued to look around interestedly as Sadie led him along the path, but seemed otherwise unperturbed when Kye eventually walked down the steps from the weighing room and was legged up into the saddle by Mr Sampfield. The absence of Travis, who was at home in charge of the yard today, ensured that Kye had not been bombarded with complex riding instructions before the race.

Mr Sampfield's instructions had been as brief, as always.

"Enjoy the ride, Kye," he had said, "Trust yourself. You know this horse better than I do."

Kye and Highlander Park gave an excellent account of themselves in the last race of the Aintree Festival. Both horse and jockey were calm and focused by the time they had reached the extended two mile start, a journey which involved a leisurely canter to the far end of the level course. The race soon went off at a terrific pace, with Kye and Highlander sitting in the centre of the field. Luke Cunningham's horse, Merriott Marsh, was highly excited by the tumult of the large field and was pulling hard as the runners passed the stands and swept around to the left past the point at which the Grand National Chase had so recently started. Merriott Marsh continued to pull and tug at his bit, bumping against other horses as he leapt the first few hurdles, drawing a barrage of shouting and swearing from the other riders. Eventually, though, the over keen horse ran out of nervous energy and dropped back, leaving other runners to take up the pace.

Kye, watching for his opportunity, accelerated Highlander Park smoothly forward in the finishing straight and brought the horse home in a very respectable third place in the short race.

"We can talk about all this when we are home," Sam told his happy young jockey as they stood together in the third place spot, whilst Sadie poured two buckets of water over Highlander and covered him in a sweat sheet.

Back in the busy horsebox park, Sadie decided that Katseye should be loaded first by Jackie, and that Kye, once he was changed and ready to travel, would bring Highlander down from the stable to which he had been returned by Sadie after his race. Many of the horses which had run in the Grand National Chase were still being loaded for their journey home, and the Sampfield Grange trio and their two horses had to wait their turn to make their homeward preparation around the bustling area.

When Sadie eventually opened the ramp of the Sampfield Grange horsebox, she was annoyed to see that one of the horses' travelling rugs lay in an untidy heap onto the floor of the horsebox.

"Just wait there a moment with Katseye," she instructed Jackie, who was leading the big gelding towards the box. Kye would be following soon with Highlander Park, and the last thing the team needed was to have to spend time clearing up before the two horses could be loaded for their journey home.

Sprinting up the ramp, Sadie picked up the corner of the rug, which felt unusually heavy. Something seemed to be holding it down, but in the fading light of the April evening, she could not easily see what it was. Had a hay net fallen from its fastenings, she wondered.

Tugging at the rug, Sadie suddenly realised that it was sticky and wet. The liquid was not water. It was too thick. And it had a familiar smell. Dropping the fabric, she held her shaking hands up to her face. They were covered in fresh blood.

"What the....?" Sadie exclaimed, her heartbeat accelerating suddenly, as she walked forward further into the box.

Jackie, patiently waiting alongside with Katseye, heard an anguished gasp as Sadie stumbled backwards down the ramp.

"There's someone in there," Sadie gasped, her voice shaking with shock, "Someone who's bleeding. Get an ambulance Jackie. And the police. Quick!"

"You take Katseye and call them on my 'phone," Jackie responded, immediately, shoving the lead rope and the mobile phone into Sadie's shaking hands, "I'll deal with the casualty. I know what to do."

But even Jackie's Army training had not prepared her for the sight of Luke Cunningham with his face kicked in and a broken beer bottle embedded in his throat.

8

There were six sleek and powerful runners in the Punchestown Champion Hurdle that year. Sam followed the progress of a gleaming Curlew Landings as the horse walked purposefully, ears pricked, around the oval parade ring path, Travis stepping out confidently alongside, the leather lead rein in his right hand. Curlew looked every inch his usual lively self, all sign of his brush with party drugs having long disappeared.

It was a bright and breezy late April day at the famous Irish Festival. The yellow gorse alongside the far section of the undulating green track glowed fiercely in the clean sunlight. The winter-bare trees lining the course were working hard to produce their new season's leaves. The cool air felt clear, fresh and full of sharp energy.

"I'm glad we decided to come, you know, Teddy," Sam told his cousin, who was standing alongside him on the lawn around which the racehorses were circling, "A good run from Curlew is just what is needed to cheer everyone up – especially Sadie. She blames herself for what happened to Luke."

"Yeah, it's been a tough time for the girl," Teddy agreed, adding for the umpteenth time, "Crap business, bloody gutser, nothing else to say for it, James."

The Punchestown Festival had started on the previous day, less than two weeks after Sadie had found Luke Cunningham slumped, bloody and unconscious, on the floor of the Sampfield Grange horse lorry.

When Jackie had thrust Katseye's lead rope into her shaking hands, Sadie had, as directed, called for help, both on Jackie's phone and by shouting out loudly to the numerous nearby grooms and drivers that someone had been badly injured and needed an ambulance. Seeing a smiling Kye approaching her with a jaunty looking Highlander Park in tow, Sadie had quickly signalled to him to stay where he was. Having manoeuvred the black bulk of Katseye quickly round to face her colleague, Sadie had told Kye only that there had been a nasty accident and that both horses were to be returned to the stables until things had been sorted out.

"What sort of accident?" Kye had asked, automatically assuming that one of the grooms had been kicked or otherwise injured by a misbehaving horse, "Is anyone hurt?"

But Sadie had just shaken her head and run back into the line of horseboxes.

Leading the two horses away, Kye became aware of people passing him in the opposite direction, some giving directions to a racecourse ambulance which had just appeared in the parking area. The ambulance had been soon followed by a green SUV, and Kye had realised with a shock that the two vehicles were heading for the Sampfield Grange and Cunningham horseboxes, which stood side by side at the end of a line of similar vehicles. Other stable staff looking after nearby horses had stopped to stare at what was happening.

"It's Luke Cunningham, Luke Cunningham, you know, he rode in the last race," Kye could soon hear hushed, horrified voices saying to one another, "Someone's attacked him. With a broken bottle, it was, right in his throat. That's what I heard the woman who called the ambulance saying on the phone."

Having taken Katseye and Highlander Park back to their former billets in the racecourse stables, Kye had found Merriott Marsh and his groom waiting there, presumably for instructions from the absent Luke. The shocked member of the Cunningham support team had also heard the horrific gossip flying around the parking area. Leaving a restless Merriott Marsh in Kye's charge, she had hurried away to fetch Luke's parents from one of the Owners and Trainers hospitality areas. Kye, adrenaline pumping through his body, his hands shaking, had tied up the horses, filled up their water buckets and remained in the stables, wondering what else he should do.

Someone had tried to cut Luke Cunningham's throat. Kye's head had been pounding as he had recalled the smirking Sheryl in the crowd by The Charlton Arms, pointing at her throat and then at Kye. Had whoever had done this to Luke mistaken his target? Kye leaned against Highlander Park's warm flank and buried his face in his hands. Where were Mr Sampfield and the Urquharts? Had they been called over along with the Cunninghams? Where was Jackie, who had once said that she was his bodyguard?

Medical assistance had come to Sadie and Jackie very promptly on that terrible day. Paramedics and doctors had been on duty all afternoon at the racecourse and had been quickly dispatched to the horsebox park. Jackie, doing her best to explain to the first paramedic what had happened, had been kneeling on the horsebox floor trying to identify the source of the blood which was falling onto Highlander Park's blue travelling rug, and could only tell him that they had found the casualty in this state a few minutes earlier, and that the bleeding appeared to be from his broken nose rather than from the wound caused to his neck and throat by the bottle. The paramedics, and, very soon after, the doctor, agreed with this assessment. Luke was badly hurt, but the initial fear that a carotid artery had been severed by the jagged brown glass could at least be dismissed.

Stabilising Luke to enable him to be transported to hospital had taken some time. As Kye had already discovered, the news that Luke had apparently suffered a vicious attack in the horsebox park had spread like wildfire, and an anxious crowd had soon gathered nearby, comprising people keen to text and tweet to their friends and family about what had happened to the unfortunate victim, and, even more urgently, to find out whether whoever had done it had been identified and arrested. The police, arriving on the scene shortly after the medical staff, had quickly established a cordon around the Sampfield Grange and Cunningham horseboxes, and had set about clearing other vehicles and people away from the area.

An ambulance containing Luke had eventually left the racecourse, its blue lights and sirens being turned on only once the vehicle was clear of the racecourse exit and out in the chaos of the Melling

Road. The ambulance had pushed and ground its way through the clogged traffic surrounding the racecourse, the police on duty in the streets doing their best to assist its passage. Out on the main road, the young paramedic driving the ambulance soon faced the additional challenge of avoiding drunken and revelling pedestrians, some of whom seemed to have forgotten the function of an emergency ambulance, and were running freely into the roadway, not looking and caring where they were going, as they shouted loudly to their equally inebriated and witless friends.

Luke had been soon in the expert care of the nearby Aintree University Hospital. Unconscious when discovered by Sadie, he had started to come to his senses in the ambulance, but the pain relief which had been pumped into his system rendered his feeble attempts at speech incoherent. His white-faced mother had accompanied him in the ambulance, his father having remained at the racecourse to give support and directions to his two shocked stable staff.

At the hospital, it had been quickly ascertained that Luke's injuries, although severe, had not been life threatening. A badly broken nose and some damaged teeth would spoil his good looks until such time as cosmetic surgery could be undertaken to improve things. The smashed eye socket, or comminuted orbital wall fracture, as the Accident and Emergency doctor had termed it, inflicted by the heavy boot which had stamped viciously on the side of his head whilst he had been on the ground, was of more concern, not least because it was not yet clear whether Luke's eyesight would be permanently damaged. A deep cut to the back of his head, caused apparently by contact with the edge of the horsebox ramp, had resulted in a hairline fracture to the skull, which would require monitoring, but which at least did not appear to have been depressed into his brain. Other than that, Luke had sustained broken bones in both wrists and hands, consistent with his having tried, ultimately unsuccessfully, to defend himself against what must have been a heavy object wielded by his attacker, such as a cricket bat or a concrete fence post, which had also fractured three of his ribs. The broken bottle, it seemed, had been driven into his neck whilst he was on the floor of the horsebox, but had fortunately done nothing worse than inflict a nasty laceration, which required stitching, and would leave Luke with a permanent scar.

Once Luke had been taken to hospital, and the area around the horseboxes had been secured as a crime scene, the police had turned their attention to Jackie and Sadie, who had appeared to be the only available witnesses. The doctor and paramedics had quickly disabused the two police officers of any presumption that the young man's injuries had been caused by a horse, with the result that further investigative resources had then been called to the location, and a scrutiny of CCTV recordings undertaken with the help of the racecourse security staff. The two young women had watched in silence as the immobile Luke, an oxygen mask covering his mouth and nose, had been stretchered into the waiting ambulance, Luke's distraught parents barely registering the presence of the two frightened young women who had discovered their injured son.

Sadie and Jackie had been hugely relieved by the welcome and reassuring appearance of Mr Sampfield. The police had initially been reluctant to permit the new arrival anywhere near the scene, but, on learning that he was the owner of the vehicle in which the injured young man had been discovered, as well as the employer of the shocked young witnesses, eventually agreed that Sam could remain on the scene with his staff. Sam could see Sir Andrew Cunningham speaking to one of the police officers, his panama hat pushed back on his balding head, a stunned expression on his normally composed face. The evening sun was quickly dropping behind the nearby buildings of the Melling Road and an air of chill gloom had begun to suffuse the proceedings.

On learning the true nature of the incident affecting Luke, Sam had immediately called Lady Helen Garratt on his rarely used mobile phone. He had known that his cousins had been in the 1839 restaurant with the Garratt party and would have been unlikely to have heard what had happened in the lorry park. Sam's intention had been to ask Helen to explain to Teddy and Tessa, whose UK mobile phone number Sam had belatedly realised that he did not know, that they would have to make their way home to Sampfield Grange that evening without him. It had already been clear to Sam from the little information which he had managed to glean from the police and Jackie that the Sampfield Grange horsebox was now a crime scene and could not be used to carry the horses back to Sampfield Grange that evening, or in the foreseeable future. Sam had not known how long the horses could reasonably remain there now that the race meeting had ended, although the racecourse stables manager had already assured him that she would be happy for the horses to stay where they were for as long as was necessary.

Quickly suppressing her initial shocked reaction, Helen, with her customary efficiency and excellent contacts, had calmly taken over the task of dealing with the stranded horses. She had arranged through the helpful offices of Alto Clef's trainer for Katseye, Highlander Park and Merriott Marsh to take up spare berths in various horseboxes containing Grand National runners and to be driven back to yards in Lambourn for the night. Sir Andrew Cunningham had been grateful for the proposal, when Sam eventually managed to speak to him, as it was clear that neither of his two employees was in a fit state to drive, even assuming the police would allow the Cunningham horsebox to be taken away. The horses could be collected from Lambourn by other staff and vehicles later that weekend.

Kye had been given the task of co-ordinating the loading of the three horses into their unfamiliar lorries, following Mr Sampfield's instructions to note the contact details of the locations to which each of them was to be sent for the night. Kye, still dazed and scared, had been glad to have something practical to do. The Lambourn staff who were to be taking temporary care of Katseye, Highlander Park and Merriott Marsh had asked Kye if he knew what had happened to Luke Cunningham, but Kye had shaken his head numbly, saying that he knew no more than they did.

"Don't worry, we'll look after your three lads," one of the practical young Lambourn women had told him, reassuringly, "It'll be a nice change of scenery for them all. Anything we need to know about any of them?"

"I can tell yez anything about Merriott Marsh," Kye had replied, trying his best to be helpful, "Except that he pulls hard in his races and I think they call him Merry at home. Highlander Park, Landy, is my ride. He's a bit full of himself sometimes, but he's a nice horse. Katseye here won his race this afternoon. He's very clever, quiet too, just a big softie."

"Oh, we know all about gorgeous Katseye," the girl had agreed, confidently, patting Katseye's dark neck, as Kye had handed over the lead rope, "His brother Tabikat is the Gold Cup winner. And there's another brother, too, isn't there?"

"Another brother?" had asked Kye, puzzled, "Not at Sampfield Grange, there isn't."

"Yeah," the other groom had gone on, "A colt, a three year old, he was supposed to be in the sale on Wednesday. Katalyst his name is. My boss has got some big owners who are interested in buying him. But he was taken out before the sale started."

The information about Katalyst had been new to Kye, and he had simply shrugged in response.

Sadie's statement to the police had been short and straightforward. She had not spoken to Luke, she had said, since the morning, when the two lorries had been first parked alongside each other. Luke had invited her to join him in the Owners and Trainers bar, but she had declined, as she had had work to do, preparing the two Sampfield Grange horses for their races. She had told Luke, she had said, speaking with a catch in her voice, that she would meet up with him back at their lorries after the end of racing. She had seen Luke in the parade ring just before the last race but had not spoken to him. The next time she had seen him was when she had opened up the back of the Sampfield Grange lorry to help Jackie load Katseye, and had found Luke lying injured and bleeding on the floor. She had not seen anyone near the lorries except other grooms and stable staff.

Jackie had corroborated Sadie's account, adding that she had not seen Luke at all since that morning until the moment Sadie had shouted to her to get help. Queried as to why she had assumed the role of first aider, she had simply referred to her Army training in stabilising severely injured casualties in the field. Sam, when asked, had said he could add nothing to their accounts, as he had not been in the horsebox park nor had he seen Luke other than in the parade ring. The police had then turned their attention to Sir Andrew Cunningham and his two staff.

Kye, walking down to join his colleagues once the horses had been safely seen on their way, could see that he had received several missed calls on his mobile phone, all of which had been from either Travis, Lewis or Kelly. Fortunately, he had transferred the details of his colleagues into the Contacts list of his recently acquired new phone, which had meant that their names, rather than just their numbers, showed up on the list of Recent calls. The news of the attack on an amateur jockey at Aintree racecourse had been widely reported and gruesomely speculated over on social media, and even the mainstream media were now carrying it as Breaking News.

Judging that Travis would be the most sensible recipient of his return call, Kye had spent the next few minutes bringing his colleague up to date with what he knew, which was really very little. IIe had told Travis that either Sadie or Mr Sampfield would be in touch with news about the collection of the horses from Lambourn and that he would let Travis know when they would all be home. Before Travis could ask anything else, Kye had cut the connection.

Sadie and Sam had arrived back at Sampfield Grange in the Audi in the early hours of the morning, shortly followed by the Urquharts, who had waited behind at the racecourse and had brought Kye and Jackie back with them in their hired Volvo. Everyone had been exhausted and, ignoring the eager questions of the wideawake Lewis and Kelly, had gone straight to bed.

Sadie had spoken little during the journey home, other than to give Mr Sampfield the message that Merlin would be along in the morning to work with Curlew Landings. Otherwise she had stared fixedly ahead at the red lines of taillights on the cars in front, simply nodding when her worried employer had enquired after her welfare. She had eventually closed her eyes, but Sam had guessed, correctly, that she had not been asleep.

Seeing Merlin now approaching them across the Punchestown parade ring, sporting the red and green colours of Sampfield Grange, Sam tried his best to concentrate on the present. Curlew had a good chance of winning this short and highly competitive race.

"'ello, Mr Sampfield, Mr Urquhart," Merlin started, "'ow's things at 'ome now?"

Merlin had not, in the event, come to Sampfield Grange on the day after the Grand National, judging, as a result of the news reports which he had heard on the car radio on his way home to Chepstow, that there would be little done in the way of normal work in the Somerset yard that day. Merlin had instead joined them to work with Curlew Landings later in the week, by which time Sadie, still subdued and evidently distressed by what had happened to Luke, had been sent to stay for a while with her and Kelly's parents, who lived in a retirement village on the coast. Luke himself had still been in hospital in Liverpool and the only communication between the two young people had been by text message.

"Sadie's still with her parents," Sam told the jockey, guessing correctly that Sadie was the real focus of his interest, "She seems to blame herself for what happened to Luke Cunningham. I have no idea why, but she thinks she should have anticipated that something of this sort might happen."

Merlin shifted uneasily in his lightweight boots, remembering his conversation with Sadie on the way home from the Cuffborough point to point meeting. Sadie had been worried then about apparent threats, but those had appeared to be directed at Tabikat, or more likely, in Merlin's view, at himself. Had whoever attacked Luke thought that Luke was Merlin? After all, the horsebox was the one which had brought Katseye to the race meeting at Aintree, and Merlin was Katseye's jockey too.

Quickly dismissing the unpleasant thought from his mind, Merlin forced himself to sound cheerful, "Well, let 'er know that I'm lookin' forward to seein' 'er 'ome again soon and ridin' in some more points. That Indian Rocks needs a clever jockey on 'is back. And Curlew's lookin' good today, I can see. I expec' Mr Halstock is watchin' on TV at home. We'll 'ave to see if we can win 'im some money on 'is bets."

The Punchestown Champion Hurdle turned out to be a rather dramatic affair, which would not have helped the blood pressure of Curlew Landings' former owner, Toby Halstock, who was known to wager large sums of money on the talented horse. The whole field set off at a cracking pace and there was little to choose between the four emergent front runners until the final part of the contest. Two of the leading horses had run in the Champion Hurdle at Cheltenham and their jockeys were determined that Curlew Landings would not beat them again.

"And as they approach two out," gabbled the racecourse commentator, his Dublin accented voice rising, along with the surge of loud encouragement from the excited raceday crowd, "Rabbit Punch is just in the lead with Stonebridge Junction matching him stride for stride. Curlew Landings is still close in behind. And .. ohh .. Rabbit Punch has run out at the second last! Stonebridge Junction has nowhere to go and he's been carried out by the other horse. His jockey's on the ground. Devil Waters has been hampered too. They're all over the place. Cheltenham winner Curlew Landings has just about dodged the mess and is pressing on. The other horses in behind are all still on their feet. It's left Curlew Landings to jump the last on his own and there's nothing can touch him now if he clears that one. Which he does! And Merlin ap Rhys eases the horse down over the line. The Cheltenham champion has done it again. Who's to say whether that incident made any difference?"

As Sam and Teddy waited in the winner's enclosure for a happy Travis to bring the triumphant Curlew Landings and Merlin back along the horsewalk, Sam noticed a group of men talking with trainer Brendan Meaghan alongside the parade ring. Brendan had not entered a horse in the Champion Hurdle, but was at the racecourse with a number of other fancied runners that day. Sam could see that one of the other men was Eoghan Foley, but the other two were people he did not know.

Seeing Sam looking towards them, Eoghan said something to the others and came forward to greet Sam at the rail.

"Congratulations to you and Merlin on your win there, Sam. Will you be staying for the auction after racing today?" Eoghan asked, rather abruptly, Sam thought. He could see that Brendan and the other two men were now silent and appeared to be watching the conversation.

"Thank you, Genie. As for the auction, I regret not," Sam responded, politely, wondering why Eoghan should have asked this unexpected question, "Is there something you think might be of interest to me?"

"Indeed, there is," Eoghan responded promptly, "Katalyst is for sale today. And we should like you to buy him."

9

The large, metal framed barn in which the horses for the sale were temporarily housed was clearly not normally used as a stable. Lines of portable wooden and aluminium sided stalls had been erected along each of the two long sides of the building. The structure itself, Sam surmised, was normally used to store racecourse plant and machinery, judging by the untidy row of tractors and their agricultural attachments which now stood behind a group of neatly aligned horseboxes in a neighbouring parking area. A second line of stalls had been placed parallel to each of the outside rows, standing back to back down the centre of the building's interior, orientated so that each line faced towards the rows along the walls. This arrangement enabled the equine occupants to view one another across the two aisles which were thereby created for the use of the stable staff who were looking after the potentially valuable creatures. Buckets, wheelbarrows, brooms, shovels, and other yard equipment stood in the corners.

The barn and its entrance were busy with chattering visitors, most of them potential buyers who would soon be bidding for the horses once the auction got under way. A grass area at the side had been fenced off for the purpose of showing the horses to anyone interested in seeing them trotted up, so that their movement could be viewed and indications of their temperament assessed, or perhaps more realistically, guessed. The sale contained only horses of three years old and upward, most of them already raced, and therefore did not offer potential buyers the option of seeing short 'breeze up' runs to show the likely quality of the horses' future racing performance. A few of the horses were being led up and down the outdoor area, groups of serious faced onlookers pointing to them and making notes in the closely printed sale catalogues.

The decision to attend the post racing horse sale had had to be made quickly. Eoghan Foley's eagerness to have Sam view the young horse had been quite evident and Sam had had to admit that he had been genuinely intrigued by the opportunity of the potentially valuable purchase. Teddy, listening to the conversation, had added to the pressure in his megaphone tones, "He's a brother to your Tabikat and Katseye, that right? This is one we have to see, James."

Merlin, who had dismounted Curlew Landings and was lifting his saddle from the triumphant horse's back, as a grinning Travis had patted Curlew's neck and sluiced down his sweating coat with water from a nearby bucket, had pricked up his ears at the mention of his Cheltenham and Aintree rides.

"Did I 'ear you right, Mr Foley?" had asked Merlin, without preamble, "You got another one at 'ome from the same dam as Tabikat an' Katseye? Little Kitty Cat, the dam, isn' it? I'd like to 'ave a look at 'im too, if you don' mind me joinin' you, Mr Sampfield and Mr Urquhart."

In the face of such persuasion, it had been difficult for Sam to do anything other than accept Eoghan's invitation to consider whether he might purchase the young horse.

Fortunately for their travel arrangements, Curlew Landings had been brought to Punchestown races by a commercial horse transport company, whose driver had been accompanied by Travis in the cab of the firm's blue liveried lorry. The larger Sampfield Grange horsebox had only just been returned from Liverpool, having been released by the police, and no-one at Sampfield Grange had been keen to transport Curlew Landings in it, even though they had been assured that it had been deep cleaned by a specialist cleaning company employed by the police. The smaller lorry had been already designated to take Highlander Park, along with Jackie and Kye, to Taunton racecourse for Highlander's last race before the horse was turned away for his summer break. This at least meant that Travis had been able to start the return journey to Sampfield Grange along with Curlew Landings and the professional horsebox driver and to leave his employer to make new arrangements for his own and his cousin's travel.

Two of the junior staff of the auction company, which was the well-known firm of Cathal's, based in Ireland, were sitting at a small wooden desk by the entrance door. They looked up as Eoghan came into the converted barn.

"Good afternoon again, Mr Foley," said one of them, a young red haired woman with a multiplicity of freckles and a bright smile, "Your lovely horse is attracting a lot of interest today. Have you brought some more prospective bidders for us?"

"That I have," Eoghan told her, "This is Mr Sampfield Peveril, a trainer from England, and Mr Urquhart from Australia. And Mr ap Rhys, who is from Wales, and a jockey."

"You sound like a geography class, indeed you do, Mr Foley," replied the other staff member, an acne-afflicted young man with lank brown hair, who was holding out a clipboard towards the party, "If your guests are interested in bidding for the lots, they will need to complete these forms, if you please, sirs. Are any of you bloodstock agents, or are you all private buyers?"

"We're private buyers," Sam replied, as Teddy accepted the clipboard and a pen from the young man, "Mr ap Rhys is here to advise us. Unless you want to bid yourself, of course, Merlin? My apologies, I should have let you answer the question for yourself."

As Merlin regretfully shook his head, his dark hair still glistening wet from his hasty shower following Curlew's race and the ensuing prize giving, Teddy said quickly, "I can sort this paperwork for us, James. You go with Merlin and Genie and give the horse a look over."

As Sam followed Eoghan Foley along the nearer of the two gangways between the stalls, he was acutely conscious that he might have offended Merlin. He knew nothing of the jockey's personal circumstances and his assumption that Merlin was not in a position to bid for a prospective racehorse at an auction was, he realised, somewhat presumptuous on his own part. He recalled Merlin saying, on the day they had first met at Sampfield Grange, that he would like to have his own racing yard at some time in the future. But surely, Sam thought, a horse like Katalyst would be an overambitious, and probably highly expensive, first step – unless, of course, Merlin had a potential owner of his own in mind.

Sam could hear Teddy's loud voice receding behind him as he walked, brushing past groups of other viewers who were occupying the walkway, listening to earnest vendors extolling the virtues of their sale lots.

"You do?" Teddy was saying to one of the Cathal's staff, "Surprised people come all the way from Oz. Melbourne you say? No, I'm a Queensland man. Must be some fair crackers of horses for sale here then."

Katalyst was housed in the last stall along the central row. The young horse put his head over the door as the group approached and allowed his nose and face to be rubbed and patted. A white notice attached to the front of the stall read:

KATALYST (IRE)
3yo
Black/brown colt
Dr Lyster (IRE) x Little Kitty Cat (IRE)

Merlin had picked up one of the glossy covered sale catalogues which had been stacked on the desk by the entrance. He flicked through it to find Katalyst's entry.

"'ere we are, Mr Sampfield, Lot 20," Merlin said, holding out the little booklet for Sam to see.

"I can guess what it says," Sam replied, keen to avoid being obliged to read out the information printed on the page, "I think that Genie here can probably give us all the details we need."

"OK," replied Merlin, slightly taken aback by Sam's dismissive answer, "It says 'ere, Mr Foley, that the horse 'as run in a couple of amateur flat races at Gleannglas. Was that with Miss Foley ridin' 'im?"

"That's correct, Merlin," Eoghan responded, "We were planning to start his career over hurdles this next season. But, as he is an entire colt, we have other possibilities open to us."

"What I don't understand, Genie," Sam put in, "Is why you are wanting to sell him? I can see he is very valuable, and I am sure you will get a good price today, but you yourself could earn a lot from him in the future as a stallion at stud, with his breeding and the recent success of his two half brothers."

"Well, that is the problem, you have it right there, Sam," Eoghan replied, clearly having answered the same question before, "See what it says about his bloodline in the catalogue."

Merlin looked at the family tree tabulation set out at the top of the page which related to Lot 20 in the auction. The information in the two left hand side columns of the table was the same as that inscribed on the notice on Katalyst's stall door. The earlier generations in the horse's family tree were set out in the third and fourth columns. In the third column, the names of the sire and dam of Dr Lyster were given as Dr Lyle and Sister Susie. Below this were the names of Little Kitty Cat's parents, Alakazam and Kat's Gift. In the final column were the names of the preceding generation of Katalyst's family. But where there should have been a list of eight names, there were only six. Kat's Gift's sire and dam were listed simply as Unknown.

Further down the same page, the dreaded word Unknown appeared again and again, in the places where information on the third and fourth dams of Katalyst should have been given. Little Kitty Cat's own racing achievements as the first dam were listed, but Kat's Gift, as the second dam or granddam, was said to be 'of little account' and her parentage Unknown. In compensation, much was made on the page of the recent achievements of half-brothers Tabikat and Katseye to allow readers to infer that Katalyst was clearly from a top racing family on the dam's side too, but it was evident that it was the known ancestry on the sire's side which constituted the only properly documented information on the colt's bloodline.

As Merlin read all this information aloud, Eoghan nodded ruefully.

"You will understand, Sam and Merlin," he said, carefully, "Why we decided to keep Tabikat and Katseye in the family, and as geldings at that. Although we have never hidden any information about our horses, the fact that they were never for sale has meant no-one would need to be concerned about their bloodline, and they could compete on their own merits. Niamh's son-in-law, Ephraim Levy, bought Tabikat, as you know, for his son Daniel, who registered him to the ownership of Susan Stonehouse and her daughter TK as a gift. Now Mrs Stonehouse is no longer alive, Efe, or that is to say his business, again owns the horse nowadays. And Mrs Crosland, who is the sister of Mrs Stonehouse, had Katseye from us. Katseye, it is true, is now the property of Mr Arturo Ardizzone, but that was a private sale to him by Mrs Crosland based on the horse's own merits on the racecourse. No-one has ever had to search through such information as is required for these sale catalogues to inform themselves. So, we have not needed until now to expose ourselves to questions about these things."

"So why have you put Katalyst up for sale now?" asked Sam, puzzled, not least by Eoghan's Foley's revelation in passing that Meredith Crosland was Susan Stonehouse's sister, "Is it because you feel that buyers may overlook these things, as you call them, in the light of Tabikat and Katseye's achievements?"

"It was worth the risk," Eoghan responded, and stopped, as if unsure what to say next.

"Do you really not know anythin' of the 'istory of Little Kitty Cat's dam?" asked Merlin, who had been listening carefully so as to take in all this additional information, "You own 'er yourself, is that right?"

Sam had already heard from Brendan Meaghan the story of how Eoghan Foley had come to acquire Kat's Gift sixteen years earlier, when the mare had been young and in foal, but Merlin had no knowledge of it.

"Kat's Gift was given her name because she was a gift to Caitlin," Eoghan explained, "Caitlin chose it because, as I later learned, she was once known herself by the name Kat when she was head lass at the racing yard of Fergal Carter. The man who gave Kat's Gift to us is dead now. His name was Oisin Cassidy. He used to be an apprentice with me at Mallows."

"Did this Mr Cassidy not know anything about the mare?" asked Merlin, intrigued, not least by the information that Eoghan's partner had worked at the Carter yard, now headed by Fergal's son Niall, "He was a jockey too, I suppose, if you were apprentices together?"

"Oisin was a stud man," Eoghan informed him, "Mallows is now a stud only, as you yourself will know, but in those days it also was a racing yard. The apprentices all learned both trades. Ronan Brody, who owns Mallows now, was with us then. And Brendan Meaghan too, who, like me, became a jockey. Brendan and I were stable jockeys together at the yard of his father Cormac in County Meath. Oisin, though, took over his father's business selling horses in Gleannglas. But sixteen years ago, the business failed and the bailiffs came to take the horses and the premises. Oisin did not want to let Maire go to be sold somewhere else, so he gave her to me, or, as he said at the time, to Caitlin."

"Maire was the stable name of Kat's Gift, is that right?" clarified Merlin.

"Oisin said then that Maire was her only name," Eoghan replied, "She was a beautiful chestnut mare, as classy a horse as anything I had ever ridden in my racing days. She was in foal to Alakazam, Oisin said, a stallion then standing at Mallows."

"I was going to ask you about that Genie," Sam interjected, as Teddy came to stand alongside the little group. The dark colt noticed the arrival of a new person and put a curious nose over the door of his box. He had a small white star on his forehead. "Brendan told me that the covering by Alakazam had not been acknowledged or certificated and so he could not be recorded as the sire when Little Kitty Cat was foaled and later when she went racing."

"That is true, Sam," Eoghan answered, "But I have made things right with Ronan since then and Alakazam has now been officially confirmed as the sire and that fact is now properly recorded with the racing authorities."

Merlin's sharp mind had been working furiously during this exchange, and, to Sam's surprise, the jockey asked an unexpected question.

"Sixteen years ago, you say you 'ad the mare, Mr Foley," Merlin started, "That would be about the time that Mr Meaghan's place, *An Féarach Beag*, was destroyed by fire, isn' it? So it was not only your friend Mr Cassidy who lost 'is business then? Mr Meaghan lost 'is too."

In the silence which followed, the young colt shuffled restlessly in his box, unaware that his hidden ancestry was the cause of so much discussion. As Eoghan opened his mouth to reply, there was a sudden interruption. The young freckled woman from the reception desk had followed Teddy along the gangway. She was accompanied by a middle-aged man who wore a grey business suit brightened up by a yellow tie reminiscent of the golden gorse alongside the racecourse. Sam recognised him as one of the men who had been standing earlier in the company of Eoghan Foley.

"Hello, Genie, glad I caught you before the sale was started," said the man, "I regret that we have a problem. We're going to have to take your lot out of the sale today, I am sorry to say."

Eoghan himself said nothing, whilst the other three men looked questioningly at the newcomer.

"My apologies, gentlemen," the well-dressed man said to them, "My name is Jack Carter. I'm one of Cathal's auctioneers, in charge of the sale today. I am sorry to disappoint you if you had it in mind to bid for this animal."

"What's the problem, Mr Carter?" asked Merlin, the quickest to recover his wits after this unexpected intervention, "Some problem with 'is breeding records?"

"I have received information that the horse is not as described," Jack Carter said obliquely, "Some of the paperwork is not in order, but that is not the difficulty. There is an allegation that this colt has been stolen from his rightful owner."

"And 'oo is that then?" asked Merlin, incredulously.

"My brother, Niall Carter," came the reply.

10

The cruise liner which had slipped into the otherwise empty East side of the quiet harbour that morning was gradually getting smaller. The local ferry ship, moored at the port's western end, its grey sea lion logo and blue and yellow lettering contrasting starkly with the anonymous lines of the cruise vessel, seemed dwarfed beside it. The ferry at least looked like a ship, whereas the cruise liner resembled an elongated apartment building, threatening to tip over under its own top-heavy weight.

The little white cabins of the cable car service with their clear acrylic viewing windows were rising quietly and continuously along curving steel lines, their smooth travel over the tops of the regularly spaced stanchions scarcely producing any disruption to the peace of the ride. The downward bound cars glided in the opposite direction towards the harbour in graceful silence.

The red roofs of the city fanned out across the surrounding hills, which formed a bright and verdant backdrop spreading upwards over an irregular staircase of flat terraces. The light walls of the houses and apartment blocks mirrored the structure of the visiting ship which lay in the deceptively still blue water beyond them. The startling black and white cathedral tower, with its little pyramidal spire, protruded upwards from the centre of the old part of the city, whilst the curved climb of the main road to the airport looped dramatically beneath to reach the concrete viaduct which spanned a rocky and vegetation packed chasm alongside the cable route, distant water just visible far below.

The suspended cabin in which Isabella Hall and George Harvey were sitting had swung slowly out from the early quiet of the spacious lower station of the scenic aerial transport system, most of the tourists from the visiting floating hotel being as yet occupied with their breakfast and discussion of their options for their single day in the picturesque capital of the remote Atlantic island of Madeira. In Funchal's sloping streets, with their startling monochrome patterned surfaces, were bars, cafes and restaurants ready to accept their money when they became bored with poking around in the many small shops for cork handbags and bottles of Madeira wine. The more energetic of them might plod up the steep and narrow streets to find the historic colonial buildings whilst others, eventually working their way along the unexpected and welcome flatness of the promenade to the Monte cable car itself, would venture to the topmost point above the city of Funchal where stood Our Lady of Monte church, a vertiginous steep flight of stone steps leading to its wooden doors. A further cable car trip onward to the exotic botanical gardens was a customary next stop.

Notwithstanding the steep incline of the cable, the rooftops of the city were scarcely more than a few feet from the little gondolas which passed above them on the ascent. Terraced domestic gardens, reached by long flights of concrete steps, at the bottom of which groups of parked cars were anchored in the snaking streets, boasted banana palms, carefully tended vegetable patches, lines of flapping and colourful washing, and in a few instances, a tethered cow. The dark granite and white body of a squat church with an angular spire slipped by, barely feet away, seated securely on a little grassy terrace of its own, the grass about it dotted with small wild flowers. On another extended terrace, a group of shouting boys played football on a green artificial pitch surrounded by high fences.

Most of the houses looked smart and well kept, but the occasional ruin was also visible, upper structure collapsed, those of its fallen tiles which were not cracked or broken quickly stripped away for use elsewhere. A well-tended lawn, complete with sunbeds, moved by the cabin window. Household dogs stood on balconies to watch the world pass by, insofar as it was possible for much of the world to pass alongside such an inaccessible location. One brown canine eagerly scrutinised the cable cars as they passed, perhaps looking for its owner, its indifferent companion snoozing in the sun, knowing that the little glass boxes contained only tourists.

The pale sky visible above the harbour was empty of cloud. It was difficult, Isabella thought, to fathom where the ocean ended and the sky began, as the distance to the vague horizon gradually grew longer in line with the inexorable ascent of the cable car. Behind her, she knew, shifting and misty clouds shrouded the peaks which formed the roof of the island, hiding from view the spectacular gorges, forests and waterfalls sought after by those who came to Madeira to walk the *llevadas* and learn about the natural wonders afforded by the isolated location of the chief island of this strange formerly volcanic archipelago.

Isabella was not looking behind her. She was familiar with the view from both directions. She was looking at the man who had walked into the cabin just before the closure of the doors and was now sitting with his back to the ocean, facing toward their direction of travel up to Monte. Isabella knew that his black sunglasses covered bright blue eyes, and that under the panama straw hat was dark hair streaked with grey. He wore an open necked blue shirt with a narrow green stripe, beige chino cotton trousers and a pair of tan loafers. He looked much like any other conservatively dressed male tourist on the understated holiday island. Except that he wasn't a tourist, she reminded herself. But then, neither were they.

George Harvey shifted his walking stick across the floor between his knees. His left leg stayed straight and stiff in front of him, whilst his right knee was bent, his own straw hat resting on his right thigh. George wore grey hiking shorts, and vicious white scars along both sides of his left knee were clearly visible.

"Well, Frank," George said, "Does your presence today mean that we are free to go now?"

"Don't you like it here?" asked the other man, deliberately not answering the question, "I should have thought you would have enjoyed coming to this holiday haunt for older couples. You said that you didn't like being shut up in the other place."

Isabella cut in, quick to rise to the deliberately dangled bait. It was she who had compared their previous residence, a small flat above a restaurant on the lively Spanish island of Mallorca, to a prison.

"Well, we aren't directly supervised by gaolers here," Isabella retorted, crossly, referring to the elderly proprietors of the Agua

Blau restaurant who had acted as their minders during their brief time in the attractive little port of Faratxa, "Yes, it's true, we have begun to feel like dull and ordinary people again. Respectable British tourists spending the winter amongst an equally respectable Northern European clientele. I have hardly heard anyone speak a word of Portuguese. But, then, we don't really need gaolers in this out of the way place. It's seven hundred miles to the nearest bit of mainland Europe and the African coast is six hundred miles away, so not much nearer. Even the Canary Islands are three hundred miles South over that horizon behind you. There are only two ways in and out of Madeira - the seaport and the airport, which are, incidentally, the only flat places on the whole island. So, you know exactly who comes in and who goes out. That's pretty much like a prison, if you ask me. I assumed that is why you sent us here back at the beginning of March."

"You are right of course, Isabella," Frank told her, disarmingly, "But there is one further crucial feature of this place which you have not mentioned and which means that it is very far from being impregnable. George knows what it is."

"Excellent internet connectivity," supplied George, as Isabella looked at him questioningly, "That means Madeira is not a prison or a fortress in a cyber sense."

"But we have made plenty of use of internet services since we've been here," objected Isabella.

"All the services and connections which we have used have been encrypted," George told her, his speech becoming more thoughtful, "Although none of those is completely secure. Nothing is."

In the pause which followed, Frank Stanley said suddenly, "This cable car takes twenty minutes to travel in each direction. We are halfway up the mountain now, so I have ten minutes to deliver my message to you and another twenty minutes for us to discuss it on the way back. As you know, this is the first face to face communication we have had in over two months, and a lot has happened since we last met. No-one can overhear us in this little box. We are as near to being air gapped as is possible in today's digital environment."

"Air gapped?" queried Isabella.

"It means that we are isolated," explained George, quickly, "Connected to nothing. Insulated by the space around us. We are not using the internet and we are outside physical earshot. No-one could predict in advance which cabin we would board, even if they knew that we would be here at all. Bugging every individual cabin would be impractical. It is the nearest we can get to total privacy."

"I see," said Isabella, slowly, as they both looked at Frank Stanley with some trepidation.

"On the day after the Cheltenham Festival finished," Frank began, his tone that of the narrator of a carefully memorised story, "A body was found at the bottom of a rock face called Cleeve Cloud, which is on the side of Cleeve Hill overlooking the racecourse. The body was that of an American tourist called Damon Casey. Mr Casey had been hit over the head with a heavy object and then was either pushed or fell from the top of the escarpment. Mr Casey was identified from items found in his rental car, which was eventually located nearby. From that starting point, we were able to track down the hotel at which he had been recently staying. It was The Charlton Arms near Sampfield Grange."

"The Charlton Arms?" repeated Isabella, sitting suddenly upright on the cable car's narrow seat. George gripped the top of his stick and looked fixedly at Frank.

"Mr Casey was not, as you will have readily guessed, the man he purported to be," went on Frank, ignoring the interruption, "He had arrived at The Charlton Arms on the second day, the Wednesday, of the Cheltenham Festival. He left on the morning of Gold Cup Day, the Friday, saying that he planned to meet his wife at Birmingham Airport. The hotel staff had no reason to suppose that he had any interest in Cheltenham or the horse racing. But he did mention that he intended to fly his drone locally at Old Warnock airfield.

"You know that we expected that Dominic Katz, the man who had been attempting to bring down Ardua Industrie S.p.A through posting fake aircraft accident reports and making denial of service cyber attacks on their IT systems, would attempt to access the Altior 10 aircraft, with its Astrak Mark 2 flight control system, which was being remotely test flown from Old Warnock. Our Mr Casey did exactly that. Furthermore, he hacked into the onboard software and caused the aircraft to fly itself to Gloucestershire Airport, its usual test flight route. He did not, though, then do what we expected, which was to direct the aircraft to crash itself at the racecourse at the time when Arturo Ardizzone, the proprietor of the aircraft company and the owner of the racehorse Katseye was standing in the parade ring. Someone stopped him from doing that by striking him over the head and killing him. Dominik Katz's sister, Dr Lara Katz, was standing with Arturo in the parade ring, ready to take over control of the aircraft and direct it away from the racecourse. But in the end, her expert services were not needed.

'We know now, from DNA tests, that Damon Casey and Dominik Katz are one and the same person. We also know, as do you, George, that a man calling himself Nico Gatto tampered with the spyware which you had planted in the office computer in the Vachers' bicycle hire shop in Frossiac in early February, setting it to spew out random nonsense starting three weeks later so as to overwhelm the UK listening station. You told me yourself that someone later closed the wormhole which led back to Egzon Paloka's old systems in Tirana, which, by the way, now seem to have been largely destroyed. We assume that destruction to have been the work of Dominik Katz, who evidently left Tirana in early January and then travelled via Rome to Carcassonne using an Italian passport in the name of Nico Gatto.

"We suspect that Dominik Katz, or Nico Gatto as he then was, deliberately introduced this three week time delay between physically appearing in Frossiac and remotely activating the work he had done there in order to buy himself some planning time. Not only did this tactic put on the back foot anyone trying to track him down, but it also gave him scope to work on establishing his own negotiating position. He needed this to be ready for later in March, when he expected that Arturo Ardizzone would be dead and he himself would have become an internationally wanted assassin and saboteur, sought by both by the law enforcement authorities and by the damaged criminal enterprises which had formerly relied on the extensive dark web systems controlled by the Paloka empire.

"Enquiries by the French authorities subsequently revealed that the man calling himself Nico Gatto had booked onto a flight from Carcassonne to Rome shortly after visiting Frossiac in February. But, as we already know, Nico Gatto did not board this flight. He clearly left the area by other means, such as rail or road, or else by using another new identity, or both.

"So, we are left with a gap. Nico Gatto was last seen in person in early February in Frossiac and Damon Casey appeared at The Charlton Arms about a month later in March. Where he was between those times, what he was doing and what identity he may have been using, we have yet to discover. We have so far only one firm lead. It is in the form of the denial of service attack which was made two days before Damon Casey arrived at The Charlton Arms, that is, on the Monday of the week of the Cheltenham Festival, on Astrak Avionics plc. As we discussed by telephone at the time, George, on the day that you and Isabella left England, it was a far from fatal attack, and so was successfully overcome by the company's own security systems. It appears to have had two distinct purposes.

"The first was to send a message, which appeared on computer screens through the Astrak company offices. This message said REQUEST NEGOTIATION WITH ARTURO. LONDON. SATURDAY. On the face of it, that would suggest that the sender fully expected Arturo Ardizzone to be alive on the day after the Cheltenham Festival and wished to open a discussion of some kind with him. We have always recognised Dominik Katz to have been a devious player, often deliberately misleading us. Whether this message was designed to make us believe that he had no intention of harming Arturo at the Cheltenham Festival, as we had anticipated, we shall never know. But what is certain is that Dominik Katz did not expect that he himself would be dead. So, our working assumption is that a further message would have been sent following the death of Arturo, which would contain alternative instructions as to the party with whom Dominik wished to negotiate and, more importantly, some indication of what he might have to offer as his part of the bargain. We had assumed, as I told you at the time, that he would ask for immunity from prosecution, a new identity, lifetime protection from those who might seek to harm him, money for life, perhaps an opportunity to work in legitimate cyber security again, that sort of thing. What was not clear was what he had to offer in return, other than an undertaking not to put up for auction the unfinished prototype Astrak Mark 2 system source code to criminal enterprises or to a hostile government."

Frank's narrative stopped abruptly, as the small cabin in which they were sitting swung quietly into the glass walled upper station, where it slowed to walking place, opening its doors in silent invitation to the occupants to disembark. Frank held up his hand.

"Stay seated," he told his two companions, who were mutely trying to get to grips with the efficiently imparted information of the last ten minutes, "The staff have been told that I am an inspector from the operating company. We can stay in here for as long as is necessary."

The little cab moved at an agonisingly slow pace around its pre-prescribed arc just above the level concrete floor. The three occupants sat in silence, ignored by the uniformed staff overseeing the embarkation of the few downward bound passengers who were waiting behind a moveable barrier. At length, the little doors slid quietly shut and the cabin swung outward over the topmost terrace.

"The second purpose was the one you yourself mentioned to me, George," went on Frank, as though the interruption to his narrative had not taken place, "The attack was routed via Frossiac and it not only destroyed your little cyber spy once and for all but also finally closed Egzon's wormhole. However, it now appears that that there was more to it than that."

"Really? What?" asked George, surprised.

"After you left England," Frank told him, "Our people took steps to discontinue the redundant listening operation on the Frossiac link. And they discovered something unexpected. It appears that, although the denial of service attack on Astrak Avionics had been routed through the Frossiac computer, it had not come through the customary route of Egzon's wormhole. A new route had been created. The rubbish and cyberflak coming through your spyware had served to disguise its existence. Once that was taken away, the new wormhole became detectable.

"Have you traced its source?" asked George, instantly curious.

"London," Frank told him, "One of the universities. But it will take our people a while to unravel it properly. As you would expect, it is booby trapped at every stage of its tortuous journey, including, they believe, at the Frossiac end."

"But what does it matter now, if Dominik Katz is dead?" asked Isabella, who had been struggling to follow the details of the story, in much of which she had not previously been involved, "Or are you saying there is someone else who has taken over from him? Someone at the university to which you say the hacking route led back, for example?"

"We don't think Dominik had any allies or understudies," Frank replied, "Dominik Katz worked for himself and no-one else, for the simple reason that the type of work in which he was involved meant that his whole existence was based on mistrust and deception and consequently he himself trusted no-one. We will monitor the link of course, but we don't believe anyone else knows about it, or is in a position to use it. The university where it came from is probably just an unwitting host to the origin of the route, perhaps even originally intended as yet another of Dominik's decoys."

"So," said George, carefully piecing together the final elements of the story, "We think it possible that Dominik Katz could have been in London during the period between February and early March.

And, from what you say, he was using the time to prepare his negotiating position following Arturo Ardizzone's planned death. But that comes back to our earlier discussion. What did he have to offer that we, or anyone else, would want?"

"Have you ever heard of *prizrak*?" asked Frank, abruptly.

"No..," replied Isabella, hesitation in her voice.

"*Prizrak*," confirmed Frank, "Is a chemical weapon. It's a nerve agent."

11

"You are going to have to go over some of Frank's briefing again for me," Isabella told George, firmly, "Cybercrime is not my strong point. I assume being in this fancy aircraft counts as a form of air gapping, which is the one piece of cyberspeak that I have been able to understand. There is no-one here but us and the pilots, and I am assuming they are part of the security services, like Frank."

Isabella Hall and George Harvey were sitting opposite each other, separated by a narrow table, in an expensive looking Bombardier Learjet 70, which was taxying to line up on runway 05 at Madeira's coastal international airport. The grey uniformed captain, a smiling Kiwi with curly fair hair, who had introduced herself as Amanda, turned the smartly appointed aircraft onto the piano key markings at the start of the infamous runway extended at its further end on thick concrete pillars stretching out over the Atlantic Ocean. Isabella could see through the window the usual dense green vegetation and dark rock of the cliffs, with their now familiar lines of vermilion roofed white houses, all of which would be close by their port side when the aircraft made its take-off roll. A line of cars made their busy way along the road running alongside and above the runway.

"There's internet connectivity in this aircraft," George told her, "But we are under no obligation to use it. Once in Carcassonne, though, we shall have no option but to connect with the online world once again."

As the white Maltese registered aircraft rose smoothly into the air, not needing to use even half of the available runway, and doubtless exciting a mixture of admiration and envy from those watching from the windswept terrace outside the crowded departure lounge, Isabella asked, "So what is this advanced persistent threat that Frank was referring to when we were on our way back down from Monte in the cable car?"

"It's basically a form of computer hacking," George began, "People call it APT for short. It's not the sort of thing that your average teenager would do from his or her bedroom. It is effectively like spying, not unlike what I was doing on the little computer in Frossiac. The perpetrator will find a way to install malware or spyware onto a target system and will use it to look for and take data from something specific which is being held or developed there.

"The installation can take place either remotely over the internet or from another computer, or it can be introduced through a physical means, such as plugging in a data stick with the malware on it. I am sure you will remember from the days when you worked in an office environment that one of the main sources of viruses getting onto company IT systems was through employees bringing USBs into work which they had used on their own computers at home. These items were often infected with things which were sitting on the individual's home computer and the plugging in of the data stick at the workplace transferred the virus to the company's systems.

"Then, when technology became more portable, with laptops, iPads, smart phones, and the like, employees would bring in those devices too and connect them to their employer's systems. However hard employers might try to prevent it, including providing 'clean' devices for their staff to use, it still happened, especially in organisations where people were travelling and needing to work from all over the world. IT departments were going mad trying to secure their systems from infiltration and damage. Firewalls were used to repel anything which came in from the outside, but could do little against things which were installed from within. Virus checking software was often out of date as soon as it was installed.

"Many of the things which got onto systems this way, rather than through other routes, like known phishing scams, were not exactly harmless but were not terribly threatening either. The average employee was not interested in, or capable of, bringing down his or her employer's systems or extracting Bitcoin ransoms through denial of service cyber attacks. People like Dominik Katz, before he became involved in criminal activity, made a living from helping organisations protect themselves from these sorts of problems.

"But the term APT means something more sinister than attacks on the ordinary workplace. It normally refers to a criminal enterprise or hostile government organisation which is attempting to gather information about something which it intends to use to its own advantage in the future. The malware can be in place for many years, undetected, slowly gathering data until it has what the perpetrator needs.

"The most well-known example of an APT is a computer worm called Stuxnet. This was used by the United States to impede Iran's development of nuclear weapons. Stuxnet was not simply a silent spy, like my little device in Frossiac. It was also a saboteur. It actively targeted and damaged the control systems of thousands of computers involved in Iran's nuclear programme. The worm got into the Iranian systems through the standard Microsoft software applications which were used on their computers.

"You can see from all this that the concept of air gapping is probably the only way to ensure the security of a computer system. If it is not connected to the internet, nothing can get onto it. If no-one plugs anything into it, such as a USB, a disk or another device, then it cannot be infected. This is what computers used to be like in the old days – standalone systems whose only interface was with a human being typing on an integral keyboard and getting output in the form of paper printouts and screen displays. But a computer like that would be useless for any practical purpose nowadays.

"So, the emphasis for organisations of all sizes, including governments, now has to be on security and protection. It has to be assumed that all IT systems are hackable and that cyber threats of ever increasing sophistication exist everywhere and can come from any source. The good guys make a living from providing this protection, which is why the Stuxnet worm was eventually uncovered and counteracted, whilst the bad guys, such as Egzon Paloka and eventually Dominik Katz, who changed sides - and if what Frank surmised is correct, would have been willing to change back again - make it their business to stay one step ahead of them. It is like a war, a game of chess, a fencing match, with moves and countermoves, feints and subterfuges, requiring intelligence, and, above all, patience. Some of these APT malware spies will remain in place for years, just like deep cover human operatives did in the Cold War days."

"But what does this have to do with the computer at Frossiac?" asked Isabella, nodding to show that she had taken in George's explanation of the hurried references by Frank before they had parted from him to the suspected use of an APT, "I understood Frank to say that someone had built a new route through to it from London, not that anything like this Stuxnet thing had been installed on it. I suppose if there had been something put on there, your listening station would have been able to detect it?"

"That's just the problem, we don't know," George replied, glumly, "I am not even sure that going there personally, as we are now, will enable me to find out either. The Frossiac computer is very far from being secure, and it might simply be acting as a host for spreading the malware to a different target, something far more important than a local bicycle franchise network."

Isabella was silent for a while, as George helped himself to a glass of water from the onboard bar. The two pilots remained silent and remote behind the curtain screening the cabin from the cockpit. There were no other crew on board.

"Where does the *prizrak*, the nerve agent, come into this, then?" Isabella seemed to be speaking to herself, as she tried to get to grips with the problem, "Frank's implication, when he was briefing us as we came down in on the cable car, was that he thought it was planned to be some sort of bargaining chip for Dominik Katz. But surely, *prizrak* is a physical thing, a drug or a gas or whatever, not something on a computer?"

"Frank mentioned an APT because he thought that Dominik may have been involved in planting one somewhere," George replied, "Not necessarily on the Frossiac computer, although he may have done that as well, but on some system which was involved in and contained the sort of deeply secret information that governments need to protect. But in this case, it was not spying on and damaging a nuclear programme, like Stuxnet was. He believes Domink's APT malware was targeting information on the development of chemical weapons, *prizrak* and possibly other similar things. Information of that kind would certainly have made for an effective bargaining position for his future protection. Dominik may not have had any actual *prizrak*, but he knew who was making it, where, and probably how, it was manufactured."

"But," objected Isabella, uncertainly, "How on earth do Frank and the .. er.. security services know this? Does that mean they were APTing the so-called target as well?"

"My guess is that the foreign power which was manufacturing the stuff will have told us, and probably our allies, about it," George said, "Think about it. If it was our side who was APTing them, they would be wanting to tell us that they knew what we were up to. If it was not our side doing it, then we would both have a vested interest in finding the real perpetrator. The last thing any government wants is for this information to fall into the hands of criminal enterprises who could then produce the *prizrak* for themselves.

"Criminal enterprises which might be interested in getting hold of the information could be people like the Palokas and Mafia-type operations, or terrorist organisations such as ISIS and the old IRA. What do you think those people would do if they got hold of stuff like this? Governments are political organisations with a vested interest in not drawing attacks or invasions onto their own countries. So long as everyone knows about the *prizrak* and no-one uses it – just like the nuclear weapons stand off during the Cold War – there is a level of safety. An attack by one side might result in an even worse attack in retaliation and both nations would be in tatters. So, nothing happens. But criminal and terrorist outfits have no such concerns. They do not care about the human and political consequences of what they do, so long as it is to their own benefit.

"Frank told us that Dominik Katz, or Damon Casey, had been killed on Cleeve Hill by someone unknown. That killer could have been the foreign government whose chemical weapons facilities he had APTed. Or it could have been a killer acting for criminals like the Palokas. From what Frank said in those last few minutes before he left us, my guess is that he does not know which it is. That is why I have to go to Frossiac again, to try to get a clue as to what exactly has been going on. Sending in the police and thereby alerting this unknown assassin to the fact that we are onto them would be unhelpful."

"And Monsieur George Harvey is just a familiar face, a disabled Englishman who was researching a never-to-be-published book about the deceased Stonehouse family," Isabella added, wryly, "But are we sure that that nosy journalist is not still prying into the Stonehouse family? She was certainly trying to find out about them – or Susan Stonehouse at least."

Isabella's reference was to Jessica Moretti, an online journalist whose stock in trade was exposing the scandalous secrets of minor celebrities for the entertainment of a gossip-hungry public. Jessica had shown an unexpected interest in the story of the apparently ordinary Stonehouse family who had happened upon a crime scene and had then been instrumental in bringing to justice a depraved crime baron, Konstantin Paloka, as a result. The justice had, though, come at the price of both Peter and Susan Stonehouse's lives, Peter dying from the injuries inflicted by the Paloka bodyguards, and his wife committing suicide following a campaign of vicious online trolling by Paloka's sons, Egzon and Aleksander. Their daughters, Stevie Stone, the horse racing tipster to the Smart Girls, and TK Stonehouse, an Army Captain in the Corps of Royal Engineers, had been left to pick up the remnants of their ruined family life.

"Stevie said," Isabella continued, "That Jessica shouted at her in the Cheltenham parade ring after Katseye's race on Gold Cup day, saying not only that the Stonehouses were not dead at all but that they and Stevie were being paid to keep quiet about a murder. Luckily, Frank's plan to have Meredith at the races that day worked out and Jessica seems to have accepted that she mistook

Meredith for Susan Stonehouse. But I don't like the sound of the remark about the murder. What did she mean by that?"

"Maybe she was just trying to provoke a reaction?" George suggested, thoughtfully, "I can't see how anyone can accuse Stevie of keeping quiet about a murder. The only death which could be connected in any way to the Stonehouses was that of Konstantin Paloka in prison. The deaths of his sons, Egzon and Aleksander, even if Jessica knew about them, occurred long after the Stonehouses were dead themselves."

"But in Jessica's suspicious mind, the Stonehouses weren't dead," Isabella corrected him, "Jessica told Stevie that she thought Susan and Peter Stonehouse were at Cheltenham racecourse with Stevie and TK on Gold Cup day last year, the same day that Aleksander Paloka died."

"Whatever she meant, there's no reason for her to be in Frossiac, anyhow," George said, firmly, "I should have thought that she would continue to focus her amateur detecting efforts on Stevie and Meredith and they are quite capable of dealing with her if she turns up at a racecourse again. Stevie didn't see her at Aintree in April, although Frank had Meredith there again, just in case there was a problem. And our inquisitive Ms Moretti is not likely to see TK at all, now that TK's going to be back at Old Warnock with the helicopter test flying operation. She'll have found someone else to pursue by now, you can be sure."

As George and Isabella continued their discussion, the swift Learjet crossed the Spanish coast and forged its elegant way towards the North East, soon leaving Madrid far behind. It was early afternoon when the aircraft began its descent into Carcassonne airport. Amanda's only communication with her passengers had been to ask them to tidy away any loose objects in the cabin and to fasten their seatbelts.

Looking curiously out of the window, as the jet turned onto its final approach for runway 28 at the French regional airport, Isabella could easily pick out the walled fortification of the fairytale medieval citadel perched above the South East corner of the picturesque Aude town. The river Aude itself joined the East to West line of the Canal du Midi, which stretched away on either side of the attractive conurbation, the modern autoroute between Toulouse and Narbonne shadowing the direction of the historic channel for waterborne cargo. Frossiac, George told Isabella, was located on the Narbonne side of Carcassonne.

"The Vachers did say that they wanted to meet Madame 'Arvai," George commented, "And there is plenty of cycling to be done along the Canal du Midi. It's nice and flat, too. No mountains, like Madeira."

"I'd rather be back at Sampfield Grange," Isabella replied, wistfully.

"I have a feeling that you are going to get your chance," said George, not quite under his breath.

12

"So, you're sticking with two miles for Curlew then, Mr Sampfield?" Travis asked, as he and Sam made their leisurely way on Curlew Landings and Caladesi Island down the dried and rutted track which ran behind the creeper covered stone residence of Sampfield Grange.

It was as yet early on the bright October morning, and a light mist hung, ghostlike, over the extensive building's grey slate roof. When the riders had set out an hour earlier, the mist had been already rising and dispersing from amongst the thorny hedgerows along the track, where fat blackberries hung, waiting to be picked later by Kelly. Above the remnants of the light fog which had formed itself over the house, the sky was clear and a warm sun was burning its inexorable way through the flimsy barrier. The work riders had gone ahead on the return journey to the yard after the morning's exercise, leaving Sam and Travis to follow at the rear.

"My objective is for him to be fit to defend his title at Cheltenham next year," Sam replied, "So we'll run him over the same distance again during this season. We'll soon find out if he is still as good as before, and we can think again if it turns out that he's not. I've discussed it with Merlin, and he agrees."

"Sounds like a plan to me," Travis confirmed, as he patted the warm neck of the talented horse who was the subject of their conversation.

"Ranulph Dicks has confirmed that he's happy for you to come here to work with Curlew Landings, so long as it doesn't interfere with your commitments to him," Sam added.

The concerted attempt over the summer months by Sam and the Urquharts to raise the issue of the suspension of Travis's jockey B licence in the Australian State of Victoria had not been as successful as they had all hoped. Sam's old friend at the British Horseracing Authority had been as helpful as he reasonably could, but the BHA had no jurisdiction outside the UK. Nevertheless, the raising from an official source of such a serious allegation, namely, that the suspension of Travis's licence had been decided on planted and faked evidence, was not something which the Racing Victoria authorities could simply ignore, so the facts of the case and the transcript of the disciplinary hearing itself had both been reviewed. Whilst it was accepted that the report of drug dealing on the part of Travis had rested entirely on the uncorroborated word of colleagues at Jack Tytherleigh's training yard, which was the reason that the police had not been interested in the matter, the evidence that Travis had ingested cocaine before going out to ride in a jumps race was incontrovertible, as the result of the drug test by the doctor at Mooney Valley racecourse had demonstrated. Travis's defence that his juice bottle had been spiked was impossible to prove. The disciplinary panel had had little choice but to issue a suspension.

The report of the subsequent intimidation of Travis, Ryan Urquhart and Ryan's University tutor was, though, new information, and was taken more seriously by the Australian racing authority, particularly when Sam's friend had explained the suspicions which Travis and Ryan had had of horse doping at the Tytherleigh establishment. Although Travis's licence suspension had been for a fixed period and Travis would in a year's time be able to apply for it to be reinstated, the content of the nasty threats had been such that it was clear that the making of any such application on his part would be met with unpleasant consequences not dissimilar to those experienced earlier in the year by Luke Cunningham.

"It's not the first time we've heard things on the QT about Tytherleigh," the Australian official said, sourly, over the phone, "But there's been no proof, nothing out of the way at all. Trust me, we've made our own checks. We don't just sideline these things, whatever you folk in the UK may think."

As Sam's friend had thanked him and had asked to be kept informed of any new developments, the other man had suddenly added, "What's to stop your lad applying for a jockey licence in the UK? You say he's a British citizen, that right?"

"Well, the suspension in Victoria would count against him, for a start," had begun his BHA counterpart, "He would have to declare it and we would come to you for information. It would be up to us what we did as a result of receiving it."

"That's your answer, then," the Australian official had said, "Young Mr Byrne's done a pretty good stint as a jockey here in Victoria. I can make sure that you're given a positive picture when we supply the information on him. If he's kept his nose clean, like you say he has at the British yard, he'd be in with a fair go of getting his licence back here too. But I hear what you tell me about these so called threats if he tries that."

Sam's first reaction on hearing this ostensibly practical advice had been that he himself was not in a position to take on an additional conditional jockey. Finding sufficient numbers of suitable rides for Kye had proved difficult enough, even with the help of other trainers who sometimes needed a talented conditional who could take a few pounds off a badly handicapped horse's back. Thanking his old hunting friend for his help, Sam had broken the news to Travis.

Travis himself, whilst expressing his genuine gratitude for what had been done, had been initially disappointed, clearly having hoped that, by some miracle, his suspension would be lifted and the stain on his record expunged. Having spoken through Skype to the Urquharts, who were by then back at home in Australia, he had been encouraged by the sensible Tessa to follow up the suggestion that he apply for a jockey licence in the UK.

"You can't live your life in fear of these people," Tessa had told him, stoutly, "At least the authorities in Vic know about it now, so they'll be watching him. You need to get on with your life, Travis. Ryan too."

Travis had agreed with her, whilst not being able to rid himself of an ever growing suspicion that the attack on Luke Cunningham had been intended for himself. The police who had been investigating the violent assault had eventually concluded that the unfortunate Luke had been a victim of mistaken identity, although no-one had yet been able to suggest who the intended victim might have been. Travis himself had not been in Aintree that day, but he had been present at various televised race meetings during his time at Sampfield Grange and had always been fearful that he might be recognised. Suppose the distant Jack Tytherleigh had somehow hired some thugs in Liverpool to seek him out? Luke was about the same height and build as Travis and with similar coloured hair.

During that year's cool and disappointing June, fortune had at last moved in Travis's favour. Ranulph Dicks had called Sam, hoping to book Kye to ride one of his summer jumpers at Worcester racecourse. In the course of the conversation, Sam had learned that Ranulph's current conditional jockey had just ridden out his claim and was leaving to become stable jockey at a yard in another part of the country, closer to his family. It had not taken long for Sam to press Travis's claims as a prospective replacement, although Ranulph's confusion as to whether the person being recommended was the young man he had known as Ryan Urquhart, or someone else, had taken some time to explain.

"Sounds like a bloody rum business to me," Ranulph had stated disparagingly, when the story had been told to him, "Amelia will be interested to hear about this. She had a run in with Tytherleigh when she was in Melbourne. Happy to take young Travis on here, Sam, especially after what you say he's done with Curlew Landings."

Travis had been initially nervous at the prospect of raising his head officially above the horseracing parapet once again, but his colleagues at Sampfield Grange had had no such scruples.

"The Dicks yard is a great place to work, Sadie told us," Jackie had enthused, "She really liked it there. I bet she'll be dead jealous when she finds out."

Sadie herself had not been present when this conversation had taken place, although no doubt she would have supported Jackie's opinion. Sadie had remained with her parents until after the Punchestown Festival, Tessa Urquhart having volunteered to stay at Sampfield Grange to oversee the yard whilst Sam, Teddy and Travis had gone with Curlew Landings to a single day of the Irish event. The original plan for the soon to be separated family to spend a few days together in Ireland had been abandoned following the assault on Luke at Aintree racecourse and its associated effect on the Sampfield Grange team.

A more cheerful seeming Sadie had returned the following week to ride the lively Indian Rocks in a point to point event at Ashfordleigh Downs, during which the assault on Luke Cunningham had been still a major talking point. A number of inquisitive people had approached Sadie, Jackie and Kye in the hope of obtaining further grisly details of what exactly had happened. Sam himself had been mostly able to repel these enquiries by saying that he had been elsewhere when the attack had taken place, but his three staff had had no such defence against their prying colleagues from other racing yards.

Sadie had subsequently accepted, with Sam's agreement, the invitation from Feanna Foley to spend the rest of the summer at *Feirm Enda*. The pointing season was by then at an end. Tabikat, Katseye, and Curlew Landings had been sent to spend their summer months on the extensive estate of Lady Helen Garratt's wealthy parents, whose family was still as much involved in eventing as they had been in the long-gone days when Sam's mother had been competing. Kye and Jackie had been away together to a couple of rain dampened music festivals. Sam himself had resolved this year to accept at least some of the many invitations he received each year to racing events at Ascot, Newmarket, Goodwood and York, so his presence at home had been intermittent.

Sampfield Grange had thus been able to slumber its way through the warm months following the summer solstice, with no urgency for the services of Sadie, whose supervisory role in relation to the remaining horses, mostly now enjoying themselves eating the grass in the local Sampfield Grange fields, had been taken on by Travis. There had been no attempt to replace Bethany, whose office still remained empty. Even Lewis and Kelly had been able to sunbathe on the smooth and sunlit garden lawn when Mr Sampfield had not been around to see them.

Curlew Landings had come home earlier in the week in the small horsebox, with Tabikat and Katseye due to follow in a new and bigger horsebox which was to be delivered in the next few days. Sadie would return today and Travis would depart to take up his new role under the employment and sponsorship of Ranulph Dicks. Merlin, of whom Sam had seen and heard little over the summer, had promised to call in on Sam to discuss a campaign for Tabikat and Katseye. The Sampfield Grange operation was starting at last to gear itself up for the promising season which was to come.

Kye, Jackie and the work riders were already back in the sun soaked yard, chattering happily as they untacked their horses and looked forward to their usual breakfast in the Sampfield Grange kitchen. As Sam and Travis clattered their horses to a stop by the empty yard office, the dull humming sound of a vehicle ascending the lane from the road below could be heard. Sam dismounted Caladesi Island and handed the reins to one of the work riders just as the hitherto unseen vehicle entered the yard.

The new arrival was a green four-wheel drive SUV, which came to a prompt stop by the entrance to the yard. The driver's door opened. A tall man got out and stood facing them all.

"Good morning, Sam," the driver said, "Sorry to arrive without notice. Am I in time for breakfast?"

Sam swallowed hard. He had not seen or heard from Frank Stanley since the day of the Bowl Chase at Aintree in April. The mobile telephone number which Frank had previously given him had remained unanswered and the ringing tone had eventually been replaced by a signal to indicate that the number was unobtainable. Now, here was Frank in person, arriving at Sampfield Grange as though nothing out of the ordinary had happened – which, of course, as far as anyone but Sam himself was concerned, was quite true.

"Good morning, Frank," Sam forced himself to say, as he moved forward to shake his friend's hand, whilst the yard staff, losing interest, turned back to their tasks. It had been almost exactly two years since Frank Stanley had first appeared unexpectedly in the yard at Sampfield Grange, but he had visited a sufficient number of times since then for his presence to be accepted as normal, albeit infrequent, at Sampfield Grange, "Will you be wanting to ride out with me later? It's an ideal day for an outing."

"An excellent suggestion," Frank responded, to Sam's surprise.

"So, what's Mr Stanley doing here, then?" Kye asked Jackie, whilst they watched the retreating backs of the two men as they walked along the path which led towards the boot room door. Mr Sampfield was wearing his familiar tweed jacket whilst the visitor appeared to have left his own jacket in his car and wore only a military style pullover.

"No idea," Jackie replied, hesitation in her voice, "He's not been in touch with me since ... well, for a while now. Maybe it's just social, like he says. He and Mr Sampfield are old friends, you know."

"I don't like him having a hold over us," Kye grumbled, "It gives me the creeps when he turns up like this."

"Stop worrying about it," Jackie told him, more firmly, "Come on. Let's get the horses sorted out, if you can work that new computer in the feed room, that is. Then we can have our breakfast before we have to start tacking up the horses for them to ride."

Travis had by this time returned from settling Curlew Landings into his familiar box. He had taken off the scuffed green riding jacket he had been wearing and was carrying it over his arm. His riding helmet, purchased for him earlier in the year with the Sampfield Grange credit card, hung from his hand by the straps. Blond hair stuck up in ragged spikes from his scalp.

"Who was that bloke who just came?" Travis asked abruptly.

"It's Mr Sampfield's friend from when he was at school, Mr Stanley," Jackie told him, "Haven't you seen him here before? He comes here to ride with Mr Sampfield sometimes. We've not seen him for a long while. But Mr Sampfield has been away a lot recently, so I expect that's why."

"He was at the races in Punchestown," said Travis, unexpectedly, "I thought I recognised his face, but I couldn't think who he was at the time. I remember him now, he came indoors with you two that day we had that journo woman here months ago."

"So, he was with Mr Sampfield and Mr Urquhart at Punchestown?" queried Jackie, her curiosity aroused by this information.

"No, I copped him after they'd gone off to look at the horses in the sale," Travis replied, shifting the worn jacket onto his other arm, "When I was loading Curlew for the journey home. Perhaps he met up with them there."

Just as Jackie was about to ask another question, she was interrupted by a familiar voice from behind them. A cyclist had arrived unnoticed in the yard, and was propping a smart looking white racing bicycle against the fence behind Mr Stanley's car.

"Good morning, Kye," said the cyclist, removing her helmet as she approached the little group, "How nice to see a familiar face. I wondered if everyone might have left since I was last here. Won't you introduce your friends?"

Recognising the speaker instantly, Kye's mouth went suddenly dry and his heart began to thump hard in his chest.

"Er.. yes," he stammered, incoherently, "This is Jackie and this is Travis. They work with the horses now. Well, Jackie does. Travis is going to Mr Dicks."

"How do you do. I am very pleased to meet you, Jackie and Travis," the woman responded, in a polite and formal tone, neither she nor Jackie giving any sign of having met before, "My name is Isabella Hall. I am going to be rejoining the staff at Sampfield Grange soon.

127

I just called in to see if I could look at your new computer set up. I understand that Mr Sampfield has recently made quite an investment in new technology for the yard."

Before Kye could reply, a further interruption distracted them all. A familiar black BMW sports car came quickly up the short slope from the entrance gates and stopped abruptly alongside Mr Stanley's vehicle.

"What's this then, a welcome party?" asked Merlin ap Rhys, a grin on his face as he opened the driver's door, "You 'aven' all been missin' me that much, 'ave you?"

No-one answered. They were all too busy staring at the passenger who was emerging from the other side of the car. It was Sadie.

13

Kelly had not expected Mr Stanley to be joining Mr Sampfield for breakfast that day. Neither had she expected the return home of her sister Sadie to be in the company of Merlin ap Rhys. So, when Kye told Kelly of the presence of Isabella Hall in the yard office, Kelly was for one of the few times in her life unable to speak.

"When Lewis has found out what Mr Sampfield and Mr Stanley want for their breakfasts, I'll get them sorted and we can have a catch up," she eventually said to Sadie, deciding to ignore Merlin, who had nonchalantly followed Sadie and Kye into the kitchen, "I'm dying to know more about *Feirm Enda*. And I've got some good news about Luke Cunningham too."

Jackie had remained with Isabella Hall in the yard office, saying that she would follow Kye up to the house once Isabella had been shown round the new IT installation in the yard. Travis had gone back to his room in the cottage to change his clothes and gather together his few possessions.

"Is Mr Sampfield busy, then?" asked Merlin, not choosing to accept Kelly's cold shouldering of him.

"I am sure I don't know," replied Kelly, stiffly, unable to avoid answering the question, "Mr Stanley is with him. Lewis will tell him you are here. And that Isabella Hall is out in the yard."

Lewis was already in the kitchen pouring coffee into a silver jug, ready to take it through to the breakfast room. To Merlin's amusement, Lewis seemed agitated by the surprise influx of unannounced, and, in Merlin's own case evidently unwanted, guests. Had Merlin known it, Lewis's curiosity as to the reason for Sadie's appearance in the company of her rejected former lover, especially after the scandals which had attached to Merlin's name, was at least equalled by his desire to know why Isabella Hall had returned to Sampfield Grange. Lewis had not forgotten the reprimand which he had earned from Mr Sampfield as a result of his behaviour towards the former office manager.

"I'll tell Mr Sampfield you are here," Lewis grudgingly announced, as he left the kitchen bearing the coffee jug. Kye and the work riders were already seated around the large, square breakfast table, whilst Merlin and Sadie remained standing awkwardly alongside. Jackie could be seen coming up the path towards the door. She was alone.

"Where's Isabella Hall?" asked Kelly, sharply, as she started to set extra places at the table for Merlin and Sadie, "Is she staying for breakfast?"

"Isabella's gone," Jackie replied, "She just had a quick look round at our new computers and then she went. She was just passing on her bike. She's starting work here tomorrow, she said. I've not met her before. She seems very nice."

Mindful of the presence of the work riders, Kelly did nothing other than nod in response, unaware that Jackie's statement that she had not met Isabella before was untrue. It would not do for Kelly to appear to the casual workers to be uninformed about the arrangements for the employment of staff at Sampfield Grange. As far as the casuals were concerned, all decisions on such matters were made by Kelly and Lewis, or, in the case of yard staff, by Sadie. It was not clear into which of these two categories Isabella Hall fell, but Kelly would certainly have expected to have been at least informed of the arrangements for replacing the long-departed Bethany.

"I'll just put my things up in the flat," Sadie butted in, picking up the two red patterned holdalls she had placed on the kitchen floor, "You'd better stay here, Merlin, and see when Mr Sampfield is free to talk to you. I'll come back down for breakfast in a minute, Kelly, and we can have a good catch up later."

Returning to the kitchen shortly afterwards, a still aggrieved Lewis told Merlin that Mr Sampfield had asked Merlin to join him and Mr

Stanley in the breakfast room. Sadie had been invited to come in too, if she wished.

"Mr Sampfield said he wants to talk about races for Tabikat and Katseye," Lewis explained, as Kelly raised her eyebrows at the proposed inclusion of Sadie amongst the breakfast room guests.

"I'll 'ave scrambled eggs, no toast," Merlin informed Lewis, without waiting to be asked, "Breakfast room's on the left, isn' it? Tell Sadie to come in too when she's ready."

"Bloody cheek," snapped Kelly, not caring if the work riders heard her, as Merlin left the room, "Who does he think he is, giving us orders?"

Unaware of the discontent in the Sampfield Grange kitchen, Sam was sitting at his usual place at the breakfast table, which was covered with a pale green linen cloth onto which the usual white and gold china breakfast service had been laid. On seeing Mr Sampfield approaching the house in the company of Mr Stanley, Lewis had already set a second place. One of the leaded casement windows was propped open and a light breeze entered the room. The strengthening sun gleamed through the uneven glass panes, casting shards of light from the crystal water jug which stood in the centre of the long table amidst a carefully arranged group of matching glasses.

Sam and Frank had had only a few moments' conversation prior to the entry of Lewis with the coffee jug, their conversation halted by Lewis's announcement of the arrival of Merlin and Sadie and associated reference in disapproving tones to the presence in the yard of Isabella Hall.

Lewis had been disappointed by Mr Sampfield's lack of surprise at his information.

"Could you send Merlin and Sadie in to join us?" Mr Sampfield had said, "We can talk about my plans for Tabikat and Katseye whilst we eat. You may be interested, Frank. As for Mrs Hall, I will see her tomorrow when she arrives for work."

"Will Mrs Hall be living in again?" Lewis had ventured to ask, quickly, "It's just that Sadie's in the chauffeur's flat now, so Kelly will need to know where to put her."

Had Lewis been his usual vigilant self, he would have noticed a slight movement of Mr Stanley's head as he had posed this question to Mr Sampfield. But Lewis's attention had been focused on gauging the reaction of his employer.

"Er, no, Lewis," Sam had replied, "Mrs Hall will not be living in."

"I'd like bacon and scrambled eggs, as usual, Lewis," had cut in Frank Stanley, in pleasant but firm tones, giving Lewis no choice but to accept the instruction and leave the room.

"What the hell is going on, Frank?" Sam had asked, rather amused, as Lewis had shut the panelled door behind him, "You told me about Isabella Hall only two minutes ago. I thought she'd gone for good."

"You did say you would be happy to have her back," Frank had reminded him, with a slight smile.

"That's true, I did," had admitted Sam, ruefully, "But I wasn't quite expecting you to take me seriously. It's been a good while since we last spoke," he had added pointedly.

This brief exchange had been brought to an end by the appearance of Merlin in the breakfast room.

"Good morning, Merlin," Sam greeted the jockey, "You will recall meeting my friend Frank Stanley at Cheltenham racecourse?"

Merlin's manner betrayed nothing, as he politely shook hands with Frank Stanley. Sam was not to know that Merlin and Frank had met more than once before and in very different circumstances to those of the parade ring at the famous racecourse.

"It is some time since I last saw you, Merlin," Sam continued, as Merlin sat down on one of the unoccupied chairs, "What have you been up to over the summer?"

"I've been ridin' for a few trainers 'oo 'ave summer jumpers," Merlin replied, airily, "An' I've just now come back from Mr Foley's place in Ireland. Brought Sadie back with me too. We were booked on the same flight out of Cork."

Before Sam could respond to Merlin's comments, Sadie came through the breakfast room door. She was followed immediately by Lewis, who fussed importantly about the sunlit room, setting places for Merlin and Sadie and enquiring whether more coffee, or tea, was required. But Lewis was to hear nothing more than pleasantries between the four people now sitting around the table and was soon obliged to leave them alone. At least there would be another chance when he brought in the food, Lewis thought.

"You are looking very well, Sadie," Sam told his yard manager, "How was everyone at *Feirm Enda*?"

"All very well, Mr Sampfield," Sadie assured him, smiling, "They send their regards. I met Tabsi's dam, Little Kitty Cat, and her dam too, Kat's Gift. They're lovely mares, Mr Sampfield. No wonder Tabsi and Big Kat are so clever. When are they going to come home?"

"Later this week, I hope," Sam replied, adopting a more businesslike tone, "I have asked you both to join me to talk about my plans for them this coming season. I am assuming that you are happy to keep competing in points on Indian Rocks, Sadie? I'll be keeping Kye on Highlander Park, although I am increasingly having to share his services with other trainers nowadays. At least Ran Dicks will have his own conditional again, now Travis is about to go to him."

"Travis is goin' to Mr Dicks?" put in Merlin, "That's good news. 'e'll do well there. 'e'll be after all my rides soon."

"You and I have spoken about Curlew Landings," Sam went on, with a quick nod of agreement to Merlin's remark, "And I think we've already said that we should try Novice Chasing this season with Katseye. As far as I know, the Foleys agree with that proposal so I imagine Mr Ardizzone will fall in with their views. I am assuming that Mrs Crosland will still be representing him at Katseye's races."

"I spoke to Mrs Crosland in Ireland," Sadie interjected, "She likes the idea."

"Mrs Crosland was at *Feirm Enda*?" Sam asked, momentarily wrong footed by Sadie's statement, "Do you know why?"

"I think she was interested in buying another of Mr Foley's horses," Sadie said, hurriedly, "She's a friend of the Foley family. She's Mrs Stonehouse's sister."

The reminder that the forthright Meredith Crosland, former owner of Katseye, was the sister of the deceased Susan Stonehouse momentarily distracted Sam from his description of his plans for the horses. The slight pause was fortuitously broken by Lewis bringing in the cooked breakfasts, so Sam had had time to gather his thoughts once again when Lewis reluctantly closed the door on them.

"As for Tabikat," Sam began, "I am intending to aim him at the Cheltenham Gold Cup again. But all those questions I was asked at Aintree in April has made me think. What if we were to run him in the King George as well this year?"

"I'm up for that, Mr Sampfield," said Merlin, at once, "If the 'orse comes back as good as 'e was last season, that's a very realistic option for 'im."

"And ...," added Sam, pausing for emphasis, "I was thinking of the Lancashire Chase at Haydock Park, too."

Merlin sat bolt upright in his chair, dropping his fork onto the china plate with a rattle. Sadie gasped and stared at her employer.

Frank Stanley continued eating his bacon and eggs, watching them with interest.

"The jump racing Triple Crown!" Sadie and Merlin exclaimed, in unison.

"Why not?" asked Sam, "After what Tabikat did last season, I see no reason why he can't attempt it. What do you both think?"

"I'm more than 'appy to give it a go, you can be sure of that, Mr Sampfield, but we're going to 'ave to 'ave 'im ready for 'aydock in, what will it be, just over a month's time," calculated Merlin, quickly.

"Helen's mother's people have already started getting the horse fit again," Sam told them, "Sadie can take over the work on him as soon as he's back."

"That's fantastic, Mr Sampfield," enthused Sadie, her blue eyes shining, "I know Tabsi can do it, he's so brilliant. You agree, don't you, Merlin? You will be available to ride him in all the races, won't you?"

"You bet I will, *cariad*," replied Merlin, hardly aware of using the old endearment once again, "I'm not goin' to pass up a chance like this. But it's very ambitious, it's only been done once before."

Whilst the breakfast room party continued their exciting discussion, Lewis was informing a disappointed Kelly that the conversation had been solely about the horses, as Mr Sampfield had previously indicated it would be. Travis had by this time joined the other staff in the kitchen and was wolfing down his final Sampfield Grange breakfast.

"Have you got everything packed up, Travis?" asked Kelly.

"Pretty much," Travis told her, "I've left that old jacket in the boot room. You'll take it back for me, won't you, Lewis?"

135

"Which jacket is that? The old green one? I thought it was yours," Kelly replied.

"No, someone had left it in the pub, the one we went out to that night Curlew won the Champion Hurdle," said Travis, looking at Lewis, "You remember, the girl in the bar said it had been there a while, that no-one had claimed it, and just to bring it back next time we were in. But we've not been there again since, and I'll be too far away once I'm at the Dicks place. Anyhow, I shan't be needing bloody freebies now I'm going to be earning proper money."

Lewis was agreeing to return the tatty borrowed jacket when Sadie came into the kitchen.

"You'll never guess what, Kye and Travis," she said, excitedly, "Tabsi's going to try for the jump racing Triple Crown this season. There's a prize of a million pounds if he does it!"

Whilst Sadie was explaining the significance of this decision to Lewis and Kelly, Merlin, not wishing to run the gauntlet of the kitchen speculation and gossip, let himself out of the large, iron studded front door of the house and walked towards his car. Seeing Curlew Landings looking over the half door of his box at him, Merlin crossed the yard to pat the horse's inquisitive nose.

"Ten per cent of the million pounds goes to the jockey," Merlin told Curlew, as Curlew nodded his handsome head up and down in apparent enthusiastic agreement, "One hundred thousan' pounds, an' that's on top of the prize money. An' you're goin' to do well for me too, aren' you, boyo? Maybe I'm goin' to get my chance of a proper future at last."

Left with Sam in the breakfast room, from which the sunshine had now begun to move away, Frank Stanley commented, "That all seemed to go very well, Sam. You have a good team there. It's important to have people around you that you can trust."

Apparently deciding on a change of subject, Frank asked suddenly, "How is the Cunningham boy now?"

"Home with his family," Sam told him, "The broken bones have mended and his eyesight hasn't been damaged, thank God. His teeth have been fixed – probably look better than they did before - but there's a nasty scar still on his neck. He'll be back riding points again before long, I'm sure. The police believe he was attacked in mistake for someone else, you know, Frank. I can't imagine what anyone would have had to have done to bring an attack like that on himself. Especially in the Aintree racecourse horsebox park, with all their security arrangements."

"That suggests that the attackers had legitimate access to the site," Frank added, helpfully.

"Yes, his father, Drew, told me that the police said the same thing," Sam responded, "That means the attackers were stable staff or worked at the racecourse. Why would any of them want to do something like this?"

"If you want to know my view," Frank said quietly, "Luke was attacked to stop him stealing a valuable horse."

"Stealing a horse?" spluttered Sam in astonishment, "Which horse?"

"Katalyst," replied Frank Stanley.

14

Kelly watched from the breakfast room window as Mr Sampfield and Mr Stanley passed behind the garden hedge to begin their ascent of the uphill track on the imposing bay hunters, Caladesi Island and Ranger Station. Both horses seemed happy to be out in the warm sunshine and were walking forward purposefully. Kelly did not move until the two men had disappeared under the line of gold and copper leafed trees at the top of the track.

Lewis had already left the premises in the household's elderly VW Golf, having offered to drive Travis over to the Dicks yard. The discarded green jacket had been slung into the boot. Lewis had told Travis that he would drop into the pub on his way home to return it.

Carrying her loaded tray of used breakfast crockery and cutlery, Kelly returned to the kitchen to find Sadie sitting at the kitchen table fiddling with her mobile phone.

"I'm just updating my Contacts list," Sadie mumbled by way of explanation, as she concentrated on the tiny screen of the phone, "I checked with Kye and Jackie just now and Kye's number is well out of date and I don't think I ever had Jackie's. Kye changed his number months ago, would you believe? And Merlin sent me his new number last year, and I realised hadn't changed that either, so I'm checking with everyone. You haven't changed yours, have you Kelly?"

"No, Lewis neither," Kelly assured her, setting the heavy wooden tray down on the worktop and opening the door of the dishwasher, "What's all this with Merlin, then, Sadie? I thought you were done with him? And what about poor Luke Cunningham and all he's been through?"

A shadow crossed Sadie's face at the mention of Luke Cunningham.

"You said you had good news of him, Kelly," she parried, "What's that then?"

"He's much better," Kelly told her sister, slightly bemused by her reaction, "They say he'll be back to riding again soon."

"I know, I've spoken to him," Sadie replied, to Kelly's surprise, "His number wasn't one of the ones which was out of date. I've deleted it now anyway."

"Why?" asked Kelly, taken aback by her sister's statement.

"He made some nasty accusations," Sadie answered, "He said it was my fault that he'd got beaten up at Aintree. So I've ditched him."

"How could it be your fault?" asked Kelly, not understanding, "You weren't even there when it happened."

"Well, Luke said I'd told him to meet me back at the lorry so that the thugs could be ready there to jump him," Sadie replied.

"But why would you want anyone to attack Luke?" Kelly exclaimed, sitting down at the table, the washing-up temporarily forgotten.

"He said it was all part of a plot to stop his father from buying Katalyst," Sadie replied, her earlier calm demeanour deserting her, "And, do you know, I believed him at first. He kept calling and accusing me when I was staying with mum and dad. I already felt bad enough about it when it happened, but then, when he said those horrible things to me, I really lost it."

Kelly had no idea what to say in response to this revelation. She stayed silent, waiting to hear the rest of Sadie's anguished narrative.

"I asked him," Sadie said, tears starting from her blue eyes and running down her cheeks, "Why would I do something like that? Do you know what he said?"

Kelly shook her head, mutely.

"He said that it was all very well for me having horses like Tabsi and Big Kat to ride every day, but he'd never had a chance of getting on a Grade 1 horse," sobbed Sadie, "Luke and his father had wanted to buy Katalyst but someone else had got there first. He thought Mr Sampfield had made a private deal with Mr Foley and that Katalyst was at Aintree that day waiting for us to drive him back to Sampfield Grange. So he went to our box in the car park to find out and then someone attacked him. He said I'd sent the attacker there to warn him off going near the lorry."

"Luke Cunningham really thinks you would do something like that?" expostulated Kelly, "What sort of a person does he think you are? I've never heard anything so horrid. I thought he was a decent sort of man."

"So did I," Sadie said, rubbing her wet face with the back of one hand, "He did call me in Ireland to apologise. He said it was the shock and the medication that had made him paranoid. His mother even spoke to me too when she found out what he'd said. I can understand all that, but it's made me want to steer clear of him. I was going to finish things with him anyway. That's the real reason I said I'd meet him at the box after his race. I didn't want to tell him before he raced in case he was upset."

"That's really awful, Sadie," sympathised Kelly, rubbing her sister's arm, "You should have told me."

"I was in Ireland when the worst of it happened," Sadie reminded her, "But the Foleys were really nice. They bred Katalyst, you know, he's Tabsi's brother, Big Kat's too. They knew about what had happened to Luke from the news. But they didn't know that he and Sir Andrew wanted to buy Katalyst. They were really upset when I explained what Luke had said to me, almost as if it was their fault. It's all so dreadful, Kelly."

"It isn't your fault, Sadie," Kelly said stoutly, "And how can it be the Foleys' fault either? Mr Sampfield hasn't bought their horse, anyway, has he?"

"No, Katalyst is still in Ireland, at *An Féarach Beag*, I think," Sadie replied, "He's never been sold to anyone. It's all in Luke's imagination."

"What about Merlin? Why was he with you? Does he know what Luke said to you?" asked Kelly, wondering how the arrogant Welsh jockey fitted into the increasingly strange picture being painted by Sadie.

"No, Merlin doesn't know anything about it," Sadie replied, her composure now recovered, "He'd probably want to thump Luke if he knew what he'd said to me, and I think Luke's had enough of that already."

"What was Merlin doing at the Foleys', anyway?" asked Kelly, irritably, not appreciating the feeble humour in the last remark by Sadie.

"Mrs Crosland asked him to come and try out one of the horses for her," Sadie explained, "He was only there for a couple of days. We just travelled back to Cardiff together yesterday evening."

Did this mean that Sadie had stayed the night with Merlin, Kelly wondered to herself, as Sadie resolutely stood up, saying that she needed a cup of coffee and that then she had work to do. Kelly decided that she had asked enough questions for now. She had already garnered plenty of gossip to share with Lewis when he came back.

Kelly would have been intrigued to know that Sadie had indeed spent the night at a hotel in Cardiff along with Merlin ap Rhys, but that they had been accommodated in separate bedrooms. And even Kelly's vivid imagination could never have enabled her to guess that Frank Stanley had been their host.

Frank Stanley himself was at that moment looking from the broad back of Ranger Station at the peaceful view which opened out to the West below the top gallop. Sam, seated on Caladesi Island stood silently next to him, sharing his friend's enjoyment of an unchanging sight which they had often seen together during their many shared rides as teenagers. The remnants of the early morning mist had evaporated away into the clean air and the autumnal panorama of countryside below them was illuminated by a mellow glow which seemed to emanate from the flame tinged leaves of the trees clustered generously about the farmland. Dark hedgerows, their lines interspersed in places by wide barred gates, divided the fields, in some of which sheep and cattle were quietly grazing in companionable groups, looking like models from a children's farmyard game. Beyond the gently undulating rural landscape lay the narrow band of the sea, its surface reflecting the essence of the light like a distant grey mirror. The bark of a dog, the whistle of a man and the throaty whirr of a tractor all floated up from the scarcely visible road which led to the village of Warnock over to the right. A group of cyclists in bright colours suddenly streamed along an intersecting lane, calling enthusiastically to each other, gone from sight almost as soon as they had appeared.

Frank's attention was focused not on the country scene, attractive though it was, but on the less attractive airfield which lay alongside the mostly modern village of Warnock. A twisting stream marked the edge of the Sampfield estate, which stopped about two miles short of the village itself. The airfield lay in an open area further away from the stream, its single hard runway visible like a dark slash across an otherwise green surround. A little line of small coloured aircraft could be seen parked at a short distance from the runway, alongside a few dull coloured buildings.

Frank's sharp eyes soon picked out a couple of figures walking from a van parked by the open gates leading into the airfield. As he watched, a red hatchback car pulled up next to the van, the occupant quickly emerging to open the tailgate of the vehicle and extract a bulky object from inside. The van driver crossed over to speak to the new arrival and a discussion appeared to ensue. Eventually, the van driver pointed towards the runway and the three people moved away from their vehicles, carrying the object with them.

"Drone flyers," said Sam, whose attention had also been caught by the little scene at the airfield, "They're becoming a bit of a nuisance. They sometimes fly the things over this way. Fortunately, the horses don't seem bothered by them. I suppose they are too high up. But I don't like the idea of being watched. Do you suppose they take photographs and make video recordings with those things, Frank?"

"They certainly do," Frank replied, "A lot of aerial filming and photography is done with drones nowadays. You might think of getting one yourself, Sam, to record your training sessions with the horses. It would give you a different angle on the way the horses work, and you may learn something, you never know. Even if you don't, the recordings would be interesting to keep for viewing in later years, say, after the horses have retired."

"Like the old videos my mother used to take," Sam ventured, carefully, aware that his mother and her camera recordings might be a subject unwelcome to his erstwhile schoolfriend. Frank, however, seemed untroubled by the mention of Sam's mother and merely gave a nod of agreement.

Frank's lapse into silence emboldened Sam at last to say, "I've not seen you for a few months, Frank. The last time was on Bowl Chase day at Aintree racecourse in April. At least I think it was you. You were with some people by the parade ring."

"You are right, I was there that day," Frank agreed, without apparent surprise at Sam's question, "I was with some old friends from my former regiment. They'd come for the auction after the racing, but the lot they were interested in was withdrawn, so we left once we'd watched your two runners. They were very keen to see Tabikat and Katseye race, especially when they found out that I knew you personally."

"You should have introduced them to me," Sam exclaimed, "I should have been more than happy to discuss the horses with them."

"No time, old chap," Frank told him, "I think you would have found them pretty dull."

"I did try to call you afterwards," Sam pressed on, "But the number you gave me seems to have lapsed."

"Yes, I am aware of that," Frank replied, unapologetically, "There was a security issue with some of our mobile numbers and we had to withdraw a batch of them. I'll make sure to give you a new number before I leave this afternoon. Now, what do you say to a canter along the top?"

Without waiting for Sam to reply, Frank turned the sedate Ranger Station to the right, walked a few steps forward, and then set the horse off at a loping canter alongside the line of jumps. Sam had no choice but to follow. As he sent Caladesi Island in pursuit of his stable companion, Sam had the feeling that, although Frank had given apparently straightforward and entirely plausible answers to Sam's questions, there was something that he was not being told. Sam wondered if it mattered. He decided to stop asking questions for now and to enjoy the ride.

As Caladesi Island and Ranger Station were running their leisurely race along the ridge of the hills above Sampfield Grange, Lewis was making his way towards The Sly Fox Inn in the village of Charlton. He had left an excited Travis at the Dicks yard and had refused an offer of coffee from the yard manager, saying that he had errands to run.

The Sly Fox was one of two licensed premises in Charlton, the other being the more salubrious Charlton Arms. In contrast to the upmarket coaching inn, The Sly Fox was simply a pub, boasting two rather gloomy bars. It was mostly frequented by locals who found The Charlton Arms too snooty for their taste. It was claimed that the beer was better at The Sly Fox, although, as both establishments obtained their supplies from the same local brewery, this statement was difficult to take seriously. The Sly Fox clientele, if challenged, would simply comment that it was the good company to be found there which improved the taste.

Tabikat Gold Ale had been on sale at both hostelries since March, as Squire Sampfield, the courtesy title which the older citizenry still gave to their local landowner, had been informed, although he had not yet graced either of the inns with his personal presence. As far as The Sly Fox Inn was concerned, however, the Sampfield Grange staff had at numerous times made up for their employer's absence with their generous custom.

Lewis was well aware that The Sly Fox would not yet be open. As he had no intention of buying a drink, this did not matter. The opportunity to return the jacket, about which he had completely forgotten until Travis had mentioned it, was not to be missed. The landlord would already be inside the premises getting ready for opening time, and his barmaid would be arriving for work very shortly. Lewis would wait in the car park, if necessary, until she appeared.

Tegan Colvin had two part time jobs. In addition to her weekend job at The Charlton Arms, she worked behind the bar of The Sly Fox during the week. It was Tegan who had lent the shabby jacket to Travis on that chilly evening back in March.

The day when Curlew Landings had won the Champion Hurdle at Cheltenham races had been one of the most exciting of Tegan's life. Not that she had any interest in horse racing, but the victory of the locally trained horse had brought the handsome Australian boy from Sampfield Grange to The Sly Fox for the evening. Tegan had admired Ryan, as she had heard him called, from behind the bar on the few previous occasions on which he had visited the pub. Tegan's lonely mind had woven images of the young man surfing, bare chested, on the crashing waves of some sparkling ocean or sunbathing with Tegan lying beside him on a sunny Australian beach. Tegan could tell that Ryan did not have much money, as the two Sampfield Grange employees who usually accompanied him seemed to pay for all the drinks, but that did not matter. Tegan had overheard the young Australian promising to repay them when his parents came to visit Sampfield Grange.

Tegan had not cared for Ryan's two companions. One of them was a Northerner called Kye, who spoke a bit like a rude comedian she had seen on TV. Kye had once been a friend of her brother, Graham. The other was a ferrety little man called Lewis, who seemed always to be asking the handsome Ryan a lot of questions about himself. Lewis in particular had incurred Tegan's dislike, as he had more than once leaned over the bar to make crude remarks about her breasts bouncing up and down as she was operating the old-fashioned beer pumps. But Tegan had been prepared to tolerate all this for the sake of being able to pull a pint for Ryan's consumption.

The three young men had entered the pub in high spirits that night. There had been a number of other regular customers in the bar who had joined in with their celebrations. The blond Australian boy, whom the others were now calling Travis, for some reason, had been particularly exuberant. He had had plenty of money that evening too, so Tegan had assumed that the long-awaited parents had eventually arrived. When it had come to closing time, Travis had belatedly remembered that he had come out without a jacket, so Tegan had lent him the one she herself had worn to work that day, saying that it had been left in the pub and not claimed. This statement had been untrue, as the jacket had in fact belonged to her brother. The gesture, though, had earned her a grateful kiss from the blond boy, which had made everything worthwhile, including having to walk home with no jacket to wear herself.

The trouble was that the jacket had not been returned, as Tegan had hoped, and it had not been long before her brother Graham, who owned the jacket, had missed it. Considering the age and condition of the garment, Tegan had thought that Gray had made a ridiculous fuss about its loss, ranting and raving, and rummaging angrily through everything in their flat, his car workshop, and his van. As a result, Tegan had kept her fearful mouth shut, and hoped that her part in its disappearance would not be discovered, or, even worse, that Gray would see her Australian idol wearing it and accuse him of stealing it. They might start fighting, Tegan had thought with horror. She could not bear the thought of the Australian boy's beautiful mouth being marred by a busted lip.

Now, as she approached the pub for her lunchtime shift, Tegan could see a grey car parked in The Sly Fox car park. Out of the car was climbing the pervy Lewis, holding the missing jacket, and waving to her. To Tegan's dismay, there was no sign of Travis.

Tegan had a pepper spray in her pocket. She clutched it tight as she walked towards the car.

15

Isabella Hall had been working for three days in the Sampfield Grange yard office when Tabikat and Katseye returned home. Lady Helen Garratt had called earlier that morning to say that the two stable stars were on their way from her parents' premises in the shiny new horsebox which had been acquired to replace the one in which the injured Luke Cunningham had been found.

"I am very pleased to hear that you have joined the team at Sampfield Grange once again," Helen had told Isabella, enthusiastically, "I know I can rely on you to help me persuade Mr Sampfield to become involved in my project."

"I will do my best, Lady Helen," Isabella had assured her, politely, "Does this mean you will be coming to see Mr Sampfield yourself soon?"

"I certainly shall," the other woman assured her, "Do you know, I believe that I may soon be able to acquire some land on that old airfield, after all?"

Isabella did indeed know of the possibility to which Lady Helen Garratt was referring, as Trevor Wills, the Sampfield Grange land agent, had called the yard the previous day and had left a message with Isabella. Sam had returned the call from the yard office, which had meant that Isabella had heard most of their conversation.

"I thought you might be interested to know, Mr Sampfield," Trevor Wills had begun, "That there have been some new developments in relation to Old Warnock airfield. There has been an application to the local Council for a change of use."

"It will no longer be an airfield in the future, then?" clarified Sam, "What is the new use which has been proposed? Nothing noisy, I trust."

Trevor Wills seemed to be scanning through a file in order to provide the information Sam required. Isabella could hear the click of a computer mouse at the other end of the line.

"It is, of course, just an outline proposal at this stage," Trevor was quick to say, "The application refers to the creation of a rural enterprise park which would enable small businesses to rent property at favourable rates and possibly to apply for start-up funding from the Council itself. There is a pretty good chance of its being approved, in my view, as it ticks a number of important boxes in relation to appropriate development in the nearby area, in particular that it would provide local employment opportunities. The scale and nature of the businesses to be potentially located there should not create an unacceptable burden on the existing infrastructure. In other words, activities such as retail operations would not be permitted, as these would require the provision of extensive parking on site and improved vehicular access. Warehousing or bulk storage and distribution operations would not be accepted for the same reason. Industrial activities involving chemicals or manufacturing with heavy plant would also be ruled out."

"That seems quite restrictive," Sam commented, "What sort of businesses are they hoping to attract?"

"It's being made available to start-ups and small businesses employing fewer than fifteen people," Trevor explained, clearly working his way further through the file he was consulting, "Particularly businesses which are offering training and apprenticeships. The background is that there is a dearth of skilled work opportunities for young people in rural areas such as this, and so, unless they are part of the farming community, young people will tend to leave the area to look for work. If they do stay, they often end up in dead end jobs, such as bar work and cleaning. So, one of the objectives of the Council's area development plan is to create more opportunities for young workers in the area. The feasibility study has identified a number of small enterprises which meet the Council's criteria: a cycle hire and repair workshop, a web development company, an online greetings card business, an art studio and picture framer. They all would undertake to employ and train local young workers."

"And how soon is this likely to come about?" asked Sam, beginning to lose interest.

"The proposals are out for consultation at the moment, so I should say six months at the very earliest for the scheme even to be approved," replied Trevor, "Then, the site would have to be prepared for occupation. It would be some time after that before the first of the businesses could move in. My guess is that nothing much will happen for a year at the earliest. The drones, microlights and small aircraft will continue to use it for now."

"Well, thank you for letting me know," Sam told his land agent, assuming their discussion was at an end.

"There is one more thing, Mr Sampfield," Trevor forestalled him, "The Council has given permission for the short-term use of the airfield as a training centre for the Air Ambulance service. That means that one, perhaps two, helicopters will now be located there. I can't imagine, though, that you will notice any significant difference from the present level of activity already going on at the airfield, or the additional usage would not have been permitted."

"Hmm," grunted Sam, not entirely convinced, as he ended the call.

Although Sam and Lady Helen had been pleased to welcome Isabella Hall back to Sampfield Grange, other members of the Sampfield Grange establishment had been less happy. Lewis, who had returned home in a bad mood from his trip to return the borrowed jacket, still harboured a dislike of Isabella, whilst Kelly remained annoyed that her own efforts, together with those of Purefoy and Associates, to cover the office work during the last few months appeared not to have been appreciated.

"Do you think she's carrying on with Mr Stanley still?" Kelly had said, cattily, to her husband, "I'll say one thing for her, she's certainly looking a lot better. New hairstyle and a suntan to boot.

Perhaps they went off somewhere on holiday together and that's why he's not been here recently."

"Who cares?" was Lewis's brusque response, "At least she's not living here this time."

Lewis's foul mood had been occasioned by the fact that his attempt to corner Tegan Colvin in the car park of The Sly Fox two days ago had been thwarted by the appearance of the landlord, a garrulous and overweight ex police officer called Barnaby Vowles. Mr Vowles had engaged Lewis in a pointless conversation which had enabled Lewis's quarry to escape into the pub along with the jacket, saying only a polite word of thanks to Lewis. Fortunately for the unsuspecting Lewis, the use of the hidden pepper spray had thus proved unnecessary.

The slowing down of a powerful engine and the clunk of changing gears heralded the eagerly anticipated arrival of the horsebox carrying Tabikat and Katseye, which came slowly upwards into the yard from the wide entrance gates. From her seat behind the smart new desk in the yard office, Isabella watched as Sadie, Jackie and Kye lowered the ramp of the box and brought the two magnificent racehorses down into the open air. She observed Mr Sampfield approaching along the path from the house, shrugging on his familiar tweed jacket, and walking over to speak to the lorry driver and her companion. The two horses were soon installed in their old stables, to the accompaniment of exclamations from Sadie and Jackie about how well they were both looking, followed by similar, but rather more measured, comments from their employer.

"I'm so glad to see you, Tabsi," Isabella heard Sadie say, "You look fabulous. Did you like it at the eventing yard? We've got great plans for you this season. Big Kat and Curlew too. Merlin will be coming to see you all soon."

Isabella had reservations about Merlin. She was well aware of the part he had played in the strategy to ensnare the now deceased Dominik Katz, but the nature of his role in their present project was less evident to her. Relations between Merlin and Sadie had clearly improved, though, which was just as well, thought Isabella, given the fact that they would be working together, not only for Mr Sampfield, but for Frank Stanley as well.

Isabella had acquired the suntan to which Kelly had referred on the towpaths of the Canal du Midi where she had spent part of the summer cycling in the shade of those of the overhanging plane trees which had not already fallen prey to relentlessly destructive fungal disease. With George, she had passed an interesting few days in Carcassonne before they had hired a car to drive to the pretty canalside village of Frossiac. There they had taken up residence in one of the holiday apartments which stood alongside the shallow reeded lake bordering the Minervois bank of the ancient waterway. A blue painted footbridge gave access to the Corbieres bank, and it was over that bridge that the couple had made their way on the morning after their arrival.

George had crossed the narrow bridge on more than one occasion before, but never in the height of summer, with the burning sun drying the wooden treads of the steep steps and making the metal railings hot to the touch. The elegant walkway curled artfully over the green water of the canal, which frequently sloshed from side to side as the wakes of the boats passing underneath fanned out behind them. Notices requesting vessels to restrict their speed in order to limit the damage to the canal banks caused by the wash went largely ignored. More experienced boaters knew well that the speed of progress along the seventeenth century waterway was largely dictated by the presence and operation of the locks. The *éclusier* in charge of each lock would be reluctant to fill or drain the lock until all visible boats, as well as those notified by the keeper of the next lock as being *en route*, had been accommodated between the upper and lower gates of their lock. Those boaters who rushed ahead were thereby forced to wait for the slower movers to catch up and enter the lock basin. Only then would the gates be closed and the lock either filled or emptied, as required.

There was no lock at Frossiac itself, although an ample mooring station along the Corbieres bank was provided for those travellers who wished to stop and sample the food and drink in the local restaurants and bars, or to stock up on shopping from the nearby *supermarché.* On that hot afternoon, a man dressed in faded red shorts and a grey T-shirt had been busily loading a stack of bicycles onto one of the moored vessels.

"Ready?" George had whispered to Isabella, who had nodded silently, as they had descended the steps of the footbridge, George's stick planted firmly on each tread to provide support to his damaged leg.

"*Bonjour, Guy!*" had called out George loudly, "*Comment va t'en, aujourd'hui?*"

The Frenchman had straightened up and turned towards them. Isabella saw that he had dark hair, mirror sunglasses and the beginnings of a wide smile.

"Georges!" Guy Vacher had responded, with evident pleasure, "I did not know you would be 'ere this summer. Is this Madame 'Arvai who at last accompanies you today?"

Once the little group had come together to shake hands, Isabella had said quickly, "*Je suis heureux de vous rencontrer, Monsieur. Je m'appelle Isabella.*"

"Please, we must speak in English," Guy had responded, "Or Georges will not understand us."

"*Alors, il ne sera pas possible pour nous deux d'avoir des secrets,*" replied Isabella with a laugh. She had been gratified that Guy had laughed too.

"I think we should certainly continue to speak in English," George, who had understood the joking comment, which had been agreed in advance, "Tell me, Guy, how is the cycling business?"

"Very good, thank you, Georges," the other man had replied, "Especially in the summer months when we have many visitors."

"And your wife, Monique?" had continued George, "Is she well? Isabella and I had planned to walk along to your bar by the stone bridge and take our lunch there. Will your schedule allow you to join us?"

In this way had begun the first of many days over which George and Isabella had sought to establish themselves as nothing more than idle holidaymakers in the area. Isabella had visited the cycle shop each morning to pick up a bicycle to take out for her morning ride. George had been welcomed back by those local residents who had recognised him from his earlier stay in the village almost two years earlier, He had joined in a number of games of *boules* as a result, somehow always managing to lose. During the daily lunchtime period of suspension of the lock service along the canal, he and Isabella had visited the cosy stone-walled bar run by Monique and Guy, sometimes returning again to eat with them in the evening. George had enquired after the wellbeing of the family of Guy's brother, Maurice, now living in Toulouse following Maurice's imprisonment for his allegedly unwitting part in a money laundering scheme organised by a drug trafficking and gambling syndicate. Guy and Monique had remained completely convinced of the innocence of Maurice and his associates, and had found a sympathetic audience in Isabella, who had professed to be very shocked at such a terrible miscarriage of justice.

"But, tell me," Isabella had said, setting down her glass of Minervois wine, after hearing the sad story for the umpteenth time, "At least your bicycle hire business has been successful, has it not? I am very impressed with what you have done. I should be interested in setting up something similar myself once I am at home in England again. Is it possible that you, Guy, could give me more information about the way in which it is organised? What facilities does the company provide, apart from the opportunity to lease and purchase the bicycles at a favourable rate?"

"It is much more than that, Isabelle," Guy assured her, as Monique set another tall glass of cold beer in front of him and an attentive George, "The company provides promotional materials, financial and administrative support, a cycle maintenance and repair service, computer services, business training for those who need it …. many helpful things. If you wish I will show you tomorrow when you come to the shop."

"Thank you, Guy, I should really be most interested," replied Isabella, pleased that the kind offer had been made so readily.

The following morning, Isabella had sat with Guy in front of the desktop computer at the back of the former wine museum, its *cave* now filled with bicycles rather than the bottles which had been stored there when George had first told the Vachers the tragic story of the Stonehouse family. As Isabella had anticipated, it had not been long before Guy had been called out onto the canal bank to deal with a customer. It had been the work of seconds for Isabella to unplug the router so as to disconnect the computer from the internet. Taking a small blue USB from her pocket, she had pushed it into the vacant port on the side of the processor and had scrolled quickly through the file directory on the screen. There in the midst of the data files and programs supplied by the cycle hire franchise operator had been the file she was seeking. The item had been soon copied onto the data stick, which had been back in the pocket of her cycling shorts before Guy had yet learned how many bicycles his new customer had wished to hire that day. Plugging the router back in, Isabella had been relieved to see the elderly machine come back on line. She had stood up, as Guy had walked back inside the shop, followed by a young man and his family.

"You are busy, I see," Isabella had remarked to Guy, "So I will take out my usual bicycle and will see you again later in the day. *Amusez vous bien!*" she had added to the French family as she had passed them in the shop entrance.

Later that day, George had spoken to Frank Stanley on his mobile phone.

"My little spy has been destroyed, as we knew, Frank," George had said, "And the wormhole leading back to Tirana is now unusable. The start of the route back to London is plainly visible, so I have placed a new spy to watch it. All this I did remotely from Madeira. Probably unnecessary, given that your people are monitoring it from the UK end, but it might produce something, you never know. But the real mystery is the strange file which I found embedded in the bicycle shop accounting software."

155

"A file?" asked Frank, "What is it for? Does Guy Vacher know of its existence?"

"My guess is that he does not, or, if he has seen it, he will assume it is a part of the package provided by the cycle franchise company. As to what is in it, I have to confess that I am mystified. It has been hidden in plain sight, but there is a problem. It has been configured to be accessible solely from the machine on which it is stored and can be accessed or copied only if the machine has no live connection to the internet. This, I imagine, is designed to prevent anything being done to it remotely, either by a hacker or by someone with legitimate remote access to the machine, such as the staff of the head office of the cycle franchise."

"Are you able to find a way retrieve it yourself?" asked Frank, baldly.

"Isabella has already done it," replied George, "She has copied it onto a data stick which I will send to your team. The item seems to be a data file and nothing more. I don't want to attempt to read it myself in case it is booby trapped. But I am pretty sure that Dominik Katz had something to do with it."

"How do you know that?" asked Frank.

"Because it has his name on it," George replied.

16

The afternoon weather at Chepstow racecourse was a considerable improvement on conditions at the same time last year. The dismal downpour of the previous year's October meeting, at which Curlew Landings had started his season's successful campaign, had been replaced by a warm, still haze. The sun resembled a dull gold ball above the grandstand, illuminating the bronze-tinged foliage of the sloping woodland which overlooked the far side of the course. The mellow temperature imparted a lethargic feel to the air enveloping the hillside racecourse. Many spectators had taken off their jackets and coats, carrying them instead over their arms or shoulders.

Sam had enjoyed the easy drive to South Wales in his black Audi, having crossed the Old Severn Bridge, which spanned the glittery and opaque water of the Bristol Channel. The tide had been high and the estuary into which the Severn and the Wye emptied their well-travelled waters had been at its widest. The elderly suspension bridge was easily visible from the racecourse, standing staunch guard over the ancient seaway.

The two and a half mile race in which Katseye was to make his debut as a chaser was a small affair with only five runners. Merlin had visited Sampfield Grange the previous week to work with the talented horse and had been openly enthusiastic about his recent progress.

"Those people 'oo've been schooling him at the eventin' place 'ave done a great job," Merlin had told Sam, as they had eventually brought their horses down the rutted track behind the old house, "'e was always quick over 'is obstacles, which was great for 'urdles, an' now 'e's shown 'e can do the same over fences too. Intelligent 'e is, just like 'is brother. Feanna was right. 'e's a chaser in the makin', that's for sure."

Jackie, who was now leading the imperious black horse around the parade ring, had been overjoyed when she had heard Merlin's words.

"You're the best horse here, Big Kat," she had said to her charge as they entered the parade ring. If the favourable reaction of the spectators was anything to go by, victory was already in the bag. Katseye had the air of an emperor from an ancient world processing before massed ranks of loyally gathered vassals and admirers. Many of those watching were already pointing him out and checking his details in their racecards, their attention readily distracted from his two grey and two bay competitors.

Meredith Crosland had driven to Chepstow to represent Arturo Ardizzone, the absent owner of the striking horse. Stevie Stone was in her usual position at the side of the parade ring, working at her online tipster blog and providing Jayce's and Tabby Cat's opinions of the day's runners. Essex lad Jayce had been cautious in his recommendation concerning Katseye's race, noting that the horse had not raced over fences before, other than in the less challenging environment of two point to point meetings in Ireland. Jayce had eventually concluded that Katseye was, as he put it, well worth a punt. The small field meant that a win bet was the only realistic option for the Smart Girls that day, as there would be a poor return on any dual forecast, and each way bets paid poorly.

"Good afternoon, James," Meredith Crosland had greeted Sam on her appearance in the parade ring.

Katseye's former owner was once again wearing a green and white outfit reminiscent of the hues of the Lombardy flag, which Arturo Ardizzone had selected his racing colours, "I am very excited to see how Katseye will get on over fences. Can we assume he will be as good as Tabikat?"

"As you know," commented Sam after he had returned her greeting, "I did not train Tabikat as a novice, so it's hard for me to make a comparison. I should have thought you yourself might be in a better position to do so, Meredith. I learned from Eoghan

Foley at Punchestown in April that Mrs Stonehouse, who used to own Tabikat in those days, was your sister?"

"Yes, indeed, I thought you had always known that," stated Meredith Crosland, unhelpfully, "And I regret that I can tell you nothing about Tabikat's early racing performances, as I was not involved with the horse in those days."

"In that case, we shall both have to form our opinion about Katseye's ability on the basis of today's performance," Sam replied, taking his cue from Meredith Crosland's off-putting tone. Perhaps she did not like to hear mention of her deceased sister, he thought.

"Hi Meredith and Mr S-P. How's everyone in Ireland?" suddenly spoke up a cheerful female voice by their side, "And how's the project with Katalyst going?"

Turning, Sam saw that Stevie Stone had finished her impromptu interviews with some nearby young female spectators and had come into the parade ring to join them, her burgundy hat clamped over her flowing blonde and red coloured hair. Before he or Meredith Crosland could say any more, however, Merlin could be seen approaching them from across the parade ring lawn. Meredith Crosland stepped forward to greet him.

"I hope that you and Katseye are going to win for us, Merlin," Meredith Crosland greeted the jockey, unceremoniously, "James appears unwilling to commit to an opinion."

Sam opened his mouth to contradict her statement but changed his mind when he saw Stevie's face. She seemed to be trying not to laugh. Merlin, though, appeared to be unbothered by Mrs Crosland's comments, simply saying, "We're in with a big chance, Mrs Crosland. But you 'ave to bear in mind that chasing is new to the 'orse an' we' don' really know anythin' much about the others in the field either."

Once Merlin had been legged up by Sam onto Katseye's back, Jackie silently led horse and rider the short distance onto the track. The big screen showed Katseye bounding easily away to the left towards the start, Merlin perched lightly in the irons over the horse's withers, Jackie standing still to see them go. Sam too remained stationary for a few moments at the side of the parade ring track, wondering what this latest venture into unknown territory would bring.

Also watching the action on the trackside screen was Kye. Kye had accompanied Jackie and Katseye to Chepstow in the small horsebox, having been booked to ride in a later race for a local Welsh trainer. Kye's lack of personal transport had put him at something of a disadvantage in his ability to accept bookings for rides. Arranging lifts to racecourses was often a problem, particularly if the horse which he was riding was travelling to the course from a different area of the country. The opportunity to accept a booking on a day on which one of the Sampfield Grange horses was running at the same course was a godsend to Kye. He had previously attempted to negotiate with Lewis and Kelly the occasional use of the household's VW Golf, but his attempts had met with determined resistance from Lewis, who liked to regard the car as his own. Kye was sure that Mr Sampfield would have been quite happy for Kye to make more use of the vehicle, which was, after all, Sampfield Grange property, but antagonising Lewis was not something Kye was prepared to risk. Lewis could make life very uncomfortable for people he did not like. Kye could see that Isabella Hall was one such person and he did not wish to join her.

The small group of five runners looked relaxed as the starter dropped his flag at the far end of the course, pressing the hand-held lever to release the orange tape, which sprang back to allow the horses to gallop forward towards the first of five jumps in the home straight. Katseye and Merlin were soon tucked in between two other runners at the back of the field. The horse, Sam was pleased to see, was not pulling and appeared well balanced as he and Merlin negotiated the first fence. The pace of the race was generous, and all the jockeys seemed content with it. The horses continued to jump confidently as the field passed the parade ring and the massed spectators in the grandstand, where they were greeted with encouraging, but not yet frantic, cheers.

"The whole field is moving well as they start to turn uphill," announced the racecourse commentator, "The two greys Milk Run and Cloud Atlas vie for the lead, with Katseye in between horses behind them. Nobody is making a move as yet. Six fences await them at the top of the hill."

Following the stiff climb towards the trees at the far side of the course, the horses were now working their purposeful way along the contour of the sloping ground, a coloured parade of silks with grey, black and brown bodies lobbing along in athletic rhythm beneath them. The field was gradually stringing itself out as it passed the tumbled ruins of the manor house which overlooked the back straight. Merlin's green and white jacket was clearly visible as Katseye crossed in front of the burnished foliage of the tall trees which provided the backdrop to the track.

"Milk Run just reached for that one," went on the commentator, fishing for things to say, "But this classy field of chase debutantes is doing an excellent job. There is little to choose between the first three as they descend the hill back to their starting point."

No sooner had the commentator made this observation than the complexion of the race began to change. As the horses turned towards the five fences in the homeward run, Katseye's chief rivals Milk Run and Cloud Atlas were clearly beginning to tire. In contrast, Katseye hardly seemed to have made any effort, and, without really seeming to do anything, Merlin took his charge quickly into the lead. Katseye jumped the remaining five fences with such ease that the only element of the race to leave any doubt in the minds of the cheering and applauding spectators was which horse would take second place. Katseye had been the favourite with many of those watching, if not with all the bookmakers, not least because he was being ridden by a local jockey.

"Katseye has won in some style!' cried the commentator, "That's a classy performance from the Liverpool Hurdle champion. And Cloud Atlas overhauls Milk Run for a weary second place."

Sam had watched the unfolding action of the race with a sense of disbelief. Notwithstanding Meredith Crosland's comments, he had been quietly confident that the horse would win, but the comfortable nature of the victory over a tough course in soft conditions had surprised him. Katseye had seemed entirely happy within himself and had tackled the course like an experienced professional.

"That was some performance, Merlin," the TV interviewer stated, as Merlin walked the victorious horse round in a circle by the finishing post, allowing Jackie to come forward to catch his rein, "Did he surprise you with how easily he did it?"

"I was expecting somethin' special from 'im," Merlin replied, speaking into the microphone which had been held up to him on a stick, "This 'orse and 'is brother Tabikat are top class. This one could win the Gold Cup too once day."

"Where's he going next, Merlin?" asked the smart, bearded interviewer, "Cheltenham in November maybe?"

"You'll 'ave to ask the trainer," Merlin gave his customary reply.

"And Tabikat, how's he?" asked the interviewer, determined to wring as much information out of the winning jockey as he could, "Will he be back to contest the big race at Newbury at the beginning of December?"

"No, I believe Mr Sampfield has different plans for Tabikat this year," Merlin told his interlocutor, "Again, it's 'is decision, and the owners', not mine."

Sam and Meredith Crosland had been surrounded by potential interviewers by the time Katseye returned to the winner's station. Stevie Stone, though, had quickly taken advantage of her privileged position to interview them both whilst the reporters for the major racing news outlets had to be content to eavesdrop, holding out an array of mobile phones to record what was being said.

"Meredith Crosland, representing the owner of Katseye," began Stevie, "You must be very pleased with that performance. Where is the horse going next?"

"To Cheltenham in November," stated Meredith Crosland, firmly, "Mr Ardizzone, the owner, is very keen to see him race there again."

"I believe you used to own Katseye yourself previously," Stevie went on, "Do you regret having sold him now?"

"Katseye did very well when I briefly owned him," Meredith Crosland replied, not answering the question, "And I am hoping to buy a colt out of the same dam in the near future."

When Stevie turned her iPad towards Sam, half a dozen mobile phones simultaneously swivelled towards him, fascinated to hear his reaction to the information given by the owner's representative. But Stevie had other questions in mind.

"Can you tell us your plans for Tabikat, Mr Sampfield Peveril?" she asked, "He's not been seen since winning the Bowl Chase at Aintree in April. Your jockey has just dropped a tantalising hint."

Although relieved not to be asked to elaborate on Meredith Crosland's unexpected remarks, Sam was completely wrong footed at being asked a question about Tabikat.

"Merlin and I have had discussions," he began, carefully, "And we are thinking in terms of the Lancashire Chase at Haydock Park in November this year. Nothing has been finally decided as yet, though."

"And then the King George, maybe?" prompted Stevie, as more reporters clustered around, scenting the presence of important breaking news.

"That's a possibility," Sam added, conscious that Merlin was now standing alongside them, having taken his tiny saddle from Katseye's broad back. Jackie was holding a yellow bucket under the horse's black nose. Katseye took a few gulps and then turned his handsome head towards his groom. He scarcely seemed to have broken a sweat, despite the warm conditions.

"That could mean a chance of the jump racing Triple Crown, couldn't it?" Stevie insisted, "What about that, Merlin?"

"It's Mr Sampfield's and the owners' call," Merlin conceded, "But Tabikat's capable of achieving it, in my book. These two 'orses are the best I've ridden by a long way. Superstars, they are. 'ooever buys that sibling of theirs will be onto a gold mine."

"A sibling?" asked Stevie, as the reporters strained their ears to catch what was being said, "Is this the colt you are planning to buy, Mrs Crosland? Or perhaps you are after him too, Mr Sampfield Peveril?"

Sam did not know how to respond to this question. The last time he had expressed an interest in the youngest offspring of Little Kitty Cat, the discussion had been interrupted by a dispute over the ownership of the colt. But this was hardly the kind of thing which he could talk about in public. He was saved by the authoritative intervention of Meredith Crosland.

"Nothing has been decided yet," she stated, firmly, "Katalyst is still the property of the breeder. He's an entire colt, so Mr Foley may even elect to keep him and send him to stud. In that case, there may be many future opportunities for his progeny to be seen on our racecourses."

"It all sounds very exciting," Stevie commented, "Tabby Cat and Jayce will make sure the Smart Girls are kept informed. Now I think you, Merlin, must go to weigh in. Thank you all for your time."

Sam was for once in his life in danger of forgetting his customary good manners.

"What on earth was all that about?" he asked Stevie Stone, curtly, "I don't like being surprised by journalists, as I am sure you are aware."

"I apologise, Mr S-P," Stevie replied, "It had to sound genuine. Meredith did her best to give you a lead. I realise you must be cross."

Meredith Crosland said nothing, apparently looking at Stevie to calm the trainer down.

"Genuine?" repeated Sam, "I don't know what you mean. And why have you brought the Foley colt into a public discussion like this? The last I heard, there was an argument over who owned the animal."

"Oh, there's no argument," Stevie responded, "But we would really like people to think there is."

"Why?" asked Sam, bewildered.

"Because we are trying to raise a ghost," said Stevie.

17

The easy victory of Katseye in the Novices' chase at Chepstow had been a source of great satisfaction at *Feirm Enda*. The soporific weather had also favoured the West of Ireland that day, so the guests who were staying in the holiday cottages had been making the most of their opportunity to be outdoors in the benign sunshine. Feanna and young Enda had taken four of them out into the hills on the resident ponies, whilst an older American couple had decided to walk into the nearby town of Gleannglas.

Eoghan, Caitlin and Niamh had been left alone at the farm at the time the race took place and had promised to record it for Feanna to watch when she was at home later in the day.

The unexpected visit of the terminally ill Oisin Cassidy almost one year ago had produced many changes in the dynamics of the hard-working household at *Feirm Enda*. The revelation by the now deceased Oisin that the defunct horse dealing business which he had inherited from his father had been used by Callan Sullivan as a front to buy illegal weapons and bomb-making equipment had unsettled Eoghan's quiet world as if there had been an earth tremor. Eoghan had remembered Oisin as a shy and awkward young man with whom he had shared his days as an apprentice at Mallows stud, and, many years later, as the sympathetic friend who had given him and Caitlin the pregnant mare which had come to be known as Kat's Gift.

By contrast, Caitlin and Niamh had known or suspected more of the truth about the extent of the criminal activities of Eoghan's uncle, Callan Sullivan, who had murdered Niamh's husband, Enda. The two women had been troubled, but less surprised than Eoghan, by what Oisin had told them. Niamh had always known that more people than her long dead husband, after whom their holiday enterprise was now named, had been involved with Uncle Callan's evil activities.

The ghastly trauma of Enda's violent death, now over thirty years in the past, and the subsequent trial and conviction of Uncle Callan, had had the immediate effect of forcing the three young adults into an unspoken and tacitly agreed pact never to discuss Uncle Callan or his works ever again. Uncle Callan had been sent to a far-away prison and the three of them, including the newly disabled Eoghan, had had a living to earn if they were to survive as a family. Niamh had been left with four young children who had needed to be given the chance of a future. So, a bond of silence had been created thirty years ago and not one of them had broken it until Oisin had turned up at the remote farm on a moonlit November evening and had shattered the silence for ever.

Oisin's revelations, in particular his reference to having brought trouble onto Eoghan's head by giving him the pregnant mare sixteen years ago and that he had pretended that the animal had been hidden by Brendan Meaghan, had been overshadowed both by Oisin's death and then by Caitlin's revelations as to her whereabouts during the ten years she had spent away from the Foley farm, as it had been called in those days. Niamh had known some of the tortuous story, but Eoghan had heard none of it before, and had listened in expressionless and unmoving silence as Caitlin had pressed on with her narrative.

Caitlin had told without interruption of her three years spent with the traveller family of her father's cousin, Eirnin, during which she had witnessed the arms and drugs smuggling operation at first hand. This had been followed by an account of her six years working in the racing yard of Fergal Carter in County Meath, during which she had lived as jockey Niall Carter's girlfriend and the yard's head lass. She had watched Eoghan's successful career as a jockey, during which he had often raced against her unfaithful partner Niall. But Eoghan had never noticed Caitlin, or Kat as she was known in those days, when she had accompanied the Carter horses to their races.

Eoghan had broken his silence only once, which was when Caitlin had haltingly related how Arnaldo, Eirnin's son, had helped her to obstruct the sniper sent to kill Eoghan at Navan racecourse by blinding the man with a mirror intended to reflect the rays of the sun into his eyes. But the flashes had instead distracted Eoghan's powerful chaser, Langham Light and had brought them down in a crashing fall over a jump. Eoghan's career as a jockey had been ended by the injuries he had sustained in the horrific fall and Langham Light had had to be put down on the course. Arnaldo had murdered the sniper with his knife.

Eoghan's audible reaction to the narrative had been nothing more than a sharp intake of breath at the resurrection of the terrible memory and the simultaneous realisation that he owed both his life and his shattered knee to the woman whom he had known since childhood and who was the mother of his three sons. The news that the loyal Caitlin, whose very existence he had put to the back of his mind in the years during which he had pursued his burning ambition to be a successful jockey, and the gypsy Arnaldo, a man he did not know, had taken such risks to protect him, had both humbled and shocked him. His brother Enda's death and his own career had not been the only consequences of his outright refusal to stop racehorses in those now distant days. Caitlin and Arnaldo had had to carry the harrowing knowledge of the roles they had played too.

In this way had been finally assembled more fragments of the Foleys' broken secrets, the secrets which they had kept from each other, not out of a lack of trust, but because the memories and their implications might have destroyed everything that they had so laboriously built for themselves at *Feirm Enda*. The old house itself had been deathly quiet, keeping watch whilst the forgotten ghosts of its inhabitants' mutual past had come crawling from their hiding places in the cracks of the stone walls and had shrouded the family once again in the dark fears which they had all thought had been erased from their collective memory.

By the time Caitlin had finished speaking, her final words being of her decision to return home after almost ten years away, the weak November sun had climbed steadily to its noonday position in a grey cloud-blurred sky. A sharp edged breeze had made itself felt down the narrow chimney of the living room in which they had still been sitting, the pale and shrivelled body of Oisin Cassidy having been removed by the ambulance crew two hours earlier.

Eoghan had stood up slowly and had held out his hand to Caitlin. Caitlin had stood wordlessly to grasp it with her own small hand. Niamh had remained seated, but after the others had left the room, she had slowly got to her feet to look out of the leaded paned window.

Niamh had seen the compact figures of Eoghan and Caitlin crossing the farmyard and entering the stables, where they had quickly tacked up two of the farm's sturdy riding horses. Young Enda had come forward to help, but Caitlin had motioned him gently away. The last sight Niamh had had of her sister and Eoghan that day had been of their upright backs moving with the motion of the horses as they had slowly ascended the dulled green slope of the hill behind the remote farm.

Niamh had watched that same scene from that same window on numerous occasions many years ago, her beloved husband Enda sometimes standing beside her. In those days, before Niamh had had children of her own, the two people she had loved most in the world, after her enigmatic husband, had been those two young teenagers, one of them a kind and introspective boy and the other a bright brave girl with untidy black hair, who had ridden their Connemara ponies, Tarragon and Branna, up into the quiet of the empty landscape in which they had enjoyed the best times of their youthful lives.

Was everyone's trust and innocence doomed to be destroyed like this, Niamh had wondered, as she had clutched the window ledge, unchecked tears running down her tired face. At that moment, she had been immensely proud of her sister. The selfish Niall Carter had not deserved her. Perhaps even Eoghan did not. Niamh herself had a story still to tell but it had not yet been the time to tell it, she had thought. Perhaps it would never be the time.

Eoghan and Caitlin had not returned until the chill morning of the next day. Young Enda and Feanna had feared that an accident had occurred, as their mobile phone calls to the older couple had gone unanswered. Niamh had reassured them, as best she could, by telling them a little of what Caitlin had said that morning, but leaving the impression that the main cause of Eoghan's taciturn behaviour the previous day had been the sudden and unpleasant death of his old friend.

Eleven months had now passed since that day when long-kept secrets had been made known, and on the afternoon of Katseye's popular win at Chepstow the normal business of *Feirm Enda* was coming to the end of another season.

The return of Eoghan and Caitlin on that gloomy November morning had been followed by a family discussion over breakfast in the large kitchen of the stone farmhouse, the same kitchen in which Eoghan and his older brothers, and more recently, Enda and Niamh's children and Eoghan's own sons, had all spent their time as children. Nowadays, it had become a pleasant space in which holiday guests could take their meals, and was no longer the dark and smoky environment which it had been in the time when Eoghan's careworn mother had been alive.

Eoghan's words that day to his family had been unexpected to everyone except Caitlin.

"I learned things yesterday," Eoghan had said, as his son and niece had listened to him with a mixture of relief at his return and surprise at his sudden eloquence, "These things have made me realise that I can no longer ignore the events which have happened in the past. I have been wrong to do this for so long. My only excuse is that I did not know everything that I know now. My brother, your father, Feanna, became entrapped in the work of evil people. But I did not know until yesterday that other people had been entrapped by it too – your mother, Enda, and, now I realise, I myself – were being dragged into the wickedness. Like my brother, I too should be long dead, had your mother not intervened to save my life. My dead friend Oisin too has carried a secret with him, a secret which I do not yet fully understand. The time has come for these secrets to be explained. Our whole family, your brothers, Enda, your sisters, Feanna, will be needed to help with this. The Stonehouse family, or what is left of them, will be wanted too. The racing people in England, who have cared for and trained Tabikat and Katseye, we will ask also for their help."

"What are you saying, dad?" young Enda had asked, unnerved by his father's tone, "What are these secrets you are speaking about?"

Caitlin, who had been sitting next to Eoghan at the long table, had spoken for the first time. Her face had been drawn and pale in the gloom of the low- ceilinged room.

"Your father is talking about Kat's Gift, Enda," Catlin had told her son, "We need now to understand who she is and where she came from."

Enda had given a sigh of relief.

"I thought you were talking about something more serious," he had said to Eoghan, "Surely knowing about Kat's Gift is not important to us now. Our Tabikat and Katseye have shown for themselves what they can do by their making their own success in their racing careers. Does it matter about their history?"

"I believe it does," Eoghan had replied, "Although not for the reasons you have given. I have long suspected that the gift to us of Maire, as she was called in those days, was not the chance event that it seemed. Oisin, who died here yesterday, said to me when he brought her to us that his business was bankrupt and that he did not want this mare to be taken by the bailiffs and sold. Oisin told me that she was in foal to Alakazam, the grand old stallion who stood then at Mallows, but that Ronan Brody did not know that the covering had been successful. I thought then that his only reason for concealing the mare's pregnancy from Ronan was because the full fee would be demanded, which Oisin did not have the money to pay. But I now think that there was more about it than that."

"What more?" had asked Feanna, "And why should Oisin have taken the mare to Alakazam at all, if he knew could not pay the covering fee?"

"That is because he knew that Maire was a valuable horse," Eoghan had replied, "And that breeding from her with a top stallion would produce a valuable foal. Oisin was right. Little Kitty Cat was the outcome."

"But Kitty was not valuable," had objected Enda, "No-one knew anything about her bloodline. We still know nothing. If we are now so very concerned, surely we should have a DNA test done? It might tell us at least if the story that Alakazam was her sire is true. We have never been able to claim that relationship in the past because of the absence of any certificate from Mallows."

"We could indeed do that," Eoghan had said, "But that will not tell us what we need to know."

The others had looked at him in silence.

"We need to know from whom Maire was taken," Eoghan had continued, "I do not believe that Oisin himself took her. I think she was one of the horses which went through his business when it was still being used as a screen for the activities which had been set up by Uncle Callan Sullivan. As Oisin said, these activities did not stop when Uncle Callan went to prison. Oisin was an experienced stud man. As I have already said, he will have recognised Maire at once as a high quality breeding mare. He will have wanted, I am sure, to keep her in his stables, instead of selling her on at an inflated price, maybe to whoever was providing the money to pay for the guns and the other evil things, maybe to someone else. When his business went down, Oisin gave her to me to try to protect his plan. But someone came looking for the mare, someone who had probably paid for her and expected to receive her from Oisin. So Oisin told them that Brendan Meaghan had hidden her. Whether he told that person that Maire was in foal, I doubt."

"Brendan's old yard was burned down at about that time," Niamh had spoken up suddenly, horror in her voice, "Do you think that this same person was responsible for that? That they were looking for Maire?"

"And they had their revenge when Brendan told them, quite truthfully, that he knew nothing of the mare," Caitlin had supplied, "They will have suspected that he had sold her on and was lying to them."

"We are speaking of events which happened over fifteen years ago," Feanna had interjected, "The people involved may be dead or no longer interested in finding the mare. After all, if they did not know that she was in foal, surely they would assume that there would be no living trace of her now?"

"Yes, that is true, because that's exactly what has happened," responded Eoghan, "Consider this, Fee. Our Kitty raced all those years ago without having a pedigree. She was a home bred horse from *Feirm Enda* with an unnamed sire and a dam of little account called Kat's Gift, a name which your aunt Caitlin herself chose for Maire. Kitty came back here after her racing career ended. There was nothing at all to connect her with Maire. Then we bred from Kitty first with Mallows' Tabloid News to produce Tabikat and then again with Night Vision to get Katseye. Tabikat and Katseye have never been put up for public sale and no-one has ever needed to look into their bloodline. They are both geldings and could not be used for breeding. They have both won a great deal of money for their owners, trainers, and for us too, as the breeder. But there is no reason to suppose any connection with Maire. No-one knew that she was ever here with us. Oisin was aware of that, and he deliberately put the people who were looking for her onto the wrong track. *Feirm Enda* did not breed any sort of horses at the time Maire went missing, so why should anyone look here for her or any of her progeny?"

"It seems to me, Eoghan," Niamh had said, slowly, "That you have done an excellent job in hiding the mare which Oisin brought to you. Indeed, she is still here with us, in the paddock over there, old and content. Who else but ourselves would want her now? Is it really necessary to rake up this evil work of the past?"

"It is not necessary, but I shall be doing it, just the same," Eoghan had told her, fiercely, "I am tired of this world of secrecy and lies. These people with whom Uncle Callan was involved have been guilty of crimes for which I do not believe they have ever been brought to account. It is because of them that I lost my brother, you your husband, and your children their father. Caitlin and her friend Arnaldo have been made into criminals. The loss of my career as a jockey is also a part of what has been done to our family, although I count that as nothing compared to what you and Caitlin have suffered."

"Surely, Eoghan," Niamh had responded, as the younger members of the family started at the passion in Eoghan's unfamiliar tone of voice, "This is a matter for the *garda*? The violence of which you speak is now a thing of history. Uncle Callan himself died in prison five years ago. If there are people still unpunished, is it your responsibility to seek them out? What will you do if they are found? Perhaps they will still wish to murder you and we will have more misery heaped on our family."

"If we involve the *garda,* your sister will be arrested, Arnaldo too, if they can find him," had said Eoghan flatly, "I think we have no choice, Niamh."

As Niamh had dropped her head in reluctant assent, Caitlin had put her arm around her older sister, and Eoghan had started to outline the plan which had been agreed last night in a house in the town of Monamar.

Listening to the televised comments of Mrs Crosland and Stevie Stone at Chepstow racecourse on the sunlit October day eleven months later, Eoghan still remained confident that the plan would achieve the outcome he had hoped. It was a plan requiring patience, in which he would sit off the pace, watch the progress of the race ahead of him, and judge when to make his move.

It had always worked for him in the past. But then, in those days, he had known against whom he was racing.

18

The relentless tide had receded by the time that Jackie drove the small horsebox containing the dark shape of Katseye towards the English coastline over the Old Severn Bridge. The now narrower channel of water in between the sloping and muddy banks looked dull and sluggish. A screen of nondescript cloud had begun to obscure the sun and a feeling of damp tainted the still air. A small blue and white aircraft buzzed slowly above them heading North East towards the extravagant bends of the River Severn and the bird sanctuaries further up the rapidly tapering channel.

Kye's race had been the last on the Chepstow card. His ride had been an experienced chaser which had given him little trouble in the Conditional Jockeys' Handicap Chase, plugging on gamely to the end of nearly three miles in the soft conditions to take second place. The local Welsh trainer who, on Merlin's recommendation, had given Kye the ride had been pleased with the performance of the eleven year old horse which had clearly benefited from the reduced weight, and had indicated that she would be happy to book Kye to ride for her again. Kye had been gratified to see that Merlin and Mr Sampfield had remained at Chepstow racecourse to watch his race and had both congratulated him on his performance.

"If Miss Roberts wants me to ride her horses again," a previously quiet Kye suddenly said to Jackie from the passenger seat of the horsebox, "I am defo going to need some wheels of my own. I can't keep on hoping that someone will be around to take me places."

"We could buy a second-hand car between us," Jackie suggested, "You've been earning money from your rides for a bit now and my mum and dad would probably lend me a few hundred pounds if I asked."

"Yez don't need a car, Jackie," Kye told her, "And I don't want your mum and dad paying out for a car for me to use. It's my problem. I'll think of something, don't worry."

Sam's decision to remain behind at the quickly emptying Chepstow racecourse for Kye's ride had been additionally prompted by a proposal from Stevie Stone to explain to him her unexpected remarks about Katalyst, in particular the cryptic, and, to Sam's ears, ridiculous reference to raising a ghost. Having ensured that Jackie and Kye were safely on their way back to Sampfield Grange, he had agreed to join Stevie in the bar of The Boat Inn, a tiny eighteenth century establishment, scenically located on the Welsh bank of the nearby River Wye.

Arriving at the riverside pub, Sam was surprised to discover Merlin ap Rhys sprawled in a chair alongside Stevie at a small corner table in the compact galleried bar. The inn was still relatively quiet and the few drinkers propping up the well-stocked bar took no notice of him.

"Not your usual sort of place, I imagine, Mr S-P?" Stevie said, whilst Merlin stood up to drag a third chair across to the wooden topped table, "But if we are recognised, then people will just assume that I'm interviewing you again about Katseye's win."

"I think I should be the one who is asking the questions on this occasion," Sam replied, trying to keep the impatience out of his voice, "Is Merlin involved in this mysterious business too, then?"

"Yes," Stevie responded in turn, "And a lot more people besides, including yourself, Mr S-P, if you will hear me out."

"Please continue," said Sam, shortly, "I'm listening. Although I suppose we ought to order some drinks if we are to be here for any length of time."

"Let me do that," Merlin offered, getting up from his chair, "I'll get us somethin' without alcohol, seein' as we're all drivin'."

Whilst Merlin was standing at the bar, answering eager questions from a small number of local racegoers who had recognised him, Stevie began her narrative.

"I'm sure you remember the background story which Brendan Meaghan will have told you just before you first took on Tabikat in January last year," Stevie started, "That Tabikat's dam was the foal of a pregnant mare which had been given to Eoghan Foley by an old friend called Oisin Cassidy?"

"Yes," replied Sam, who, in the course a lifetime of being unable easily to write anything down, had developed a highly retentive memory, "And that Oisin Cassidy told him that the sire of the foal was Alakazam, but that this could not be confirmed with Mallows stud because no payment had been made for the covering."

"Good," Stevie said, as if approving the correctly recited knowledge of a trainee, "Well, Oisin Cassidy died almost a year ago and more information has come to light as a result of his death. It appears that Oisin's horse dealing business, which belonged to his father before him, was being used as a front for criminal activity by a man called Callan Sullivan. Money which seemed to be for buying horses was actually buying guns and drugs. Some genuine horse sales went through the business too so as to make it look legitimate. Then Callan Sullivan went to prison and the whole thing came to a temporary stop."

"Callan Sullivan is the man who killed Genie Foley's brother, is he not?" interjected Sam, "Because Genie wouldn't stop horses for him, as I recall?"

"Yes, that is what everyone has believed for thirty years," Stevie confirmed, "But after Oisin came to see him, the Foleys learned, I am not entirely sure how, that Eoghan's brother Enda had been involved in Callan Sullivan's arms and drug smuggling enterprise, bringing in the goods from abroad. Being the family connection who would pressurise Eoghan to stop horses for betting gains was only one part of Enda's involvement. The Foleys also learned that the accident to Eoghan at Navan was more than it appeared at the time. It was an unsuccessful attempt by a hired gunman to kill Eoghan too."

"Good God," exclaimed Sam, as Merlin returned from the bar and set a small jug of lime juice, some ginger cordial, three glasses and two large bottles of sparkling water on the table, "But, forgive me, what has this to do with Katalyst and your reference to a ghost?"

"The first thing to understand," Stevie went on, "Is that Oisin Cassidy did not come into possession of Maire until many years after Enda was killed and Eoghan injured. With Callan Sullivan in prison, Oisin at first thought that no-one would need to use his business as a front any more. But he was wrong. Callan Sullivan's associates resurrected the operation within a short time and Oisin was drawn into it again. But this time, genuinely valuable horses were also being put through the business. Some of the proceeds from the drug dealing were being spent not on arms but on top quality equine bloodstock. Another way of laundering the drug money as well as an investment for the future, one would suppose. Oisin, though, was not in on this part of the activity. Someone else, I don't know who, explained it all to Eoghan after Oisin died. Most of the horses which went through Oisin's books were completely fictitious. But he had to operate a legitimate business too, in order to remain beyond suspicion. It seems that, for whatever reason, the people who were operating the business involving the bloodstock had to move some of their horses out of their usual place quickly, and so one of them came to Oisin."

"Maire," said Sam, following the story with increasing interest.

"Yes, and Oisin, it seems, was told to hold on to Maire. The Foleys are not sure what happened next. Oisin never got around to explaining it, and their other source of information, which they did not divulge to me, told them that there was a big falling out in the drugs operation. People were arrested, other people were killed, but the upshot was that the whole thing fell apart."

"And this man Oisin was left with the mare, and 'e no idea where she came from, except that 'e could see that she was well bred," put in Merlin, who had remained silent until now.

"This Oisin Cassidy was a trained stud man, as I recall," Sam said thoughtfully, "So my guess is that he decided to breed from her and put her in foal to Alakazam. Then his business failed, once the

178

illegal activity was not there to prop it up any more. So, he gave the mare to Genie."

"That's about the size of it, Mr S-P," Stevie replied, approvingly, "And no-one ever came looking for her, perhaps because there was nobody around to do the looking, or perhaps because they had no idea where to look."

"The Foleys think that someone did come once, at the beginning," Merlin corrected her, "The person who burned down Brendan Meaghan's place sixteen years ago. And now someone's been threatenin' Brendan again, as his son Declan tol' you last year, Mr Sampfield. Maybe someone still thinks Brendan knows somethin'."

"Let me get this straight," Sam said, reaching for one of the bottles of water and slowly unscrewing the cap, "Thirty years ago, Callan Sullivan shot Enda Foley and he or someone working with him in this … er.. illegal operation tried and failed to have Genie Foley killed too. Then sixteen years ago, Brendan has his yard burned down. Then last year he gets threatened. My question is, how do we know the things are all connected? And is it the same people? Surely after thirty years, some of them could be dead or too old to be involved still?"

"Eoghan Foley is pretty sure it is the same people or their successors," Stevie told him, "I think Eoghan has more information than he has given to me and to the others who he has asked to help him. My understanding is that the original criminal enterprise was set up to help fund the republican cause and provide the means to commit terrorist acts in Northern Ireland and on the British mainland. Now that all that violence is – or should be - over and done with since the Good Friday Agreement, those original objectives have changed. The people involved nowadays are just out to make money for themselves. No-one is going to give up a valuable network like that one just because an end to armed hostilities has been negotiated and agreed."

"And Genie now wants to know who they and their predecessors are," declared Sam, with sudden insight, "I can't say I blame him, given the damage they have done to him and his family. He thinks that finding out more about Maire, or Kat's Gift as they named her themselves, will help him discover their identity."

"Eoghan is something of a changed man," Stevie said, "Or, more accurately, the real Eoghan has now emerged again. I have known him ever since my sister TK was involved with his family. He's always been a kind and introspective person, someone who has kept his head down for the last thirty years. What he learned from Oisin has made him start asking questions about the things he had deliberately put to the back of his mind. The old jump jockey mentality has come out in him again as a result. He won't give up now until he has found out who these people are and ..."

"And what?" asked Sam, suddenly alarmed, "It sounds as if these are very dangerous and ruthless people. Does Genie know what he is getting himself into?"

"I think 'e does," Merlin put in, "'e's 'ad enough, Mr Sampfield."

"So, what is his plan?" asked Sam, doubtfully, "I have seen for myself that Alakazam's place in the bloodline has now been officially recognised. I assume that means Mallows stud is involved too?"

"Ronan Brody's father was apparently mixed up somehow with these people as well," Stevie explained, "Mallows used to be a racing yard as well as a stud, you will remember, and there were clearly things going on there too. Don't ask me what, Mr S-P. There was a lot that Eoghan wouldn't tell me, probably because it would mean that friends of his might face criminal charges if the information came out."

"Tell me the plan," Sam instructed, "I still don't follow how Genie is hoping to achieve what he wants."

"It's quite a slow burn," Steve said, "The first step was to get the issue into the public domain, starting at the beginning of this year. Tabikat and Katseye are both pretty famous nowadays, but their connection to Maire was known to no-one other than the Foleys and Ronan Brody. Maire's name was recorded as being Kat's Gift, and there was self-evidently no account of her anywhere in any official record.

"The first step was to reveal that Alakazam was the sire of Little Kitty Cat. That was in itself an indication that the mare Kat's Gift must have been something more than a common creature. The second step was to put Little Kitty Cat's third produce up for public sale. Tabikat and Katseye had not been sold to anyone outside the family, so their ancestry was never checked into by anyone involved in buying bloodstock. In any case, they are both geldings, so if anyone did work out that their bloodline could go back to the missing Maire, they would be no use to someone looking to make money in the future. They have won a lot of money for their current owners, but their careers will not last for ever, and neither Levy Brothers International nor Mr Ardizzone would agree to sell them. But an entire colt coming up for public sale would certainly catch the attention of whoever Eoghan is seeking, the ghosts of his family's terrible past."

"It's a bit of a long shot," Sam said, slowly, filling his glass with water again, "Genie is assuming that someone will now be able to work out that Oisin Cassidy gave Maire to him all that time ago."

"It's not such a long shot as all that," Stevie replied, "Think about it, Mr S-P. Ronan Brody, Oisin Cassidy and Brendan Meaghan were apprentices together at Mallows. If Ronan Brody and Brendan Meaghan didn't have the mare, then the only person with the knowledge to take her off Oisin's hands would be Eoghan Foley. A few years later a racing champion, Little Kitty Cat, comes out of an obscure farm in the hills above Gleannglas, the very town where Oisin ran his business. Kitty herself is sent to two top class stallions and produces two Grade 1 level chasers. Nothing else bred on *Feirm Enda* is in the same league, Mr S-P. The rest of their output are riding horses and pointers."

"So, the word goes out that Katalyst, an entire colt out of Little Kitty Cat, is up for sale by Cathal's," Merlin continued, as Stevie stopped to take a drink from the glass which Merlin had filled for her whilst she was speaking, "It's the first time anyone 'as 'ad chance to get their 'ands on a colt related to Tabikat and Katseye.

181

Then the colt is withdrawn from the first two sales, at Cheltenham in March and Aintree in April, but only late on, mind, so people get to 'ear about 'im and see 'is profile in the catalogue. If that doesn't interest these people Mr Foley is after, I don' know what would."

"And the business at the Punchestown sale, with Niall Carter claiming ownership of the colt," remembered Sam, "That was part of this too? To generate more publicity?"

"It was all reported in the Irish racing press," Stevie said, "And it was stated by Cathal's themselves that they would not agree to put the colt up for auction again until the matter had been resolved. Caitlin, Eoghan's partner, used to be the head lass at the Carter yard years ago, Eoghan told me, so they got Niall Carter involved too. Niall was a jockey at the same time as Eoghan and he remembers the accident at Navan. It was thought at the time to be more than just an accident, but no-one had any proof of anything and the *garda* got nowhere with following up the suspicions."

"Cathal's said they'd 'elp as much as they could," Merlin added, "Mr Carter's brother is one of the partners there."

A sudden memory flashed into Sam's mind. It was the memory of Frank Stanley at breakfast two weeks ago saying that he guessed that Luke Cunningham had been attacked in the horsebox park at Aintree racecourse because he was thought to be trying to steal a valuable horse. Frank had even suggested that Katalyst was the name of the horse concerned.

Sam was on the verge of asking Stevie and Merlin whether Frank Stanley was involved in Eoghan Foley's plan to smoke out the people who had caused so much pain to his family, but quickly decided against it. Merlin did not even know Frank Stanley, or so Sam thought, and Stevie's involvement with Frank related only to tragic death of her own parents and its complex consequences. Sam decided that he would ask Frank himself when he got the chance.

"What is your role in this, Stevie?" he asked, instead, "And yours, Merlin?"

"Our role is to create publicity in England," Stevie said simply, "So I and Tabby Cat mention Katalyst in my vlogs and get the racing press listening in to my interviews with you and Meredith. Meredith talks about what great things Katseye is going to achieve this season and where and when he will be racing. You and Merlin talk about Tabikat being aimed at the jump racing Triple Crown. We slip in references to Katalyst at every opportunity."

"You two are being very supportive to the Foley family," commented Sam, thoughtfully, "Why get involved in something which could become very dangerous if these people are as terrible as you are making out? From what you say, they're drug dealers, arms smugglers, horse thieves, murderers, republican dissidents, people maybe still capable of terrorist acts."

"Because the Foleys have helped my family," Stevie stated firmly, "They helped to entrap the Paloka brothers, the disgusting bastards who destroyed my parents, which in turn put the authorities in the way of dismantling their horrific criminal enterprises. They have helped to stop and prevent untold suffering in terms of the human lives which the Palokas preyed on and used for their own personal gain."

"And I 'ave 'ad the chance to ride these great 'orses," added Merlin, speaking equally firmly, "It's 'elped my career and won me a lot of money. Mr Foley was once a jockey like me, an' what' appened to 'im is fuckin' unacceptable. Gettin' shot at for refusin' to stop a 'orse. That could 'appen to any of us jocks, Mr Sampfield."

"And I've trained a Cheltenham Gold Cup winner," said Sam, quietly, "Something I never even dreamed I would do. You are right. We all owe them a lot. What is it Genie wants me to do? I have already agreed to consider buying Katalyst. Is that what he is asking?"

"I think you will find that you already own him, Mr S-P," Stevie told him, "Weatherbys have been sent all the paperwork this afternoon."

As Sam stared at Stevie and Merlin wordlessly, the hubbub of the pub grew ever louder around them.

19

Merlin ap Rhys was, as ever, feeling confident. On the morning of the Friday of Cheltenham's three day November meeting, the cold Autumn air slanted sharp sunlight into his eyes as he steered his BMW sports car along the undulating A48 towards Gloucester. There he would join the Northbound carriageway of the M5 to Cheltenham.

Merlin's journeys to the South and West usually took him over the Old Severn bridge towards the busy M4, where the task of driving took on the character of a challenging race in which the slower vehicles had to be passed without exceeding the speed limit, or at least not in any way which could be detected, and no-one received any prizes. By contrast the mostly single carriageway road which meandered parallel to the Northern coast of the Bristol Channel, as it narrowed back into the River Severn, was a slowly navigated affair laid down over gently sloping hills and making its way through wayside towns with old pubs and twisting high streets. It was impossible, or highly inadvisable, to drive fast, and for that reason the journey could be thought of as a calming experience, notwithstanding the dire roadside notices announcing the number of casualties caused by the more impatient users of the route.

Merlin was due to ride Katseye on that sunny day in an extended two and a half mile Chase at the famous Gloucestershire racecourse. His agent, Jackson Argyrides, had booked him two rides in the other races, one for Dorset trainer Justin Venn, for whom Merlin had ridden many times in the past, and the other for Hafren Roberts, the trainer whose horse Kye had ridden at Chepstow the previous month.

Steering through the descending turns of the little town of Newnham, Merlin wondered if Sadie would be accompanying the magnificent Sampfield Grange runner that day. He knew that Jackie, the horse's usual groom, was likely to lead up the novice chaser in the parade ring, but he could not guess whether it would be Sadie or Kye who would accompany her to the meeting. It would have been easy to call Sadie to ask, but Merlin was still treading carefully around Sadie, even after the unexpected intervention of Frank Stanley over a month ago.

Merlin had been surprised to be asked, through Jackson, to come to *Feirm Enda* in early October.

"It's Mrs Crosland what used to own de black 'orse," Jackson had told him in his strange hybrid accent, "She want you out there to try out another 'orse for 'er. She's payin' travel and a riding fee, she says."

Knowing that Sadie had been staying with the Foleys over the summer, Merlin had seen a chance to capitalise on his determination to renew his enjoyable relationship with Sadie and had accepted the offer straightaway. In the event, the purpose of the visit had proved somewhat different to that described to Jackson by Mrs Crosland, and Merlin had found himself brought into the plan of Eoghan Foley to track down the origins of the horse officially known as Kat's Gift. Sadie, fascinated by the story of Tabikat's past, had also been keen to support the venture, but only on the understanding that Mr Sampfield would be informed of the activity relating to the two racehorses which he was training, a promise which Stevie Stone and Merlin had subsequently fulfilled.

Merlin and Sadie had travelled on a budget airline back to Cardiff airport together. Merlin had been regretfully aware that the last time the two of them had shared a flight from Ireland, they had been returning from the previous year's Punchestown Festival, which had occurred just before the breakdown of their torrid relationship. It had taken all of Merlin's self-control not to put his hand on Sadie's warm thigh as the two of them had sat primly side by side whilst the aircraft made its swift way over Southern Ireland.

Sadie had chattered brightly about her relaxing summer weeks riding out on the Foley horses with the holiday guests and then of her plans for competing with Indian Rocks in point to point races during the coming season. The sombre mood which had overshadowed the weeks following her horrific discovery of the injured Luke Cunningham seemed to have been dispelled. Watching her from the corner of his eye, Merlin had wanted nothing more than to silence her guileless narrative with his own mouth and to feel her perfect breasts pressing hard against his chest. Erotic images of the two of them enjoying each other in the cosy attic bedroom in Chepstow had floated unchecked into his mind. Merlin had been obliged to sit uncomfortably on the aircraft seat, trying to concentrate on what Sadie was telling him, carefully keeping a folded racing paper on his lap to prevent his unruly body from betraying his lascivious thoughts.

On their arrival at Cardiff Airport, Merlin had been taken to one side by an armed police officer.

"Your companion can wait for you in the entrance area," the stony-faced man had said to him curtly, as Sadie had stared at Merlin in consternation, "Your bags will be brought to you there."

"What the 'ell is all this about?" Merlin had protested crossly as he was led towards an anonymous grey door with a small, security-wired window set into it.

Sitting behind an ancient metal desk in the bare room had been a tall man whom Merlin had recognised with a stomach-churning jolt of trepidation.

"Mr Stanley," Merlin had said, without enthusiasm, remaining standing defiantly whilst the forbidding police officer had left them alone in the utilitarian surroundings.

"Good afternoon, Mr ap Rhys," had replied his companion, "I am sorry if you or Miss Shinkins have been alarmed. I am hoping you will consent to be of assistance to me once again."

"I am not sure what assistance, as you call it, I gave you last time," Merlin had replied, referring to his memory of the anti-climax when nothing out of the ordinary had appeared to have happened before Katseye's race on Gold Cup day, "But I promised I'd drive Sadie to the station in Cardiff, so I can't 'ang around 'ere for long."

"Yes, I should like to involve your companion, Miss Shinkins, too," Frank Stanley had said, unexpectedly, "But only with your agreement."

"Sadie isn't exac'ly my companion," Merlin had objected, quickly, "An' it's not up to me what she does, any'ow."

"I ask only because I may in due course need to refer to the person through whom you first came to my attention," Frank Stanley had said, carefully, "I would not wish to cause you any embarrassment."

Merlin had pondered this oblique remark for a moment and had then ventured, "You mean that woman Lara in Liverpool? What does she 'ave to do with all this?"

"Lara – not her real name as you know – is one of my operatives," had come the reply, "I may need to involve her."

It had been as a consequence of this short conversation that Merlin had driven a mystified Sadie to a bland hotel in the centre of Cardiff and they had spent part of the evening in discussion with Frank Stanley.

Sadie had been astonished to see Merlin in the company of the man she knew only as her employer's old school friend and the suspected lover of former Sampfield Grange employee Isabella Hall. Sadie had been even more astonished to hear what he had to ask of them.

"Eoghan Foley has told you both of the events which led to his acquisition of the mare from which Tabikat and Katseye are descended," Frank Stanley had begun, as they had sat at a corner table in the far end of the unimaginatively decorated hotel restaurant, "And of the death of his brother Enda at the hands of Callan Sullivan following the attempt on Eoghan's own life at Navan racecourse."

Sadie and Merlin had both nodded.

"Eoghan will have also described to you," Frank Stanley had continued, "A smuggling operation which Callan Sullivan was running at the time. Callan Sullivan was, though, merely one cog in a much larger machine which supplied the Irish republican cause with illegal arms and ready cash earned from drug dealing. The networks through which these people operated at the time were extensive and sophisticated. What Eoghan may not understand, though, is that although the terrorist violence is, or should be, over, the lines through which the illegal arms and drugs were brought into the South of Ireland and thence to the North and to the British mainland have been carefully preserved over the years, even expanded. But there is no political idealism now. It is plain criminal activity, designed to make money for gangsters - gangsters we believe to be based in Belfast and Liverpool, the route through which the original supply chain eventually reached mainland Britain."

"That means that if Eoghan Foley finds out where the mare came from, you think 'e could find 'imself faced with these gangsters," had supplied Merlin.

"Is this to do with what happened to Luke?" Sadie had suddenly butted in, "That was in Liverpool, and we had Katseye with us that day. Was it these gangsters who attacked him?"

Both men had looked at her in surprise.

"There may well be a connection," Frank Stanley had told her, thoughtfully, "Although I think it more likely that someone was looking for the elusive Katalyst and thought Luke was some kind of threat to them."

"What is it you want from us?" Merlin had demanded, determined to get to the point of the meeting, not least because he had hoped to get some time alone with Sadie, "With respect, Mr Stanley, I don' understand your involvement in this. You asked me to 'elp you before with that business with Katseye and Mr Ardizzone, but us 'elping Eoghan Foley 'as nothin' to do with any of that."

189

"My involvement, as you describe it," Frank had replied, "Is not in Eoghan Foley's plan to uncover the ancestry of his horses. That is a matter for the Foley family. But the effect of Eoghan's actions may well put him and his family in danger of repercussions from the present criminal operation, as you yourself have just suggested, and that possibility does affect my current work. I am therefore trying to ensure, as far as I can, that he, and those who are assisting him, are protected. That includes the people involved with the horses in England, such as yourselves."

"Why are you telling us all this, Mr Stanley?" had asked Sadie, worry sounding in her question, "Are you saying that someone might attack Merlin or me, like they did Luke? Or try to hurt the horses? Are you saying we shouldn't help Mr Foley?"

"I am saying, Miss Shinkins," Frank Stanley had replied, "That there are potential unintended consequences to Mr Foley's plan. My purpose this evening is to ensure that you and Mr ap Rhys understand that fact and to ask that you comply with some actions which I will be taking to minimise the likelihood of the occurrence of those consequences. As to your personal safety, no-one outside the family, and the close friends who were with you at *Feirm Enda* this summer, is aware that you are party to what Eoghan Foley is doing, so there is no reason that you should be targets. As I have already said, I believe the attack on Mr Cunningham to have been motivated by something entirely different."

"OK," had said Merlin, impatiently, whilst Sadie had seemed to be thinking over what she had just been told, "But you still 'aven't said what you want from the two of us."

"Nothing, at the moment," Frank Stanley had replied, "Carry out your part in Eoghan Foley's plan, as you have already promised him. I understand this to consist simply of publicising the ambitious racing plans for Tabikat and Katseye and making known the existence of the younger horse, Katalyst. The information I will now add, Miss Shinkins, is that, when you return to Sampfield Grange, you will find that Isabella Hall will once again join the staff in order to support you in progressing Eoghan Foley's plan. I am confident that you will be able to work with her co-operatively. As to Liverpool, Mr ap Rhys, the woman that you know as Lara will contact you if your help is needed there."

Frank Stanley had then stood up abruptly and pushed back his metal framed chair.

"There are two rooms booked in your names in this hotel for you to use tonight, if you wish," he had said, "In any event, I will see you both at Sampfield Grange tomorrow morning."

Such had been the abrupt conclusion of the so-called briefing which Frank Stanley had provided that evening. Merlin's subsequent attempt to explain to Sadie the other man's reference to Lara had been met with a firm rebuff.

"I've already told you, Merlin, that it isn't my business and you don't need to explain," Sadie had reminded him, flatly, "And now I am going to call Kelly to tell her that I will be home tomorrow morning instead of this evening and then I am going to go to the room which Mr Stanley said he'd booked for me here."

"At least let me drive us both to Sampfield Grange, tomorrow," Merlin had said to her, "It'll save you a train fare. If I'm goin' to 'elp, I need to talk to Mr Sampfield about the plans for the horses, any'ow. And Sadie, just one question I want to ask. You don' 'ave to answer, if you don' want. But that Luke Cunningham. Is 'e still your boyfriend?"

"No," Sadie had said, and had left him alone in the half empty restaurant.

The Friday morning traffic on the M5 was far busier than that on the winding country road to Gloucester, but Merlin was soon turning his car through the white gates of Cheltenham racecourse. Glancing over the hedge and railings to his right, he tried without success to spot the Sampfield Grange horsebox. Doing what he did best, Merlin mentally shrugged his shoulders and resolved to concentrate on his day's work. He would put the problem of Sadie into the back of his mind until he could achieve something useful.

Katseye's race was the fourth on the six race card. Merlin's rides for Justin Venn and Hafren Roberts were in the second and third races, so Merlin had been kept fully occupied by the time the four horses for the Novices' Chase were brought down to the pre-parade area. Walking out from the weighing room, Merlin could see Mr Sampfield and Sadie standing in the centre of the parade ring, talking intently to Mrs Crosland, who appeared to have abandoned her customary green and white outfit for a black coat with a high collar. Notwithstanding the bright sunshine, there was a crispy chill in the air and the hedge patterned shape of Cleeve Hill stood out starkly against a clean blue sky.

Katseye soon stalked grandly into the parade ring, the first of the four horses to appear, dwarfing the diminutive figure of Jackie, who was dressed in a zipped red jacket and a dark bobble hat. The members of the small field had plenty of space around them as they all walked obediently clockwise along the pink coloured path. Warmly clad spectators clustered along the glass and metal barriers of the extensive viewing areas overlooking the smartly mown parade ring. With only four horses to choose from, there might not have been a great deal for the watchers to discuss, but the small size of the field belied its calibre, and the choice of a winner was no easy decision.

Tabby Cat and Jayce had stayed loyal to Katseye, and the bookies seemed to agree with them. The second favourite was a Lambourn trained horse called Petit Zazou, which Merlin could not recall seeing before. Having spoken to the jockey in the weighing room, Merlin had learned that the dark bay gelding with a narrow white blaze down its nose had raced previously in France.

"I've only seen recordings of him racing," the other jockey had said to Merlin, "But he schools nice enough at home. We're still finding out about him."

Merlin, to his surprise, had been legged up into Katseye's saddle by Sadie.

"Stay safe, Merlin," was all Sadie said, as Katseye continued his grand and uninterrupted way along the path towards the horsewalk, Merlin perched in the tiny saddle, his black booted toes pushed into the irons on either side. Sadie continued to monitor their progress as Jackie released her hold on Katseye's rein and Merlin cantered the stunning horse in front of the grandstand. Petit Zazou was the last horse to enter the horsewalk and seemed suddenly to wake from the quiet trance in which he had walked around the parade ring, bucking excitedly, but without malice, as his jockey put him into a canter.

The four horses were more or less in a line as they set off from the starting point on the far side of the Old course. The field soon began to swing to the left, and two expensive looking helicopters became visible on the viewing screen, parked on the grass beyond the course. Next to them, the smaller shape of a bright yellow Air Ambulance could also be seen.

"As the field approaches the first of the sixteen fences there is little to choose between them," the amplified commentator said in an even tone, clearly not expecting anything interesting to happen for some time, immediately afterwards suddenly crying out, "And Petit Zazou has blundered badly at the first and has scattered the birch. He's stayed on his feet, but he's hampered the favourite, Katseye, who's been relegated to last place. Cloud Atlas has not been done any favours either."

"Fuck that!" yelled Merlin angrily, as the French horse recovered his balance and sped off, pulling hard against the contact. Merlin could hear Cloud Atlas's jockey shouting out something similar.

After the unexpectedly dramatic start, the race continued relatively uneventfully. The lively Petit Zazou retained the lead but the field gradually closed up behind him. All four horses were measuring their fences well and the neatly packed birch of the remaining jumps stayed intact.

"Thought you said 'e was well be'aved," shouted Merlin at Petit Zazou's jockey as he brought Katseye to race upsides the miscreant, who was still pulling hard. The other jockey emitted a grunt which could have meant anything, but most probably that he was saving his breath.

"Katseye's motoring up to pass Petit Zazou," the commentator told the crowd, as the runners approached the second last obstacle, "Petit Zazou's having none of it and they take the fence together."

Approaching the final fence, Merlin could hear the roar of the excited crowd reverberating from the packed stands at the top of the famous hill. The dipping sun was in his eyes as the last jump loomed large ahead of them. Beyond it was the finish line, the course narrowing into a white railed funnel between the animated and noisy spectator areas.

'Go, Katseye, *bachgen*," urged Merlin, as the big black horse gathered itself beneath him to power them over the fence, "We've got this!"

The two leaders landed together, but Petit Zazou's earlier pulling against his bit had not served him well and Katseye gradually drew inexorably ahead to cross the line in first place by little more than a length.

Standing in the parade ring whilst Merlin gave his post-race interview from Katseye's steaming back for the benefit of the television audience, Sam and Meredith Crosland gave a simultaneous sigh of relief. Both of them had been rattled by Katseye's early misfortune in running. The fact that it had occurred so early in the race had been the saving grace which had given the game Katseye the chance to make up the lost ground.

Merlin and Katseye returned to the winner's place amidst the cheers of the numerous spectators assembled on the steppings to greet them. The slowly expiring sun had begun to descend behind the buildings and the air felt heavier and colder. Merlin was gratified to see the smiling face of Sadie amongst the happy group awaiting him.

Sadie's cheerful smile, though, was forced. Merlin might have forgotten, but she had not. The illiterate threatening message **I cu at Chlets agen I brak ur legs** thumped persistently through her head.

20

Curlew Landings' second attempt to win the Greatwood Hurdle required the Sampfield Grange team to make a second trip to Cheltenham racecourse on the Sunday of the three day meeting.

The notoriously variable November weather had changed considerably from the bright and chilly conditions which had prevailed on the Friday. The loitering sun seemed at last to have accepted the arrival of winter and had shrouded itself in a mass of scudding and chaotic grey clouds, which occasionally ripped and parted before a strong wind, providing only fleeting glimpses of the blue which had been so generously displayed two days earlier. Those few of the decaying leaves which still clung to the branches of the trees above the rutted and sloping track behind the stone built racing yard and house were being flung hectically skywards, soon whirling to the ground in a frenzied spin, only to be swept aloft again by the next gust of turbulent air.

Curlew Landings was the sole Sampfield Grange horse to travel to the races that day. With the exception of Katseye, who was still on light exercise following his recent run, the remainder of the string had been out as usual in the morning's breezy conditions, shaking their heads irritably as the wind whipped around their warm bodies, ready to leap away in alarm from every piece of flapping foliage or rush of skittering loose earth and stones around their hooves.

Tabikat, with only six days remaining before his first attempt at the Lancashire Chase at the unfamiliar Haydock Park, led the edgy equine group up onto the top gallop, a windswept Sadie wrapped up warmly on his back. Mr Sampfield was already on his way to Cheltenham, where he would meet Curlew's customary fan club, consisting of Sam's red-haired cousin Gilbert Peveril and his wife Philippa, together with the talented horse's former owner, Toby Halstock.

Notwithstanding the blustery conditions, Curlew Landings had loaded without trouble into the small horsebox whilst his stable companions were out on the gallops. Travis had cycled over from the Dicks yard to Sampfield Grange twice during the week to work with Curlew, Merlin's riding commitments having prevented him from coming to Sampfield Grange during the now increasingly limited daylight hours.

Travis had been as enthusiastic as ever about his former charge.

"Curlew's fair dinkum, Mr Sampfield," Travis had assured Sam, "Sure, he'll be carrying a lot more weight this time, but he can still win it, I reckon."

Travis's remark had referenced one of Sam's principal concerns about Curlew's upcoming race. Curlew liked to run his races from the front, so he and Merlin necessarily dictated a fast pace from the outset to avoid being passed. The ground conditions were likely to be in his favour, as the combination of Friday's sunshine and the blustery weather which had followed had ensured good going. Galloping into a headwind at the head of affairs would be required for a good part of the race, however, including the uphill finish. It would be a tough task for any horse carrying top weight, even a horse as strong and fit as Curlew Landings.

Jackie and Kye were assigned to accompany Curlew Landings in the lorry that day. Kye had been booked to ride once again for Welsh trainer Hafren Roberts in the first race, a Conditional Jockeys' Handicap Hurdle. The Dicks yard's aristocratic Fan Court was running in the second race, the same two mile Chase in which he had been so narrowly beaten last year. Travis would be travelling with Fan Court and would as a result be present for Curlew's attempt to win the Greatwood Hurdle, which followed immediately afterwards. Curlew Landings too had been beaten into second place last year and his connections were determined that that result should not be repeated.

The northbound carriageway of the M5 was quiet that morning, but the constant aggressive tugging of the wind gusts at the lorry meant that Jackie had to concentrate as she steered the horsebox along the inside lane. There was no other sound but the hum of the engine and the tinny tones of music playing from the elderly radio.

Kye's phone suddenly rang.

"Hello?" he said, pressing the key showing the symbol of an old fashioned green telephone receiver, "Gray? Yez don't say? That's great. I owe yez, Gray, mate. I'll be round this evening after we're back from Chelts."

"That was Gray Colvin," Kye said, unnecessarily, to Jackie, as he slid his phone back in his jacket pocket, "He's found me a car. I shan't need to be cadging lifts with people anymore."

"You sure you want to get involved with him again?" asked Jackie, doubtfully, "What if he tries to get you back into that drug dealing stuff?"

"Look, he's a mechanic, he runs a garage," Kye said, nettled by Jackie's objection, "I'm just getting a car off him, straight business deal, nothing dodgy. He knows I can't be his bagman now I'm a legit jockey."

"If you say so," replied Jackie, "Just watch out for him, that's all. I don't trust him."

Jackie would not have been happy to know that her poor opinion of Graham Colvin had been amply confirmed by a scene which had been played out in the Colvin family's comfortless flat half an hour earlier.

"What do you mean, you just found it?" Graham had been hissing angrily at his sister Tegan, preventing her from moving by gripping her arm below the elbow and simultaneously twisting it so that his hapless sister had been bent sideways in her effort to escape the pain, "It's been missing for months and now it suddenly turns up hanging in the hall. What have you been up to, Teegs, nicking my gear? Been selling it yourself, have you?"

"I've not sold nothing," Tegan had squealed, fearfully, "Your jacket's there, isn't it? I only had a lend of it to wear on a cold day. I left it at the pub and forgot to bring it home, that's all. You're hurting me, Gray. Stop it. I'll scream and Mum'll hear."

"Mum? She can't do nothing to help you," Graham had snapped, contemptuously, "So you've been doing a bit of business at the pub on your own account have you, girl?"

"I don't know what you mean," Tegan had gasped, in genuine puzzlement, still trying to extract her skinny arm from Graham's cruel grip, "The jacket's here. I put it back. I know it's a bit dirty but it's still here."

"I don't mean the fucking jacket," Graham's voice had begun to rise as he became angrier, "I mean the stuff what was in the pocket. You sell it, did you?"

Tegan had looked at him blankly, fear in her pale eyes.

"I've not sold nothing," she had repeated, wanly, "Please, Gray. Leave me be."

"Well, where is it then? The ket?" had persisted Gray, unmoved by her plea, "And don't say you used it yourself, because I won't believe you."

"I don't know nothing about your ket," Tegan had shouted suddenly into his face, losing her temper as the pain in her arm intensified, "I don't do filthy drugs like you!"

"You fucking sold it and you've hid the money," Gray had shouted back, shaking her in his fury, "I know where you keep your stuff, under that floorboard over there. You think I'm stupid?"

With that, he had twisted Tegan's arm behind her back and flung her face downwards onto the narrow bed, where she had remained, sobbing, as Gray had knelt on the floor and ripped back the carpet from the skirting board. Raising the loose flooring, he had begun rummaging angrily in the dark space beneath, the space Tegan had thought was secret.

"What the fuck is this?" he had snarled towards his tearful victim, as his hand had emerged from the cavity clutching the gold ingot on its chain, "Someone give you this for my ket, did they?"

"It's a gold ingot, you can have it," Tegan had stammered pathetically through streaming tears, "I found it in The Charlton Arms. A guest dropped it in his bedroom."

"A gold ingot!" had sneered Graham, nastily, "You really are a thick cow, Teegs. This is a flash drive. It's for a computer. Look, you dimbo."

So saying, Graham had tugged apart the two ends of the little cuboid object to reveal the rectangular metal shape of the business end of a USB stick.

"You plug this bit into the computer, thickshit," Graham had said, pointing at it.

Tegan had sat up and stared at him silently, snot running freely from her small nose.

"You've not heard the last of this, Teegs," Graham had gone on, in a menacing tone, "I'll find out who it is you sold the ket to, don't you worry, and they'll get what's coming to them. You too. Meantime, I'll keep this for myself. Might come in handy."

With that threat left hanging in the air, Graham had slammed out of the bedroom, Tegan looking hopelessly after him. Then she had put her head in her hands and wept. After a while, though, she had gulped down her misery and had started to think.

Jackie and Kye arrived at Cheltenham racecourse in good time for the race in which Kye would be riding. The Dicks horsebox bringing Fan Court and Travis was yet to arrive in the car park as Curlew Landings was installed in his temporary accommodation in the smart red brick racecourse stables as the wind continued to whip and eddy around the buildings.

"You go ahead, Kye," Jackie told her colleague, kissing his cheek, as they saw Hafren Roberts' head lad unloading the horse which Kye was booked to ride, "I can see to Curlew now, and Travis will be here soon, I'm sure. I'll be watching your race. Make sure you win, now."

Whilst Jackie was busy turning out Curlew Landings for his forthcoming race, Isabella Hall and Sadie Shinkins were sitting together in the Sampfield Grange yard office, looking at the screen of the new desktop computer.

Sadie had had a great deal to think about following the unexpected briefing that she and Merlin had received from Frank Stanley over a month ago. Sadie had already been aware that Isabella was still resident somewhere in the local district, because she had seen her former colleague spectating at a point to point meeting almost a year earlier. Lewis, too, had claimed to have seen Isabella, this time in the company of Frank Stanley. As a result, Lewis and Kelly remained convinced that Isabella's recent return to Sampfield Grange signalled a resumption of her clandestine affair with the man with whom she had apparently shared a room on more than one occasion at The Charlton Arms.

Having listened to Mr Stanley's words on that strange evening in Cardiff, Sadie had come to realise that there was certainly a connection between Mr Sampfield's old friend and this strange middle-aged woman whom they had all treated with such suspicion and hostility when she had previously lived and worked with them at Sampfield Grange. But this was not the connection of lovers. It was a work relationship. Isabella Hall, Sadie had since discovered, had a different partner, an older man who kept himself well outside the range of Lewis and Kelly's gossipy speculation. Sadie knew only that his name was George, as she had seen it on the unguarded screen of Isabella's mobile phone one day.

The journey home from Ireland to Cardiff had been challenging for Sadie. Her determination to remain on friendly but neutral terms with Merlin had proved far more difficult to manage than her previous strategy of ignoring him completely. Being obliged to interact with her former lover as if she were nothing more than a friend and colleague had served only to emphasise that both her physical desire and emotional need for Merlin were as overwhelming as ever. Although she no longer blindly idolised the self-confident Welsh jockey to the extent that she once had, Sadie still loved him unconditionally, and she knew that that would never change.

Sadie's resolve to remain in control of her feelings for Merlin had been put under tremendous strain. Refusing to travel on the same homebound flight as Merlin had been impossible without causing inconvenience to the kind Foley family, who had driven them both to the airport. Then the clerk at the check-in desk had allocated them seats alongside each other, assuming that they were a couple. Sadie had not felt able to object to this arrangement without creating embarrassment, and, in truth, had found the experience of sitting close to Merlin a tantalising reminder of their old intimacy. It had taken all her willpower not to turn to him and tell him she still loved him desperately and that she wanted nothing more than to have sex with him on the aircraft seats, even if it meant shocking everyone around them and probably getting arrested. Instead, she had talked incessantly to distract herself, whilst Merlin had sat mostly silently, holding a folded racing paper, which he clearly would have preferred to have been reading rather than being bored by her chatter.

Later, after they had concluded their odd meeting with Mr Stanley, Sadie had been determined to take herself away to her own room in the hotel before she could succumb to any temptation which might arise to join Merlin in his bed, especially when Merlin had ascertained that her relationship with Luke Cunningham was over. Then there had been the hotel breakfast and the car journey to Sampfield Grange to get through, which she had done very successfully, she thought, and she had used the time taking her bags up to the flat as a chance to draw a deep breath and regroup.

Once back into her usual work routine at Sampfield Grange, Sadie had been uncertain how to approach Isabella Hall. Lewis and Kelly had had few qualms about giving the other woman what they imagined was the cold shoulder, behaviour which was of limited effect now that Isabella no longer lived on the premises. Isabella herself remained apparently immune to their ill manners and got on with her work in the yard office as though she had not been absent for the previous eighteen months. Sadie's indecision about her own role in relation to her aloof and business-like colleague had been resolved by Isabella herself.

"I understand from Frank Stanley that he asked you to assist me, Sadie," Isabella had said to her one morning as Sadie had been efficiently brushing the stable dust from Tabikat's mahogany coat whilst the handsome horse had stood compliantly in the weak sunshine outside his stable.

"Yes," had replied Sadie, feeling uncomfortable, remembering her former unfriendly behaviour towards Isabella, and wondering if Isabella resented her for it, "But he didn't say what you wanted me to do."

Tabikat had turned his dark head towards Isabella and given a little breathy snort. Isabella had stroked the horse's soft nose and had said something to him in a whisper which Sadie could not make out.

"I need your help with the training tracker," Isabella had replied, "We have to keep up a record for each of the horses."

It was the computerised training monitoring and tracking system, a recent innovation at Sampfield Grange, which Sadie and Isabella were now looking at on the windy morning of the Greatwood Hurdle. Pressed persistently over the summer by Travis, with support from Jackie, Sam had eventually agreed to the purchase of a software product on which records of the horses' training, exercise and nutrition could be kept. Detailed information on heart rates, stride lengths, and speeds in various states of exercise and rest could be held and analysed, generating information which could be displayed in numerous graphs and charts. Other parameters such as weather and the type and state of the ground could be included to assist in the analysis whilst extensive records of the content and frequency of feeds, as well as veterinary notes and medical information, could be added to the basic data. The equipment associated with the system included a handheld tablet device which could be taken out onto the gallops, and two desktop computers, one located in the feed room and the other in the yard office. The system also offered scope to add real time exercise videos recorded by a drone, but, to Travis's disappointment, Mr Sampfield had drawn the line at that element of the technology, saying that he did not want the horses upset by the presence of potentially frightening aerial objects.

Sam, for his part, had been quite certain that none of the information which the system would generate would tell him anything more than his many years of experience, together with the training methods learned from generations of Sampfields, had already taught him. His ability to keep large amounts of complex information in his head was something of which his yard staff were very well aware, but, as the enthusiastic Travis had hopefully pointed out, the information might come in useful for the rest of the staff, whose memories and analytic abilities were less proficient.

Sadie had returned from Ireland to find the new system, which was the same as had been in regular use at the Dicks yard, already in place.

"I thought Travis and Jackie had done all the set up work before Travis left," Sadie told Isabella, "We just have to keep putting the information into it. Look, here are Tabsi's records, all his heartrate measurements, notes from the vet checks, his feed times and what we give him."

"There's no record for Katalyst, though," Isabella said quietly, "I've started to set that up but there's no data for him."

Sadie stared.

"That's because he isn't here," she said, carefully, wondering if Isabella was playing some kind of trick on her.

"I know," Isabella replied, "So we're going to have to make something up that looks realistic. I don't have the knowledge to do that. You do."

21

The Greatwood Hurdle was clearly not destined to be a lucky race for Curlew Landings.

The blustery afternoon had started well for the Sampfield Grange team. Kye's ride for trainer Hafren Roberts had proved to be the best of his short career when he had brought her bright young gelding home in first place in the two mile and five furlong race. The result, as published later, succinctly summarised their winning performance in the words *Kept wide, mid-division, headway from 7th, tracked leader between last 2, led turning in, stayed on to win.*

Travis had been in the sheltered pre-parade ring with a restless Fan Court when Kye's race took place and had been able only to send his former work colleague a quick text message which read **'bloody bonzer mate'**. Jackie too had watched the race on the course's big screens and had sent her own **'brill xx'** text to Kye before she had, with some difficulty, led an unco-operative Curlew Landings down the black rubber surfaced path whilst Fan Court's Chase event was in progress. Merlin had passed Kye in the weighing room after Kye had returned from picking up his share of the prize and had added his own congratulations to those of Hafren Roberts and her horse's highly pleased owners. Kye himself had been ecstatic at his success, particularly as it has been achieved at such a famous course.

"Maybe things are going my way at last," Kye thought, unable to stop smiling, as he ran across from the weighing room to the nearby pre-parade area in which an increasingly irritable Curlew Landings was being made ready for the Greatwood Hurdle. Mr Sampfield himself was working there with Jackie and said simply "Excellent ride, Kye" as Curlew shifted peevishly about in his temporary stall, objecting to his girth being tightened.

Curlew had quite clearly decided that he did not like the gusty wind blowing around the racecourse buildings, sending paper cups and mangled copies of the racing papers scurrying along the ground. He had tossed his head crossly and skittered around on the walkway all the way down from the racecourse stables at the top of the hill. Jackie's usually calming influence had had little effect on his mood and she had gratefully accepted Kye's offer to help lead the jittery horse into the parade ring. Travis, to whom Curlew was more accustomed as his usual handler on racedays, was still waiting by the horsewalk in front of the grandstand to receive Fan Court and Merlin when their race ended, so could not be asked to assist. Mr Sampfield walked into the parade ring alongside his two young staff in case his help with their upset charge should also be needed.

By the time Merlin was legged up onto Curlew's back, the horse had calmed down slightly. The discipline of walking in procession around the oval parade ring, which was more sheltered than the higher parts of the racecourse, seemed to have settled him. Merlin, for all his arrogance with people, was a sympathetic and well-balanced rider, whose considerable success with his mounts was to a large degree attributable to his instinctively good riding position and quiet physical empathy with the horse's natural movement. Had Merlin known it, his invaluable ability, honed by years of practice and experience, had also been at the root of Genie Foley's success as a jockey many years previously.

Merlin's skills ensured that Curlew arrived in a relatively calm mood at the race's starting point at the bottom of the sloping racecourse, but there was little which Merlin could do to influence the behaviour of the other runners. A number of Curlew Landings' usual foes were present in the group, but there were also a number of new names in the field. One of these, a big bay gelding, had planted himself behind the start line and it had required the assistance of the trainer to bring him forward towards the rest of the field, where the horse promptly reared violently and threw his unfortunate jockey to the ground. The gelding then took off like a rocket towards the centre of the course, and several minutes were wasted before the errant animal was cornered and caught alongside one of the bigger obstacles on the cross country course. The horse was soon withdrawn from the line up and the remaining members of the Greatwood Hurdle field were sent on their belated way by the patient starter.

If the starter had been patient, some of the horses had not. The delay and disruption, coupled with the gusting wind, had unsettled a number of the runners, and there was an awkward looking unseating of one of the jockeys at the first obstacle. The young man was flung sideways, almost going through the white plastic rails, whilst his mount, free of its unwanted burden, charged off with the rest of the runners towards the second hurdle, which it cleared with an extravagant and lopsided jump, reins flailing above its brown ears. The second hurdle was the last before the upward sloping bend to the left, and it appeared at first that the loose horse would continue to run forward towards the finish line, located straight ahead, where it could have been quickly caught.

The errant horse, though, had ideas of its own that day. The commentator continued to call the progress of the race, confirming to the spectators that Curlew Landings was leading the field down the back straight, with Southern Cross and Devil Waters tracking him about a length behind. Those of the Smart Girls and other followers of Stevie Stone's vlogs, who had heeded the earlier advice of Tabby Cat and Jayce as to Curlew Landings' excellent chances of winning the race were doubtless feeling happy with their selection. But the riderless horse was about to dash their hopes of an easy profit.

Rounding the turn at the bottom of the hill, Merlin and Curlew remained at the head of affairs, the commentator notifying the crowd that only two hurdles remained to be crossed before the final uphill run to the finish. Notwithstanding the desperate efforts of people on the course to catch it, the loose horse had whipped around and had cantered back down the hill towards the approaching field. Whether it intended to try to join in the race again, or was simply feeling lonely, only the horse itself would ever know, but the effect of its thought process was that it made a sudden dash to the right, immediately in front of the second last hurdle. Merlin and Curlew were unable to avoid the moving obstacle and collided at full tilt with the confused creature.

Both horses were knocked to the ground by the force of the collision. Merlin was catapulted through the air and landed several feet ahead of them. Both horses and the jockey lay still for what seemed like an eternity as the remaining runners thundered past.

Sadie's anguished scream in the kitchen of Sampfield Grange, where she was watching the afternoon's racing with Kelly and Lewis, was heard by Isabella from the yard office. Reluctant to leave the yard unattended but fearing that some awful accident had occurred in the house, Isabella ran to the boot room's heavy wooden door and shoved both it and then the kitchen door open.

"What's happened?" she asked, immediately realising that the three people in the kitchen were all still staring at the television screen and fortunately seemed not to be injured in any way.

"Curlew's been brought down!" gasped Sadie, "They're bringing out the screens for him. Oh no, no!"

The television coverage cruelly concentrated on the finishing stages of the race, which was eventually won by an unhindered Southern Cross for the second year running. But Curlew Landings' status as the reigning Champion Hurdle trophy holder, not to mention Merlin ap Rhys's as a Gold Cup winning jockey, meant that even the television commentators were concerned to keep viewers informed. Nevertheless, the interview with today's first placed rider needed to be conducted first.

Sadie grabbed her mobile phone and stabbed in the link to Jackie's number. When there was no response, she tried to reach Kye and then Travis. Travis answered at once, his shaking voice scarcely under control.

"Travis? Are the screens still round Curlew?" demanded Sadie, urgently, "What's happening? We can't see anything on TV."

"Curlew's just stood up and so has the other horse," Travis informed her, breathlessly, seeming to be running as he spoke, "But Merlin's still on the deck."

Turning back to the television screen, Sadie could see an ambulance parked near the remaining green screen, the paramedics clearly attending to a person on the ground behind it. The doctor's car was also stopped nearby. Sadie observed Jackie and Kye leading Curlew slowly up the hill towards the horsewalk, the horse walking evenly, with no obvious sign of injury. The runner which had caused the collision was standing quietly close to the spot where it had come down, held by a groom, being checked over by the racecourse vet.

"Merlin ap Rhys is still on the ground," the televised voice in the kitchen announced, the pictures on the screen showing the three suitably glum looking TV presenters clustered within their compact work area in the parade ring, "We'll bring you news of him as soon as we have it. Meanwhile, Southern Cross is returning behind us to rapturous applause from his large group of owners."

"I'm nearly down where Merlin is," Travis gasped, "I can see him now. They're folding up the screens. He's walking across to the ambo. Looks OK to me. Hope so."

Seeing that there was little she could do, Isabella returned to her desk in the yard office. Accidents on the course had always been the aspect of jump racing which bothered her, so she was grateful that neither of the horses nor the jockey appeared to have been seriously hurt. Isabella had little time for the self-centred Merlin, but she would not have wished him injured. She had hoped for an opportunity to go out on a cycle ride, in spite of the unpleasant wind, but the light was already beginning to fade and a quick journey home to the whitewashed cottage in Warnock was all that she now felt prepared to attempt.

The sun had dipped below the horizon when Isabella had eventually heard footsteps coming into the yard. Isabella saw Sadie walking hurriedly past the office door towards Tabikat's stable. Sadie was oblivious to the other woman's presence, as she entered the stable, putting her arms around the unprotesting horse's neck.

"Tabsi," Isabella heard Sadie say, as Tabikat shifted his feet in the straw bedding, "Merlin's come off Curlew at Cheltenham this afternoon. He went in an ambulance to the hospital. What if he can't ride you at Haydock Park on Saturday? There's no-one who rides you like Merlin does. We need him to be OK, Tabsi, don't we?"

The return of the Sampfield Grange party early in the dismal evening was a depressing affair. Jackie and Kye led Curlew Landings into his stable, a call having already been put out to Rachel Horwood, asking her to come into the yard the following morning. The racecourse vet had decided that Curlew, although probably battered and bruised, had only been winded, but there was no point in taking any chances with the horse's wellbeing. Mr Sampfield was clearly disappointed at what had happened, but this, Jackie told a goggle-eyed Lewis and Kelly, had been nothing to the anguish shown by Mr Halstock, who appeared to have bet a large amount of money on his former possession, and had practically collapsed when the incident had occurred.

"Mr Peveril and his wife had to take him off to the bar," Jackie said, "I thought he might need a doctor too, he was in such a state."

Later that evening, Kye was standing outside Graham Colvin's dingy motor workshop, his hand resting on the roof of the elderly black Fiat Punto which Graham had said he would be willing to sell to Kye for a few hundred pounds. The tired vehicle, in spite of the many miles it had travelled, appeared to be in roadworthy condition. Kye had spent fifteen minutes checking it over himself, making good use of his teenage training as a mechanic.

"I'll get the tax and insurance sorted out tomorrow," Kye told Gray, who had been standing in the workshop yard, watching him.

"You could have it for free," Gray offered, speaking quietly, "If you'd do some running for me. I'm branching out a bit. Got a new supplier."

"No way, Gray," Kye responded, hurriedly, "I can't risk it. I get checked up on all the time now I'm a jockey."

"Shame," replied Gray, "It's good stuff. Comes down from your way, up North. Regular shipments. I pick it up in the van at the service station on the M5. I'd shift a lot more if I had a team. There's be good money in it for you too."

Kye froze.

"My way? Yez mean Liverpool?" he asked, trying to keep the tremor out of his voice.

Gray shrugged and then laughed suddenly.

"You lot all sound the same to me," he said, "Liverpool, Manchester, wherever. It's a woman that organises it all. I can't hardly understand what she says sometimes."

"Does she come here to see you?" Kye asked in what he hoped was a normal sounding voice, an unwelcome image of the hard-faced Sheryl rearing up in his panicked imagination.

"Offering to translate, are you?" Gray sneered, "No, she came here once, months ago - to check out the territory, I guess - but it's all done by phone now."

"Well, like I say Gray, I can't help yez nowadays," Kye repeated, keen now to get as far away as possible from the Colvin garage, "I'd better be getting back. I'll bring the money for the car tomorrow. Cheers, Gray."

Gray watched thoughtfully as Kye disappeared into the dark lane beyond the old stone building which housed his car repair business and the flat above it. Kye had been a dead loss ever since he started riding horses in races for posh people and got himself that little bimbo of a girlfriend, Gray thought enviously. Things had been better when Kye was a just a stable skivvy and needed the money. He'd been a pretty good bagman in those days.

Sitting down in front of the workshop computer, Gray had been about to log into the DVLA site to register the sale of the Fiat Punto to Kye when the little gold flash drive that he had wrested from the wretched Tegan earlier in the day caught his eye. Tegan had gone off to work her weekend shift at The Charlton Arms at lunchtime, slipping past Gray on the stairs of the flat, a baleful look in her red rimmed eyes.

Gray picked up the data stick by its silver chain and looked at it carefully. No wonder the stupid Tegan had thought it was a gold ingot. It was nicely made and had characters engraved on the side, like hallmarks. But they were not hallmarks. They were some kind of foreign language, Gray thought, turning on a grubby desk lamp in order to squint at them. The letters read **призрак**.

"Let's see if there's anything on it," Gray said under his breath, plugging the USB stick into his computer, ignorantly oblivious to the risk of viruses or other online damage to his tatty office machine.

The flash drive appeared to contain only one file. Clicking on it, Gray was rewarded with a short piece of text on the grease smeared screen.

Keep
1355 - 280992
72 - 160885

Gray puzzled over the strange text for a while. It appeared to be the only data recorded on the snazzy flash drive. Eventually deciding that it was not worth his further attention, and that the pornography on the tablet computer in his bedroom would prove more rewarding, Gray turned off the light and locked up the garage premises for the night.

At the same time as Graham Colvin was turning the key in the lock, a denial of service cyber attack hit the IT systems of Ardua Industrie S.p.A in faraway Milan. Nearer to home, an encrypted message made its way via a circuitous and carefully guarded route to a fake staff account on a computer at a University in London where the person monitoring the account had long given up all expectation of ever receiving it.

22

Merlin had ridden at Haydock Park racecourse many times, but this was the first occasion on which he been riding the favourite to win the Lancashire Steeple Chase, nowadays more commonly known by the name of the bookmaker acting as sponsor. Today, Merlin faced the additional pressure of knowing that the prestigious race represented the first step towards the award of the jump racing Triple Crown. If Tabikat did not win this race, then winning the remaining two, whilst still a significant and lucrative achievement in its own right, would not bring the additional financial reward that Merlin now had in his sights. The wealthy Levy Brothers International and James Sampfield Peveril would doubtless scarcely notice their respective shares of the million pound prize, but the 10% which would go to the Sampfield Grange yard staff and the 10% for Merlin himself could potentially change their lives and careers. All three trophies were on display at the racecourse today, together with one additional tall, three-sided pyramidal trophy which would be awarded only in the event that any horse achieved this stupendous feat.

Merlin, as he walked the beautifully groomed Tabikat calmly around behind the rails near the extended three mile and one furlong start, was being eagerly watched by a large and excited crowd further ahead and to the right of the straight section of the elongated track. Haydock Park racecourse was an unusual shape, having two long sides, one with a kink in it, and hairpin turns at either end. It was also characterised by a lengthy run in to the finish after the final jump, a plain fence which was the first to be crossed after the start and the only one of the nineteen obstacles which made up the route which had to be jumped three times. The course was flat and required galloping and staying ability from competitors, particularly in the soft conditions prevailing today.

The sky above the parkland course was a dull and evenly distributed grey with no definition or contour to impart artistic interest to the solid cloud base. The air beneath the featureless clouds hung damp and cold, sitting heavily over the towering evergreen trees which bordered part of the not entirely straight back straight. Pounding rain and chaotic gales had favoured the North West of England earlier in the week, as a series of low pressure systems from the Atlantic Ocean had crossed the country. Areas of higher pressure had since intervened to push the unwelcome weather further to the North and had left behind the static and dank conditions which prevailed today, conditions which were ideal for Tabikat's first attempt to win the race.

Merlin could see the paddock area in the distance beyond the spectators massed against the rails and in the grandstands. In the tree studded parade ring he had left a tense Mr Sampfield, who had legged him up onto Tabikat's strong back. Merlin had successfully suppressed a grimace at the pressure on the damaged muscles in his leg and the jarringly painful protest made by his two cracked ribs. With Mr Sampfield had been a nervous Sadie, whose efforts to turn out Tabikat like the king he was for this important race had earned the horse many admiring glances from the warmly dressed racegoers crowded along the rails surrounding the parade ring. Brendan Meaghan and Niamh Foley, both wearing winter coats, had been standing alongside the Sampfield Grange team when Merlin had entered the already darkening arena alongside his fellow jockeys.

Although Sadie had informed Tabikat that Merlin had been taken to hospital six days ago by ambulance, this had not in fact been the case. Merlin had walked into the ambulance and had walked out again minutes later having convinced the racecourse doctor that the reason for his lack of movement on the ground after his fall had been only because he had been winded. The truth was that Merlin could not remember the ten seconds which had elapsed between his enforced flight over Curlew Landings' ears and the appearance of the paramedic running to his aid. Merlin was well practised at minimising injury to himself from a fall, but the unusual nature of this accident had caused him to hit the ground at an awkward angle and the side of his helmet, now replaced, had made heavy contact with the unyielding turf. Like a boxer caught unawares by a powerful left hook, Merlin had literally seen not just stars but jagged bursts of light and orange spots as he had fought to stay conscious. Any diagnosis by the racecourse doctor that Merlin had concussion would result in an automatic suspension from riding of at least six days on medical grounds. The sixth day was the day of the Lancashire Steeple Chase.

Merlin had employed theatrical distraction tactics as the young paramedic had come running towards him.

"Let me get my breath," he had gasped and wheezed, convincingly, he had hoped, thereby gaining a valuable additional few seconds to allow his vision to return to normal before anyone could examine him, "Then I'll get up." As the paramedic had stood ready to support him, he had declined her proffered arm and had walked steadily into the ambulance before the doctor could get near him on the ground.

The initial medical examination had taken place in the ambulance. The doctor had been insistent in his questioning as to whether Merlin had struck his head when he fell, but Merlin had been stout in his denials, and had answered all questions and satisfied the initial checks to the doctor's eventual satisfaction.

"I know you lot," had grumbled the white-haired medic, "Your bloody leg could be hanging off and you'd swear it was just a scratch."

"Well, my leg isn' 'angin' off," Merlin had said, crossly, "Though I think there'll be a load of bruises all over it soon. An' I think I might 'ave cracked a rib or two."

The reference to the possibility of cracked ribs diverted the doctor's attention towards that alternative focus, one on which both men were able to agree.

"Nothing to be done about that," the elderly doctor had grunted, "You know the drill - ice, painkillers and rest."

"I'm not booked to ride for a few days any'ow," Merlin had told him, "An' I've nothin' else this afternoon. So that's not a problem."

"I'm standing you down for the rest of the day," the doctor had said, firmly, "I don't want you hopping on any spare rides."

"OK," Merlin had agreed, not least because his head had been pounding and he was trying to suppress a feeling of nausea which was churning up his insides, "An' I'd like to walk back now, get some air and find out 'ow the 'orse is. I'll see you in the med room if you need me to sign anythin'."

Merlin had then left the doctor to his paperwork in the ambulance and had made his way up the side of the course, feeling like a drunk. He had had no intention whatever of staying off a horse during the week. He had been telling the truth when he had said that he was not race riding, but he had planned to be at Sampfield Grange on at least one day to work with Tabikat.

There were five highly experienced Grade 1 horses competing in the Lancashire Chase. All the other four were familiar opponents to Tabikat and any of them could at the present time be a contender for the Triple Crown. After today, though, only one would still be in the running for the trophy. The little company consisted of former Cheltenham Gold Cup winner Macalantern, Aintree Bowl Chase runner Inkspot, and old foes Less Than Ross and Stormlighter. The Page of Cups, which had run Tabikat so close in the Cheltenham Gold Cup, was, fortunately, not amongst the contenders.

Tabikat, fit and athletic thanks to the daily work put into him by Sadie, had performed well and enthusiastically when Merlin had visited Sampfield Grange on the previous Thursday. By that time, Merlin's feeling of nausea and lightheadedness had largely dissipated and his only remaining problems had been the throbbing pain in his ribs, two of which an X-ray had since confirmed were indeed cracked, and an array of black bruises and pulled muscles in various parts of his strong body. Questions from Sadie and Mr Sampfield as to his recovery had been met by Merlin with a dismissive "Still a bit stiff, but I'm fine" from the jockey.

Sadie had nevertheless caught Merlin by the arm as he was leaving the yard, after Merlin had been checking with Kye on the wellbeing

216

of an also rather stiff Curlew Landings. Sadie had asked, "You're fit to ride, aren't you, Merlin? I know you're in pain, so don't try to hide it. It's nothing serious, is it? You didn't hit your head or anything? Or break any bones?"

"Look, *cariad*, I'm fine, like I said," Merlin had insisted, "I wouldn' miss this race for the world."

"That's what I'm worried about," Sadie had replied.

Merlin brought Tabikat onto the course in the middle of the little group of classy horses as the starter climbed her flight of mobile steps. Tabikat's dark ears were upright in front of Merlin, and the horse seemed, as usual, calm but alert as they faced the yellow flag held by the woman who would send the field on its way. The first fence was directly ahead of them all, the white coated flagman holding his own yellow flag high above his head. Then the starter's flag dropped, the starting tape was released with a quick squeeze of the lever, and the five horses set off on their journey over the nineteen fences.

"And they're off!" cried the racecourse commentator, as a ragged cheer arose from the eager spectators, "It's a steady pace, and they all clear the first. Macalantern is leading the field as they make the long run to the second fence. Tabikat and Inkspot are tracking him, with Less Than Ross and Stormlighter tucked in behind."

The small field swept grandly past the paddock area where Tabikat's connections were standing, their attention focused on the big viewing screen. Sam raised his field glasses to see that Merlin and Tabikat looked relaxed and focused as they lobbed along behind the leader. Sadie was standing down by the paddock corner of the famous track, repeating Tabikat's and Merlin's names over and over under her breath. Brendan Meaghan and Niamh Foley were silent by Sam's side. Stevie Stone stood by the parade ring rails, iPad in hand, ready to prepare her post-race vlog for the Smart Girls, hoping desperately that Jayce's and Tabby Cat's advice to put a forecast on Tabikat to beat Inkspot into second place would prove correct. Back in Somerset, the Sampfield Grange staff were staring at the television screen in the kitchen, fists clenched in nervous anticipation. Isabella Hall and TK Stonehouse occupied two armchairs in front of another TV set in the living room of the little cottage in the nearby village of Warnock.

Rounding the hairpin bend at the wider western end of the course, the runners eventually reached the second fence, all clearing it safely, and continued to run along against the attractive background of a small wood of bare-branched tall trees. The course sloped slightly downhill.

There was little for the commentator to say at this stage of the race, although he kept up his customary stream of words as the horses progressed, reminding the watchers of the colours worn by the jockeys and some of the previous successful performances of the top quality runners. There were five fences in the back straight, the last of which was an open ditch.

"There's been no change in the order," announced the commentator, "Less Than Ross put himself right at the ditch. The entire field is going well as they round the bend back into the home straight, where four fences await them."

Merlin needed no reminder of why he enjoyed riding Tabikat so much. The horse had taken all the jumps cleanly and without effort. The adrenalin created by the occasion had made him forget his throbbing ribcage and his whole world had now become focused on himself and the magnificent chaser and their route to victory. None of the other jockeys had much to say when the field turned into the home straight, but, then, the race had yet to develop. The first circuit had seemed to Merlin like a practice run.

Merlin could hear the anticipatory buzz of the crowd as the horses approached the open ditch, which was the eighth obstacle.

"Macalantern still has a two length advantage," said the commentator, calmly, "But the field is in touch. Merlin ap Rhys has brought Tabikat up behind the leader as they clear the ditch and continue along the straight."

Merlin was indeed keeping a close watch on Macalantern. Aidan Scanlon, the jockey, seemed relaxed, letting his mount jump around the course in its naturally quiet and economical style, but Merlin and Tabikat needed to be ready to respond to any injection of pace by their tricky rival. Inkspot continued to sit just behind Tabikat's quarters with the other two runners still close behind.

Reaching the paddock turn once again, the field had strung itself out a little more, the horses now one behind the other, Macalantern retaining the lead. Aidan Scanlon had not moved. The roar of the crowd was loud in Merlin's ears as the horses completed the left turn. Merlin fancied he could hear Sadie's voice shouting Tabikat's name.

Entering the dog leg of the back straight once again, Merlin began to see his chance. The light was fading fast as the sun dropped towards the horizon on his right, painting the dull clouds a shade of pale coral behind the line of tall trees. Macalantern's jockey had shifted his weight slightly, quietly urging his mount to pick up its efforts. Macalantern responded, and Merlin reacted. As the field reached the final jump in the back straight, Merlin brought Tabikat up alongside the leader. The pace had lifted and the back two runners had dropped further behind. A new urgency had entered the race.

Landing after the ditch, Merlin shouted, "Gotcha, Aidan!"

"Not a feckin' chance," yelled the Irish jockey back at him, as the two horses rounded the bend which led into the final straight.

"Tabikat's come up to challenge the leader," announced the commentator, sounding more animated, "They take the fourth last together. Inkspot's not far behind. Less Than Ross and Stormlighter haven't been shaken off yet."

Merlin could see that Macalantern, notwithstanding Aidan Scanlon's confident riposte, was beginning to tire. Tabikat was still taking the fences fluently, but Inkspot was close on their heels and did not seem likely to give up. He could hear Inkspot's jockey, Jenna Roberts, encouraging her horse in a determined voice.

"Come on Inky, keep going, good lad, we're onto them," Jenna shouted. Her voice sounded a bit like Sadie's, thought Merlin, irrelevantly.

Clearing the second last, Tabikat drew ahead. Macalantern had taken the jump laboriously and Merlin could sense that his rival was dropping back, in spite of Aidan Scanlon's best efforts to rouse him. Inkspot's jockey was still calling out encouragement to her horse and very clearly had Tabikat and Merlin in her sights.

Tabikat's ears were pricked as they cleared the last. The swelling noise of the spectators boomed across the course as they started the long run into the finishing post.

"Tabikat's going for the line, but Inkspot's not going down without a fight," shouted the commentator, "Inkspot's being driven out to the finish and he's making ground on Tabikat. Macalantern is leaden-legged in third and may even be passed by one of the others. Merlin ap Rhys is asking Tabikat for more effort. The horse is responding....... And Tabikat wins!"

As Tabikat passed the finishing post in first place, Merlin felt as if Inkspot's jockey had been screaming into his own ears rather than those of her horse. Tabikat had won, but by only half a length. As Merlin sat gratefully back in the saddle, bringing Tabikat quickly to a walk, the young woman manoeuvred the defeated and steaming Inkspot alongside him.

"Nearly had you there, Merlin," she said, with a grin, "Well done."

"Thanks, Jen," replied Merlin, slightly breathlessly, as the pain in his ribs made itself felt again, "See you at the King George next, will I?"

"You can see me before that, if you want," the other jockey replied, laughing, "Call in when you're passing".

Giving Merlin no time to answer, Jenna Roberts quickly turned Inkspot away to allow an ecstatic Sadie to grab Tabikat's bridle whilst the warmly-dressed TV interviewer walked towards them holding her microphone.

Merlin wondered if Sadie had heard what Jenna Roberts had had to say to him, but Sadie seemed completely preoccupied with making a fuss of Tabikat whilst the horse gradually resumed his customary air of regal self-possession. Sadie's only words to Merlin were an excited "Great ride, Merlin! Tabikat's on his way!"

Perhaps I need to move on from trying to get back with Sadie, Merlin suddenly thought. Maybe her only interest in me now is because I'm Tabikat's jockey. Admitting defeat was not in Merlin's nature, but neither was flogging a dead horse, however much he might want to revive it.

23

"That was exciting," said TK Stonehouse, as she got up from the deep cushion of the armchair from which she had been watching Tabikat win the Lancashire Chase, "Even if the sight of Merlin ap Rhys was spoiling Isabella's view."

George Harvey and Frank Stanley, who had previously been sitting in the little dining room across the narrow hall, had come in to watch the race through the open doorway.

Isabella was listening to the post-race interviews.

"Niamh Foley's telling them about Katalyst again," she said, drawing the attention of the others back to the television coverage still showing on the living room screen, "Including that he now belongs to Mr Sampfield."

"Do you really think this is going to work?" TK asked her, "It seems a bit of a hopeless task to me, trying to smoke out people who traded a horse illegally over fifteen years ago."

"Young Katalyst is potentially very valuable," Isabella said, "Any foals he sires in the future could make someone lots of money if they were to turn out like Tabikat and Katseye, not to mention the stud fees which could be charged. There's every reason for these people to want to try to get their hands on him. Their twisted logic will say that the colt effectively is their property and that neither Eoghan Foley nor James Sampfield Peveril have any right to him."

TK shrugged and reached for the charcoal grey leather jacket which lay over the back of the armchair she had occupied.

"Well, I'll be leaving," she told them all, "We have another test run on the rotary wing this evening. Astrak's Mark 3 version of the Artificial Intelligence fly by wire software still has some issues to iron out, so we've been putting a human pilot in the cockpit so far, for safety. If this one makes it to Glos and then to Chelts Heliport without intervention, we'll try a pilotless run next week. Fancy a free flight to the racecourse, any of you?"

"That Air Ambulance liveried helicopter has become quite a feature round here," Isabella commented, ignoring the flippant suggestion, "Not sure you could get many patients in an Ardocopter A Series but I suppose that isn't the point."

"Actually, the absence of personnel has been a bit of a problem for us," TK admitted, "When we've been working on the low level manoeuvres over the airfield, we've had to put a pilot in there just to maintain the illusion that we're training pilots rather than testing software."

As the throaty sound of the TK's Land Rover Defender's engine made itself heard, George turned to Frank Stanley.

"Come into the living room, Frank," he said, "Maybe we can get Isabella's thoughts on this, too."

"Is this a whisky job?" asked Isabella, not entirely seriously, "I'll get it anyway."

As the three of them sat in the little lamplit room around the circular wooden coffee table, whisky and glasses on a tray before them, the television switched off, blinds closed against the encroaching darkness, Frank began the discussion.

"Dominik Katz has become active again," he said.

"Dominik Katz?" repeated Isabella, "I thought you told us he was dead?"

"He is," Frank confirmed, "But his works continue."

"What sort of works?" asked Isabella, mystified.

"The first is a denial of service attack on Ardua Industrie S.p.A," began Frank, "It happened six days ago."

"But another cyber attacker could have done that," Isabella objected, "Why do you think it is anything to do with Dominik Katz?"

"The nature and style of the attack," Frank said, "There was no request for a ransom, and the attack didn't cause any real damage to the Ardua systems. It seemed designed solely to let Ardua know that Dominik still had them in his sights and was a continuing threat to them. But, the interesting thing was that the message which came up on all the office screens referred to the fact that Arturo Ardizzone was dead. It said I KILLED YOUR BOSS AND NOW IT'S THE REST OF YOU."

"Well, if Dominik Katz himself is dead, he can't have sent the message," Isabella said, reasonably, "It must have been someone else. Someone who knew he wanted Arturo dead."

"It would have to be someone who thought Arturo was actually dead," George put in, "And Arturo isn't."

"The obvious explanation is that the message had been set up to be sent automatically once Dominik's plan to kill Arturo at Cheltenham in March had been carried out," Frank put in, evidently becoming impatient to move the conversation forward, "The fact that Dominik himself is no longer around is not something which even Dominik had factored into his planning. He didn't expect to be dead himself."

"All right," said George, "Two questions for you, then, Frank. One, what would Dominik have been doing if he had still been alive? Two, why did it take so long for the message to be sent?"

"And three," added Isabella, "You mentioned works in the plural. What else has happened?"

"Our assumption, as I told you in Madeira," Frank said, "Is that Dominik would have tried to negotiate with us and perhaps with others. In the previous denial of service attack, he demanded to meet Arturo in London on the day after the Cheltenham Festival ended. Dominik's body was found at the bottom of Cleeve Cloud, after he had failed to carry out his plan to kill Arturo. The circumstances of his death are unclear, but we are still assuming that someone murdered him. As I told you, he had been hit over the head with a heavy object and pushed over the edge of the rock face.

"We know that Dominik was a devious and clever opponent. What if he had no real intention of negotiating with us? What if the message he sent before Katseye's race at the Festival in March about a meeting in London was a distraction? After all, he would not have expected Arturo himself to be there because Arturo should have been dead. We assumed at the time that the message was solely to make us believe that we were wrong about the attempt Dominik intended to make on Arturo's life. What then was the original purpose of this recent message other than to crow about his achievement in killing Arturo? It doesn't ask to negotiate with anyone else from our side. It just makes a threat to destroy Arturo's company. This suggests that Dominik had a different plan in mind than the one we originally supposed. It suggests that that didn't want the protection of the British Government at all. And why would that be?"

"Because he had already secured the protection of someone else," George and Isabella almost chorused.

"Quite," Frank Stanley replied, approvingly, "Dominik would always leave himself a back door, or perhaps an alternative door. Perhaps he intended to play us off against this other party, offering us information about them in return for more concessions, or, more likely, he intended to offer them his professional services as a cybermaster.

"You asked, Isabella, what other activities had been detected. The answer also responds to George's second question about the delay in sending the message. The people who would be keen to use the services of an international criminal like Dominik would be another powerful organised crime outfit like the one the Palokas used to control. Dominik could not be employed in a legitimate business without the sort of protection that only a Government could give him. Given that Dominik would have murdered not only

225

Arturo Ardizzone but everyone else in the Cheltenham parade ring that day, not to mention the collateral damage in terms of the deaths and injuries to bystanders plus the destruction of horses, damage to the racecourse buildings, and so on, it is most unlikely that anyone, including us, would have been willing to do that for him without some really serious incentive in the form of, say, a significant higher political or humanitarian end. Preventing mass murder, that kind of thing. Therefore, his only realistic choice, if he wanted protection, would have been to re-enter the criminal world, working for someone to whom the sort of carnage he had wreaked at Cheltenham racecourse was not a concern.

"We have already sought for any vestige of a trail that Dominik Katz might have left behind him. Naturally, he has covered his tracks expertly as far as his online presence is concerned. Until a few days ago, the only thing we had discovered was the file in the computer in Frossiac."

"Which was a dead end," George put in, "Put there to waste our time."

"Indeed," said Frank, "But the second thing, which happened six days ago, was that a message was generated which went to an IT user account at a University in London and then on to another computer facility in Liverpool."

"What was the origin of the message?" asked George, sitting up suddenly.

"We don't know yet," Frank told him, "The source in London was a fake staff IT account at a University. Needless to say, the person whose name was on the account is not an employee at that institution. It was set up in February in the name of Merlin ap Rhys, a man whom Dominik had in his sights at that time because he thought Merlin had been involved in killing his sister. The dummy account was set up when Dominik Katz was in London, using, as we have now discovered, a forged British passport in the name of Dominic Kitson. He stayed at a budget hotel in Kensington. They had a photocopy of the passport still there."

"If you don't know where the message came from," Isabella said, "You do seem to know where it was sent."

"It went," Frank told her, "To a data storage facility which had been rented in one of the names which we believe to belong to a criminal operation in Liverpool. This operation isn't - yet - the size of that which was once operated by the Palokas. It is a former IRA-founded drugs and arms smuggling operation which has now grown into something much larger and just as nasty. It is the same organisation in which Kye McMahon recently played a small part. It also is the same organisation in which Kye's brothers and their associate, Sheryl Mavers, continue to play a slightly larger part. And it is the same organisation which Eoghan Foley may well soon find is wanting to acquire the horse he has just sold to James Sampfield."

"For God's sake, Frank!" Isabella exclaimed, "You said Liverpool. Was it those people who had Luke Cunningham beaten up at Aintree? Because they were looking for the horse and Luke was in their way?"

"I think that is more than likely," Frank replied, "Mr Cunningham was just in the wrong place at the wrong time. I imagine the people we are dealing with would have had no difficulty obtaining entry into the Aintree racecourse horsebox area. Locations in Ireland and Sampfield Grange would, I expect, present only slightly more difficulties."

"Well, that begs a lot of questions," Isabella began, "Such as how much danger we are all now in at Sampfield Grange, for a start."

"I'll come back to that," replied Frank, irritatingly, "But first let me finish telling you about the message."

"All right," said George, though privately sharing Isabella's concern, "We're listening."

"We believe that the reason for the long delay in sending the message was because Dominik Katz was dead," Frank went on, "The message, which I will describe in a moment, was clearly an element in his negotiation with his prospective new protectors. In the circumstances, it should never have been sent at all, so our assumption is that it has been sent unintentionally. Someone, somewhere has unintentionally triggered it, probably by ..."

"Plugging a flash drive into a PC," finished George, "A flash drive which has been lying around unused since March. So, Dominik's message has effectively lain dormant for all these months. Now someone's found the device and decided to plug it into their computer. That's what will have triggered the recent DoS attack on Ardua too."

"So where is this flash drive? Do we know?" asked Isabella.

"The police are working on that," Frank told her, "It wasn't amongst the things found in the car hired by the man calling himself Damon Casey, so the next steps are to go back to all the places he stayed – the hotels in Carcassonne and Kensington, and The Charlton Arms. But that has a pretty low percentage chance of success, especially after all this time. The thing could have been dropped or hidden anywhere. Our best hope is tracing back the route the message took to reach the fake staff IT account at the University in London."

"What did the message say?" asked George, "This one clearly wasn't a cyberattack if it was part of a negotiation."

"You are correct, George," Frank replied, "We think it was intended as a signal of Dominik's good faith in the negotiations. The communication was encrypted for security during its transmission, twice in fact. The message was picked up in our routine monitoring of this criminal organisation. It's by no means as well protected as the Paloka systems were, which is why they needed someone like Dominik Katz. They're about to expand their operations, we believe, and they can't afford their systems to be hackable."

"Do you think they know Dominik is dead?" asked Isabella, "After all, they could have been the people who killed him."

"It's possible, but it seems unlikely," Frank replied, "It is hard to imagine why they would kill someone who was about to be useful to them. And it would not have been in Dominik Katz's interests to get on the wrong side of them. Not just then, anyway."

"What was his gesture of good faith, I wonder?" George seemed to be thinking aloud, "Could it be something to do with the information he got from his APT operation, perhaps? You said it was a nerve agent he was targeting, *prizrak*, is that right? That would be a serious weapon for a criminal gang to get their hands on."

"And what about Katalyst and Sampfield Grange?" Isabella wanted to know, "I realise the horse isn't actually there, but we have set things up now to make everyone think he's in training at the Sampfield yard. Anyone hacking the system, which wouldn't exactly be difficult for a professional, will find a training record for him, as you know."

"We've got that covered," Frank said, "If anyone does hack into the system at Sampfield Grange, George will know about it. If there's a physical threat, then Jackie has instructions to call for armed back up."

The reassurances being given in the little house in Warnock would have been justified, but for one unexpected event - the interference of Graham Colvin.

24

In the weeks leading up to Christmas, The Charlton Arms was busy. People who had worked in barely concealed disharmony throughout the year suddenly felt the need to mark their successful tolerance of each other by eating a roast turkey dinner and drinking too much festive wine together in a quaint village pub. Garish crackers containing cheap plastic toys and tatty paper crowns added to the manufactured jollity of the atmosphere as the revellers ritually groaned and complained at the familiar bad jokes printed on small slips of paper which quickly fell to the floor and were trodden underfoot.

The weather outside the dining room's leaded windows had been unremittingly miserable throughout the last month. Heavy vertical rain had dropped from the skies as if squirted from clustered pipes. During the brief periods when the tap appeared to have been turned off, leaden clouds had darkened the skies, resting their fat bellies on the sodden hills around the villages of Charlton and Warnock. The defeated sun had spent the few daily hours when it had been above the horizon smothered behind the turgid mass of bloated air, sending local citizens scurrying for their homes or propping up the bars in both The Charlton Arms and The Sly Fox.

Tegan Colvin had benefited from the miserable early winter weather. Extra shifts had been available at The Charlton Arms and even Barnaby Vowles at the Fox called on her assistance during periods when he would normally have managed the premises alone. The only problem Tegan had had was in keeping her meagre wages out of the reach of her brother, who still seemed determined to extract payment for the loss of the ketamine which had apparently been in the pocket of the jacket she had loaned to the Australian boy. Not that Gray had any idea that the Australian boy – Travis, a cool name, Tegan thought – had kept the drug for himself, because Tegan had been determined that Gray should not find out.

One dismal December evening, whilst working her shift in The Sly Fox, Tegan at last saw her idol again in the flesh. He came crashing in through the door with his two usual friends, the Northerner and the slimy one who had commented on Tegan's breasts. The three men were laughing together as they pushed the battered red door open and walked across the stone-flagged floor with its patchy cover of disreputable looking patterned rugs.

Tegan hung back. She was waiting to see which of the three customers came to the bar to order the drinks. To her horror, it was the creepy Lewis, the man who had returned Gray's jacket without the ket stash in its pocket, who detached himself from the group and approached the bar counter.

"Good evening, young lady. Three pints of Tabikat Gold," Lewis said with a wink at Tegan, "I'm watching you."

"That's fine, Tegan, you go out now and collect up some glasses," intervened landlord Barnaby Vowles, who seemed, notwithstanding his bulk, to have appeared from nowhere, "I'll get the gentleman's order."

Tegan scuttled away, relieved to have escaped the horrible Lewis. She could see that Travis and the other young man had sat down at a table by the window, on which a number of dead glasses had been left. She might as well start there, she thought.

"Hello," she said shyly, as she gathered the glassware together in the green plastic carrier, "Are you celebrating something?"

"We both had wins at Taunton today," Kye exclaimed, unable to refrain from telling anyone and everyone of the two young jockeys' respective achievements that afternoon, "Yerz Gray's sister, aren't yez?"

"Yes," Tegan admitted, not wanting to talk about her brother.

"And it was you that loaned me the jacket," the gorgeous Travis added, evidently in a talkative mood, "Did Lewis bring it back?"

"Yes, he did," Tegan told him, realising for the first time that it might have been Lewis rather than Travis who had taken the drugs from the jacket pocket, and that this might an opportunity to get her revenge, "Just as well, because the owner came back for it after all. He said there was something missing out of the pocket, but that was his own fault, I told him."

Seeing the aforementioned Lewis returning to the table with the drinks, Tegan quickly tried to move away, but Travis stopped her.

"Something missing?" he asked, "Did he say what?"

"No, I think he was just trying it on," Tegan replied, fearfully, realising she had just dug a big hole for herself, "Trying to blame us for losing something, so he could get free drinks out of Mr Vowles. Sorry, I'm busy. I need to get on clearing tables."

Ever since the experience of being set up at Mooney Park racecourse with a drink spiked with an illegal drug, Travis had been extremely careful to check anything which might be in his possession when he attended a racecourse or, indeed, any other public place. The fact that he had lived in at Sampfield Grange for so long had made him feel safer, but the thought that something might have been planted in the borrowed jacket in an attempt to incriminate him now loomed threateningly in his mind. He looked at the retreating back of the skinny barmaid as she gathered empty glasses from the neighbouring tables. Could she have been asked to set him up, he wondered. Did Jack Tytherleigh's influence stretch to a village pub in rural England?

"You said you knew that girl, Kye," Travis said, suddenly.

"Yeah, she's called Tegan," Kye told him, carelessly, "She's Gray Colvin's sister, yez know, at the garage."

Travis's mind was continuing to work overtime.

"Is there drug dealing in this pub?" he asked suddenly, nearly causing Kye to spill the drink which Lewis had placed on the table in front of him.

"Not that I know of," Kye said, cautiously.

"I doubt it," butted in Lewis, "That landlord's an ex-copper. He wouldn't have anything like that going on in here."

"That's good," Travis replied, "I just get paranoid after that business at Mooney Valley."

The three of them soon returned to the discussion of Travis's and Kye's winning rides at Taunton races, until Travis eventually got to his feet.

"Just going to splash me boots," he told the others, who had now moved onto the topic, introduced by Lewis, of the stuck-up Isabella Hall who seemed to be all pally with Sadie these days. Travis cared little about Isabella Hall and judged it a good time to absent himself.

Travis's real purpose in leaving the table was to speak to Tegan, who was now wiping up spilt beer from the unoccupied end of the bar nearest to the toilets.

"That jacket," Travis said to her without preamble, making Tegan jump and give him a frightened look, "Did you know the bloke who came back for it?"

"No, never seen him before," Tegan lied, her heart pounding beneath the breasts which had attracted Lewis's unwanted attention. "He wasn't from round here."

"If you see him again, let me know," Travis instructed her, "I'd like to speak to him, say cheers for the lend of the jacket. I'm not with Mr Sampfield anymore, Tegan. I work for Mr Dicks now, further away from here. I'll give you my number."

Tegan was completely overwhelmed. The lovely Australian boy knew her name. Now she had been given his mobile phone number and she hadn't even asked for it.

"Yes, 'course," she stuttered, carefully writing down the number on a conveniently located cardboard beer mat behind the bar. She had no intention of telling Travis the truth about the ownership of the jacket. Her idol must have used the ket himself, she thought, and maybe now he wanted to get more. Tegan knew just where she could get it for him.

Had she known what Travis was really thinking, Tegan would have not been nearly so keen to write down his contact number. Travis's persistent fears about drugs being planted on him again had coincidentally led him to the correct conclusion about what had been left in the jacket pocket. In the fortunately deserted men's toilets, Travis slumped against the wall, sweat running down his face and trickling down his back between his shoulder blades. The item which the jacket owner had lost was a stash of ketamine, he realised, and Curlew Landings had eaten it. Either it had fallen out of the jacket pocket into the horse's feed, or, perhaps more likely, his equine charge had snaffled it from the jacket pocket when the garment was hanging outside the stable, with Curlew tied up nearby whilst Travis mucked out.

Had someone set this up, or was it pure chance, Travis wondered, as he tried to calm himself down. Tegan could have been telling the truth, that the jacket had simply been left behind by someone who had been annoyed subsequently to discover that his illicit drugs had gone missing. The other option was that someone had deliberately put the stuff into the jacket pocket and then paid the mousy barmaid to lend Travis the jacket.

Either way, no-one must ever know what had happened. The incident was many months in the past and Curlew Landings, still nursing bruised ribs from his unlucky collision at Cheltenham, had come to no harm in the end. Meanwhile, Travis had to return to the others and behave normally. Maybe Tegan would call his phone, he thought, and the matter would be resolved one way or the other. In the meantime, he needed to be nice to the girl, if he were to see her again, to keep her onside. If it was Jack Tytherleigh, or someone working for him, Travis would be ready for him this time.

Whilst Travis was trying to pull himself back together in The Sly Fox, Graham Colvin was sitting in his grimy car workshop, two gift-wrapped bottles of duty free spirits standing on his dirty wooden desk behind the computer screen. They would make good Christmas presents for someone, Graham thought. He disliked whisky himself, having had it breathed over him on many an unpleasant occasion as a child by his long-departed father, but the vodka looked good.

The consignment of illegal drugs which Gray had picked up a week ago from the local M5 service station was still secreted in a metal container welded into a recess in the side of the inspection pit behind him. That afternoon's delivery arrangements had been straightforward, as usual. Graham, driving his white van bearing the words **Colvin's Garage, Motor Repairs MOTs and Servicing** had gone out to an Irish registered lorry which apparently required mechanical attention in the service station HGV park. The exchange of the shipment of drugs would have appeared to any onlooker to be part of the work involved in the services rendered to repair the vehicle. Gray had even produced a credit card payment machine for the benefit of watching CCTV. The CCTV coverage in the lorry park had been well researched some time ago and the apparently defective lorry had been stopped in the area which had the least comprehensive coverage. The bogus work on the lorry had taken place in full view of the nearest camera, whilst the delivery of the shipment and Gray's payment had been made whilst the Northern Irish driver and Gray were on the less well scrutinised side of the large vehicle.

Driving out of the service station in the crepuscular light of the miserable early December afternoon, Graham's attention had been suddenly attracted to a large warehouse to the left of the exit road. The ugly building had been a storage facility of the sort used by householders who had run out of room at home to store items not in everyday use, or by small businesses to hold and distribute stock for which they had no warehousing of their own.

Gray had not been interested in renting a storage unit for his own use. What had stopped him in his tracks that afternoon had been the large sign emblazoned across the fascia of the two-storey blue-painted premises. It had shown an outline of a battlemented castle, labelled with large black letters, which read **THE KEEP**. Beneath, in smaller letters, the sign had said 'Secure Storage at Low Prices'.

Acting on an impulse, which he would later come to regret, Gray had stopped his van on the slip road by the warehouse car park and had switched off the engine. Fumbling in the pocket of his messy overalls, Gray had found the piece of folded paper onto which he had previously copied the mysterious message from the file on the stolen flash drive. Gray had been intending to show the piece of paper to a fellow drone flyer whom he knew to enjoy solving puzzles and participating in quizzes, to find out what he might make of the strange conundrum. It was the word **KEEP** on the warehouse sign which Gray had noticed. That had been the first and only word in the message.

Gray had been well aware that storage hire facilities kept their prices low by employing as few staff as possible. Instead, all access was controlled by numbered codes, selected by the person renting the facilities. It was worth a try, he had thought, getting out of his van and locking it up, with its valuable illegal cargo, very carefully. The slip road on which he had left the vehicle had no CCTV cameras that Gray could see, although helpful notices announced that the car park itself was under constant video surveillance.

A number pad with a small screen above it had been attached to the wall alongside the blue door of the building. **Enter your PIN** read the words showing on the grubby display. Turning up the collar of his jacket and keeping his back to the security camera, which was trained on the door itself rather than the number pad, Gray carefully pressed **1355** into the keypad. No-one else was to be seen anywhere nearby. A second message appeared on the screen. **PIN accepted. Enter your personal code.** Gray had dutifully typed in **280992**. The door had slid silently open.

Gray had felt excited. His suspicions had been confirmed. The flash drive lost by the guest at The Charlton Arms had contained clues for a real-life treasure hunt, the sort which imitated the missions played out in online video games. The premises selected to hold the treasure had even had a suitably medieval sounding name. In opening the door, he had completed Level 1 of the game and had successfully broken through to Level 2 of his mission. The prize must be hidden somewhere inside the building.

Gray had soon worked out exactly where to look next. The following number in the message was **72**. Direction signs within ground floor of the building had pointed to **Units 1-50**. A second sign with an upward pointing arrow had indicated **Units 51-100**. Turning his back towards the camera fixed in one of the upper corners of the large lift, Gray had ascended instead by the stairs to the first floor. He had soon located Unit 72, one of the smaller cabinets, no larger than a domestic freezer, in the third row. Soft music had played continuously and soothingly in the unpleasantly cold building, adding to the surreal atmosphere.

Gray had spotted two people at the further end of the facility, loading camping equipment from a trolley into one of the larger units. Harmless bystanders, not a threat, he had thought, his mind now firmly in video game mode. He had contemplated the innocuous Unit 72, which had been secured by a padlock with six number reels. It had taken only seconds for Gray to twist the reels so that they read **160885**. The padlock had clicked open.

Gray had slowly opened the door of the metal storage cabinet, holding his breath. Almost at once, he had let it out again. There was no Holy Grail or Tiger Eye diamond which it would require further skills on his part to release safely. Instead, Gray had been confronted with two bottles of booze in presentation boxes. They had stood on top of a brown folder. The folder had a mysterious looking Chinese pictogram 鬼 printed on the cover.

Deflated, Gray had taken out the bottles and put them down on the concrete floor by the open door of the cabinet. He had flicked open the folder in the hope that mysterious symbol on the front had been intended to indicate that it contained more codes and challenges to be overcome. Disappointingly, he had been able to make no sense of the pages contained inside, as they had been written in an unrecognisable, at least to Gray, foreign language. The pages had included numerous diagrams, tables and lists of numbers interspersed between the text. Whatever it was, it was of no use to him, Gray had decided, shoving it back onto the shelf. Maybe the prize for cracking this level of the game was the expensive looking alcohol, he had decided, and the clues to the rest of the game lay elsewhere.

Gray had picked up the bottles from the floor and shoved them into the deep pockets of his jacket. After a moment's thought, he had removed the garment and folded it over his left arm. The bulges in the pockets had been too noticeable. He had not wanted to be challenged by any previously unseen observer on his way out of the building. Even though Gray did not like whisky, he had been quite sure that someone else would be happy to buy it from him at a suitably bargain price, and the vodka he could drink himself. Shutting the door and re-attaching the padlock, Gray had twisted the reels round to show a random selection of numbers once again.

In the days following Gray's excursion into real world video gaming, two things happened.

A man and a woman arrived at the branch of The Keep by the service station and accessed Unit 72. They found the folder, the contents of which they photographed and then put it back in place. At the same time, two police officers attended The Charlton Arms, asking to speak to the member of staff who had cleaned the room immediately after it had been vacated in March by the deceased American guest, Mr Damon Casey.

25

The sluggish Boxing Day sun had made a tardy appearance above the eastern horizon, but its dull orange disk had done little to illuminate the landscape alongside the almost deserted A303 when the new Sampfield Grange horsebox, driven by Sadie, made its way past Stonehenge. The Winter Solstice, the shortest day of the year, had only a few days ago been celebrated at the famous sun temple by large numbers of enthusiasts for prehistory and ancient religion, but the lightless days had yet to show any noticeable sign of lengthening. Today, more encouragingly, the sky was a clear, cold blue, with elongated fingers of furrowed cloud exploding from a bank of low-lying mist in the East, resembling the veins of a glowing feather fan reaching outwards above the moving vehicle. Spindly, bare branched trees could be seen marking the sides of the empty road as it curved away ahead.

The M3 motorway had been slightly busier, suggesting that some citizens had shaken off the torpor of the previous day and intended to use the second public holiday to more pro-active effect. Some of these people would be on their way, Sadie and Jackie were sure, to the first day of the Winter Festival at Kempton Park racecourse. Many more would be watching the events of the famous race day from the warm comfort of their living rooms.

Tabikat was well rugged up and protected in the back of the smartly appointed lorry, standing quietly on one side of the barrier dividing him from the now successfully rehabilitated Curlew Landings.

Tabikat's forthcoming attempt to win the three mile King George VI Gold Cup Chase that day had been well publicised and endlessly discussed in the racing media. Trainer James Sampfield Peveril and jockey Merlin ap Rhys had given many interviews and answered numerous questions about the now famous horse's chances of winning the big race. The English racing festival had been less prominently covered in the Irish press, given that it coincided with the four day Christmas Festival at Leopardstown racecourse, the meeting at which the prolific Tabikat had customarily raced in previous years when still trained by Brendan Meaghan. Nevertheless, the Foley family had been asked for their comments on what the equine superstar which had been bred at their remote country farm might achieve in the tough English race.

"I have every confidence in the horse," Eoghan Foley had stated firmly both on TV and in press previews, "The track at Kempton will suit him, and the recent wet weather will help. He's a good strong galloper and very clever over his fences, wherever he's racing."

Tabikat and Curlew Landings had schooled together earlier in the week on the now dank and unwelcoming gallops above Sampfield Grange. Merlin had earlier visited the Dicks establishment to work with Fan Court, who was due to run in a two mile Chase on the second day of the Kempton festival, having already notched up a third place in a Grade 1 Chase at Sandown Park earlier in the month. Merlin had then come on to Sampfield Grange to work with Tabikat.

With him, Merlin had brought an eager Travis, who had helped in the preceding weeks to bring Curlew Landings back into full work following his bad experience at Cheltenham over a month earlier. Mr Sampfield had remained ready to take Curlew out of the Boxing Day race at the slightest indication that he might not be fit to run, but both Travis and Rachel Horwood had considered that the horse deserved to take his chance. Merlin would be under instructions on the day to pull Curlew Landings up if there was any sign of a continuing problem during the race.

Sadie had accompanied Mr Sampfield up onto the gallops during the exercise session, riding the enthusiastic Indian Rocks, who had joined in with Tabikat's and Curlew's exhibition of top class jumping. Indian Rocks had worked with Curlew over a line of hurdles, after which they had all stood to watch Merlin and Tabikat showing them all just how fences should be jumped. Sadie had observed Merlin's well-balanced frame with envy, watching her beloved Tabikat skimming over the obstacles, scarcely needing any direction from his jockey, who had seemed content to let the intelligent horse get on with his job. Sadie had wished that she could ride as apparently effortlessly as the talented Merlin, although she had been confident that her own hard work over the last few weeks had at least ensured that Tabikat was fit and ready to meet his next challenge.

Indian Rocks had followed his stable companions down the puddled and muddy track which sloped into the yard behind the rear wall of the chauffeur's flat and garden of the main house, the brown bulk of Caladesi Island, with Mr Sampfield on his broad back, walking by the young horse's side. The short-lived day had been gloomy and dull and the only sound to be heard was the harsh and eerie cry of invisible crows somewhere in the distance. A small yellow helicopter had buzzed briefly into view in the colourless sky but had been soon gone.

Travis and Merlin had been chatting companionably as their now relaxed horses had negotiated the familiar homeward route. Most of their discussion had been about Curlew Landings, the horse Merlin would be riding in the Christmas Hurdle race, due to take place immediately before the King George VI Chase on Boxing Day. Merlin had not asked any questions of Sadie and she had felt disappointed that her former lover had seemed to have little to say to her that day. A feeling of loss had suddenly threatened to upset Sadie's well suppressed emotions, but she had quickly damped the feeling down. After all, she had agreed with Merlin that their relationship was now to be that of friends and work colleagues. There was no reason for them to engage in personal conversation.

Sadie tried to shake off this unwelcome memory as the horsebox passed the exit from the M3 signposted to Ascot racecourse, the course to which Merlin had been travelling on the evening of that depressing afternoon. He had been due to ride in three races on the following day, including a two mile and five furlongs Novices' Chase in which Katseye had been entered.

Katseye had been driven to the famous Berkshire course that day by Jackie and Kye whilst Sadie had been preparing to ride Indian Rocks in a point to point race at Ashfordleigh Downs the same afternoon. Gilbert Peveril and his wife had represented Sampfield

241

Grange at the attractive rural course, whilst the trainer himself had followed the horsebox containing Katseye further East to Ascot.

The Ascot event had been a four horse race, as at Cheltenham, and had included both the unruly Petit Zazou and the more patient Cloud Atlas once again. The French horse had been on its best behaviour that day but had been unable to get the better of Katseye on the less undulating right-handed course with its stiff fences. Katseye's size and power had stood him in good stead and Merlin had been well in control of the race as they had left Swinley Bottom for the second time. Much to the Sampfield Grange camp's dismay, however, a horse against which Katseye had not raced before had been similarly suited by the course and conditions, and had eventually overhauled Katseye on the final run in. Katseye, though a tough stayer, had been unable to fend off his new rival and Merlin had had to settle for second place.

Both Arturo Ardizzone and Meredith Crosland had been at Ascot racecourse with Sam that day, and had accepted the result with resignation, the owner nevertheless commenting favourably on his horse's gritty performance. Most pleased by the result had been the bookmakers. The winner, Altimeter, had been the rank outsider in the race. His respectable but not outstanding form, acquired mostly at northern racecourses, had not led anyone, including Jayce and Tabby Cat, to believe that he could stay on so dourly at the finish against the powerful Katseye.

"That 'orse Altimeter is flying today. Maybe 'e's on steroids," Arturo Ardizzone had commented, as they had watched the owner of the victorious runner being given his prize, the youthful trainer from the Cheshire yard where the horse was based standing alongside.

"If he is, then it will be picked up by the routine drug testing of the winner," Sam remarked, although he was sure that the charismatic Italian business owner was not being serious.

As the lorry containing Tabikat and Curlew Landings approached the end of the M3, Jackie was snoozing in the cab seat next to

Sadie, the radio volume turned low so as not to wake her until they were nearer to Kempton Park.

Sam was also on his way to the well-known suburban London course, accompanied in the Range Rover by his cousin Gilbert. Pippa Peveril had chosen to remain at home with their teenaged children and various of Pippa's relatives who had spent the Christmas holiday with them. There had been no sign of Toby Halstock.

"Old Toby's a bit out of sorts these days," Gilbert had told Sam, mysteriously, "Let's hope that Curlew Landings can restore his good mood."

Kempton Park racecourse seemed to be a magnet that day. The sun had gradually faded to a pale yellow as it had climbed into the sky above the grandstand with its spectacular cantilevered roof. The narrow road leading from the roundabout at the end of the M3 motorway towards the entrance for horsebox parking was clogged with traffic and overrun with groups of pedestrians eager to arrive early at the racecourse and secure a seat in one of the soon to be overcrowded bars. The small station by the car park was, unhelpfully, closed in deference to the public holiday.

Sadie was relieved to get the lorry through the milling crowds without running anyone over. Tabikat and Curlew Landings both emerged into the cold sunlight bright and happy after their journey. They were soon joined by Mr Sampfield and Mr Peveril in the racecourse stables. Curlew's race was to be preceded by three earlier races, so there was as yet no urgency to prepare the horses.

Sam had found a short text message on his phone, which showed an icon of a racehorse with the words **Good Luck** next to it. It was from Helen Garratt, who would be at Chepstow races on the following day for Alto Clef's attempt to win the Welsh National for the third time. Tabikat had missed his customary annual run against Helen's grey gelding, as Sam had this year bypassed the race at Newbury formerly known as the Hennessy Gold Cup Chase at the beginning of December. Alto Clef had run into second place in that event behind The Page of Cups, trained by Niall Carter.

Sadie saw no sign of Merlin until after she and Jackie had brought Curlew Landings into the well-attended parade ring. Curlew was on his toes and seemed excited to be back at a racecourse once again. Sadie left Jackie to lead the horse around the large oval arena, whilst the final interviews following the prize-giving for the previous race, a Grade 1 Novices Chase, named after the former prolific champion, Kauto Star, who had been immortalised in the form of a statue in the parade ring, were being completed. Sadie could see Mr Sampfield and Mr Peveril standing near the statue in the centre of the parade ring, the former answering questions from the TV interviewer roaming amongst the assembled groups to obtain comments from owners and trainers for the edification of the home-based spectators. Stevie Stone was standing at the end of the tiered viewing section on the far side of the arena, just in front of the statue of the famous Desert Orchid.

Sadie heard Merlin before she saw him. The weighing room at Kempton Park was some distance away from the parade ring, back in the direction of the pre-parade area, which meant that the jockeys had to follow the horses along the paved track which led into and out of the parade ring itself. Merlin appeared to be chatting to another jockey. Sadie, turning to greet him, saw that his companion was Jenna Roberts, who would later be riding Inkspot in Tabikat's race. So engrossed in their discussion were the two jockeys that they passed Sadie without noticing her. Sadie, who had been about to greet Merlin, closed her mouth abruptly, simply watching as Merlin walked briskly forward to greet Mr Sampfield in the parade ring.

Curlew Landings' race was fast and furious. Curlew had always enjoyed racing on flat courses and zoomed off ahead, as usual, as soon as the starter had dropped his yellow flag. The two mile start was towards the right of the grandstand and Curlew had bounced down the track past the spectators, tossing his handsome head, as if to tell everyone that he was back. By the time the field of four horses had progressed towards the far side of the course beyond the lake, from the surface of which a gaggle of geese arose in a panic as the horses approached, Curlew Landings had a two length advantage over his nearest competitor. Customary rivals Southern Cross and Devil Waters were being towed in his wake. The fourth horse, Rabbit Punch, was ridden today by Jenna Roberts, who had taken the chance ride following an injury in an earlier race to the horse's usual jockey. The combination, still finding out about each other, remained in touch, Jenna seemingly confident that her horse could stay the course and take advantage of any error by the other three.

Coming down towards the final bend into the finishing straight, Merlin could feel that Curlew was beginning to tire. The distance of the race was too short to get much of a breather into the horse, and it was not clear to Merlin that a two length advantage was going to be enough to hold the lead. The instruction to pull Curlew up if there was any sign of a physical problem was foremost in his mind, but they were not at that stage yet. He could hear the roar of the huge Boxing Day crowd ahead of them and was sure Curlew could too.

"Come on, Curlew," Merlin urged, under his breath, "Keep fightin', *bachgen*. They want us to win."

Merlin was right. Notwithstanding the recent incident at Cheltenham, the Champion Hurdle winner was the Even money favourite with the punters.

There were two hurdles to clear before the finish. Curlew rattled through the top of the first, causing a gasp from the spectators, but his momentum kept him on his feet. The mistake, though, had cost him some ground. The field closed up before they reached the final obstacle.

"They're all still in with a chance!" yelled the racecourse commentator, as the frenzied shrieking and shouting of the many thousands congregated in the grandstand and by the rails boomed and echoed to the left of the runners, "Southern Cross is coming at Curlew Landings. The leader's being caught. Curlew Landings needs the line!"

Merlin and Curlew Landings were stretched to the limit. Merlin was working like a madman, his usual poise now left behind, as he willed his horse past the finishing post. He could hear the snorting breath of Southern Cross loud on his right side, the jockey also shoving and pushing and shouting at his mount to overtake Curlew. The two horses passed the finishing post together.

"It's going to the judge in a photo finish," announced the commentator, "Rabbit Punch and Devil Waters are in close order behind, coming third and fourth respectively."

As the agonising wait for the decision on the placings was awaited, Sadie was putting the final touches to Tabikat before bringing him out into the pre-parade area. As she led him towards the saddling boxes, where Mr Sampfield would meet them, Sadie was talking as usual to her handsome charge.

"You're the cleverest and most talented horse in the world, Tabsi," Sadie told him, "And you've got the best jockey. You and Merlin are going to win again today, I know you will."

Tabikat's mahogany coloured ears flicked about and he gave a few soft snorts into Sadie's ear. He seemed to be looking at something over her shoulder. Sadie turned. A youngish man in a waxed jacket and wearing a tweed cap was leaning on the railings at the other side of the pre-parade area. Like many people on that day, he was wearing dark glasses. He seemed to be looking at them.

More horses and people were now drifting into the pre-parade area, but the man did not move from his position. Ever since the receipt of the threatening message on the child's drawing of Tabikat, Sadie had been hyper vigilant when accompanying the special horse.

Turning her back towards the stationary figure, Sadie held up her mobile phone and pretended to take a selfie whilst she stood alongside Tabikat's dark head.

"He's probably just one of the owners, but I'm not taking any chances with you," Sadie told Tabikat as she started to lead the magnificent horse around the little oval lawn, eager spectators now coming thick and fast towards the white rails, "Look, Tabsi, your fans are arriving."

Over the racecourse loudspeaker system came the result of Curlew Landings' race. It had been a dead heat.

26

Merlin ap Rhys was enjoying his new relationship with fellow jockey Jenna Roberts. After over eighteen months of casual sex with a succession of disinterested young women, finding a regular partner in his bed had, to his surprise, been a positive change in his life. Merlin had known Jenna since they were children, but it was only in the last year that she had reappeared as an ambitious professional jockey on the British racing scene. It had never occurred to Merlin see her as a prospective bedfellow, but her very clear hint to him after the race at Haydock Park had made him think again.

Jenna was the younger sister of Welsh trainer Hafren Roberts. Jenna had spent much of her riding career in the South East of England and had lost most of her Welsh accent in the process. Merlin had been under the impression that she had been engaged to the assistant trainer at the yard where she had previously worked, but, if this had ever been the case, it appeared to be no longer. Jenna had recently returned to live in Wales but rode for a number of trainers, including her sister.

Jenna's approach to their relationship suited Merlin very well. Jenna seemed to want nothing from him but a good time in bed. Her attitude to sex was rather like that which she brought to the gym sessions which they sometimes shared - a form of regular exercise to be undertaken with the objective of getting fit. A tiny nagging voice in the back of Merlin's mind suggested to him that his own physical fitness was probably the main attraction for his new partner. For a man accustomed to using women for his own fun, this was a novel experience, so he banished the warnings and concentrated on having a good time, in much the same way as Sadie had originally done with him, had he but known it, nearly two years ago.

As Merlin walked past the excited spectators lining the horsewalk towards the Kempton Park parade ring, he had nothing in his mind other than the forthcoming race. Jenna Roberts was now just another jockey who was riding one of Tabikat's rivals for the coveted prize. Merlin's ability to compartmentalise his thoughts was absolute. There would be plenty of time to enjoy themselves later after the racing was over.

There were seven horses competing in the cold and sunlit King George VI Chase. Tabikat would almost certainly be going off favourite, as the book had scarcely altered since the final declarations. The six horses Tabikat and Merlin needed to beat were Inkspot, who had come second to Tabikat at Haydock Park; former Cheltenham Gold Cup winner Macalantern; the light grey Bees and Mist; Poseidon's Gold, who had ditched his jockey in the Bowl Chase at Aintree; and familiar rivals Less Than Ross and Stormlighter, who were both still firmly in the picture, although showing at the longest odds. Fortunately, Cheltenham Gold Cup runner up, The Page of Cups, was running instead at Leopardstown. None of the horses was a complete outsider, and all of them had the potential to run into a place, even if not all of them were realistic selections to win. Tabikat was the only horse now still in with the chance of winning the Triple Crown, which meant that the pressure on him and Merlin that day was even greater than that on the other runners.

Sam watched Merlin as the self-confident jockey, wearing the Levy Brothers' blue and gold racing colours, approached Tabikat's little party of connections who were standing on the lawn in the parade ring. Sam had been surprised to learn the previous week that Niamh and Feanna Foley planned to make the trip to Kempton Park over the holiday period to watch Tabikat run. Mother and daughter were with Sam now, Feanna chatting to Gilbert Peveril about their shared interest in point to point riding, whilst Niamh stood in silence, observing the spectacularly turned out Tabikat being led around the parade ring path by Sadie.

Sam had never been sure how to approach Niamh Foley. He was well aware that her son in law, Ephraim Levy, was, through his international banking and commodities trading company, the sole owner of Tabikat since the death of previous owner Susan Stonehouse. It had, though, become increasingly clear to him that the current ownership was unofficially vested in Niamh Foley herself, particularly in the last year and a half, during which time Niamh had regularly appeared in person at racecourses to support the talented horse. Sometimes she had been accompanied by her brother in law Eoghan Foley, or Tabikat's former trainer Brendan Meaghan, or by employees from the Levy Brothers International bank. Niamh herself was a business manager rather than a horsewoman, and her knowledge of racing came entirely from her family connections and the fact that she had been brought up at Gleannglas racecourse where her father had worked. Sam had found Caitlin's older sister to be a self-contained individual, occasionally outspoken, but mostly calm and focused as she watched her breathtaking horse in his races. Niamh's composed features revealed little of her inner thoughts, and Sam had more than once wondered what was going through her mind.

The two of them had greeted each other with polite pleasure, like old acquaintances at a social event.

"You would be very welcome to visit us at Sampfield Grange, Mrs Foley," Sam had already told her as they waited for Merlin to join them, "Then you will be able to see for yourself what we are doing with your horse. It has been a great privilege for us to train him at our small yard."

"I am pleased to hear you say so," Niamh had replied, carefully avoiding responding to the invitation to visit Sampfield Grange, "Tabikat and Katseye have been a precious gift to our family."

"And now Katalyst too," Sam had added, "I am very much looking forward to receiving him at home. As you know, I agreed with Genie that the colt would remain in Ireland until the New Year and that we would start to look for opportunities for him in England after that."

If Niamh had intended to respond to this comment, the arrival of Merlin by their side quickly put an end to the conversation.

Sadie, leading Tabikat along the dull red path within a few feet of the clustered spectators, noted Merlin's appearance alongside Mr Sampfield and his party. She wondered whether she should tell

Merlin, once the much-anticipated race was over, about the unnerving man she had seen lurking near the pre-parade ring. Although Sadie had not forgotten the oddly spelt threatening note on the child's drawing of Tabikat, she was aware that Merlin had taken it less seriously than she had and would probably think that she was worrying about nothing. The note had, after all, referred specifically to Cheltenham. Sadie also sensed that something had changed in Merlin's attitude towards her. Merlin had once seemed keen to become friends with her again, but, having achieved that objective, he now appeared to Sadie to have allowed the new trust which had arisen between them to lapse back into a purely professional relationship.

"But that was what you wanted," Sadie told herself fiercely, as she strode briskly around the parade ring, Tabikat's lightly-shod hooves making little sound on the cushioned surface of the path, "It was your own decision to keep him at arm's length. If he's found someone else, then that's a good thing."

Alongside Sadie came the chatter and mutter of the many voices which made up the Boxing Day crowd, "There's Inkspot – his jockey's a girl, you know, must be tough for her..... Tabikat's amazing, he's the one with a chance at the million pounds, just think..... Bees and Mist, what a weird name, he's really gorgeous, like a unicorn......"

Sadie soon passed Stevie Stone, long hair flowing loose down the back of her cream jacket, surrounded by her usual coterie of Smart Girls, talking animatedly into an iPad. Tabby Cat and Jayce had confidently tipped Tabikat to win the King George that day. The harder task had been that of predicting who would cross the finishing line immediately behind him. The bookmakers mostly had Inkspot as the second favourite although some preferred Macalantern.

The clang of the bell telling the jockeys to mount sounded suddenly in Sadie's ears.

"Here we go, Tabsi," she told the unperturbed horse, as she pulled down the lightweight stirrup irons into which Merlin would soon slot his toes, "Come back safe. I'll be waiting for you."

Tabikat looked straight ahead but flicked one dark ear towards Sadie's quiet voice. Then Mr Sampfield came to the horse's side to leg Merlin up into the tiny saddle and the combination made its stately way towards with horsewalk, Sadie silently holding the rein.

"Tabikat's lookin' good today, Sadie," Merlin commented, "You've done a great job with 'im, as usual."

Sadie heard this compliment as one which Merlin might give to any groom, noting only the absence of the customary endearment *cariad* from Merlin's words to her.

"You two had better win," Sadie said, unintentionally brusquely, her sharp tone taking Merlin aback.

"We'll do our best," he replied shortly, as they joined the back of the pre-race parade on the turf of the track in front of the heaving grandstand.

Tabikat was the last horse in the alphabetical ordering of the seven runners. The nearly white Bees and Mist led the procession, looking like an equine character from a fantasy adventure story. Behind him, Inkspot with Jenna Roberts on board, strode out purposefully. Poseidon's Gold, fifth in the line, was already becoming jittery, wanting to get on with the race. Tabikat, Merlin and Sadie, bringing up the rear, moved together as one, hearing the enthusiastic cheering of the crowd as the racecourse commentator announced Tabikat's name.

"And, finally, Tabikat, the favourite, ridden by Merlin ap Rhys for trainer James Sampfield Peveril. Tabikat has won the best turned out prize today. Well done to his groom and work rider, Sadie Shinkins."

"We're the top team," Sadie said under her breath to Tabikat, pleased to hear her own contribution acknowledged.

Watching Tabikat finally cantering away towards the three mile start, Sadie stared after horse and jockey for a few moments before trudging back to the horsewalk, where Jackie had come to join her to watch the race.

Back in the emptying parade ring, Sam was accosted by the ever-present TV interviewer.

"This is a big day for Tabikat's connections," the colourfully-attired young woman stated, unnecessarily, "How confident are you feeling, Mr Sampfield Peveril?"

"All that I can say," Sam responded, firmly, "Is that we've done the work with him, and we can only watch him now. Merlin will give him a good ride, of that I am very confident."

The start of the King George VI Chase was greeted by the massed spectators with a deafening cheer. The race commenced towards the left of the packed grandstand, close to where the all-weather course intersected the Chase course. There were two fences to be taken on that side of the track, the first a plain fence and the second an open ditch. The experienced chasers approached them both at a controlled pace and cleared them expertly and without mishap.

"The leaders are setting a good pace and the field is closely grouped," announced the commentator, "Bees and Mist stood off a mile from the second there. Now they swing right handed into the back straight where the next four of the remaining sixteen fences await them."

Merlin was keeping Tabikat settled in the middle of the comfortably progressing group. At his side was the light grey Bees and Mist, his Cheshire-based jockey known to Merlin only by sight. Inkspot and Macalantern were immediately behind them, the talkative Aidan Scanlon already needling Jenna, who was ignoring him, refusing to allow her concentration to be diverted. Aidan had not forgiven Jenna and Inkspot for beating him into third place at Haydock Park.

"Poseidon's Gold is out ahead as they reach the third," went on the commentator, "Stormlighter is on his heels, the others content to sit and watch at this stage."

The race progressed in good order for the next half mile. Running alongside a backdrop of scrubby, bare trees, the flat track widening slightly, the entire field soon cleared the sixth fence and began the long sweeping turn which would bring them back in front of the grandstand. Three fences lay ahead on this section of the course, the third of which would represent the halfway point of the contest.

A burst of scattered cheering and encouragement arose from the stands when the closely grouped horses passed the spectators and made the wide turn over the all-weather corner of the course to complete a full circuit back to the starting point.

"Less Than Ross has taken it very wide," indicated the commentator, as the field spread out across the grey surface, "They're approaching the tenth with nothing to choose between them."

As if by some invisible signal, the structure of the race changed after the eleventh fence had been cleared. Less Than Ross began to drop back and lose touch as the horses rounded the turn which led once again to the four jumps in the back straight. Tabikat and Bees and Mist were starting to overhaul Stormlighter and Poseidon's Gold, whose jockeys were nudging and pushing their horses to try to stay in the lead.

"The pace is lifting as they approach the end of the back straight," called the voice of the commentator, "Poseidon's Gold surrenders the lead. Stormlighter is beginning to struggle. Bees and Mist and Tabikat take the fourteenth together. And a bad mistake from Stormlighter drops him right back through the field."

Rounding the final bend with three fences left to jump, it was clear to Sam as he watched the parade ring screen that there were only three horses who could still challenge Tabikat for victory. Less Than Ross and Poseidon's Gold had both been pulled up, whilst Stormlighter was continuing, but well out of touch. Tabikat and Merlin motored to the head of affairs just as the runners straightened up to face the final three fences. Bees and Mist was sticking to Tabikat like unwanted white glue, whilst Macalantern and Inkspot hammered determinedly onward behind the leaders with little to choose between them.

The thousands of crammed and yelling spectators were beside themselves as the horses approached the grandstand. The tumult which had greeted Merlin and Curlew Landings in the previous race seemed muted compared to the wall of roaring sound into which Tabikat was now running. To Merlin, the experience was completely exhilarating as the adrenalin coursed through his strong body.

All the jockeys were shouting and shoving hard now. Merlin could hear Aidan's and Jenna's voices sounding loud and urgent behind and to either side of him, the heavy panting of their horses like a pair of steam engines. The Northern Irish accent of Bees and Mist's jockey boomed closer, nearby to his right. Tabikat's dark head and black tipped ears bounced rhythmically up and down in front of Merlin's eyes, the courageous horse's breath coming in sharp snorts as he powered his way over the final two jumps.

Sadie and Jackie could see Tabikat approaching them with Bees and Mist close on his heels. Merlin's head was down as he and Tabikat fought to keep their grey challenger behind them. Sadie was almost beside herself with fear as Tabikat tackled the final fence, landing neatly before gathering his energy for the run in to the finish.

"Tabikat's made the better jump at the last," screamed the commentator, "Bees and Mist is not giving up. Bees and Mist is gaining on Tabikat. Tabikat's not having any of it. Tabikat's grimly sticking on to the finish. Bees and Mist is still coming. Tabikat won't be caught..... And it's Tabikat by a length from Bees and Mist!

Tabikat's won the King George at the first attempt! There's a tussle for third between Macalantern and Inkspot. Macalantern just gets it."

Merlin realised that he was completely out of breath. He was well accustomed to the strenuous physical activity, but the stress of the occasion suddenly caught up with him, and he had to take a few deep breaths as the tired Tabikat's forward momentum slackened after the finish line. The noise of the crowd reverberated and echoed from behind him as Tabikat came to a graceful walk in the corner of the course, where he was soon joined by the other horses and jockeys.

"Good ride, Merlin," said Bees and Mists' jockey, holding out a hand, as his elegant horse, puffing and snorting, walked briefly alongside Tabikat, "Thought we had you there."

The next few minutes were frantic. Aidan Scanlon and Jenna Roberts added their congratulations to Merlin before leaving him and Tabikat to walk back in front of the grandstand to receive the roaring adulation of the crowd. Sadie ran onto the course to take hold of Tabikat's bridle, her tensions over Merlin's changed behaviour towards her temporarily forgotten. The required on-course TV interview and the subsequent return along the long horsewalk to the winner's enclosure through ranks of cheering onlookers passed by as if part of a quickly accelerating movie reel.

Sam, Gilbert and the Foleys found themselves at the centre of the attention of all the other owners and trainers in the parade ring. Sam was familiar with most of the trainers, if not the owners, and accepted their congratulations with pleasure. The last to come forward to greet him was a man of medium height with dark eyes and thick grey hair. He was wearing a heavy coat with the collar turned up against the cold, a black fedora hat held in leather gloved hands before him.

"Congratulations, Mr Sampfield Peveril," the newcomer said, his accent vaguely Irish, holding out his hand, "I am the owner of Bees and Mist. We gave you a good run there, I think?"

As Sam was about to agree, the man turned to Niamh Foley, who was standing next to Sam with a beaming smile on her usually serious face, looking towards the horsewalk along which Tabikat would soon arrive, "And this is the lucky owner? Congratulations to you, Mrs Foley. Your horse is certainly something special."

As Niamh Foley turned to shake hands with the man who had said he was the owner of Bees and Mist, Sam saw her bright smile suddenly fade. In contrast, the other owner's smile became only broader and Sam realised with surprise that Niamh Foley had recognised him.

"How very kind of you to say so," Niamh Foley muttered, and turned away without taking the man's proffered hand.

Sam had no time to try to understand what had just happened between the two owners, and soon forgot the incident completely in the excitement of Tabikat's triumphant return to the winner's enclosure.

Unfortunately, the happy day was to have a less happy conclusion. Listening to the news on the radio in the Range Rover on the way home to Sampfield Grange, Sam and Gilbert were shocked to learn that Merlin ap Rhys had been attacked by an unknown assailant in the jockeys' car park at Kempton Park racecourse and had been taken to hospital by emergency ambulance.

27

The January weather had done nothing to lift the mood of the Sampfield Grange staff. An unstable mass of warm air had brought more heavy rain and driving wind to the South West corner of the country, with the result that any outdoor task, however normally undemanding or pleasurable, had now become a wearisome chore.

The boot room was full of muddy footwear and wet jackets as the yard staff sat at the breakfast table, rain beating against the leaded panes of the warm kitchen. The work riders had left for the day and the remaining staff, with the exception of Isabella Hall, who had remained in the yard office, had come indoors for a welcome mid-morning cup of coffee with a temporarily unoccupied Kelly and Lewis. Travis too was sitting with them, having spent a couple of hours at the yard that morning to work with Curlew Landings.

"I just don't understand what's going on," Sadie moaned, for the umpteenth time, repeatedly running her hand through her wet pony tail as she slumped on one of the wooden kitchen chairs, "First we had that nasty note about Tabsi, then someone had a go at Curlew, Luke got attacked at Aintree, and, just when things seemed to be going right again, Merlin's been punched in the face by some lunatic. Has someone got it in for us all this year? Who's going to be next?"

Kye shifted uncomfortably in his seat, not noticing that Travis was doing something similar in his own chair beside him.

"Do yez think these things are all related, then?" Kye asked Sadie, "That it's the same person doing it all?"

"This nasty note," asked Jackie, practically, "What exactly did it say, again?"

"It had a child's drawing of Tabsi winning the Gold Cup on one side," Sadie told her, "And on the other side it said **I cu at Chelts agen I brak ur legs**, like it was a text message. I talked to Merlin about it at the time, and he thought it must be written like that because the person couldn't actually send it as a text because they didn't have the right number to send it to."

"Well, it must have been aimed at a particular person then," Kelly put in, suddenly, "Who was there on the day you were given it? It was you, Kye, and Travis, wasn't it? If it was meant for someone else there would have been no point giving it to you lot, would there? Anyway, Luke and Merlin weren't attacked at Cheltenham racecourse."

"So, yez don't think the things are connected then?" Kye persisted, "I thought... well...."

"What, Kye?" asked Jackie, sharply.

Kye drew a deep breath. The thought of saying anything which might cause Mr Sampfield to find out about his drug dealing past had so far deterred him from speaking up, but he was beginning to realise that things could continue to become even more serious. If he said nothing, and someone else was injured, killed even, then the fact that he had kept his suspicions to himself would count against him even more.

"That day we took Tabikat and Curlew out into Charlton village," Kye said, hesitantly, "I saw someone in the crowd that I used to know in Liverpool. Someone who doesn't like me. A real piece of work, she is. She made a sign at me, like cutting my throat. So, I thought that maybe it was her that had sent the note. She meant it for me."

There was a pause, as the others thought about the implications of this information.

"This woman, did she know your mobile number?" asked Sadie.

"I changed it," Kye reminded her, "No-one knew it. Even you didn't."

"So, if the message was meant for you, Kye, this woman, whoever she is, wrote it down instead of texting, is that what you're suggesting?" asked Kelly, "I suppose she could have just picked up the piece of paper with the drawing on it. Maybe the child had dropped it and she used it to write on."

"Why should she want to break your legs, Kye?" asked Lewis, his sense of curiosity on high alert, "What have you done to upset her?"

"Shopped her to the bizzies," Kye said shortly, deciding to tell the truth insofar as this was possible, "For drug dealing. It was a while ago."

"Drug dealing?" asked Travis, suddenly, "You don't think she had anything to do with what happened to Curlew?"

"I wondered that, too," Kye replied, miserably, "I was leading Curlew with you that day so maybe it looked to her like he was my horse. But I can't see how she could have done it. I never saw her again after that day. If she'd come up to the yard someone would have seen her. And I don't think she would know the first thing about how to give drugs to a horse. Then when Luke got beaten up at Aintree, I thought it might be her doing too and the people were really after me. But the thing with Merlin, that can't be anything to do with her, surely?"

"Why did the note mention Cheltenham?" asked Sadie, trying to banish the picture of the injured Luke which had flooded back, unwanted, into her mind. She had been trying hard not to think about Merlin either.

Kye realised that he was in danger of being forced to say more than he wanted, and simply shrugged.

"Maybe she saw you on TV when you were riding there?" suggested Jackie, quickly, saving Kye from answering, "She wouldn't want you doing well at being a jockey if she hates you that much."

The discussion was brought to a temporary halt by the shrilling of the house telephone in the hall. Lewis quickly jumped up to answer it.

"So, this horrible woman could be at the bottom of all these things, except maybe the attack on Merlin," Kelly said, thoughtfully, "No wonder you left Liverpool to come down here, Kye. Should we tell the police?"

"What, and make it worse?" exclaimed Kye, horrified at the mention of the police, "I don't have any proof anyway. They wouldn't even listen."

Sadie had lapsed into a moody silence ever since the mention of Luke Cunningham whilst Jackie seemed suddenly keen to get back to work, so the little group began to disperse. Kelly was gathering together the empty coffee cups when Lewis returned to the kitchen to find that Kye and Jackie were leaving to go back into the yard.

"Just someone from the BHA for Mr Sampfield," Lewis announced, clearly disappointed that the interesting chat in the kitchen seemed to have been terminated in his absence.

"You heard anything more about Merlin?" he asked Sadie, keen to prolong the discussion and perhaps also to find out the latest state of play between the former lovers.

"No, why would I?" Sadie replied, irritably, "Travis is more likely to know than I am. Mr Dicks will have had to find another jockey to ride Fan Court the next day."

"Yeah, Mr Dicks booked Jenna Roberts," Travis told them, "She's sister to that Welsh trainer that Kye rides for sometimes. Jen was in the car park at Kempton when Merlin got hit and went with Merlin to the hospital. Merlin's got a black eye and concussion, she said, so he can't ride until he's cleared by the BHA medical people. She's going to get some of his bookings, but she didn't seem too stoked about it."

There was a clatter as Sadie's chair fell over.

"Sorry," Sadie muttered, bending down to pick up the chair, as sudden tears of realisation started into her eyes.

Travis had been gathering his possessions together in readiness to leave Sampfield Grange to return home to the Dicks yard. Kye's revelation had unsettled him. Travis had become quite sure that the ketamine which Curlew had ingested had come from the pocket of the jacket which he had been lent by Tegan Colvin. Kye had mentioned that the woman from Liverpool was a drug dealer. Was there a connection between her and Tegan Colvin? Was she the source of the gear which was in the jacket? Had Jack Tytherleigh's people somehow got her to plant it on him?

Sadie had quickly left the kitchen, saying that she had things to do. Travis had started to follow her into the boot room, when Mr Sampfield unexpectedly opened the door from the hall.

"Ah, Travis," Mr Sampfield said, "I'm glad I caught you. I have some interesting news for you. Would you come through to the study with me for a few moments? Bring me in some coffee, would you, Lewis?"

Sitting in the comfortable study as the rain continued to stream down the glass of the window overlooking the sheep paddock, Travis was bemused to be told that the telephone call recently received at Sampfield Grange had been from the hunting acquaintance of Mr Sampfield who had previously been in touch with the authorities at Racing Victoria.

"There has been a development in the case of your young jockey from Australia," Sam's friend had told him, "It relates to the testing of samples taken from some of the Tytherleigh horses. It appears that the Racing Victoria people have had their eyes on Mr Tytherleigh for a while and some of the samples from his horses which previously came up clean have been recently retested. New techniques for detection are coming up all the time, of course, as we try to keep up with the latest substances which come into circulation. One of these techniques has picked up a new finding. It looks as if your young lad and his scientific friend may have been right."

"May I tell Travis about this?" Sam had asked, "He happens to be here riding out for me today."

"There's nothing official yet," the friend had cautioned, "The Racing Victoria people are biding their time. So, please ask him to keep it to himself. The authorities there want to make sure they are on solid ground before they make a move. This in itself won't solve your lad's problems, of course. He will still have to deal with the findings made against himself, even if Racing Victoria is able to charge the trainer with doping his own horses. But this may be enough at least to have his case re-opened in due course."

Whilst Sam was summarising this information for Travis's exclusive benefit, once Lewis had reluctantly left the study after bringing the coffee, Kye and Jackie were in angry discussion in the tack room.

"I'm going to tell Mr Stanley about Sheryl Mavers being seen round here," Jackie insisted, "It is her, isn't it? The one you got arrested along with your brother Bronz on Gold Cup day the year before last? You should have said something before, Kye. Then maybe Luke Cunningham wouldn't have got beaten up. I'm supposed to be here to help you, but I can't help you if you won't trust me."

"I didn't know about that note on the picture," Kye snapped back at her, "Sadie kept it and I didn't see what it said until later. All I saw was Sheryl making the throat cutting sign at me."

"And what about that Graham Colvin at the garage?" demanded Jackie, "You back in league with him, then, like before? You promised me you wouldn't get involved with him again. Is that how you paid for the car?"

"No, it fucking isn't," hissed Kye back at her, "I paid for that car out of my riding fees and prize money."

"So, he's not asked you to start dealing again?" Jackie wanted to know.

"He did, but I said no," Kye raged at her, "He was boasting about a new supplier in the North. He said there was good money to be made. He picks the stuff up on the M5 somewhere, he said. Oh..... no, Christ, Jax ....."

Kye's angry rant trailed off into silence as Jackie looked at him in despair.

"It's Sheryl, isn't it?" Kye said, slowly, "The stuff's coming through Liverpool under the Irish lorries. Nothing's changed at all. I'm still trapped, after everything that's happened. I can't believe it, Jax."

Kye sat down suddenly on a nearby wooden stool and rested his dark, curly head in his hands. Jackie stood by his side, not knowing how to comfort him.

Fortunately for Kye, there was no-one else in the yard to witness his misery. Sadie had walked as calmly as she could from the kitchen up to her flat above the garage and had shut the wooden door behind her. Normally, she would have taken comfort from one of the horses, but they were all safely in their stables, sheltered from the pouring rain, and she could not go to talk to one of them without attracting attention.

The recognition that Merlin could be in a relationship with fellow jockey Jenna Roberts had just rocked Sadie's carefully constructed defences to their foundations. She was very well aware that Merlin's sex life would not have simply come to a halt after they had parted, but she had assumed that this would not involve any personal commitment on Merlin's part. The existence of a relationship which might replace the one she had enjoyed with Merlin was an entirely different matter. Had Merlin felt like this when he had seen her with Luke, she wondered, belatedly?

Sadie knew she was as much in love with Merlin as she ever had been. Her attempts to convince herself that her feelings could be got over by willpower alone had been brutally shown to be unrealistic. When she had heard on the radio that Merlin had been attacked at Kempton Park, Sadie had sent him a text message, framed to sound like the sort of sympathetic query which might be sent by any concerned friend, asking after his wellbeing. She had received a brief reply.

OK thx. No rides 4 me 4 a wk or 2.

The bland tone of the reply had deterred Sadie from asking further questions, so she had consulted the news and social media for more information on exactly what had happened on that late Boxing Day afternoon. The most useful information had come from the animated mouth of a sad looking Tabby Cat on the Smart Girls vlog, where the charismatic Merlin ap Rhys had always been a popular attraction. The blue-eyed kitten had reported that 'our favourite jockey, magic Merlin' had been walking towards his car in the jockeys' car park when a man had jumped out from behind a van and punched him the face. Merlin, taken by surprise, had been knocked sideways and had struck his head on one of the parked vehicles nearby. The assailant, as yet untraced, had run off before Merlin could see anything which might help identify the person who had ambushed him.

Mr Stanley, Sadie remembered, had thought the attack on Luke to have been connected with Katalyst, rather than with Kye's female enemy. This explanation had made some sense to Sadie, for the simple reason that Kye himself had been at Aintree on that dreadful day, so if anyone had wanted to attack him, they could have easily done so. Furthermore, Luke Cunningham's angry tirade at her on the telephone had suggested that Luke had indeed had some interest in acquiring Katalyst for his family, rather than allowing the horse to be sold to Mr Sampfield, as Luke had apparently suspected might have already happened. The attack on Merlin, though, sounded more like something that someone might have carried out in a fit of drunken rage, like a pub fight rather than a sustained and vicious beating.

The sound of a car engine roused Sadie from her inconclusive thoughts. Peering through the small, rain-streaked window overlooking the entrance to the yard, she was astonished to see none other than Mr Stanley himself getting out of his green SUV and shrugging on a beige raincoat. She was even more surprised to see Kye and Jackie come out from the shelter of the tack room and walk over to join him.

Together, the three of them made their way through the pouring rain towards the main door of the house.

28

Cyber and Computer Security student Rajesh Mallik had been happy when the University's libraries and computer rooms had introduced twenty-four hour opening. He had been ecstatic when, in the April of his first postgraduate year at the University, he had discovered the fake staff account in the strange name of Merlin ap Rhys.

Rajesh's family had been determined that Rajesh would study either Medicine or Law at University. His Bangladeshi immigrant father had worked long hours in the family's East London corner shop, braving opportunist thieves, knife attackers and aggressive drunks in order to keep the little store open during the unpopular but lucrative hours leading up to midnight. Rajesh's mother had helped her husband in the shop whilst their three children were at school and again in the late hours of the evening when their children were occupied with their homework or had gone to bed. Both parents had wanted nothing more dearly than that their children should never have to do what they themselves were doing.

Rajesh was the first of their three children and on him the family hopes had chiefly rested. As a doctor or a lawyer, he could become rich and successful, make a good marriage, and look after the needs of his parents in their old age, when they were unable any longer to run the shop. The two younger siblings, a girl and a boy, would also benefit from their older brother's success. The Mallik parents had foreseen an advantageous marriage into a good family for their daughter and an equally fortunate career for the younger son in whichever of the options of Medicine or Law had not already been selected by Rajesh. Rajesh's father had worshipped at the local mosque on a regular basis, lived a quiet and law-abiding existence as a respected member of their local community, and had had no reason to believe that his plans for his apparently equally quiet and law-abiding children would not come to fruition. His two sons had been clever and had done well at the local school whilst his daughter had never shown anything other than submissive respect for her father's wishes for her future.

As with many a parent's ambitious plans for his children, Rajesh Mallik senior's vision for his family's future had been doomed to be cruelly crushed. The plan had progressed well at first. Young Rajesh had achieved sufficiently good grades to be offered a place on a Law degree course at one of the central London universities. Daughter Ranya had dutifully accepted the respectable young man whose neighbouring family had proposed their son as a suitable match for the Malliks' daughter. Second son Ashik had seemed destined to follow his brother to University until he had suddenly seemed to be more interested in sitting in his room with his laptop computer open on his desk, playing games which involved ancient and unending battles in which blood was liberally shed, and in which murder and rape appeared to be part of the fake entertainment.

Unfortunately, the Mallik parents had been unaware of Ashik's interests, or they might have taken steps to prevent Ashik accessing the material. But they were from another era and understood computer technology very poorly. Games to them had been innocent recreational activities for children, not violent and subversive filth poured relentlessly into their younger son's bedroom every evening.

"Ashik is studying," they would tell their neighbours, "He is going to be a doctor."

In one respect, they had been correct. Ashik had been studying the advertising and propaganda which came onto the screen before and after the violent games. The smartly created videos had offered those who enjoyed playing out the aggressive fantasies in the games the opportunity to experience them in real life. Depictions of the oppression and murder of Muslim brothers and sisters had been shown on the well-designed screenshots, together with clear statements to the effect that these atrocities were the work of the *kuffar,* the unbelievers, in particular those of them who were the modern version of cruel medieval crusaders. The teachings of the *Quran* required Muslims to wage *jihad* on these worthless individuals, who were worse than dogs and had no place in the world of the devout. *Allah* would reward those who carried out his will, said the persuasive male voices in the videos.

Pictures of young, bearded men on horseback carrying assault rifles, black-checked desert *shemaghs* wound round their heads, had appeared on the slickly produced videos. Other young men had been crouched behind ruined walls, dressed in dusty combat gear, holding impressive looking rocket launchers. Anonymous, *burka* clad women had been visible in the background, tending to vegetable patches, carrying water and cooking food. "Join us and live the life of the righteous" the message had urged.

Ashik had joined them. Aged only seventeen, he had somehow slipped the country on a false passport and made his way to Syria. Within months he had been killed in a mortar bomb attack on one of the cities in the faraway country in which he had made his new and dangerous home. Whether he had now become a posthumously rewarded martyr in heaven, his family could only imagine.

The anger and grief of the remaining Malliks had been overwhelming and ultimately destructive. Although devout Muslims, the parents had had no interest in terrorist activities, and had failed to understand the discontent of their younger son with the future which they had mapped out for him in one of the most opportunity-rich cities in the Western world. Granted, the country was full of *kuffar*, and morals were lax, but the Muslim communities were strong and numerous and there was no reason for anyone to be drawn into evil ways whilst surrounded by the protective circle of their faith. Quite apart from the senseless loss of a beloved child, the shame brought on the family by the boy's reckless and disrespectful actions towards his parents had only added to their burden of grief.

The respectable family into which Ranya had been destined to marry, fearing that their future daughter in law might have inherited a family trait of instability and criminal tendencies, had broken off the engagement with little hesitation, reducing the two young people, who had become accustomed to the plans for their union and had in the process come to like each other, to desperation. One evening, they had packed their bags and taken a train to Birmingham, where they had entered into a contract of marriage without the presence of their London relations. There had been little that either family could do to express their disapproval other than to ban the newly-wed couple from ever returning to their homes in the East End, thereby forcing the unfortunate youngsters into poverty and homelessness as they tried to support themselves in their new environment.

Rajesh had remained the one hope for his stricken parents. His mother had scarcely appeared out of doors since the departure of her daughter, although, Rajesh knew, she had wept and begged his father to allow the couple to return home, especially when it had been reported to her that Ranya was now pregnant. Eventually, Rajesh's father had relented to the extent of asking a relative to offer a job to Ranya's husband on condition that the couple remained in Wolverhampton, where the job as a waiter in an Indian restaurant was located.

Rajesh had by then reached the end of his first year as a Law student and had been by that time quite sure that the last thing he wished to be in life was a lawyer. The profession might well be a lucrative one for those who were good at the work, but Rajesh had found his studies tedious and mind-numbing. Rajesh had a lively imagination and a creative mind, neither of which were useful characteristics for the sort of workaday lawyer which he, along with most of his fellow students, was likely to become. His lack of interest had showed through in his coursework marks, which were uniformly mediocre.

Rajesh had been astonished by his younger brother's decision to leave the safety of London for the dangers of Syria. Rajesh too had watched the propaganda videos, but his admiration for them had been limited to the slickness of their production and the means by which they had found their way onto his brother's computer. Rajesh had been well aware that TV and film production was taught in the University where he was studying and had been quite sure that those who had developed the clever videos had probably been trained in their craft in the very establishment in which he was studying. But what had interested Rajesh had been the technical means by which the internet had been used to deliver the propaganda to the very people on whom it would have the greatest impact. The people who knew how to achieve this, the IT experts, the user data collectors, the analysts of internet traffic and usage, had very powerful and influential tools at their disposal.

What little teaching Rajesh had by that time received in the law relating to information technology, social media and data piracy had shown him that the regulation was woefully behind what was actually going on over the internet. It was clearly illegal to access, steal or corrupt computer users' confidential data in order to commit fraud or theft, but the process of detecting the perpetrators of such common crimes was often beyond the capacity of the police, not least because many such activities were orchestrated from outside the country and subject to multiple jurisdictions. These same activities thereby had the potential to become very lucrative for those who carried them out successfully with little risk of being caught. Rajesh had quickly seen that the key to that success lay in a good understanding of cyber security and the systems to which it applied, and most particularly how that security could be overcome and manipulated.

Without telling his parents, Rajesh had abandoned his Law degree and re-enrolled on a degree course in Cyber and Computer Security. The atmosphere at his family home had become unbearable, with the result that he had spent as little time there as possible, telling his benighted parents that he had been studying hard in the University library during the evenings. In reality, he had been in the computer laboratories, learning everything he could about the sort of ethical hacking which was permitted as part of the course which he was now studying. As far as his fellow students knew, Rajesh had his sights set on becoming a computer security consultant. This would have been no surprise, for Rajesh had been very proficient, achieving high marks for his coursework and being generally regarded by his tutors as one of the course's most successful students.

It had been at the start of the final year of the undergraduate course that Rajesh had first come across Watchman. Watchman had been the online name of a cyber security consultant who worked for a company called Katz:i d.o.o. in Rijeka, Croatia. Watchman's services had been widely advertised across Europe by his employer and the company had had many satisfied clients. Rajesh had admired from a distance the work which Watchman did and had eventually contacted him for advice on developing his own IT security skills. Watchman had responded generously and had introduced Rajesh, who now went by his chosen hacker name of Orphan, to an online circle in which professional hackers had honed their skills against each other. The members had been all, ostensibly at least, legitimate cyber security consultants, the so-called white hat hackers who would use their skills to prevent the proliferation of cyber crime, in particular by protecting the IT systems of major corporations from attack and from being held to lucrative ransom to be paid by the victim in Bitcoins.

Rajesh had enjoyed belonging to this exclusive and clever club, which had replaced the family which had rejected him, and had as a result been upset when Watchman had suddenly disappeared from the virtual scene. Learning from online news about the collapse of Katz:i d.o.o. and a subsequent series of denial of service attacks on one of their major clients, Ardua Industrie S.p.A, Rajesh had quickly concluded that Watchman must not only have left the Croatian company but that things had clearly turned very sour between his online idol and the people by whom he had been employed. Rajesh had not wished to lose contact with Watchman, who he had still hoped might give him a job in the future, so had decided to use his own, by then very extensive, skills to find him. Orphan knew enough now of Watchman's style to recognise his hallmarks, or so he had hoped.

Watchman, though, had seemed to have gone quiet and Rajesh had spent several months monitoring various cyber attacks around the world without learning anything useful. Eventually, in the January of his final year as an undergraduate student, he had had a breakthrough, although he did not recognise it as such at first. News had filtered through the hacker community that King Zog, a prolific member of their exclusive band, had been found dead. King Zog, it appeared, had in reality been a member of a vicious criminal family, based in Tirana, who had used his considerable skills to enable the family to perpetrate serious organised crime through the dark web. There had been no computer system which King Zog, whose real-world name had been Egzon Paloka, could not hack, corrupt and destroy, and no purpose too disgusting or evil in which his skills could not be used. The word was that the apparently impregnable King Zog had been taken on by an unknown online assailant and had lost.

Had Rajesh had any real sense of the danger to which he was about to expose himself, he would have stopped his investigations at that point. By then, though, Rajesh had become no stranger to online crime, having designed various scams of his own to defraud unsuspecting members of the public who showed poor knowledge of how to protect themselves online, by making attacks on their bank balances and credit card accounts. The Mallik parents had eventually realised that their son had abandoned his Law course and had thrown him out of their home, thereby relinquishing the last of their dreams for their three children, not wanting to offer a future even for their only grandchild, now growing up amongst strangers in Wolverhampton.

Rajesh had not cared. His criminal activities had by then earned him enough money to live and eat and he had also for some time held down a legitimate job with a computer retailer. As a postgraduate student at the University he had in addition been able to secure employment on the unpopular night time helpdesk shift in the computer laboratories, a role which gave him free rein to use the University's systems as a host for his own online activities. Unbeknown to his parents, he had been sending some of his ill-gotten earnings regularly to his struggling sister and her husband, in generous recognition of the fact that his young brother-in-law had once been his friend and their child deserved the chance of a decent future.

Rajesh had continued to be fascinated by Watchman and had wanted nothing more than to find him. But Watchman had vanished, so Rajesh had set his mind to how he might locate him. His only lead had been the company on which the denial of service and data corruption attack had been launched. It had been called Ardua Industrie S.p.A. Rajesh's researches had revealed it to be an

Italian family owned company, headed by a man called Arturo Ardizzone, which manufactured light aircraft and small helicopters. The company had been a major investor in Katz:i d.o.o. which had developed advanced Artificial Intelligence fly by wire software which had been tested in the Ardua aircraft. Following the demise of Katz:i d.o.o. the work had been taken over by a company in the UK called Astrak Avionics plc, based in Cheltenham. Rajesh had checked to see whether Astrak's IT systems had been protected by Watchman, but the protection in place when he had tried to hack in, had borne none of Watchman's hallmarks.

Rajesh's next step had been to investigate Ardua Industrie S.p.A more carefully. He had discovered that one of their most popular products was a light aircraft called the Altior 10, which had been the subject of a number of air accident reports, all of which had turned out to have been cleverly faked. Perhaps Watchman had posted these fake reports by hacking the legitimate government accident investigation sites on which the reports appeared, Rajesh had speculated. The latest report, which seemed this time to be genuine, had been posted only recently, in November, and had been followed by a televised press conference in which Arturo Ardizzone had himself appeared and had publicly denounced the people from Katz:i d.o.o. as criminals and crooks who had acted to damage his company.

Rajesh had by then been sure that Watchman had been the source of the fake reports. Watchman had had reason to hold a grudge against the Ardua organisation, which had failed to rescue from bankruptcy the company which had employed the clever cyber security consultant. Perhaps, though, thought Rajesh, Watchman had been more than just an employee. Seeking information about the directors of the now defunct Katz:i d.o.o., Rajesh had discovered that it had been owned by a family named Katz, whose historic business before it entered the emergent technology and cyber security world had been in watch and clock making. The younger generation of the family consisted of a brother and sister called Dominik and Lara Katz.

Further research had quickly told Rajesh that Lara Katz had been a junior chess champion and was now part of a research team working in Artificial Intelligence applications at the University of Liverpool. She had previously studied Mathematics at the University of Cambridge. A further reference to a murder, also in Liverpool, of a sex worker going by the same name had been initially discounted as a coincidence by Rajesh until he had read a report indicating that a jockey called Merlin ap Rhys had initially been suspected of having been responsible for the crime. In researching the name Merlin ap Rhys, Rajesh had then discovered that Arturo Ardizzone of Ardua Industrie owned a racehorse called Katseye which was being ridden in prestigious sounding horse races by this very same jockey.

It had been the discovery of the fake University staff IT account in the name of Merlin ap Rhys which had finally made Rajesh absolutely certain that Dominik Katz and Watchman were one and the same person and that the fake account at the University had been created by Watchman himself.

Rajesh's next problem had been to decide exactly what Watchman had intended by creating the apparently spurious account. He was sure that Watchman was aware that the fellow hacker he would know as Orphan was a student at the central London University. Had the account been placed there deliberately to attract Rajesh's attention? Poking carefully at the account, Rakesh had discovered that the virtual traffic which had been routed through the account had been sent via a well-protected link which led to a poorly protected desktop computer in a place with an unpronounceable name the South of France. The last time the route had been used had been in March and had consisted of a further denial of service attack on Ardua Industrie S.p.A.

At this point, Rajesh's detective work had run into a dead end. Watchman had gone completely silent and many months had passed with no apparent activity from him. Rajesh had even dared to try to elicit a response from his idol by placing a little file, which included both the names Watchman and Dominik Katz, on the remote computer in France. If nothing else, it would tell Watchman that, if he were trying to contact Orphan, then Orphan was ready to respond. The file was booby trapped to destroy itself in the event of being accessed online, but no-one had seemed to be interested in it.

There had been nothing obvious left for Rajesh to do but to monitor the Merlin ap Rhys staff account for evidence of further activity. To his frustration, there had been none. For want of anything else to try, he had for a few months followed the riding career of the real Merlin ap Rhys and Katseye, once the horse had resumed racing in the Autumn, learning for the first time in his life a great deal about horse racing, and, rather more interestingly, about online gambling and the systems through which it was carried out. The internet bookmakers had expert levels of cyber security, he had soon discovered, and Rajesh idly wondered whether these organisations might prove to be a source of employment for him, whether legitimate or otherwise, in the future.

Then one day, quite unexpectedly, in December a heavily encrypted message appeared in the Merlin ap Rhys account. It came from a computer somewhere in Somerset and was routed, with changed encryption, to a computer facility in Liverpool. At the same time, another denial of service attack was launched on Ardua Industrie S.p.A.

Rajesh finally understood. The fake account was acting as both a weapon and an automated encryption device. Watchman was surpassing himself.

29

Tegan Colvin had been summarily dismissed from her weekend job at The Charlton Arms. The two police officers had had no difficulty in securing from Tegan the information that she had found a USB stick which had been left behind in the room once occupied by Damon Casey. The police officers had been surprised at their easy success, having initially assumed their task to be a hopeless one. It had seemed highly unlikely to them that the item in question would have been left in the room at The Charlton Arms, given that this was only one of a large number of places which they had understood were also being searched. The chances of someone confessing to having found the missing flash drive after the passage of something like nine months had seemed even more remote.

The police officers had reckoned without Tegan's burning desire to wreak revenge on her abusive brother. Tegan had meekly confessed to finding the flash drive but had quickly informed the officers that she had been unable to return it to the manager of the inn, because it had been forcibly taken from her by her brother, Graham. She had not wanted to get her brother into trouble, Tegan had said tremulously and with downcast eyes, so she had kept quiet about her find. It had not seemed to be anything valuable, she had lied, so she had not thought that it would be missed.

Accompanied by Tegan, the police officers had proceeded to the workshop of Colvin's Garage, where they had been received by the agitated proprietor. Graham face had become ashen beneath the oil streaks from the car he had been servicing when he had seen the officers crossing the outside yard. Their request for the flash drive which he had taken from his sister, who had hovered nervously in the background throughout the proceedings, had come as a considerable relief to him.

"Yeah, it's here," Gray had said, picking up the gold USB stick from his cluttered little desk, "I didn't think it belonged to anyone. I thought Tegan had found it in the pub or somewhere. She said I could have it."

The police officers had come across many liars in their careers and had not believed the information which had been given by either of the siblings. Their concern, however, had been to follow their superior's instructions to recover the flash drive with the minimum fuss, and, rather alarmingly, to call for armed back up should they encounter any resistance. Anyone who had the item in their possession must not suspect that it might contain material which was a matter of national security.

"The owner of the property has reported it missing," the first police officer had told Gray, "I will take it from you now, sir, please."

"No problem," Gray had replied hurriedly, handing the little gold flash drive to the officer, "I didn't think it was worth anything to anyone. It's just a data stick."

"In the light of your and your sister's co-operation," the second police officer had continued, deliberately ponderous, "We shall not be bringing charges in relation to this matter. Please be aware, however, that the physical removal of an object without consent and with the intent of depriving its owner of it permanently is theft, a serious criminal offence."

As the officers had left the workshop to report that the flash drive had been located and retrieved, they had failed to notice Graham Colvin step menacingly towards his cowering sister.

The January rain was still lashing down relentlessly when Frank Stanley's green SUV pulled up once again outside the little whitewashed cottage in the village of Warnock. In deference to the time of day, no whisky was produced, and the three occupants of the sitting room had to be content with coffee. Unlike the coffee which Frank had recently consumed in the drawing room at Sampfield Grange, this coffee was served in a variety of non-matching mugs.

"This is the culprit, then? Where was it?" were George's first questions, as he accepted the gold flash drive from Frank.

"I have a technical report here for you," Frank told him, handing over another, more utilitarian-looking, USB storage device, "But I can give you the gist of what's been happening. Then I need to update you on my meeting just now with James Sampfield."

"These two flash drives," Frank went on, "Are only to be used in a stand-alone computer. The fancy gold drive was recovered from the room at The Charlton Arms once occupied by the man calling himself Damon Casey, who, as we know, was Dominik Katz. One of the service staff found it after he had left and kept it. Her name is Tegan Colvin."

"Tegan Colvin?" repeated Isabella, in surprise, "The sister of Graham Colvin, the garage owner, who supplied Kye with the drugs he used to sell at the point to point meetings? I remember her bringing us tea once when we were waiting at The Charlton Arms for George to contact us from Frossiac. I shouldn't have thought she would know what this thing was."

"I don't know whether she did know what it was," Frank went on, "But in any event, it passed into Graham Colvin's hands and he plugged it into his desktop computer, setting off the messages and the cyberattack on Ardua Industrie that I told you about. When Graham Colvin used the flash drive, he would have seen a short message consisting of some numbers and a single word. This was the unencrypted version of the simple text file which resides on the device. As I told you before, this file was at the same time sent to the fake staff IT account in the University in central London, but in encrypted form, the encryption having been created by a hidden file on the flash drive, which Graham Colvin would not have seen. A second hidden file launched the denial of service attack on Ardua Industrie, using a detonator device residing in Ardua's own systems, which must have been planted by Dominik Katz during the previous attack. The text file was then automatically re-encrypted by the fake staff account in London and sent on to Liverpool, where the recipient should have had the double de-encryption key."

"All this encryption and re-encryption seems a bit pointless," put in George, sounding puzzled, "If the contents of the message were plain for anyone to see on this flash drive. Why not just give or send it physically to the recipient? Surely that would have been more secure and drawn less attention?"

"We think," Frank responded, "That Dominik Katz organised like this precisely in order to draw what he was doing to our attention. What was not intended, though, was that several months should elapse before the flash drive was used. Our guess is that this was all supposed to have happened shortly after the planned atrocity with the aircraft crash at Cheltenham racecourse."

"What did the text file say?" asked Isabella.

"It turned out to be something very simple. Our technical people were hampered for a while by the encryption. Graham Colvin would have had no such difficulty because his version was in plain text. So, he managed to work out what it meant before we did."

Isabella and George stared at Frank in surprise.

"The text was a list of the access codes for the door and padlock to a secure storage facility not far from here by the M5," Frank told them, "The storage had been rented during the week of the Cheltenham Festival by Damon Casey. We think it must have been intended as a secure drop facility for his communication with the people with whom he was negotiating. It was an old-fashioned method of dealing with the passing on of secret information which avoided the risk of passing any detailed information over the internet. Dominik Katz put just enough of his activity online to enable us eventually to find out what he was doing - but not until after the party with whom he was in discussion had got there first."

"Dominik Katz does not sound like the sort of person who would carelessly leave an important flash drive behind in his hotel room," Isabella commented, thoughtfully.

"I agree, Isabella," replied Frank, "I don't think it was a matter of being careless. It was deliberate. It was a way of making sure the origin of the message was obscured but not completely hidden. I think Dominik Katz's intention was to call The Charlton Arms in the evening of the day he went to Cheltenham and ask them if the flash drive had been found. He would have then asked them if they could kindly plug it into their computer and forward by email attachment a copy of the file which was on it. Something along those lines. He would have then told them they could keep the flash drive for themselves as he needed only the data in the file. The process which Graham Colvin unwittingly set in motion would then have happened at that time rather than just recently. If the hotel had not admitted to finding the flash drive, I imagine he would have had some alternative plan up his sleeve."

"So, what has been left in this storage facility?" asked George.

"According to the paperwork which was completed when the secure cabinet was rented to Damon Casey," said Frank, "The contents were "confidential business documents". Indeed, when my people went to the place and opened the cabinet, that is exactly what they found. They photographed the documents and left them in place."

"That means that the people in Liverpool had not been there already, then?" asked Isabella, "Or Graham Colvin even?"

"The people in Liverpool and Graham Colvin may be one and the same," Frank replied, "I told you that the criminal operation in Liverpool includes a well organised operation in drug trafficking and distribution. Kye McMahon is no longer involved, as you know, but Graham Colvin certainly is. He is hoping, I would guess, to set himself up as their dealer in this part of the world. Graham Colvin went into that storage facility and opened the secure cabinet using the codes in the text file. What we don't know is whether he did it on his own account, having somehow worked out what the information in the data file referred to, or whether he did it on the direct instructions of the Liverpool outfit. The storage facility is unstaffed and relies heavily on CCTV and access code technology for its security. We have recordings of Graham Colvin entering and leaving the floor where Damon Casey's secure cabinet is located. What we don't have, though, is a clear vision of what Graham Colvin did when he opened the cabinet. The door obscures his upper body from the camera. There were certainly some paper files in the cabinet when we got there, the contents of which I will come back to, but whether anything else was previously removed by Graham Colvin, we don't know. We do see him walking out of the facility with his jacket folded over his arm – it is possible that there could be something hidden under it or in the pockets. I will save you the trouble of asking me what was in the paper files. Have a look at what is printed on the side of the flash drive."

George held the small item up to the light. It twisted round on its chain as he squinted at it.

"It's in Cyrillic script," he said, "My guess is that it says *prizrak*. I am guessing that the information in the so-called confidential business files is about *prizrak* too, in other words the information Dominik Katz obtained through his APT work on the manufacturing facility. I'm sorry Frank, but this all seems a bit theatrical to me, another hoax, designed to waste our time. What reaction was Dominik Katz trying to provoke from us, anyway?"

"I think he was trying to provoke us into interfering with his negotiations with the Liverpool people," Frank replied, "He wanted us to think that he was handing over the means to manufacture a chemical weapon to a criminal gang. Obviously, we would have tried to stop that happening once we found out."

"Do we have any evidence that the criminal gang has actually received any of this information?" asked Isabella, "Other than possibly sending Graham Colvin to open the storage unit, have they done anything else in response to the encrypted message? Such as trying to reply to it, for instance."

"No, there has been no sign of any response, or not one that our monitor has seen," Frank replied, "But we have an entirely different problem, which I have also come to discuss with you, George. Dominik Katz has a stalker."

"A stalker?" repeated George, "You mean a cyber stalker, I assume? We always thought Dominik Katz was a lone operator. Does this mean that someone other than ourselves has been following what Dominik Katz has been doing?"

"They have been doing more than that," Frank told him, "They have been interfering in it. This stalker was responsible for putting that pointless file onto the Frossiac computer which you and Isabella found there. The one that had Dominik Katz's name on it. It also had another name on it too, did it not?"

"It did," George agreed, "It said Watchman. But that's just Dominik Katz's online identity, I'm guessing. Why would the stalker put such a file on the Vachers' computer?"

"To tell Dominik Katz that he or she knew who Dominik Katz was?" hazarded Isabella, "And also that he or she knew about the Frossiac link? But why? Does this person not know that Dominik Katz is dead?"

"I doubt this individual knows that Dominik Katz is dead," Frank replied, "If the stalker even knew about the unfortunate death of an American tourist near Cheltenham in March, he would not have connected it with the cybermaster known as Watchman. As to why, we think this individual wanted to play a part in what he thought Dominik Katz was doing."

"This stalker, then, whoever he or she is, thinks that Dominik Katz is currently in the process of negotiating with the Liverpool drugs trafficking gang to sell them information to enable the manufacture of *prizrak*," clarified George, "How could the stalker get him or herself involved in that?"

'You haven't asked me how we located this stalker," Frank prompted him, "So I'll tell you. His online name is Orphan, real name Rajesh Mallik, and he too is a member of the cyber security and hacker community. He also has links with international terrorism, in his case, Islamic *jihad*. We have had him on a watch list for some time.

"That means we potentially have two criminal groups wanting to get their hands on the information which Dominik Katz has apparently touted out for sale. One, a Liverpool-based drugs trafficking outfit which is about to expand its sources from South America and its distribution activities within the UK and Europe. The other, Islamic militant forces who are losing the current war and need to step up their terrorist activities in Europe with something more comprehensive and organised than fanatical suicide bombers and individual knife attackers."

"You say that the paper file is still in the storage place," George said, slowly, "So neither group has taken it. Why not?"

"Because there is nothing in it worth taking," Frank replied, "It is just a lot of garbled information which looks impressive. It does include the word **призрак** several times, though. The folder also has a Chinese pictogram on the front cover, just to add the effect."

"Another false trail, then," George said, "The file must have been put there to make whoever found it think that Dominik Katz had something which he didn't actually possess. But you said that Graham Colvin took something from the security cabinet. There must have been something else in there which was recognisable as what they had been discussing."

"I think the clue lies somewhere in the fact that these people are drug traffickers," Frank replied, "If they think Dominik Katz is still around, and what Graham Colvin has collected for them is what they are expecting, it seems likely that they will eventually try to contact Dominik Katz. We will have to wait for that to happen."

"You know what *prizrak* means, don't you?" suddenly asked Isabella, "I looked it up."

"Yes," replied Frank Stanley, "It means the same thing as the Chinese pictogram and it is what Dominik Katz has now become – a ghost. And you, George, are about to create another ghost. We want you to stalk Dominik Katz's stalker."

30

The relentless grey January rain had been suggestive of Noah's Flood, but had at least given Sam, imprisoned alternately in the drawing room or in his study, ample opportunity to give thought to his racing plans. The normal exercise programme for the Sampfield Grange horses had been severely disrupted during the first two weeks of the miserable month by the increasingly poached and bottomless ground on the usually attractive upper gallop, which had turned tackling the jumps and hurdles on the sodden hilltop into a hazardous affair.

The winter sky and its distant sun had been sights of the past. No warmth or brightness had penetrated the cloying thickness of the multiple layers of heavy cloud. Rain had run freely down the track behind the big house, swamping the grassy verges, filling the numerous holes and ruts with muddy water and forming gurgling rivulets on either side of the churned surface of the equine thoroughfare. The lawn outside the drawing room window had lain miserably waterlogged, whilst the rosebushes by the lawn had dripped and bowed sadly under their wet load. Raindrops had drummed a muffled tune on the metal surface of the sundial.

The only member of the yard who had truly revelled in the unpleasant conditions had been Highlander Park. On Sam's instructions, Isabella Hall had entered the young horse in a Novices' Hurdle event at Taunton racecourse on a date in the middle of the month, a race in which Kye would ride. Sam had acceded to an odd request from Frank Stanley, who had called in, unexpectedly as usual, one morning in the previous week, that Kye should not be booked to ride at the Cheltenham meeting at the end of the month. Kye and Jackie should instead both act as drivers and grooms that day, if Sam would be so kind as to agree to the request.

Curlew Landings was to be aimed at the challenging Kingwell Hurdle at Wincanton in February once again. Sam had secured the agreement of Ranulph Dicks that Travis would be made available to accompany his former charge to the important race on that day. Curlew's dead heat with Southern Cross for first place at Kempton Park had been a sharp reminder that it would be tough for the horse to defend his Cheltenham title as Champion Hurdler at the Festival in March.

Indian Rocks had been entered into a point to point race, where he would be ridden once again by Sadie, at Ashfordleigh Downs on the weekend following.

Katseye, it had been agreed with Arturo Ardizzone through the usual efficient intermediary of Meredith Crosland, would be entered in a Novices' Chase at the end of January Cheltenham meeting. There had therefore been little difficulty in accommodating Frank Stanley's request concerning the driving arrangements that day. Kye, it had appeared, was required to identify to the police someone associated with his former racing yard in Cheshire and Frank had wanted to secure Kye's full attention on the task that day.

The brief explanation which Frank, in the presence of the two young stable staff, had given Sam for the arrangement had reminded Sam how little he really knew about the work of his former schoolfriend and teenage lover. As if reading Sam's thoughts, Frank had remained in the drawing room with Sam for over an hour after Kye and Jackie had left them, and Sam was still trying to come to terms with what Frank had told him during that time. Sam had promised himself that he would think more carefully about the information Frank had imparted once he had his own plans in order.

Tabikat was still scheduled to run in the Gold Cup race at the Cheltenham Festival in March. Sam had told the eager members of the racing press at Kempton Park on Boxing Day that Tabikat would not be seen again on any racecourse until that day, but this decision required careful thought to be given to a programme of preparation for the horse. He did not want to run the risk of losing the Gold Cup, and hence the Triple Crown, through lack of race fitness. Sam had wanted to discuss the requirements with Merlin, but the sidelining of the jockey with concussion during the first two weeks of January, not to mention the poor ground which had restricted all the horses' training schedules, had meant that Merlin could not yet be involved.

Sam and Gilbert had been horrified to hear on the radio of the Range Rover of the attack on the jockey who had just won the King George VI Chase with Tabikat. The concussive force of the collision of Merlin's head with a parked vehicle had succeeded in creating the very problem which Merlin had so dexterously avoided following the incident with Curlew Landings at Cheltenham racecourse. On this occasion, the fact that Merlin had been knocked unconscious was a matter of official record in the log of the ambulance paramedics who had been called to the car park, whilst the diagnosis of severe concussion had later been made formally by a doctor at the West Middlesex University Hospital. Fortunately, it had been confirmed, the scan of Merlin's head had revealed no fractures nor any obvious brain damage. The fact that the injury had occurred in a public place rather than on the racecourse itself had, though, made no difference to the rules of the BHA Medical Department on Merlin's fitness or otherwise to ride.

Jenna Roberts had provided a statement to the police but had told them little of use to the identification of the attacker. Jenna had said that she had been walking with Merlin to his car in the dark of the late afternoon when the unknown assailant had ambushed them and had targeted Merlin with a vicious punch to the face which had caused him to fall and hit his unprotected head against a nearby vehicle. Merlin himself had had no memory of the event and had recalled only waking up in the ambulance with a throbbing pain in his head and vomiting into a cardboard bowl held out for him by a young male paramedic.

Merlin's initial reaction to his confusing situation had been that he and Tabikat had come to grief at one of the Kempton Park fences during the big race, so his first question had been about the welfare of the precious horse.

"Sadie'll never forgive me if anythin's 'appened to 'im," he had mumbled, to the mystification of the green-uniformed paramedic, who, having found out his name from Jenna, had told him firmly, "Don't try to talk, Merlin, we're looking after you now."

Merlin had ignored the instruction, asking more urgently, "Is Tabikat all right? Tell Sadie to call me," before falling back into a pain-filled and brain-whirling doze.

Once Merlin had been brought home to Chepstow the following morning, he had been delivered into the care of his sister. Rhian had been nervous about allowing Merlin to sleep alone in his attic bedroom with its steep stairs and had insisted that he stay at her home for the first two days. Merlin had tried to protest but both his balance and voice had been shaky, and he had eventually given in to his sister's fiercely expressed instructions. Rhian herself, not used to seeing her tough brother so incapacitated, had been seriously worried.

"Whyever did 'e break up with that nice girl who used to think so much of 'im?" Rhian lamented to Thomas, her stoic husband, "She would have looked after 'im. Not like that Roberts girl, 'oo's only out for 'erself. She's after takin' 'is rides, she is. Wouldn' surprise me if she 'adn' arranged this muggin' 'erself."

Jackson Argyrides, Merlin's agent, having ascertained that Merlin would be out of action for at least a fortnight, at which time he would need to undergo a further medical assessment, had ensured that all Merlin's bookings for the first two weeks of January had been cancelled. Although Merlin had not been due to ride for Sampfield Grange during that period, Jackson had nevertheless spoken to Isabella Hall to confirm that he would let her know when Merlin would be bookable once again. Isabella had asked for the good wishes of everyone at the yard to be passed to Merlin.

Merlin's recovery had progressed rapidly once the initial nausea and dizziness had abated. He had had a spectacular black eye and big lump on the side of his head where his skull had made heavy contact with a parked van. Otherwise, apart from feeling very tired, the effects of the concussion itself had mostly left him after a few days of enforced rest. He had soon realised that his initial impression that his injury had happened in the course of a race had been incorrect, not least because of the buzzing and ill-informed speculation on social media about the reason for the attack and the number of text messages and tweets which had made their way onto the screen of his mobile phone. Looking at the phone for any length of time had worsened his headache during the first few days, so he had restricted his replies to those messages he had deemed the most important and had kept his own texts deliberately short. He had avoided answering phone calls at all as he had not trusted his voice to remain steady as he spoke.

Sadie's text message had been one of the few which he had answered. There had been no direct enquiry after his wellbeing from Jenna Roberts, although Jenna's sister Hafren had called Rhian to let her know that Jenna planned to call in at Merlin's house on her way home from the New Year's Day meeting at Cheltenham.

Jenna's visit had been devastatingly brief. She had perched on the edge of an armchair in Merlin's living room, fresh from driving back home from a race meeting. After enquiring after Merlin's welfare, Jenna had suddenly said, "And I've come to tell you, Merlin, that we can't see each other anymore."

"That's a bit sudden, isn' it?" Merlin had replied, stung by the abruptness of the communication, and abandoning the tentative plan he had made to ask Jenna to stay the night, "What's made you decide that, then, Jen? I thought we were doin' all right together?"

"We are, well, we were," the other jockey had replied, looking uncomfortable, "But it's just not possible, Merlin. I don't want you getting hurt."

"The sex isn' that crazy," Merlin had tried to joke, as his injured head had throbbed and pounded, "I didn' get this black eye from you, Jen."

Jenna had given him a small smile.

"The sex has been great, Merlin," she had told him, earnestly, "I like you too. But that isn't what I meant. I can't explain. Just accept it. Please."

Merlin, more annoyed than upset, had let his now former squeeze out of the panelled front door and had flopped back into one of the armchairs in the small living room wondering what the hell was going on with his life. He had not guessed that the steel-willed Jenna Roberts had been crying like a child as she had driven herself home.

In mid January, the clouds parted and an exhausted sun pushed its way back into the world. Creatures both animal and human poked their tentative heads outside and decided it was now safe to emerge. Along with the rest of the sodden local community, the orderly world of Sampfield Grange swung back into action. For those who lived in the lower lying areas of the Somerset Levels, the recovery process would be slower, but the well-drained hills above the Sampfield yard quickly resumed their normal attractive demeanour and were soon decorated with their customary annual clumps of hopeful white snowdrops.

Kye and Highlander Park came a close second in their Novices' Hurdle race at Taunton. Much to the relief of Sam, Ranulph Dicks and a number of other trainers who wished to make use of his services during the last two weeks of January, Merlin ap Rhys's black eye faded to its normal colour and he was passed by the BHA as fit to ride in races once again. The police had as yet been unable to identify the assailant who had caused the disruption to Merlin's career and it had been generally assumed that the attacker was either a chance mugger or a disgruntled punter who had bet against Tabikat or Curlew Landings, or both, on that day. Lighting and security arrangements in the car park at Kempton Park racecourse had been duly reviewed.

The one person who had a different view as to the identity of Merlin's attacker was Sadie. Sadie's solitary musings following the conversation in the Sampfield Grange kitchen on the day of Mr Stanley's unexpected visit had soon brought to mind the unknown man who had been watching her and Tabikat near the pre-parade area at Kempton Park.

Kye, Jackie and the work riders were busy hosing down and sweeping the stone surface of the yard, the resultant puddles weakly reflecting a washed out blue and hectic cloud-spattered sky, when Sadie, sitting alone in the chilly tack room, took out her mobile phone for the umpteenth time to look at her selfie with Tabikat, the suspicious stranger clearly visible in the background. Merlin was due at Sampfield Grange later in the morning and Sadie had already resolved to show him the picture and to ask whether Merlin recognised the man as his assailant that day. In the meantime, she reminded herself, as she slipped the phone back into the pocket of her green fleece jacket, she should help Isabella Hall to update the information in the horse training database following the string's now resumed regular exercise programme.

Creating the fictitious training record for the absent Katalyst had proved to be quite amusing at first, but Sadie had found it difficult to understand the purpose of the strange project. Katalyst, as far as she knew, was still in Ireland, being trained either by the Meaghans, or perhaps by Niall Carter, who, so she had been told by Merlin during their difficult car journey from Cardiff in October, had claimed to own the colt. Although Mr Sampfield was now officially registered as Katalyst's owner and Sadie had been expecting the horse to arrive at Sampfield Grange at any time during January, a series of obstacles appeared to have arisen which had delayed the delivery of the presumably expensive equine purchase. Sadie had been secretly relieved, fearing that the arrival of the coveted colt might induce a visit from either Sir Andrew or the now recovered Luke Cunningham. But no-one had explained why a fictitious record for Katalyst had to be created on the computer system at Sampfield Grange.

Unbeknown to Sadie, her employer was sitting rather more comfortably in his warm study, debating whether to call Eoghan Foley to discuss the plans for Katalyst. Although Sam was unaware of the fanciful information being created on the yard computer, the activity surrounding Katalyst remained a mystery to him as much as to Sadie. Sam had had no difficulty in accepting the proposals that the colt should remain in Ireland for the present if this assisted Eoghan's mysterious plans, but he had yet to understand the purpose of his own involvement as the horse's apparent owner.

Sam was about to reach for the handset of the telephone on the desk, when the old-fashioned device suddenly emitted its customary shrill ring. Normally Sam would have allowed the ever-present Lewis to answer the call from the extension in the hall, but Sam's hand was already so near the receiver that he instinctively picked it up.

"James Sampfield," he said curtly into the mouthpiece.

"James? That you?" boomed a familiar Australian voice through the earpiece, adding superfluously, "Teddy here. Sorry to call so late but I wanted to get you soonest."

"Good day to you, Teddy. It's only morning here," Sam reminded his cousin, whilst his stomach lurched in reaction to the urgent tone of Teddy's voice on the phone, "Is something wrong? Is mother well?"

"Fact is, James," Teddy began, sounding as if he was trying to avoid coming to the point, "It's bad news."

There was a scuffling sound at the other end of the line, and Sam heard Tessa's voice say, "Let me speak to him, Teddy."

Tessa, once on the line, was prompt and compassionate with her explanation. Sam's mother, she said, had gone walkabout during the night. Raldi, normally a good sleeper, had never done such a thing before, so no-one had taken any precautions to prevent her from having free run of the remotely located property and its extensive surroundings. The former Australian team event rider, as the news media subsequently described her, and widow of respected English racehorse trainer Richard Sampfield Peveril, had had no difficulty in accessing the stables in which the stock horses had been bedded down for the night. Notwithstanding the arthritis in her spine and the associated weakness of her hands,

Raldi had selected one of the horses, tacked it up, and ridden out into the open outback of the cattle station. The horse had returned alone during the early light of morning. Finding Raldi herself had proved more difficult, but she had eventually been discovered that afternoon, lying on her face in a dried-up stream bed close to a dirt road, where her lifeless shape had been spotted by a passing truck driver.

"Aunt Raldi didn't suffer, James," Tessa assured Sam, more than once, whilst he sat in stunned silence as the weak and scattered light of the English January day drifted quietly over his polished desk, "The doc said she'd broken her neck when she came off the horse. Her death would have been instantaneous. God knows what she was doing. Thought she was out there riding a cross country stage again, I shouldn't wonder."

Later, Sam could not remember the rest of their conversation. But within a few minutes, he had summoned Lewis, correctly assuming that the household stickybeak, as Teddy had once called him, would not be far away from the extension of the house telephone located in the wide hallway.

"I need to go to Brisbane as soon as possible, Lewis," was all that Sam said.

A twenty-four hour journey to the other side of the world would at least give him the time to grapple with the implications of what Frank Stanley had told him on that rainy day two weeks ago.

31

The damp streets of the historic Northern Irish town of Fermagarrick were lined with a variety of drab vehicles when the young man known in those days only as Gerry drove a dark blue Ford Escort slowly along Market Street, the rain-drizzled thoroughfare stretching long and straight ahead of him. The barely functional car heater blew uselessly onto the inside of the nicotine stained windscreen, scarcely clearing the condensation which continued to form as the wet air cooled the outer surface of the glass.

It was like driving through a cloud, thought Gerry, or at least how he imagined driving through a cloud would feel. When he was a boy, he had lived in green countryside, where clean streams and small rivers had twisted through shallow valleys and clouds had clung onto the low hilltops until a breeze from a not too distant ocean had picked them up and moved them onwards into the heart of Ireland. Gerry had walked, run, and ridden ponies through those whispering ghostlike presences, which had disappeared as soon as they were approached, just like the legendary pots of gold at the end of the frequent rainbows. That was before his parents had died and his remaining family had been scattered abroad like seeds to grow into their own place in the world.

Today the clouds stayed where they were, pressing down on the car exhaust polluted urban street, hovering on the windscreen, from which the wipers could scarcely clear the moisture away before it returned, glue-like, to obscure Gerry's sharp vision. Nevertheless, Gerry was sure that his pot of gold existed somewhere in the early April dampness and that his purpose in being in this town today would be a step towards finding it. A vision of a galloping black horse flitted across his inner eye and then was gone.

The car he was driving was not his own. It had been brought to him, complete with fake number plates, having been driven by another driver using different plates through the guarded border crossing ten miles away. The components of the bomb had been brought to the car through three separate routes, carefully disguised within farm machinery. The block of plastic explosive had been hidden in a lined case in the centre of a haybale. More technically-minded people than Gerry had assembled the improvised device which would turn an unremarkable little vehicle into a lethal weapon when it exploded into a fireball of flying shrapnel and ear-splitting noise and blast pressure, killing those closest to it as well as maiming and damaging anyone and anything within a far wider range.

Gerry had no intention of being anywhere nearby when the bomb was detonated. He had been taught how to set the timing device which would inexorably count down to the moment of completion of the electrical circuit connected through the car battery. The explosive load itself was concealed in a small brown suitcase located under the front seat of the passenger side of the car. Black trailing wires had been neatly run under the rubber mat of the same colour on the floor into the engine compartment. It was a professional job.

The town of Fermagarrick had been chosen not for its attractive location by Lough Far, nor for its famous annual festival and ancient stone castle with its magical legends, but for the fact that a division of a British Army regiment was stationed there. Illicit intelligence on the plans and movements of the regiment had recently been good, thanks to the efforts of local young women, secret republican sympathisers, who had obtained all kinds of useful information from the bored British soldiers through the old fashioned and carefully combined expedients of sex and drink. In theory, these local girls should have been loyal to the official preference of their birthplace to remain part of the United Kingdom rather than to become part of the republic of Ireland, but the loyalties of youth are influenced in mysterious ways, not least by the excitement of doing something illegal and dangerous which would upset the authorities, whomever they might happen to be. The consequences for these young women would be serious if their activities were ever to be exposed, most especially those few who had re-crossed the line into becoming double agents and informers. They would have no friends on either side of the deep-rooted political and military stand-off and could expect to be tortured and killed if it suited any malicious individual to expose them. It was all part of the only glamour in this otherwise sleepy town.

Gerry could understand the girls' motivation for seeking excitement. Although he came from the rural South, his life too had hitherto been hard, tedious and purposeless. The theatrical escapism and dangerous thrill of being a murderous bomber, whatever the cause, was intoxicating. The man who had sought to persuade Gerry to join his side in the viciously prosecuted struggle had not had to try very hard.

The carefully nurtured intelligence had told the faceless men who handled the activities of the bored young people that visitors were expected that day to the garrison building in Fermagarrick. A minor royal and a member of the British Parliament were due to attend the well-guarded building to show support and bolster the morale of the equally bored young soldiers living there. The event was to take place in the greatest secrecy, the two VIPs with their accompanying officers and staff being set to arrive in a small cavalcade of unmarked, albeit reinforced, vehicles. By the time they appeared in the town, it would be too late for any ill-wisher to set a trap for them. The route, the date and time of arrival had been changed several times, intending to confuse any informer who had slipped through the mesh of the British Army intelligence net. The security presence around the town would be unobtrusive. There would be no clearing of roads nor cordoning off of parking areas, both of which might draw attention to the fact that something unusual was happening. Such patrols as were mounted would be done by men in civvies or made to look like routine exercises for those in uniform.

Had the intention been to kill the minor royal and the politician, these precautions might well have achieved the objective of protecting them from harm. But these individuals were not the target of Gerry's handlers. The target was the town itself. The detonation of a lethal car bomb on the date when the important visitors were due to congratulate the occupants of the garrison, a fact which would be widely publicised after the event, was designed to demonstrate the dangers of having a division of the Fermagarrick Infantry Brigade in their midst, as well as signalling brutally to the British Army itself that its own security that day had been comprehensively compromised and to suggest that the civilian casualties were a consequence of its own failure and weakness.

Gerry cruised casually along the crowded street looking for somewhere to park the Ford Escort. The chosen spot had to be near the cobbled town centre, alive with shoppers and commercial activities, and near to the sloping road which led from the central square up to the military establishment. He was in luck. A brown Renault 16 manoeuvred laboriously out of a space by the kerb as the Escort approached. It was the work of seconds for Gerry to slot the smaller vehicle into the vacated spot. The space was outside the public library, its glass-paned and wooden-framed doors opening and closing as members of the Fermagarrick populace pushed their way in and out of the grey stone civic building. There was no inkling of the chaos to come.

A surprisingly bright sun was now flickering in and out of the quickly thinning clouds when Gerry reached down for the little timer connected to the hidden wires. The device itself had been hidden inside a packet now empty of its cigarettes, an item which would appear to anyone peering through the car window to have been dropped carelessly on the floor. There was a faint click as Gerry pushed across the metal tab to start the internal clock. He had one hour. There was no need to rush.

Gerry's next instructions were simple. After leaving the car and setting the timer, he was to walk to the far side of the busy central square and wait at the bus stop outside the Northern Bank. There he would be picked up and driven to Belfast, where a legitimate and permanent job with a haulage company awaited him.

The planned arrangements worked perfectly in all but one respect. About quarter of an hour after Gerry had left the town and was riding towards Belfast in the passenger seat of an electrician's van, someone unknown telephoned the local branch of the Samaritans with a warning of the presence of the bomb. The Samaritans at once called the police. The visit of the minor royal and the member of the UK Parliament, who were about to enter the town, was immediately cancelled. The people in the streets around the central square of Fermagarrick were hastily evacuated. The haste was not, though, enough to save everyone. The warning had come too late and was expressed in terms too vague for the frantic police and soldiers to locate the lethal blue Ford Escort before the bomb was detonated by the mercilessly counting timer.

Two police officers, three soldiers and six users of the town library were killed outright. Countless other passers-by and even those in nearby streets were injured, some with subsequently fatal consequences, their injuries including loss of limbs, spinal damage resulting in paralysis, multiple broken bones, and permanent damage to eyes and other vulnerable organs. Metal shrapnel from what was once the Escort caused traumatic penetrative injury to human bodies and property alike. Nearby cars, street furniture, paving stones, drain covers and trees were all ripped from their places along the street and flung into the air, raining down again in thousands of pieces onto the road surface. The car at the centre of the blast became unrecognisable under a pile of jumbled rubble comprising stones, bricks, rooftiles, wooden beams, glass and concrete, not to mention human limbs separated from their bodies. The doors of the library were amongst the many which were blasted from their hinges and flung to the other end of the building into the terrified faces of two of the staff employed there.

The work of the explosion was not finished. The shock of the blast wave travelled outwards, faster than the speed of sound, streaking along the nearby streets, the vacuum created in its wake sucking out windows and doors, dragging fleeing pedestrians to the ground, injuring lungs, bursting eardrums, shaking and echoing through the town with a sonic boom like that created by the famous Anglo-French Concorde. Not that any of the Fermagarrick citizens could have heard it. Those who were not dead or unconscious had been rendered stone deaf.

The passage of the shock wave was followed by a silence, punctuated only by the pathetic ringing of alarm bells from ruined business premises, the gushing of water from burst water mains, and the slow clatter of late falling debris. For many minutes, no-one moved. Some would never move again. Others would move in their own time, damaged forever both in mind and body. Slowly, cautiously, the emergency response began, as the town of Fermagarrick started to realise just what had happened on that ordinary April morning.

By the time the ambulances and fire engines were streaking frantically towards the stricken town from all over the province and from both sides of the disputed border, Gerry was sitting in a betting shop in the centre of Belfast listening to the racing commentary from Navan. The electrician had dropped his youthful passenger off outside a pub in the now sunlit Falls Road and had left him there without a word of farewell. Gerry now had the afternoon to himself.

A radio in the corner of the dingy shop was chattering away as Gerry studied the racing papers which were pinned on the shop walls. He had a special interest in one of the races due to be run at Navan racecourse, eighty-five miles to the South. The voice on the radio barely penetrated Gerry's consciousness, as it told of a massive car bomb having exploded in the market town of Fermagarrick. At least ten people had been killed and many others injured. A warning had been telephoned but it had not included the known codeword and had in any case come too late. No-one had yet claimed responsibility for planting the lethal device.

The only part of the radio news report which was news to Gerry was that there had been a warning. He filed the information away for future reference and concentrated instead on the racing commentary which was coming from the crackling fabric-fronted tannoy mounted in its black plastic case in the upper corner of the smoke-filled room. Other punters perched on the wooden stools or leaned against the counter as the disembodied voice with its Dublin accent gabbled the information about the current race into the foetid air.

"And they're off. There are ten of them in contention as they approach the bend. First to show is Langham Light, ridden by

Genie Foley, and trained by Cormac Meagan. They're followed by ….."

Gerry tuned out the quickfire recitation of the remaining horses in the field. He was interested only in Langham Light, or, more accurately, in Langham Light's star jockey, Eoghan Foley.

What happened in the first race at Navan that afternoon made headlines in the racing papers, although not for the right reasons. Rounding the first bend in the lead on the second circuit and approaching an open ditch, Langham Light failed to take off at the fence. The horse crashed through the top of the birch and landed awkwardly on its side. Eoghan was catapulted from the saddle and landed with his full weight on his left knee. As he tried to roll away, another horse came over the fence, and, in its efforts to avoid the stricken Langham Light, stepped with full force on Eoghan's already injured knee and shattered the bones to pieces. Eoghan was left screaming in agony on the ground. He had effectively been kneecapped and would never ride in a race again.

Meanwhile, a sniper's bullet buried itself harmlessly in the ground in the centre of the course.

Gerry stayed in the betting shop until it closed, but the man he was supposed to meet in the nearby pub that evening never arrived. It was the second betrayal of the day.

Over the ensuing desperate years, and notwithstanding extensive and lengthy police enquiries, those responsible for the evil of the Fermagarrick bombing had not been brought to justice for their crimes. In total, sixteen people had been either killed on the spot or had died from their injuries in, or on the way to, hospital. Over fifty more people had been injured, some of them left with serious disabilities as a result, and even more had suffered trauma and flashback episodes. The one small ray of light in the impenetrable darkness of the horror was the knowledge that the warning which had been belatedly telephoned to the office of the Fermagarrick Samaritans had resulted in fewer deaths and injuries than might otherwise have been the case, because a partial evacuation of the town centre had at least been achieved in the short time available before the bomb had been triggered.

A group of determined families who had lost loved ones in the atrocity had later attempted to bring private prosecutions against a number of people whom enquiries suggested had been involved in the incident, but with little success. An official enquiry by a distinguished judge had identified and criticised many failings in the use of the intelligence held by the police and the British military, but the judicial castigation of those who should have protected them had been of no help to the shattered families, nor had it done anything to mitigate the legacy of grief and trauma which they had been forever condemned to share.

The poorly deployed police and military intelligence had identified an established supply line for arms and drugs which had stretched back to the port of Cork and into the South of Spain and North Africa. With the help of itinerant travellers, this line had snaked its hidden way around the Irish countryside until it had reached the North. Shortly after the day of the explosion, a number of people had been arrested, including one Callan Sullivan, now deceased, who had controlled that part of the smuggling operation which had run through a town called Gleannglas. In detaining Callan Sullivan, action by the authorities on their intelligence, the learned judge had noted disparagingly, had been forced by another, apparently unrelated, incident. Callan Sullivan had been arrested by the Gleannglas *garda* on suspicion of the murder of his nephew, a local farmer called Enda Foley, ostensibly in a personal dispute over the refusal by Enda's younger brother, jump jockey Eoghan Foley, to stop horses for money in races.

Callan Sullivan's trial could not be conducted in public for reasons of national security and it had been equally unclear what information Callan Sullivan had been apparently able to offer at the trial in order to obtain a reduced sentence for his nephew's murder. The Fermagarrick families remained, even to the present day, convinced that this agreement with Callan Sullivan had cheated them of their chance of justice, as there was no doubt that the components of the bomb had been delivered through the network of which Callan Sullivan had been part. The network itself had at last been dismantled, or had gone to ground, perhaps as part of the bargaining that Callan Sullivan had been able to do on his own behalf. The setter of the car bomb had never been identified or caught.

More than thirty years later, the man once known only as Gerry had become the owner of a successful road haulage business operating out of Liverpool and Belfast. His fleet of lorries was liveried in the same red and black colours as his numerous racehorses. Gerry had never discovered who had telephoned the warning which had reduced the impact of the devastating bomb which he had planted on that April day in Fermagarrick. Nor did he know who had killed the sniper whose job it had been to shoot Eoghan Foley in the head on the same afternoon and who had been supposed to join him to celebrate in the pub in the Falls Road in the evening.

Gerry had been willing to wait to take his revenge on these traitors – or perhaps it was one and the same traitor - an opportunity which he was sure would present itself eventually, even after the passage of years. Gerry knew that many of the people who had been enmeshed in the two very different crimes committed on that sunny day would be still alive, now living respectable existences, the knowledge of the events for which they had been responsible carefully boxed up in their secret souls like a vicious and festering tumour, a scar on the soul which the person who had harboured it would at some inevitable time in the future no longer be able to hide. Deathbed confessions, the inability to take the secret with them to the grave, or a chance utterance which would arouse suspicion, one of these would trip them up eventually.

Perhaps unremarkably, it did not occur to Gerry that the people he thought of as traitors might themselves have considered their long ago actions to have been justified and that the guilt with which they still lived was not of the creeping and poisonous type, but was instead a guilt that they had not been able to do more to save the traumatised Fermagarrick families whose lives had been so ruthlessly blighted and the ambitious young jockey whose career had been destroyed.

After building the businesses, the one successful and legitimate and the others equally successful but criminal, which had made him wealthy, Gerry's remaining goal was now to recover what belonged to him, which was possession of the bloodline of the stallion which had been pledged to him as payment over thirty years ago. For this too, he had waited several years, until there came into the world the most valuable and promising of the carefully nurtured progeny of this animal. This foal was a mare carrying ancient Barb and Arabian blood, infused more recently with modern Andalucian lines, and lately crossed with illegally sourced Irish thoroughbred mares officially recorded as having died during foaling. The horse breeding activity which had produced Gerry's promised reward had been an interesting sideline for the Callan Sullivan smuggling operation, but it had been the centre of Gerry's interest, and had led to his request for one of the progeny of El Heredero de Sevilla as part of the reward for his evil work.

The proud stallion himself had been powerful, dark and imperious and had lived like a farmer's horse in a small town in County Kerry called Monamar. But those who rode and schooled him on the remote rural property were not the farmer's sons. They were Andalucian *gitanos* who returned to the area every year and who had been responsible for the illegal introduction of the genes of El Heredero de Sevilla into the Irish thoroughbred stock. The mares serviced by El Heredero had been properly registered in the Irish Stud book and came mostly from the prestigious established stud called Mallows not far from Gleannglas. But the mares did not live there. Some were recorded as deceased and those which were alive were shown as being the property of a horse dealership run by a family called Cassidy in Gleannglas.

Gerry had had high hopes for the eventual achievement of his dream to breed a new thoroughbred line for himself when the filly known as Maria la Herederita de Sevilla, or, at her Irish home, as Maire, was foaled. The fact of Maire's existence was, as usual, protected through her apparent ownership by a quiet farming family in Monamar. Later, she would be entered into the books of Cassidy's horse dealership, described as a common riding horse, at which point she was to be passed into the ownership of Gerry. But someone had not kept their part of the bargain.

Although the private prosecutions brought many years after the Fermagarrick bombing did not achieve their objective of bringing to justice those who had built and planted the bomb, these actions and the judicial enquiry which followed eventually brought to a halt, mainly through fear of discovery, that part of the smuggling activity which had been operated by the Andalucian travellers though Cork and Monamar. In consequence, the equine breeding operation at Monamar also came to a halt and Maire was sold on quite legitimately at the age of six years to Cassidy's. There, Oisin Cassidy, recognising her quality, although not completely understanding its origins, put the mare in foal to Alakazam, an Irish stallion standing at the nearby Mallows stud where Oisin had once worked, and which was now run by Ronan Brody, the son of the previous owner.

Oisin had then no idea that anyone would want to claim the mare after several years of inactivity by the illicit horse breeding operation. The farm and its paddocks and pastureland at Monamar were soon sold to a genuine local farmer and no horses of any type were ever kept there again. The subsequent demise of Oisin's chaotic business through bankruptcy led him to give the pregnant mare as a gift to Eoghan Foley and Caitlin Kennelly, Oisin knowing that Eoghan was the only man of his acquaintance who could be trusted to see Maire's potential.

Gerry did not know the details of this chain of events, but he could readily guess at most of them. Gerry did not care about the people involved, but he did care about the mare Maria la Herederita. Tracking down Oisin Cassidy after the latter had abandoned his Gleannglas business and subsequent employment at Mallows stud had proved easy enough. A terrified Oisin had told Gerry's persuasive messenger that the mare of which Gerry claimed to be the rightful owner had been sent to trainer Brendan Meaghan in County Meath. Frustratingly, Brendan Meaghan, when approached, had denied all knowledge of the mare, standing surprisingly firm against the threats from Gerry's representative. Gerry had had the premises burnt down in an act of retaliation, but it had made no difference. Maria la Herederita de Sevilla was gone.

Over the ensuing sixteen years, Gerry had attempted to realise his dream as the owner of top racehorses by buying the best of those available using the wealth which his businesses brought him. Ruthless and cold-hearted, the qualities which had marked him out as the ideal candidate to commit mass murder, he selected and discarded horses and trainers alike based entirely on the success they brought him. Gerry soon became the most consistent of Cathal's clients.

But none of the expensively and legitimately bred racehorses which he had acquired in recent years had brought him the success he craved, not even with the undetectable illegal dope sourced from the Far East now coursing in the veins of some of them.

Because Gerry bought his horses through the established auction houses and bloodstock agents, he almost missed the vital clues which would at last reveal to him what had happened to the mare who had slipped through his fingers. Gerry became in due course the owner of a steeplechaser called Less Than Ross which achieved considerable success, including second place in both the Cheltenham Gold Cup and the Punchestown Gold Cup. Gerry had been confident that Less Than Ross would win the latter race, given that the Cheltenham winner, Macalantern, was not running that day. He had not been pleased to note that Tabikat, the handsome horse which had snatched the Punchestown Gold Cup from his grasp, was the runner who had achieved third place in the big Cheltenham race. Gerry had been even more displeased to discover that Tabikat was trained by Brendan Meaghan, having previously been for a short time with another, somewhat obscure, trainer in England.

Standing in the second place spot at Punchestown, Gerry watched the connections of Tabikat as they assembled themselves around their victorious and highly striking horse. The race card told him that the owners were an organisation called Levy Brothers International, a name which meant nothing to Gerry at the time, but it was the name of the breeder which gave Gerry his first jolt of recognition. The breeder's name was listed as E Foley. As far as Gerry could see, as he observed the excited group, the E Foley who had survived the shot from the sniper all those years ago was not amongst the connections. They mostly looked like young business people invited along for a day out at their employer's expense, so maybe the name was merely a coincidence, Gerry thought at first.

One member of Tabikat's party, though, caught Gerry's attention. An older woman, who had been holding Brendan Meaghan's arm during the race, looked vaguely familiar, although Gerry was not sure why this should be. Gerry generally took little interest in women, except as a source of sexual satisfaction, as his two discarded wives and numerous casual mistresses and paid escorts could testify, so he could see no reason why he should know this relatively unattractive woman. Probably she was the trainer's wife, Gerry decided, as he followed his sweating horse out of the parade ring, leaving the victors to their enthusiastic celebrations.

From that day forward, Gerry followed Tabikat's career, which was soon being shadowed by the horse's younger half-brother, Katseye. Researching the two horses' bloodline, he quickly discovered that they were the first and second produce of a mare called Little Kitty Cat, who had three wins and three second places in races under Rules, and was owned by a little known breeder called Eoghan Foley of *Feirm Enda* in County Kerry. There was no doubt now in Gerry's mind that E Foley and Genie Foley, the jockey whose career had ended in the mud of Navan racecourse, were one and the same person. No sire was listed for Little Kitty Cat, but her dam was recorded as being called Kat's Gift, a mare of little account with no known parentage. Both Tabikat and Katseye had top class pedigrees on their respective sires' sides, the stallions which had produced them, Tabloid News and Night Vision, being both from Mallows stud.

Furthermore, Gerry' enquiries told him, neither of the two geldings had ever come up for public sale. Tabikat had been owned by a family by the name of Stonehouse prior to his acquisition by the Levy Brothers International bank. Katseye had belonged to a family called Crosland who appeared to have sold him on to Arturo

Ardizzone, the owner of an aircraft company based in Milan. Both geldings had started their lives as colts at Enda's Farm.

Watching the continuing success of Tabikat, including the recent winning of the Cheltenham Gold Cup, against his own runner Less Than Ross, Gerry knew that he had at last found the family of Maria la Herederita de Sevilla. Oisin Cassidy had not given Maire to Brendan Meaghan at all. He had given her to Eoghan Foley, who had renamed her Kat's Gift. Eoghan Foley had produced from Maire another top-class mare, who in turn had produced Tabikat and Katseye. Frustratingly, both these colts had been gelded and sent jump racing, which meant that the known line of El Heredero de Sevilla had come to an end. Maria La Herederita herself, if she was still alive, would be too old to produce more foals, and there had been no mention of any third produce of Little Kitty Cat. Until now.

When it came to Gerry's attention that a colt by the name of Katalyst from the same dam was due to be sold at the Aintree racecourse sale earlier that year, Gerry was certain that in Katalyst's veins ran one quarter of the blood of that valuable mare. Gerry wanted it back.

The quest for ownership of Katalyst had required much patience on Gerry's part. He had been well aware that the promise to him of one of the progeny of the original stallion El Heredero de Sevilla was likely to be known to the sort of craven people who would have given information to the British Army Intelligence officers in return for immunity from prosecution for themselves. Callan Sullivan was an example of one such individual but there were likely to be others, such as whoever had called in the bomb warning that day in Fermagarrick over thirty years ago, not to mention the person who had murdered the sniper hired to kill Eoghan Foley on the same day. Any attempt on Gerry's part to assert his rights to his payment through the remnants of the old republican channels would provide a clear alert to those still determined to discover the planter of Fermagarrick car bomb.

Gerry's carefully assumed new identity of Nathan G Lowry had been taken from the owner of the haulage company which employed him in Belfast, where he had been passed off as the owner's nephew. The faked documents had over time acquired an authenticity which had been assisted by a mixed approach of blackmail and the payment of bribes to selected corrupt officials, most of whom were now deceased. Now an apparently respectable Belfast business owner following the retirement of the original Mr Lowry, Gerry had the means to pursue his objective to obtain the horse through a legitimate channel. Nathan G Lowry was a well-known racehorse owner and employed a respected bloodstock agent to source his horses at public sales.

Unknown to those who were pleased to source his string of racehorses, the Lowry haulage company's major involvement in drugs, arms and, lately, people trafficking was the highly lucrative activity which had been built up over many years previously and had given Gerry most of his carefully concealed wealth. Gerry had had new plans for this side of his business activity. The horse performance enhancer *gui*, to which he had been introduced at the Parry yard, where some of his horses were based, was not only undetectable in the horses but, he quickly realised, had been brought undetected into the country too. The process which enabled the stimulant *gui* to be masked and undetectable when dissolved in liquid was of great interest to Gerry. The horses pissed the drug out after a short time, but it was the possibility of putting similar substances into bottled or canned liquids so they could be afterwards recovered intact which was of interest to Gerry.

The disintegration of the criminal Paloka enterprise in Tirana had suddenly provided Gerry with his opportunity. Those individuals overseeing the many evil trades of the deceased brothers had been looking elsewhere for new protectors. Gerry, keen to expand his own operations had been interested to know what these people might do for him. Gerry's criminal activities were of the old-fashioned type, involving the physical movement and exploitation of people and things, readily facilitated by his haulage enterprise, as well as prostitution, blackmail and protection racketeering. Gerry had become acutely aware that cybercrime was nowadays a more lucrative and less risky way of making illegal money and he had been keen to find himself a quick way into that type of activity.

Then, just over one year ago, an individual known online as Watchman had approached him directly via Gerry's fledgling IT operation with an irresistible proposal.

Watchman, it appeared, had been at the forefront of the Paloka online cybercriminal operation. According to the excited head of Gerry's newly assembled cybercrime group, Watchman was one of the world's most prolific criminal cybermasters. Watchman had been looking for a new protector, preferably in the UK, and had not only his considerable technical skills, but another secret to offer. Over the ensuing weeks, after the process of Advanced Persistent Threat had been explained to Gerry by one of his well-educated young team, the same technonerd had acted as the go-between in the negotiations, conducted through encrypted messages run through a fake staff account at a University in London.

The goods on offer had been precisely what Gerry had been seeking: the technical knowledge of the process by which certain chemical substances could be disguised in liquids and carried undetected across borders. Watchman, Gerry was informed, had originally stolen the intelligence for use by the Palokas from a chemical weapons research establishment in Russia. The demise of the Albanian family criminal enterprise had prevented their exploitation of the technology and Chinese cybercriminals had quickly occupied the territory vacated by the Palokas' demise. Watchman had offered the details of the technical process to Gerry in return for his protection. Watchman said he could provide samples which he had previously smuggled successfully into Western Europe out of Tirana. Everything had seemed to be falling into Gerry's lap.

Watchman, though, had let Gerry down spectacularly. After a month of online negotiation, a drop had been agreed. Watchman would send a message providing the location of samples, as well as associated information concerning the process itself, which would enable Gerry to verify Watchman's claims. The promised message, though, had never arrived and Watchman himself had disappeared. Gerry had concluded that his IT operatives had been the victims of a hoax and had instructed them to stick in future to their usual business of online scamming and financial fraud. The currently more lucrative cocaine had continued to be smuggled through Nathan G Lowry's usual channels.

The appearance in Cathal's Aintree sale catalogue of the colt Katalyst had occurred shortly after Watchman had gone silent. The details of the lot had served to confirm Gerry's suspicions as to the eventual whereabouts of the mare which had been promised to him. Gerry had been at Aintree racecourse to watch the grandsons of Kat's Gift run to victory in their respective races and had learned with irritation from his agent that their half-brother Katalyst had been withdrawn from the sale because the necessary paperwork had not been completed on time.

Gerry's agent had also told him that, unsurprisingly, there had been much interest in the colt, in particular on the part of a family called Cunningham, who appeared to have tried to make behind the scenes enquiries about the colt. Fearing that a private deal might had been done with the family, Gerry had quickly obtained fake racecourse credentials for two of his employees to check that the horse was not concealed in the Cunningham horsebox. The two men had accomplished their task by following the son of the Cunningham family, an amateur jockey who had ridden in one of the day's races, into the horsebox park. More used to getting the information they needed by brute force, the thugs had carried out their brief with their usual enthusiasm, resulting in serious injury to the unsuspecting young man. This was precisely the sort of publicity which Gerry did not want and the two individuals were no longer in his, or anyone else's, service.

Gerry's next opportunity to purchase Katalyst had come very soon afterwards, at the Punchestown sale in Ireland later that month. There could be no difficulties this time about travel documents and Gerry had been confident that his agent could secure the purchase for him. Neither Tabikat nor Katseye had raced at Punchestown, although the trainer James Sampfield Peveril had entered another runner, the recent Cheltenham Champion Hurdle winner, Curlew Landings. Gerry had been unsurprised to learn that Mr Sampfield Peveril appeared too to have an interest in obtaining Katalyst, as he had been spotted, accompanied by the

Welsh jockey who rode Katalyst's siblings, entering the barn where the equine lots were held prior to the sale. That sale though had been frustrated by a sudden claim by an Irish trainer called Niall Carter to own the colt. The lot had been withdrawn from sale until the dispute could be resolved.

After that, much to Gerry's frustration, there had been no sign of the colt in any public bloodstock sale either in the UK or Ireland. The horse's older half-siblings had continued to excel in their top class races and Gerry had learned more than he wanted to hear about the owners' ambitious plans for them. He had eventually realised for himself that the woman he had seen with Brendan Meaghan the previous year at Punchestown and who had appeared to be taking centre stage in talking about the horses, was Niamh Foley, formerly Niamh Kennelly, now the mother in law of Tabikat's owner and the widow of Enda Foley, the man who had been killed by the traitor Callan Sullivan.

With the help of the *gui,* Gerry had put his own horses up against Tabikat and Katseye, with some success, particularly at Ascot shortly before Christmas. His accomplished light grey horse, Bees and Mist, had come close to beating Tabikat at Kempton Park in the King George VI Chase and that day Gerry had taken the risk of congratulating the woman he now knew to be Niamh Foley on Tabikat's victory. Gerry had not imagined for one second that the widow of Enda Foley would, after more than thirty years, either remember or recognise his face in the context of a racecourse in England. After all, he had not at first recognised her.

Gerry had been wrong. Niamh Foley had indeed recognised him that day. It had been the first false step Gerry had taken in over thirty years. But Enda's widow had been, in any case, a non-entity of a human being, a farmer's wife doing nothing other than producing a succession of children for her cowardly husband. There was nothing the woman once known as Niamh Kennelly could do to harm Nathan G Lowry.

32

If the young man near the Cheltenham winners' enclosure had not been arrested right by his side, Kye would have not even noticed him.

Kye and Jackie were being managed that January Saturday by Sadie, Mr Sampfield having now been absent for two weeks from Sampfield Grange, attending to the complex affairs ensuing from the sudden death of his mother in Australia. Raldi's dramatic demise through an unwitnessed riding accident had entailed a formal investigation through the Queensland Coroner's Court before Raldi's body could be released to her family and a funeral held.

Fortunately, the trainer's plans for his horses for the rest of January had been shared with Sadie before Sam's hurried departure in the Audi in the weak January sunshine to catch the flight from Heathrow Airport to Brisbane via Hong Kong, a journey which the efficient Lewis had fortunately been able to arrange promptly for his employer. A few telephone calls had since been received from the trainer to check on progress in the yard, but otherwise Mr Sampfield had seemed content to leave matters in Sadie's increasingly capable hands until his expected return home in early February.

Mr Sampfield had spoken directly to Sadie before his departure, telling her that she should consult Merlin for help in relation to maintaining Tabikat's fitness, given that the horse would not be racing again until the day of the Cheltenham Gold Cup, still two months hence. Following an equally efficient conversation with Merlin, who had fortuitously arrived at Sampfield Grange shortly after the shocking news had been received from Teddy Urquhart, Sam had agreed to book several days of Merlin's time, as if the jockey were temporarily engaged as an additional member of staff at the yard in Sam's absence.

Merlin, pleased to receive this unexpected commission, had had little hesitation in agreeing to Mr Sampfield's plan, not least because it had enabled him to phase in his return to full-time race riding during the second part of the month, not to mention providing him with useful practical experience towards a project which was slowly beginning to assemble itself in his mind. The arrangement had also served to facilitate his avoidance of fellow jockey Jenna Roberts with whom he had become increasingly annoyed. Merlin had not believed for a moment that Jenna had had concerns for his wellbeing, as she had suggested, and had come to the typically self-centred conclusion that Jenna had dumped him because he had been unavailable for sex or for training with her in the gym whilst he had been injured. Rose-tinted memories of an affectionate Sadie looking after him on a previous occasion when he had been stuck at home injured had crowded unhelpfully into Merlin's jumbled thoughts whilst he had tried to capture some elusive sleep alone in his attic bedroom.

Following Mr Sampfield's hasty departure, Merlin had carried out his scheduled schooling session with Katseye. Having given the imposing black horse back into the conscientious care of Jackie, Merlin had gone to find Sadie in the tack room, intending to discuss with her the programme for Tabikat and Curlew Landings.

Sadie, though, had forestalled him.

"Do you know who this is?" she had asked Merlin abruptly, holding up her mobile phone in front of him.

"As far as I can see, it's you an' Tabikat before the King George at Kempton Park," Merlin had responded, puzzled, after glancing at the little picture.

"Not us, Merlin," Sadie had chided him, "The man in the background. He was watching us. I thought he might be the person who attacked you that day. Do you recognise him?"

Merlin, more interested, had taken the phone from her and fiddled about with the screenshot so as to enlarge the part of the picture which showed the unknown watcher.

"Can't say that I do, *cariad*," he had responded, finally, the familiar endearment slipping out unintentionally once again, as they had stood together in the chilly timber-lined room, the racks loaded with leather saddles and neatly hanging bridles, a worn wooden saddlehorse standing in the centre of the space. Sadie had taken off her waterproof jacket, which had been hanging on a peg by the door, although her fleece body warmer had still been required to combat the chilly atmosphere of the unheated storage room. The rest of the yard staff had been finishing the mucking out and the preparation of the next set of feeds, whilst some had already left for the day or had gone for lunch in the warm kitchen. It was the first time the two former lovers had been truly alone together since their awkward journey back from Ireland over three months ago.

"It's really scary that you got attacked like that, Merlin," Sadie had said, abruptly, "I wish I understood what all this horrible stuff is about. After what was on that drawing and what happened to Luke Cunningham, I've been really worried about you and Tabikat. And now it looks as if I was right to be."

Merlin swallowed hard. Pushing the mobile phone into one of the pockets of Sadie's blue fleece, Merlin had put a hand on each of her shoulders, looked her in the face and spoke as firmly as he could, "Look, Sadie, there could be a million and one explanations for what 'appened to me at Kempton Park. I don' remember anything about it and didn' even see the person 'oo did it. But you send me that picture, *cariad*, an' I'll show it to the other jocks and see whether any of them recognise 'im. I've got a cousin does photography, too. Maybe 'e could do something to improve the image, maybe even search for the person online."

As Sadie's blue eyes had looked back at him, Merlin had been suddenly unable to control his suppressed emotions any longer. Hardly knowing what he was doing, he had leaned forward and pressed his open mouth over Sadie's. Much to his relief, after a brief stiffening of her athletic body, Merlin had felt no further resistance from Sadie. Her almost instant physical response to his kiss had brought every memory of their old relationship rushing back, just as though the last twenty months apart had simply not happened. Merlin had pulled her towards him and had run his hands down her strong back and buttocks. Sadie had reached out and pulled him forward by the waist until he had been pressed against her.

"Not here, Merlin," was all that Sadie had said as she had felt the well-remembered erection pushing hard into her lower abdomen, "Come up to the flat with me."

After that eventful day, it had been impossible for anyone at Sampfield Grange to ignore that fact that Sadie and Merlin were a couple once again, not least because Merlin had spent a good part of his time in the run up to Katseye's race at Cheltenham at the end of the month not just at the yard, as arranged with Mr Sampfield, but sharing the former chauffeur's flat with a noticeably happier Sadie.

Merlin, rather to his surprise, had found the experience of participating in Sadie's working life at the rural racing yard to be an enjoyable addition to their resumed sexual relationship, which had certainly retained every bit of its original explosive chemistry. During their work time, the two of them had successfully prepared the headstrong Indian Rocks for a point to point race at Ashfordleigh Downs, in which the young horse had been ridden into first place by Sadie, who had benefited from both Merlin's professional advice and personal encouragement. Merlin, used only to concentrating on his own performance in jump races, had for the first time experienced the satisfaction resulting from coaching a pair of talented protegees to victory.

Less enthusiastic about the resumption of Sadie's relationship with Merlin had been Kelly and Lewis, both of whom harboured a rooted dislike of Merlin's self-confident character. During the time he had spent at Sampfield Grange, Merlin had taken his meals with the staff in the busy kitchen. He had been accorded by his fellow workers a deference which even Kelly and Lewis had had to concede had been justified by his extensive knowledge and experience, but which it had nevertheless been very galling for them to witness. Merlin, for his part, had appeared to hold no ill will towards the couple for their less than friendly attitude towards him, with the result that, knowing the high regard in which Mr Sampfield held the jockey, Lewis had eventually suggested to Kelly that it would be expedient for them to treat Merlin with friendly courtesy, to his face at least.

"Just so long as he doesn't upset Sadie again," was all that Kelly had said, crossly, in response. Judging by the amount of time, the reunited lovers had recently spent exercising the ancient springs of the old-fashioned bed in the chauffeur's flat, Lewis had not thought there to be much prospect of Sadie being in any way upset, but he had kept his envious thoughts to himself.

Katseye was now making his darkly magnificent way around the Cheltenham parade ring, Jackie holding the smart leather lead rein with its brass coloured fastenings clipped onto the horse's bridle. The horse had been entered in the second race to be run on the bright and cold afternoon, a Novices' Chase, the same race in which Fan Court had run in the previous season. Sadie, as the trainer's representative, was standing rather nervously in the centre of the parade ring with Arturo Ardizzone and Meredith Crosland, having followed a smiling Jackie from the pre-parade area where the two of them had saddled the horse for his race. The Italian industrialist was clad in an expensive looking black coat and wore an equally black fedora hat over his dark hair, the gloom of the outfit relieved only by a green and white scarf tucked carefully around the collar and lapels of the coat. Mrs Crosland had resurrected her previous season's black coat which was smartly decorated by a diagonal row of silver buttons. Were it not for their enthusiastic mood, Sadie thought privately, they would not be out of place at a fashionable funeral.

As if reading Sadie's thoughts, Mrs Crosland suddenly asked, "And how is James? I was very sorry to hear about the death of his mother. Will he be coming home soon?"

"Next week, Mrs Crosland," Sadie responded, as Arturo Ardizzone turned to greet Merlin, who had just joined them, wearing the rather more cheerful green and white silks of the owner.

"It must have been good experience for you, Sadie, running the yard on your own for a while," Mrs Crosland added, unexpectedly, "I am sure you will have done an excellent job. Katseye is looking splendid today."

"Well, Merlin helped me, and the yard staff are very hard working," Sadie responded, not wanting to receive all the praise for something which had truly been a team effort.

"Don't let others take the credit for your personal achievements," Mrs Crosland stated, firmly, clearly unwilling to revise her view of how matters had been arranged at Sampfield Grange over the past two weeks. Merlin and Arturo Ardizzone suppressed smiles as they listened in silence to the conversation.

The sun cut brightly through the crisp winter air as the bell rang for the jockeys to mount. Legging Merlin up into Katseye's tiny saddle, Sadie whispered, "I hope you'll be following the trainer's instructions today, Merlin."

"Depends what she asks me to do," Merlin replied with a grin, receiving a conspiratorial smile from Sadie in return. Jackie walked quietly onwards, pretending that she had heard nothing.

Kye, standing expectantly in the spectators' area, watched Merlin and Katseye cantering towards the two mile and five furlongs starting point, located in the central area of Prestbury Park. The large viewing screen was situated at the far end of the parade ring, directly opposite where Kye was standing, and above the heads of those of the connections of the six runners who had chosen to stay in the parade ring to watch their horses in the race. Most of the racegoers who had come to view the beautifully turned out horses in the parade ring had by now gravitated towards the grandstand areas to watch the action on the track, but a significant few had decided to remain where they stood. Kye could see Stevie Stone, wearing her usual burgundy hat, standing alongside the parade ring, chatting to a small group of inappropriately clad female racegoers. Tabby Cat and Jayce had confidently tipped Katseye to win his race that day.

Kye was still not sure for whom he was supposed to be looking. At first, he had feared that his targets were to be Kye's brother Bronz, or Bronz's girlfriend and henchwoman, Sheryl. But, as Jackie had pointed out as they had travelled together in the small horsebox containing Katseye along the M5 in the early morning sunlight, Mr Stanley and those who worked for him needed no help from Kye to identify the two Liverpudlian drug dealers. In any case, Kye had seen neither of these unwelcome individuals at the racecourse, so far, at least.

Katseye's competitors in the Novices' Chase that day included Altimeter, the horse which had beaten him into second place at Ascot a month ago. Previous rivals Petit Zazou and Cloud Atlas, were in the field today, as was Milk Run, the grey who had claimed third place in Katseye's runaway debut chase appearance at Chepstow. Kye could see that Katseye and Merlin had a stiff challenge before them today. Enough time had passed since the cessation of the deluges which had characterised the early part of the month to allow the ground to improve significantly, so today's going had been officially described as good to soft, which Kye was sure would help not only Katseye but some of his rivals as well. Over the past two weeks, Kye too had benefited from Merlin's advice, and had been left even more in awe of the star jockey's knowledge and skill. If anyone could pull a win out of the bag, thought Kye, it would be Merlin.

Seeing the starter drop the yellow flag to send the six horses on their way, Kye noticed some movement in the parade ring. One of the groups of connections had changed their standing position, apparently to gain a better sight of the viewing screen, and in the course of this change, someone had accidentally bumped into a member of another group. During the ensuing apologies and polite repositioning of the individuals concerned, a middle-aged man wearing a grey coat with a red and black scarf draped around his neck turned briefly towards the concrete steppings on which Kye was standing. It was but a second's glimpse, but it was enough to trigger something in Kye's memory. Perhaps this was the person Mr Stanley had expected him to recognise, Kye thought.

Ignoring the progress of the competitive steeplechase which was currently taking place on the New course, Kye walked quickly down the steppings and around to the side of the parade ring, eventually positioning himself where he could get a better view of the faces of the people which included the familiar seeming man. Kye quickly identified them as the connections of Altimeter, the winner who had beaten Katseye at Ascot. Kye then realised with a sudden shock that the man in the grey coat was not the only familiar face in the group. One of the others was the son of the trainer for whom Kye had previously worked in Cheshire. Kye studied them all for a while longer, but recognised neither of the remaining two men. The group itself seemed to be otherwise unexceptional. They watched the viewing screen with the same tense and excited demeanour as all the other people standing on the neatly mown lawn, including Katseye's supporters, becoming more animated once the horses turned up the final hill to aim for the finish.

"There are two fences still to take!" shouted the commentator, excitedly, as the noise from the other side of the two grandstands began to swell and explode in volume, "Cloud Atlas keeps the lead as they round the final turn. Katseye and Altimeter are locked together in behind, with Petit Zazou hard on their heels. Milk Run is the only other runner still continuing but he's detached by three lengths. As they come to the second last, Altimeter takes off on a long one and comes upsides Cloud Atlas. Petit Zazou and Katseye are matching the pace. It's anyone's race!"

Kye could not take his eyes off the exciting finish being played out on the screen. Much would depend on how much fuel each of the horses had left in the tank after the final fence. The fierce fight for the lead which he could see going on in the tense dying stages of the race would be a taxing affair. Already Kye could see Merlin working hard on Katseye's dark back, the jockey doing his utmost to motivate his mount to ever greater efforts. By the time the leaders had reached the run in, three of the horses were in line, the watching crowd surging with excitement on either side of the track, screaming and calling the names of the horses and jockeys involved.

"There's nothing at all between them!" yelled the disembodied voice of the commentator, "Altimeter, Katseye and Cloud Atlas are all locked together as they run to the line. Altimeter seems to be getting the better of the others. It's very close. The others aren't giving up. It's neck and neck over the final few yards. Altimeter gets it! Katseye and Cloud Atlas are in a photo for second. Petit Zazou is a close fourth. Milk Run is the only other finisher."

Kye could hardly contain his disappointment. After all the work Merlin and Sadie had put in to prepare Katseye for the race, it would have been a real triumph to be able to report a victory to Mr Sampfield when he returned home. Ignoring the jubilant celebrations of the previously interesting Altimeter connections, Kye moved round the exterior path towards the post marking the second place stand in the winners' enclosure intending to wait for Sadie, Mr Ardizzone and Mrs Crosland to join Katseye, Merlin and Jackie there.

In his selected location Kye found a young Asian man already pressing tensely against the white rail. Slightly annoyed, Kye positioned himself alongside this fellow spectator, who in turn ignored the newcomer. The young man was gazing fixedly at Arturo Ardizzone as the party of connections approached, shaking their heads ruefully at each other as they discussed the frustrating closeness of the finish. Jackie walked behind them, leading a weary-looking Katseye, Merlin talking downwards to Sadie from the horse's back. Spotting Kye by the rails, Merlin gave him a quick wave as he swung himself from the horse, removing the saddle to allow Jackie to cover the sweating animal with a sheet and offer him a well-earned drink from one of the yellow water buckets.

Something then happened, the details of which Kye could not afterwards fully recall. There was a sudden movement from the young man by his side, who seemed to be trying to vault the rails, holding in his right hand an object which he had taken from his jacket pocket. He was shouting words which Kye could not make out but which seemed to include Arturo Ardizzone's name. Frightened by the sudden and apparently threatening movement just in front of his nose, Katseye shied suddenly backwards, almost pulling Jackie to the ground as she grabbed at his bridle. Kye saw

Sadie and Merlin springing to Jackie's assistance as she tried to calm the spooked horse. Mr Ardizzone and Mrs Crosland moved hurriedly out of the way to avoid being knocked over.

As if by magic, two dark-clad and heavily armed police officers appeared from behind Kye and grabbed the back of the young man's black leather jacket, yanking him backwards, then flipping him over like a doll to pin him face down onto the concrete by the rails. There was a gasp, followed by a stunned silence, from those of the spectators who had already returned to that side of the parade ring and whose attention was not focused on the progress of Altimeter down the horsewalk from the finish. Before Kye, or anyone else, could move, the officers dragged the unresisting young man to his feet and half-marched and half-pulled him up the steppings, and were gone. The incident was over in seconds, almost as though it had never happened, and, after a bit of puzzled muttering from those nearby, attention soon returned to the triumphant arrival of Altimeter and his jockey in the parade ring.

Merlin had soon left to weigh in and to get ready to ride Ranulph Dicks's Fan Court in the next race. Jackie led Katseye towards the parade ring exit next to the weighing room, Sadie by her side. Meredith Crosland and Arturo Ardizzone walked away in the direction of the Owners and Trainers bar in the Princess Royal Stand, where they were soon joined by Stevie Stone, whose followers were no doubt regretting following Tabby Cat's tip that day. Kye, left alone, turned his attention to the faces of the Altimeter connections who were about to go up to the platform where the race sponsor would present their prizes. There was no doubt about it. One of the men was his former employer's son, the man's previously clean-shaven face now adorned with a ginger beard. Kye now realised that the older man in the grey coat was Altimeter's owner. Kye could only assume that he must have previously seen the man when he had come to visit the racing yard.

At that moment, Amelia Dicks appeared at the entrance to the parade ring, talking urgently to Sadie, and pointing to Kye. Sadie was nodding her head in apparent agreement and the two women signalled to Kye to make his way towards them around the white perimeter fence.

"Will you lead up Fan Court for me, please, Kye?" Amelia asked him, sounding flustered, "Travis doesn't dare go into the parade ring. He says that the people who framed him in Australia are there."

33

"I assume we're not up here to admire the view," commented a slightly breathless George Harvey, who was leaning on his stick whilst he and his companions looked out from the top of Cleeve Hill towards the Severn Estuary. The many paths of the Cotswold Way wound their uneven route to either side of them, tracking along the edge of the presently deserted greens and bunkers of the Cleeve Hill golf course. The unmissable, hump-backed silhouettes of the Malvern Hills lay prominently against the bright blue sky to the North West.

The buildings and roads of Regency Cheltenham lay below and to the South West of the vantage point, the round grey roof of GCHQ with the open space of Gloucestershire Airport beyond it, visible on the far side of the orderly conurbation. Closer to where the watchers were standing, almost directly above the golden rock face of Cleeve Cloud, could be seen the distinctive layout of Prestbury Park. This sloping green space housed not only Cheltenham racecourse, with its attendant buildings and car parks, but a steam railway line and station and numerous open fields, including that in which affluent racegoers, usually the more prolific racehorse owners, landed their helicopters. Cheltenham Heliport, the aviation charts called it.

The cold of the February air felt sharp in Isabella Hall's lungs. The clean afternoon sun was starting to move down into the West, causing Isabella to shade her eyes as she tried to pick out the nearer of the two Severn Bridges which could sometimes be discerned against the background of the darker shapes of the rising hills of South Wales. A red kite floated on the thermals below them, suddenly plunging to the slope beneath to grasp in its vicious talons some unlucky prey which it had spied.

"In one sense, that is exactly why we are here," Frank Stanley replied, "The information we obtained from Mr Mallik, alongside another development, has significantly changed our perspective. Have you ever looked at the racecourse from up here before?"

"Is this some clever way of saying that we have been too close to the action to see the bigger picture?" suggested Isabella, trying to grasp Frank's implied meaning.

"Something like that, Isabella," Frank replied, "And the other reason we have come here is because it is the place where Dominik Katz met his death."

"So, what did that Mallik boy tell you, then?" asked George, becoming irritated by Frank's oblique approach to the briefing session which he had insisted be held in this spectacular but inconvenient and, at the moment, rather cold location.

Rajesh Mallik had been taken completely by surprise when he had been so roughly arrested at Cheltenham racecourse. Years of existing in his own bubble of undetected – or so he had thought - online financial fraud, not to mention the fantastic cybergames in which everyone used fake names, had imbued in him a sense of isolated invulnerability. That armed police should arrest him so peremptorily in such a public location was something which had left him feeling both baffled and extremely scared. When he had been informed that his arrest and detention had been made under the provisions of Anti-Terrorism legislation, his confusion and fear had increased still more.

"I ain't no terrorist, man," he had shouted to no avail at the unmoving figure of the armed police officer who had been standing, still holding his semi-automatic carbine, by the closed door of the small featureless room to which Rajesh had been taken following his arrest. Rajesh had had no idea where he was. The journey in the police van had been short, but not too short to enable the arresting officers to relieve him of his few possessions, including his state of the art mobile phone, all of which had been bundled into a large plastic bag and placed on a chair in the room.

Rajesh had repeated this same statement to a tall man with greying dark hair, who had subsequently entered the room and had sat opposite him, his hands resting on the empty surface of a table, whilst the silent police officer had looked impassively on.

"Suppose you tell me what you were doing at Cheltenham racecourse?" the man had suggested, helpfully, making no attempt to introduce himself,

"I come to see that Mr Ardiz-izon," had replied Rajesh, stumbling over the pronunciation of the Italian name, "I 'ad to speak to 'im."

"About what?" the nameless man had asked, pleasantly.

"About my mate Watchman, what's 'appened to 'im," Rajesh had told him, "I thought this bloke might be able to tell me something."

"Your mate?" the man had repeated, his blue eyes staring apparently interestedly at Rajesh, "When did you last see this Watchman?"

"I didn't," Rajesh had tried to clarify, "I only know him from online."

"I think you know him better than that," the older man had objected, calmly, "You've been stalking him. Did you fall out? Was it you that killed him?"

Rajesh's horrified and open-mouthed silence had given Frank Stanley the first piece of information he had wanted. Orphan had had no idea that Watchman was dead.

Much of what an almost comically deflated Rajesh Mallik had revealed during his subsequent interrogation, apparently as a suspected terrorist, had served to confirm what George had already found out by tracking the cyber security student's online activity. Rajesh had been horrified to hear his history of online internet crime set out in some detail by the unknown man on the other side of the table, but it was the information which related to his estranged family which had made him realise just how much trouble he was really in. The mosque regularly attended by his father was known to harbour dangerous hate preachers, his brother had been a soldier of ISIS in Syria and had participated in video-recorded hostage executions, and Rajesh himself had regularly sent money to finance a suspected Islamic terrorist cell in Wolverhampton.

"I don't know about none of this stuff, sir, you must believe me," Rajesh had begged eventually, his voice shaking with fear, "The money's for my sister's kid. Our dad chucked 'er out an' she needs it."

"Tell me about the IT account at your University in the name of Merlin ap Rhys," had been the next question, one to which Rajesh was by now more than willing to give as helpful an answer as he could.

"I was looking for Watchman," Rajesh had begun, "You know who 'e is, right? Top hacker, cybermaster, best in the world, innit? I thought he could 'elp me, get me a job. I worked out who 'e was, found out about 'is company Katz:i an' the security work e'd done for this Mr Ardi-whatever. Then Watchman's just went away for ages. I tries to track 'im down through this bloke's company. There was all these fake reports about accidents to the planes that the Ardi company 'ad made. I figured out then that it was Watchman 'ad done it. That owner must 'ave really pissed 'im off some'ow, something to do with 'is dad's company goin' under, I'm guessin'. So, then, I looked into the Ardi bloke. One thing is, 'e's got racehorses, like that one that was racin' today. After I done all that, I found the IT account at the Uni, the one you're askin' about. It's got the same foreign name on it as that jockey what rides the 'orse. So it 'ad to be connected some'ow."

"What happened then?" had prompted the questioner, as Rajesh had seemed to hesitate.

"I knew it was Watchman 'ad put the fake account there," Rajesh went on, more slowly, "But it didn' seem to do nothin' except go to some site in France. I put a shout-out on the French place to tell Watchman I'd found it, but there was nothin' came back. I thought maybe e'd gone working with that online betting stuff they do with the 'orses, but that's pretty stitched up, no way in. Then that DoS attack 'appened at the Ardi place a few weeks back, an' I could see that it was the fake account what 'ad done it. It 'ad got a message from Watchman. It was clever stuff, code and whatnot, set off a real neat bomb in the Ardi IT set-up."

"Did you do anything with the account yourself?" had asked the questioner, who already know most of this information.

"You're kidding me," Rajesh, having got into his story, had seemed to forget to whom he was speaking, "That file was genius, man. But it was weird, you know. The DoS message said the Ardi bloke was dead, when 'e wasn't, innit? And the message went to Liverpool just went straight to trash. That's when I figured Watchman was playin' somethin' deep."

"What do you mean by that?" had responded the other man.

"Watchman, 'e's a fuckin' clever geezer," Rajesh had mused aloud, as if to himself, "Tries to put people off, lays traps, that sort of crap. But that trashcan in Liverpool was mean. I tried to read it, but it was like a black hole, those things they 'ave in space. Things went in, nothin' came out. Like it was air gapped, but just one way. Like one of those dead-end roads, you know, that name like a sack."

'Why do you think Watchman launched that most recent DoS attack?" had been the final question that Rajesh had answered that day, although many, rather more basic, questions were to come his way after the file concerning his online financial crimes had been passed to the police.

"I couldn' work it out," Rajesh had replied, "It said that Mr Ardi-thing was dead, but he wasn', was 'e? That's why I wanted to talk to the bloke, innit, get 'is answers recorded on my phone, find out what 'e'd done to Watchman. But your lot came an' stopped me."

Frank Stanley looked at his attentive audience, which now also included TK Stonehouse, who had walked across the sloping hillside to join them whilst Frank had been speaking. She wore a white quilted jacket with the collar turned up again the cold air.

"With permission, sir, the rest of the briefing's going to have to wait," TK butted in, raising her arm, "The Altior's nearly here."

As TK pointed, the four people on the hilltop turned to see a small black speck in the clear sky to the South. As it drew nearer, TK pulled an object which looked like a large mobile phone from one of the pockets of her warm jacket and studied the screen.

"Taking a photo are you, TK?" asked Isabella, surprised, "There's a pretty impressive view of the racecourse from here, I have to say. You could be up here and watch the racing for free if you had some good field glasses. You can even see the parade ring."

"Watch the aircraft," TK told her, concentrating on the device in her hand. "It's approaching the interception point for the localiser at Gloucestershire Airport over there. Here we go. I have control."

Although the others could not see the screen, the virtual pilot which until then had been flying the Altior 10 on its regular test route from Old Warnock airfield, promptly texted back the words "You have control". Instead of continuing with its previous instruction to intercept the localiser and to descend on a westerly heading with the glide slope procedure into Gloucestershire Airport, the little aircraft continued instead to fly towards the place where its new pilot was standing above Cleeve Cloud, overlooking Cheltenham racecourse.

The Altio 10 continued to make its way at an altitude of two thousand feet towards TK. The ground where she was standing was almost one thousand feet above sea level, which meant that the aircraft would be a similar distance above her head on reaching the point at which she would direct it towards the racecourse.

The aircraft was almost overhead. TK initiated a steep turn to the left onto a compass heading of 260 degrees. Looking up, everyone saw the aircraft bank steeply above them as the software responded to the instruction from the handset.

"I'm disabling this control now," announced TK suddenly.

Recognising the signing off of the human controller, the Artificial Intelligence of the virtual pilot in the aircraft above Cleeve Hill immediately took charge of the flight once again. Reverting to its original instructions, it continued the left hand turn to take it back towards the localiser. Descending the glide slope in accordance with the published procedure, the Altior 10 made an uneventful landing on runway 27 at Gloucestershire Airport.

"And that," announced TK, quietly, "Is how Dominik Katz was killed."

"You're really going to have to explain this, TK," George told her, with a sigh.

"You will remember that these flights were part of a test programme for the Artificial Intelligence fly by wire software," TK responded, "All the recorded parameters from the test flights were analysed back in the Astrak lab after the aircraft had completed each of the runs. The flight we have just reproduced was obviously not part of the scheduled programme because Dominik Katz had hi-jacked the aircraft for his own purposes. As a consequence, there was no routine analysis undertaken on this flight after it landed. We were all just glad that Dr Katz had not had to intervene to prevent her brother crashing the Altior into the racecourse parade ring.

"More recently, though, this omission was put right and the flight parameters were belatedly included in the final sets of analyses which were produced following the termination of the fixed-wing test programme. It became immediately clear that there had been something different about this flight, especially the recording of power settings both on take-off and in the air and then the trim once the aircraft was flying. These anomalies ceased shortly after the aircraft had passed over Cleeve Hill and had turned to intercept the localiser, a position during which a human controller, Dominik Katz, that is, had for a short time taken over from the onboard software.

"Without boring you with all the figures, it was evident that there was some kind of dead weight towards the front of the aircraft which had pushed forward the centre of gravity and upset the normal flight characteristics. The software had responded to this

329

by altering the trim and power settings and using frequent small heading corrections. It looked as if something was pulling down on the main wheel of the landing gear, something which came off when the aircraft made the steep turn just above Dominik Katz's head.

"I'd always thought the Altior's towbar had been stolen from Old Warnock airfield, but it hadn't. It looks like it had been left attached to the aircraft, probably by one of the other owners at the field, who moved it for some reason. That's what killed our nasty Mr Katz. No-one murdered him. It was just a freak accident. If we could have just found the towbar, that would have clinched it, but by the time we got onto this, it would have been long gone. Detectorists, scrap metal scavengers, who knows who might have picked it up."

After TK stopped speaking, there was a long silence during which Isabella and George took in the implications of the story. Frank, who had already been informed of the conclusions reached by the Astrak analysts, spoke first.

"We now think it significant," Frank said, "That, apart from our Mr Mallik, no-one went looking online for Dominik Katz after his death. That suggests that no-one was expecting him to contact them online. As such, it sheds a new light on the full purpose of the data stick which the Colvin siblings found.

"What I told you about Mr Mallik is a highly summarised version of a conversation which took place over a period of a couple of hours. The young man subsequently wasted a great deal of energy trying to persuade us not to pass our evidence of his criminal activities onto the police. He seemed to think that his rejection by his parents justified his preying on vulnerable individuals on the internet to steal their money. More importantly, though, he genuinely didn't seem to be involved with anything Dominik Katz was planning, in particular the hacking of the Artificial Intelligence fly by wire system on the Altior 10 and the attempt to crash the aircraft at the racecourse."

"Mallik does seem to have tried to hack into the Astrak systems once," George pointed out, "But he didn't get very far. Having followed him over the past few weeks, I'd say he'd be a pretty ineffective attacker of any properly secured system. That's why targeting people who don't know how to protect their data was more lucrative for him. But there's one thing which you've told us, Frank, which I hadn't picked up – his comment about the destination of the encrypted message in Liverpool being a trashcan, or a black hole, or something. Has anyone looked into that yet?"

"My operative in Liverpool has done exactly that," replied Frank, "Mr Mallik was correct. The message went to a rented server in a data centre on Merseyside, where, along with thousands of other messages, it has remained unread. And, as I told you before, the data storage in question was allocated to a fake company set up by someone who gave a false name."

"What on earth was Dominik Katz up to?" exclaimed Isabella, "This doesn't make any sense. Even if the message was sent automatically after his death, why would it be sent to an account which no-one used?"

"This is where the change of perspective comes in," Frank replied, "We have been assuming all along that we have been dealing with cybercrime. That was what Dominik Katz did for a living, either perpetrating it himself or protecting others from being the victims of it. But what if what he was involved in just before he died was not cybercrime at all? What if it was good old-fashioned, traditional real-world crime?"

"Such as?" asked Isabella.

"Such as murder, drug trafficking, and race fixing," answered Frank, starkly.

34

On the day of Curlew Landings' attempt to win the Kingwell Hurdle for the second time, Graham Colvin was driving an inconspicuous and recently renovated small white Peugeot towards Wincanton racecourse. Beside him sat a cowed and nervous Tegan, the black thumb-shaped bruises on her right arm bearing witness to her reluctance to comply with her brother's wish that she should accompany him that day. Only the thought that she might see the lovely Travis again had made Tegan feel any better.

Gray had been furious when Tegan had been dismissed from her part-time job at The Charlton Arms. After he had calmed down, however, he had begun to wonder whether he might make good use of Tegan's weekend presence at the flat they both shared with their disabled mother. Now that he no longer had Kye to act as his runner at horseracing events, the inconspicuous and submissive Tegan might make a good substitute, Gray thought. If she were unlucky enough to be spotted handing over the gear, he could just let her take the rap and deny all knowledge of what his stupid sister was doing.

Gray had not seen his contact Sheryl for some months, which suited him very well, so long as the shipments continued to arrive at the motorway service station on schedule. Their occasional communication had been through apparently innocuous text messages exchanged via pay-as-you-go mobile phones which he changed every few weeks, sending Sheryl the new number by means of a private chat on an online dating site, the replacement numbers conveyed in the form of times and dates on which the fake couple might hook up.

Inducting Tegan into her role as a bagwoman for Gray had not been discussed with Sheryl, but Gray had persuaded himself that Sheryl would approve. Gray was both sexually attracted and a little frightened by the hard-faced young woman whose crush-vowelled accent he barely understood. Gray had not liked to think about the black and yellow taser which she had left with him when she had visited him in his workshop nearly a year ago, the day after Mr Sampfield Peveril's racehorse had won the Cheltenham Gold Cup. Sheryl had not needed to remind Gray that there were 'dead nasty crewks' to be found in this line of work but packing a device which looked like a handgun every time he went out had seemed a bit strong in the context of rural Somerset, so Gray had put it in the bottom of his toolbox in the workshop. Since the visit by the police to retrieve the stolen flash drive, Gray had thought the illicit weapon would be safer indoors, and had stowed it in the secret storage area under the floorboards in Tegan's bedroom.

"That means I've got it handy, if you give me any more trouble," he had snarled at a terrified Tegan.

Also making their separate ways to Wincanton racecourse, in a rather happier frame of mind than Tegan's, were Sadie and Travis with a bright Curlew Landings behind them in the small horsebox, and, further ahead along the picturesque country route, Merlin ap Rhys speeding contentedly along in his black BMW sports car. Mr Sampfield was due to arrive at Heathrow Airport on an overnight flight from Hong Kong and had told Lewis over the phone that he would drive directly to Wincanton racecourse in time to watch Curlew compete at 2.45pm. Gilbert Peveril had notified Isabella Hall that he too intended to join the owners' group that day and that he would be accompanied by Curlew Landings' former owner, the eccentric Toby Halstock.

Fortunately for the many spectators attending the popular meeting, the mid-February day was unseasonably warm, a soft breeze barely discernible in the soft air. A promise of Spring in the not too far away future seemed to hover around the flat contours of the rural racecourse, the hazy sun creating a faint mist between the branches of the winter trees which provided the backdrop to the further side of the track.

"James not here yet?" asked Gilbert, surprising Sadie and Travis in the horsebox park, where they were unloading Curlew Landings, who stopped at the bottom of the ramp to undertake a comprehensive review of the area, as if checking that he was in the right place.

"Mr Sampfield plans to be here in time to see Curlew Landings run, Mr Peveril," Sadie replied, whilst Travis started to lead their inquisitive charge away from the lorry.

"I didn't realise you were still working at Sampfield Grange," said Toby Halstock, who was smartly dressed in his customary tweed jacket and buff shirt with a green tie, as he walked alongside Travis for a few steps, "I'm sure I saw you riding at Warwick recently. On one of Ranulph Dicks's horses."

Whilst Travis was attempting to explain his present working arrangements to the garrulous Toby Halstock, who in reality only wanted an excuse to accompany in suitably proprietorial fashion the successful horse which he had formerly owned, Merlin was in the jockeys' changing room, a small cluster of fellow riders grouped curiously around him. They were looking at the selfie of Sadie and Tabikat which showed the suspicious stranger standing in the background. Merlin had already touted the picture around his fellow riders during the Cheltenham meeting at the end of January, but no-one had admitted to recognising the man. As a consequence, many of today's jockeys had seen the image before, but there were a few different individuals at Wincanton racecourse that day.

"You reckon that's the fella that decked you at Kempton, Merlin?" asked one of his colleagues, peering at the phone which Merlin was holding up, adding, "Never seen him before in me life. Sexy bitta stuff next to the horse, though."

The Kingwell Hurdle was the third race on the afternoon's card. Merlin, thanks to the efforts of Jackson Argyrides on his behalf was now back to his former work routine, and had just completed his ride for Dorset trainer Justin Venn in the second race, a two mile handicap Chase. Rather to Sadie's disappointment, when the six horses running in the Kingwell Hurdle were being brought into the parade ring, there was still no sign of Mr Sampfield.

Sadie watched the expensive and familiar runners circling the parade ring, their grooms marching proudly along by their sides, Curlew Landings and Travis amongst them. Tabby Cat and Jayce had tipped Curlew Landings as an uneasy favourite that morning, but Sadie could not forget that Curlew's victory last year had been partly due to Mr Venn's runner, Southern Cross, having been hampered by The Squire's Tale, competing here again today, who had fallen at the last hurdle. It had been Southern Cross with whom Curlew had dead-heated at Kempton Park, ahead of Rabbit Punch and Devil Waters, and Southern Cross who had won the Greatwood Hurdle, in which Curlew had been brought down. Southern Cross was amongst the runners again today, looking in magnificent condition, as indeed did all the horses. Sadie knew that Merlin needed no riding instructions from the trainer, but she was certain that the other connections would have found Mr Sampfield's presence in the parade ring reassuring.

Travis, leading the now more settled Curlew Landings, had honoured his commitment to Mr Sampfield to prepare and lead out the horse for this important race in the horse's schedule, but the sighting of his former accusers from the Tytherleigh yard in the Cheltenham parade ring in January continued to worry him. Amelia Dicks had been sufficiently concerned by Travis's evident panic that day to ask Kye to take Travis's place as Fan Court's handler in the parade ring, but this was clearly not a sustainable remedy. Following a conversation with Amelia's father, Ranulph Dicks, Travis had confirmed that he would report any further sightings of the men concerned to Mr Dicks, who had said he would 'deal with things' on Travis's behalf. Travis was not sure exactly what that meant in practice but felt a little happier to have a supportive ally on his side.

In the event, Mr Sampfield and Merlin arrived in the parade ring at more or less the same time. Legging up Merlin, who was now wearing the red and green colours of Sampfield Grange, Sadie quickly said "Good luck, stay safe" to horse and rider, earning a cheeky comment from Merlin in return, whilst Mr Sampfield joined his cousin and Toby Halstock on the damp lawn in the centre of the paddock. Mr Sampfield, Sadie now realised, had brought another man with him to watch the race, someone she had not seen before. The newcomer was short and stocky and was smartly dressed in a dark blazer over a striped shirt and a blue tie with some kind of monogram on it. As Sadie watched, the stranger briefly removed and replaced his wide brimmed hat as he was being introduced to the rest of the party and Sadie got a glimpse only of a balding head before the party walked away to secure a good position from which to view the race.

The Kingwell Hurdle that year was destined to produce a shock result. Although Curlew Landings and Southern Cross flip-flopped for favouritism right up until the start, neither of them won.

Curlew and Merlin set off purposefully in front as soon as the race starter had dropped her yellow flag. The two mile start was positioned to the right of the viewing stands, so the horses soon passed the spectators massed on their left as they galloped towards the first of the two turns opposite the horsebox park. The remaining five runners remained well bunched in behind, with no-one inclined to chase too hard after the fleet Curlew at this stage, just so long as they kept tabs on the leader and did not allow him to get too far ahead.

When coming out onto the course from the short horsewalk, Merlin had been conscious of the presence behind him of Jenna Roberts, who had kept the ride on Rabbit Punch. Merlin had seen nothing of his short-lived love interest since their sudden parting at his home in Chepstow when he had been still on the sidelines through concussion. The two of them had exchanged polite greetings before today's race but otherwise had had nothing to say to each other. The upshot was that Merlin had not yet shown to Jenna the selfie depicting the mysterious stranger, notwithstanding the fact that Merlin knew that Jenna was the most likely person to have seen who had attacked him, given that she had been with him when the assailant had struck.

As the determined Curlew Landings powered his way down the back straight, leaping with aplomb the three hurdles set out there, Merlin had nothing now in his mind other than winning the race. All that mattered at the moment was keeping Curlew at the front and not allowing any of the other horses to pass them.

Merlin was much too experienced a rider to need to look around to see where pursuers were located. He could hear the snorting breath of the horses, the rattle and clatter of the tack and the voices of the jockeys. Jenna's female voice was easy to pick out, as were the West Country tones of Southern Cross's rider. The accents of the three remaining jockeys were from different parts of Ireland.

"*Ewch i fynd, bachgen*," urged Merlin, as Curlew's mane, neatly plaited and stitched into golf balls by Jackie earlier in the day, rose up and down rhythmically in front of him. Between Curlew's pricked ears, Merlin could see the right-hand bend at the end of the back straight drawing quickly nearer. The babble of the on-course commentary sounded continuously in his right ear.

Rounding the first of the two turns which would bring them back into the home straight where they would ride the finish of the short race, Merlin could sense that some of the field were gaining on them. The fit and powerful Curlew was not yet operating in top gear, so had plenty of energy yet in reserve, but Merlin would have preferred to enter the final half mile well in the lead. Clearing the final hurdle on the bend, Merlin could feel another horse coming up on his left to join Curlew.

"It's Devil Waters coming to challenge the leader!" he heard the commentator shout, "Southern Cross is on their heels. They're approaching the second last...."

Merlin had no choice now but to step on the gas. The dark shape of Devil Waters loomed up at Curlew Landings side, the jockey pressing his mount forward, shouting repeatedly 'get on, get on, good lad'. Curlew, for his part, took exception to the attempt by Devil Waters to pass him, and sped forward with increased determination. The two horses cleared the second last together, Southern Cross half a length behind.

The finish of the race seemed to the Sampfield Grange connections to take forever, even though it was run at breakneck speed. The battle between Curlew Landings and Devil Waters was like a grim duel to the death with neither of the horses and their jockeys giving ground. Even Southern Cross was unable to stay the pace and was soon two lengths behind as the leaders approached the last hurdle.

"Curlew Landings and Devil Waters are locked together!" shouted the commentator over the barrage of frenzied sound coming from the stands, "They're in the air with nothing between them."

Merlin had never needed to work so hard on Curlew Landings at the finish. The opponent was matching them, stride for stride and he could feel that Curlew, although game, was beginning to struggle to keep abreast of the other horse. As if in slow motion, the head of Devil Waters drew ahead of Curlew's and the frenziedly moving arm and shoulder of the black and red clad jockey came into the left side of Merlin's vision. The two horses flashed past the finishing post. Devil Waters had won by half a length.

Curlew soon came down to a walk not far past the finishing post, whilst Merlin sat back on the small saddle, breathless and deflated. Devil Waters and his jockey had cantered on further ahead and were about to turn back to join the others, who had streamed past the winning post, Southern Cross in third place, the remaining runners close behind.

"Hard luck, Merlin," Merlin heard Jenna's voice say behind him, but Merlin's attention was on the approaching Devil Waters.

"Good ride, *fy frrind*," Merlin told the winning jockey, realising that he did not know the other man's first name. He was the same jockey who had ridden both Devil Waters and Bees and Mist at Kempton Park on Boxing Day, and Merlin had assumed him to be a recently recruited stable jockey for Dean Parry, who was listed as the trainer. Curlew Landings had not met Devil Waters in a race before that day, whilst a different jockey had ridden Bees and Mist in the Bowl Chase ten months ago. The same jockey, Merlin now recalled, had more recently also been piloting Altimeter, the horse which had beaten Katseye at Ascot before Christmas and again on Festival Trials Day at Cheltenham. All three of the other horses had been trained by Dean Parry and had run in the same black and red colours.

"*Diolch*," replied the other jockey, unexpectedly, adding rather unnecessarily, "Good horse, this one."

Merlin left the winning jockey to his post-race interview with the enthusiastic TV presenter and trotted the sweating Curlew to where a glum-looking Travis was standing waiting for them by the entrance to the horsewalk.

"What went on there, Merlin, mate?" asked Travis, sounding dazed, "Curlew looked to be going bonzer to me."

"'e was," Merlin replied, "Nothing wrong with 'im. That other 'orse was just too good. We're goin' to 'ave to up our game, we are."

As Curlew Landings plodded dutifully out of the TV camera shot towards the second place spot in the winners' enclosure, where his connections awaited him, a disappointed Kelly reached for the remote control to switch off the television screen in the Sampfield Grange kitchen.

"No, leave it on, Kelly," Kye stopped her, "I want to hear what the winners have to say. Curlew's not been beaten by this horse before. Wonder if they're thinking of going to the Champion Hurdle at the Festival with him?"

Kelly shrugged and left Kye and Jackie sitting on their own. Lewis had already disappeared into the hall, saying that he and Kelly needed to ensure that everything was ready for Mr Sampfield's imminent return home and for the accommodation of the house guest who would reportedly be accompanying him.

The TV interview with Devil Waters' Northern Irish accented jockey revealed little information other than that he was pleased with the win and that it was up to the horse's connections where he ran next. Kye and Jackie continued to watch the coverage together, wondering if either the owner or trainer would be interviewed on screen about their horse's surprise win, as it seemed to the tipsters and pundits at least.

The TV presenters did not let them down. And in the course of the informative interviews, Kye learned not only that Devil Waters was indeed to be aimed at the Champion Hurdle, but also that both the trainer and owner were familiar faces. The trainer, Dean Parry, was the son of Kye's former employer in Cheshire and the owner, whom the presenter addressed as Mr Lowry, was the man Kye had thought he recognised in the parade ring at Cheltenham. This time, though, Kye now remembered with a sudden shock exactly where he had seen the familiar man before. It was in the road haulage depot where Kye had once helped make so-called chassis mods to the black and red liveried lorries.

The delighted owner of winner Devil Waters also owned the haulage company.

35

Kingwell Hurdle day was destined to spring a few more surprises.

The unexpected victory of Devil Waters had rankled with Merlin, and, having listened to the enthusiastic but bland comments of the happy owner following the prize giving, he had resolved to speak further to the unfamiliar jockey who had now beaten him on three occasions, when the latter came back into the changing room, to see what more he could learn about the background of the winning horse. The racecard indicated that the jockey's name was Joel Edge. According also to the racecard, Joel had no more rides that day at Wincanton whilst Merlin himself had no other commitments until the race due to take place at 4.30pm. Merlin was sure he could easily catch up with his fellow rider in the intervening period.

Merlin, though, found himself thwarted. It appeared that Joel Edge had left the racecourse immediately after the prizegiving, apparently in company with Devil Waters' trainer, Dean Parry. Merlin could only hope that the stable staff looking after Devil Waters might have been more forthcoming with Sadie and Travis, who no doubt would be asking questions too.

Merlin's annoyance led him to be brusquer than he had intended when he went to track down Jenna Roberts shortly after learning the news of Joel's departure. Showing Sadie's selfie to the other male jockeys in the changing room had been relatively straightforward, but the female jockeys, of whom Jenna was the sole representative that day, used a separate, smaller changing area. Stopping a female staff member who was passing nearby, Merlin asked the young woman if she could find out whether the jockey Miss Roberts was inside the room, and, if so, to ask her if she could come outside into the corridor to speak to Mr ap Rhys. The process felt like something out of a bygone era, Merlin thought, as the helpful girl pushed open the entrance door to ask whether Miss Roberts was inside.

Jenna came up to the wooden door at once, a wary look on her face.

"You can come in if you want, Merlin," she said, "I'm the only one here."

"No fear," Merlin told her, at once, "I don' wan' to be 'auled up on some disciplinary charge."

"Sorry, I should have thought of that," Jenna apologised promptly, "What did you want to talk to me about, Merlin?"

"This photo," Merlin responded, shoving the mobile phone under Jenna's nose, "It's of my Gold Cup 'orse, Tabikat, and Sadie that looks after 'im. You recognise this man in the background at all, do you?"

Merlin was quite unprepared for Jenna's reaction. He had never seen anyone turn white before, but this was a rather accurate description of what happened to Jenna's face. The normally tough young woman took a step backwards and slumped awkwardly against the door frame.

"Christ, Jen, you ok?" exclaimed Merlin, shocked by the other jockey's reaction. Fearing she might fall, he reached out to grab her by the arm.

Jenna's eyes were closed. She made no sound except for a couple of gasping gulps, as if she was trying her best not to be sick. She did not speak for several seconds, by which time Merlin had begun to suspect that she had been taken ill and was debating whether he should fetch help from the nearby medical room.

"Shall I call someone for you?" Merlin asked, eventually, not sure what to do.

"It's all right," Jenna said, standing upright once again, some of the colour returning to her cheeks, "That picture, it gave me a shock, that's all."

"Why?" asked Merlin, "Is this the wanker that jumped me at Kempton?"

"Yes," replied Jenna, quietly, "And he's not a wanker."

"Well, 'oo is 'e then?" demanded Merlin, forgetting his previous concern for Jenna's welfare, "Do you know 'im?"

"I can't talk to you," replied Jenna, more staunchly, "I'm sorry, Merlin. Please don't ask me again."

Merlin, annoyed now, felt more than justified in insisting on being told the identity of the person who had attacked him, but Jenna simply turned away and slipped through the door behind her, which she shut in Merlin's face.

As Merlin tramped angrily back to the jockey's changing room, Travis was leading a weary Curlew Landings, now rugged up and protectively dressed for travelling, back to the Sampfield Grange horsebox. Lost in his own thoughts, he did not notice a young woman standing at the entrance to the lorry park.

"Hello, Travis," said the girl in a shy voice, "Is that your horse?"

Travis looked at the speaker and for a moment struggled to remember where he had seen her before.

"You're the barmaid at the Fox," he said, after a few seconds, "Tina, that right?"

"Tegan," the young woman corrected him.

"Sorry, Tegan," repeated Travis, remembering his resolution to keep the girl onside in case she could provide any information about the source of the ketamine in the pocket of the borrowed jacket, "Enjoying the racing, are you?"

"Not really," Tegan replied, her honesty taking Travis by surprise, "I'm scared of horses. I've been in the car park all day anyway."

"Why?" Travis could not help but ask, mystified by the information.

"I had to meet some people," Tegan replied timidly, "I was wondering if you needed anything yourself today."

"What do you mean?" Travis asked, more puzzled than ever.

"That stuff in the jacket, you know," Tegan tried to clarify, "You want some more? I can get it for you."

Travis's mind whirled and his heart started to thump uncomfortably. He had not expected the pallid barmaid to approach him directly about the ketamine which he was now sure had been in the jacket pocket last year. She clearly thought he had used it himself and that he might be a customer for some future sales. It was strange, Travis thought, that such a quiet little thing should be a drug dealer. Maybe the owner of the jacket was the dealer and had put her up to it.

Curlew shifted restlessly about, earning a scared glance from Tegan, as Travis asked her, "The bloke whose jacket I had, is he here?"

Tegan had continued to eye Curlew Landings fearfully, but this question seemed to send her into a state of terror.

"Yes .. no .. you won't speak to him, will you?" she stammered.

"Who is he, then, your boyfriend or what?" asked Travis, impatiently.

The last thing that Tegan wanted Travis to think was that she had a boyfriend.

"It's my brother," she said, beginning to panic, "But he doesn't know I lent you the jacket. He was livid when he found the ket was gone. But, don't worry, Travis, please, I didn't tell him it was you that took it."

344

"Your brother, the spanner monkey in the Charlton servo?" asked Travis incredulously, "He gets you to do his running, then? You could get arrested Tegan, you're breaking the law. You could end up in the bloody clink, both of you. And I didn't take your brother's ket. I don't do drugs. It was – er - someone else that took it."

As if on cue, Curlew Landings snorted loudly and impatiently, clearly keen to get on with his homeward journey. Tegan jumped back in fright.

"It's all right, I'm holding him," Travis said, more gently, seeing that Tegan was genuinely afraid of Curlew. The idea that she or her brother could be in league with Jack Tytherleigh now seemed increasingly ludicrous. They were just a couple of local losers trying to make a bit of cash for themselves.

"I've got to take this horse home now," Travis told Tegan, "The boss'll be along soon and she'll be mad if he's not in the box and ready to go. You think about what I said, Tegan. Drugs are a bloody bag of worms, trust me."

Tegan watched Travis walk away towards the parked horseboxes leading the big brown horse behind him. Tears stung her eyes and furrowed down her pale cheeks. She wondered if her idol would even care if she told him that Gray had forced her into helping him with the drug dealing. More likely, Travis would despise her, she thought. After all, she was already a criminal who had been sacked from her weekend job for stealing a guest's computer stick and now she was delivering drugs to sleazy looking men in the car park of a racecourse whilst her brother drummed up more business from the people inside. What was there for anyone to admire about her? She wouldn't see the gorgeous Travis ever again.

Tegan went to sit in Gray's parked car. She had nowhere else to go.

Meanwhile, in the crowded paddock area, Sadie made an unexpected discovery. Once Mr Sampfield had arrived at the racecourse, Sadie had been no longer required to act as his representative, a role she was at that moment glad to relinquish, not least because she was not now required to answer the agitated questions of Toby Halstock and Gilbert Peveril concerning Curlew Landings' narrow defeat. Fortunately, the usually reckless Mr Halstock appeared to Sadie to have been more restrained with his bets than on previous occasions and seemed more perplexed than upset.

"If you don't need me, Mr Sampfield," Sadie had said, "I'll go on home now with Travis and Curlew."

The other three men, including the stranger in the cowboy hat, had already begun heading for one of the racecourse bars. Mr Sampfield had seemed anxious to keep the group together and had quickly agreed to Sadie's request, saying that he would speak to her later at Sampfield Grange.

Within a few seconds of that short conversation, Sadie suddenly caught sight of the man captured in the background of the Kempton Park selfie. He was standing by the paddock, intently watching the horses preparing to compete in the fifth race. As at Kempton Park, the man was wearing dark glasses and a cap, but the waxed jacket of the photo had now been replaced with a dark brown leather version. Sadie, trying to stay calm, remembered that Merlin was not due to ride in the upcoming race. They had agreed to meet each other later, back at her flat at Sampfield Grange, but the unanticipated sighting of the unknown man made Sadie decide that she must amend that plan.

As Sadie started to walk towards the weighing room an announcement was made on the racecourse tannoy. Jenna Roberts, due to ride horse number four, Ginger Tea, would be replaced by Sammy Mullen, claiming 5lbs, the speaker informed the racegoers clustered around the paddock. Sadie would have paid little attention to this information had the man in the cap and sunglasses not looked startled by the announcement, and, after a moment's thought, pulled out his phone to compose a text message.

Sadie could not send a text message to Merlin whilst racing was taking place. As she reached the weighing room, however, Merlin suddenly emerged from the doorway, an outdoor jacket slung around his shoulders, another jockey standing by his side and pointing towards the paddock. Merlin spoke hurriedly to his companion and ran out of the weighing room entrance, where Sadie stepped forward to intercept him.

"I've seen him, Merlin, he's here," she said urgently, gripping Merlin's arm.

"I know, Mark jus' told me," Merlin replied, grimly, "I'm goin' to speak to 'im right now."

Before the two of them could do anything further, however, the object of their concern seemed to receive a reply to his text message and immediately set off briskly away from them in the direction of the Owners and Trainers car park.

"Come on, let's get after 'im, Sadie," Merlin said, adding quickly in response to her suddenly worried look, "'e can't do anythin' to me with all these people around. It's not dark like it was at Kempton."

The stranger did not get very far before he met up with someone else. Recently replaced jockey Jenna Roberts, dressed now in a blue zip-up jacket and jeans, appeared to be waiting for him by the exit gate. As soon as the stranger reached her, Jenna appeared to launch into an agitated explanation, gesturing with her hands and talking rapidly.

By the time their quarry saw them, Merlin and Sadie were too nearby for there to be any possibility of escape. Fortunately, most of the spectators had moved to the stands to watch the current race and no-one seemed to notice either Merlin or Jenna amongst the quartet gathered by the exit.

"I'm givin' you ten seconds before I call the police," Merlin confronted the other man, who had turned to face him, a look of startled recognition evident from his posture, "I know it was you that 'it me at Kempton. 'oo the fuck are you?"

Before Merlin's alleged assailant could answer, Jenna stepped between the two men and put her hand in the centre of Merlin's chest.

"He's my husband," said Jenna, firmly, "I'm sorry, Merlin. I should have told you."

Merlin, for once in his life, was rendered completely speechless. He stood in open mouthed silence, staring first at Jenna and then at the young man she had described as her husband. Taking advantage of the pause, the other man removed his sunglasses and spoke directly to Merlin in strongly accented English, "My name is Martim Nuno de Fontes, sir. I regret sincerely for injuring you. I am not intending. I want that you go from Jeninha, is all."

As Merlin struggled to frame a suitable response, Sadie took the opportunity to make her own voice heard.

"Why were you watching Tabikat and me at Kempton Park, then?" she demanded, "Merlin and Jenna weren't even around then."

Martim Nuno de Fontes turned his newly revealed brown eyes towards Sadie and said, "Is because the 'orse is blood of El Heredero de Sevilla. 'e belong to my family."

36

"It's time we pooled our resources, Sam," Frank Stanley had said when Sam had called him from Melbourne a few days earlier.

Sam and Frank were sitting on two of the capacious sofas in the Sampfield Grange drawing room following breakfast on the morning after Kingwell Hurdle day. Outside, visible through the wide window overlooking the garden, the snowdrops were fading around the sodden lawn whilst the green shoots of the crocuses were still deciding whether or not to make their annual yellow and purple debut. A wet winter without snow had left the claggy soil dark with retained turgid moisture which the weak sun had done little to evaporate. Only the voice of an insistently chittering stonechat broke the silence of the damp garden whilst a group of foraging sparrows flitted silently between the hedges.

The overnight guest, whose silver rental car was just turning out into the lane beyond the Sampfield Grange gates been briefly introduced to a desperately inquisitive Lewis the previous evening as Mr Craig Wickham 'from the horseracing authorities in Melbourne'. Sadie had been called over from the chauffeur's flat to be introduced Mr Wickham and had taken the opportunity to remind her employer that she would be leaving shortly with Merlin, once the jockey arrived at Sampfield Grange from Wincanton, to spend the following day at Ffos Las racecourse where Merlin was booked to ride a promising novice for a South Wales trainer. Tabikat had been at the Dicks yard since Friday where his exercise programme was being temporarily overseen by assistant trainer Amelia Dicks in Sadie's absence.

Sam had not entirely kept pace with the tortuous twists and turns of the relationship between Sadie and the Welsh jockey over the previous two years. Their arrival together in Merlin's car at Sampfield Grange in October had led him vaguely to assume that whatever had happened to drive them apart eighteen months previously had been either rectified or forgiven. Sam had been aware of Sadie's intervening relationship with Luke Cunningham, which appeared to have come to an end during the period in which Luke was recovering from the vicious attack at Aintree racecourse in April. The means by which Sam had learned this was through Lady Cunningham having approached him rather hesitantly at a Newmarket race meeting in the summer to enquire after Sadie's welfare and to express her hope that she would not hold her son's angry words against him. Sam had been mystified by this communication and had simply informed Luke's mother that Sadie had not discussed the matter with him but that he did not believe her to be the sort of young woman to bear anyone a grudge.

Sam's subsequent observation that Sadie and Merlin were on apparently cordial terms once again had led him to make the proposal that Merlin take on the temporary training role at Sampfield Grange during Sam's enforced absence in Australia. Perhaps rather naively, Sam had not anticipated that the couple's former intimacy would be rekindled so suddenly during his short absence. Sam had been made aware of this development very soon after his arrival home, thanks to Lewis informing his employer that the bedroom which had been made available for Merlin in the house could be given to the visitor because Merlin normally slept in Sadie's flat when staying at the yard.

With Sadie and Tabikat both absent, the morning ride had been a more limited affair than usual, which Sam, still feeling the effects of jetlag, had asked Kye and Jackie to organise with the help of the work riders. Caladesi Island and Ranger Station had been kept in their boxes waiting for Sam and Frank Stanley to take them out later in the day.

"Thank you for meeting me this morning, Mr Wickham. My name is Frank Stanley. I believe that Sam has explained that I work for the security services," Frank had introduced himself formally to Craig Wickham as soon as they had sat down to breakfast together, "Sam tells me that he met you in Melbourne."

"That's right," the other man replied, with a glance at Sam as he heard the unfamiliar nickname, "I spoke to our contact at the BHA here in January to inform him that we've now made progress on a report of horse doping in Victoria which was made to us informally from the UK last year. My BHA contact then called me to say that James here was visiting in Oz, so I suggested we meet up. James was good enough to organise his return journey via Melbourne. I assume you are familiar with the nature of the doping report?"

"Sam has told me about the suspicions which his young cousin and his jockey friend had about the administration of performance enhancing drugs to racehorses in the yard where they were based in Australia," Frank told him, concisely, "Sam has also explained that this particular substance was not being detected through the routine testing of the horses at the racecourse. I understand, though, that the Racing Victoria authorities believe that they have progressed some enhancements to the testing process which may enable this substance to be identified. Is that correct?"

"That is correct," the other man assured him, falling suddenly silent as a bustling Lewis came into the room with a large wooden tray on which the breakfast dishes were neatly set out. The occupants of the table busied themselves politely pouring more coffee and tea for each other until Lewis had reluctantly left them alone once again.

"Sorry, sirs, I'm sure your man is trustworthy," Craig Wickham apologised, putting down his coffee cup, before continuing, rather self-importantly, "But this operation is being kept very quiet at the moment. We don't want the bird to fly the coop. The official story is that I'm in the UK on a fact-finding trip, looking at welfare arrangements at your racecourses with an eye to improving our own procedures and training. The real story is that we believe that this same substance may have made its way to some UK racecourses. You've got the same problem here, though. Your dope testing processes won't pick this stuff up. Our new test should find it. The BHA don't want anyone knowing that they're introducing this enhancement to the existing tests, hence the cover story. I'm only being allowed to tell you now because I had their permission to talk to you and James here."

"I don't need to know the details of the BHA/Racing Victoria operation," Frank assured the Australian, "My interest is in only two things: one, whether the substance concerned has indeed been brought into the UK, and two, by what means it is being introduced undetected into the horses' systems and remains undetectable after the end of the race."

"We call it Ghost,' Craig Wickham commented, tucking into his bacon and eggs, "We don't know enough about it yet to be able to classify and ban it. But I didn't know the security services had any interest in horse doping."

"We don't," Frank replied, "But we are interested in international organised crime and in the drug trafficking which is part of it. Your operation is, in effect, a small part of that larger picture. If apparently invisible drugs can be moved around the world and administered to animals, undetected, we are looking at the potential for a very serious threat to the human population. I hope you understand my point, Mr Wickham."

"What are you wanting from me?" the other man said, after a short pause during which he seemed to process the implications of Frank's statement, "Obviously, I will report any positive findings to the BHA and I assume they will inform you, as you are in contact with them already."

"There is some intelligence of which you should be aware," Frank said, appearing to ignore Craig Wickham's question, "The first is that we know that two people who worked with the trainer Jack Tytherleigh in Australia are here in the UK. They were seen and identified at a UK racecourse two weeks ago. Second, the people concerned were also seen in the company of the son of a trainer based in England. And third, we have identified an individual owner whose horses may be benefiting from the administration of this substance."

"So, you're suggesting I should focus on these horses first?" asked Craig Wickham, "That's no problem if I'm given the locations of the racecourses where they're running next. I reckon I can re-order my schedule."

"On the contrary," Frank responded, to Craig Wickham's obvious surprise, "I am asking you not to do anything which might arouse any suspicion that this activity has been detected. If you obtain a positive test on a horse, as I am confident that you eventually will, I am asking you not to give any indication whatever that you have found anything. It would be helpful to us if the people concerned in this activity should believe that they are continuing to evade detection, in other words, that the testing process remains ineffective. Instead, I should like you to report the findings only to me, using the number on this card. I have cleared this with the BHA, but obviously we require your personal co-operation in this matter."

The flummoxed Australian investigator, having hesitantly accepted the proffered card, eventually agreed to Frank's request only after asking several further questions, most of which Frank avoided answering in any useful detail, followed by a confirmatory telephone call to his contact at the BHA, who had clearly been expecting the call.

"I guess you folks know what you're doing," was all Craig Wickham had said, irritably, as he had made ready to leave, evidently feeling that his interesting overseas detective assignment had been thoroughly undermined, "Bloody rum way of doing things, if you ask me. Anyhow, I'm due at a racecourse called Ffos Las in three hours, so I'd better make tracks. Thanks for the hospitality, James. No doubt we'll speak further in due course."

"It looks as if I was right to put the two of you in touch, Frank," Sam commented cautiously, as they sat together afterwards in the drawing room, a large silver jug of fresh coffee before them, "I am assuming it was Kye who provided the so-called intelligence you described. I suppose that was why you wanted him present at Cheltenham that day. What I want to ask, though – that story you told me about the bombing in the Irish town, is it connected to this business or is that something different altogether?"

"You ask far too many sensible questions, Sam," replied Frank, standing up, "I'll try to tell you as much as I can when we are outside on the horses and our friend Lewis can't listen in. Air gapping, that's what the technonerds would call it. But first, I want to hear from you about your mother."

Whilst Kye and Jackie were tacking up the two patient hunters at Sampfield Grange, Sadie and Merlin were making swift progress in the BMW along the Westbound carriageway of the relatively quiet M4, bound, like Craig Wickham, for Ffos Las racecourse. Merlin had arrived promptly at Sampfield Grange following his final ride at Wincanton racecourse the previous day. Sadie had had no choice but to travel home ahead of him in the horsebox with Curlew Landings and Travis and had been awaiting his arrival impatiently.

"We're meetin' Jenna and 'er 'usband at my place in Chepstow this evenin'," Merlin had informed Sadie shortly, "I'm goin' to get to the bottom of this crap. You mus' believe me, Sadie, I 'ad no idea she was married when I was goin' out with 'er last year. She kept that quiet, all right."

"What was all that about Tabikat belonging to the man's family?" Sadie had asked him, her tone slightly panic stricken, "They're not going to try to take him away, are they?"

"Not if I 'ave anything to do with it," Merlin had announced, sounding angry, as he had steered the powerful black car down the darkening country lane, "We'll find out about that too, don' you worry, *cariad*."

The meeting between the four young people had taken place round the table in the stone flagged kitchen of Merlin's Chepstow cottage. It had lasted two hours and had been tense, intermittently angry and fascinating, and, in the end, rather sad. The story which Jenna had told about her marriage to Martim Nuno de Fontes, or Marti, as she called him, had been short and to the point. Following the end of her relationship with the assistant trainer at the home counties yard to which she had previously been attached, Jenna had been offered by a sympathetic friend the opportunity to spend what she called some 'me time' working at a prestigious rural stud in the South of Portugal. This offer had had the unexpected consequence that Jenna, still smarting from her rejection by her former fiancé, had entered into a reckless affair with the younger son of the owner of the stud, and, succumbing to a mad impulse to prove that she had now been made a better offer than before, had accepted the young Martim Nuno de Fontes' equally mad proposal of marriage. The opposition of the de Fontes family to a match in which the participants had known each other for less than two months had only made the rash couple more determined.

The early days of the hasty marriage had been an exercise in learning more about each other, including the fact that Jenna planned to resume her career as a jump jockey in England. An argument had ensued, Martim had told Jenna to leave, and Jenna had done so, stating that she wanted a divorce. Returning to England, she had told no-one of the ill-advised marriage, perhaps even deluding herself that it had never happened, until her distraught young husband had sought her out. Finding her in a relationship with the previously unknown Merlin ap Rhys, Martim had lost his temper and punched Merlin in the face in the car park at Kempton Park racecourse. Martim's work with the stud horses and their offspring had made him as fit and strong as the tough-muscled Merlin and the punch had also had a good measure of frustrated sexual passion behind it.

"I regret again that I injure you, *senhor*," Martim had repeated more than once, as Jenna had told the unedifying story to a glowering Merlin and a silent Sadie, "I love Jeninha and I no want her with other man. You 'ave beautiful girlfriend, I see, so I 'ope you 'appy."

"That's not the point," had snapped Merlin, leaning forward across the kitchen table which separated the two couples, "You made a fool of me, Jenna. I wouldn' 'ave gone with you if I'd known you were married."

"I'm so sorry, Merlin," Jenna had replied, desperately, "There's no excuse. I never thought Marti would come here and attack you."

"'e's lucky he took me by surprise," Merlin had bristled, "Or 'e'd 'ave been the one 'oo got 'urt."

"Tell us about Tabikat," Sadie had suddenly intervened, sensing that the conversation was descending into repeated recriminations and useless apologies. Sadie had felt little sympathy for the other couple's self-inflicted problems, although the kinder side of her nature had hoped that they would somehow resolve their differences. She had also had to admit to herself that the situation that Jenna had so thoughtlessly created had been the trigger for the resumption of her own relationship with Merlin, as Martim himself had just pointed out.

The story of Tabikat had taken up the larger part of the two hour discussion, mainly because it had been recounted by Martim Nuno de Fontes, whose command of English was limited. Jenna had picked up a little Portuguese, so with her help and that of a translation app on Merlin's mobile phone, the story of the unknown part of the bloodline of the talented and unusual racehorse bred on Enda's Farm had been eventually revealed. Even Merlin had for a short time put aside his anger as he had struggled to listen to the story, which the fragmented nature of its narrative, not to mention Martim's accent, made seem more romantic than had probably been the case. The greed, theft and deception involved had appeared less vicious only because they had been eroded by the large volume of metaphorical water which since had passed under the associated metaphorical bridge.

Had Eoghan Foley and Caitlin been present when the story was told, they would doubtless have had more pieces to contribute to the strange jigsaw puzzle which was Tabikat's past, and, by extension, that of Katseye and the still absent Katalyst too. But they were far away in Ireland at that moment.

The De Fontes stud, Martim had explained, was an old family establishment whose business was the breeding and selling of Lusitano horses.

"The Lusitano, certainly you know, sir and miss, is relative of Andalucian 'orse," Martim had explained, laboriously, "Less than one 'undred years we 'ave in Portugal separate stud book for Lusitano. Lusitano is strong and brave 'orse, very quick, we use 'im for fighting the bulls. 'e is also proud, intelligent, 'ave good temperament. These 'orses are in demand for 'igh school work."

An earlier generation of the de Fontes family had been breeding Lusitano horses, as well as cultivating vines and arable crops, when the Spanish Civil War had started in the summer of 1936 with the invasion by Nationalist troops of Andalucia. The capital city of Sevilla had been seized by the invaders and many of its citizens massacred in public executions.

"There exist a family by the name of Jimenez," Martim had staggered on, slowly, "They 'ave Andalucian 'orses for circus and performance with *flamenco.* They travel in Europe with big circus. When war begins, they are in Portugal. They bring to my great grandfather their 'orses. You know Andalucian 'orse 'ave the blood of Arab and Barb 'orse, the most ancient of the 'orse breeds. They give the Andalucian 'orse 'is pride, 'is endurance, 'is elegance. My great grandfather and the circus man Jimenez, they make project to breed great champion from their 'orses for the bullfights. They produce El Heredero de Sevilla."

El Heredero de Sevilla, it had seemed from Martim's fractured and sometimes incomprehensible narrative, had, though, never appeared in any bullring. The hospitality shown to the Jimenez family had been repaid with the theft of the colt together with two of the stud's Lusitano brood mares.

"My great grandfather and 'is, son, my grandfather, try to follow the 'orses," Martin had ploughed on, "The plan of Jimenez, though, is good. They disappear for ever. The circus travel and is gone when the war in Spain is finished. But, there is war then in Europe for many years. No business is left for circus, so it is gone. After the war, my grandfather search for El Heredero de Sevilla and maybe 'is progeny. 'e is told many things. They are in England, or maybe in Ireland."

"What makes you think that Tabikat is a descendent of this stallion?" had asked Merlin, sceptically.

"Is the Jimenez family of today, they tell my father," Martim had replied, simply, "The 'orses are in Ireland, where they take them long time ago. They have bred them there with your own thoroughbred 'orses, who 'ave also Arab ancestors. They 'ave kept the 'orses on a farm, I do not know the name. Some of the 'orses are better than others. Then they produce a mare, who is perfect. She is called Maria, Maria la Herederita de Sevilla."

"Maire!" had exclaimed Sadie, making everyone jump in the growing darkness of the small kitchen, "That's what Feanna told me that Kat's Gift was called when she was given to her uncle sixteen years ago."

"Kat's Gift?" had queried Martim, uncertainly, "This your name for Maria la Herederita de Sevilla?"

"Yes," Sadie had replied, "Kat's Gift is the granddam of Tabikat, Katseye and Katalyst."

At this point, Merlin had suddenly stood up and called a halt to the discussion, saying firmly that he and Sadie had work to do the following day. As Merlin had closed the house door on the troubled couple, Sadie had asked him, "What do you think of all that stuff they told us then?"

"I think those two need to grow up," Merlin had commented, crossly, "'e's bloody lucky I don't report 'im to the police for assault."

"I didn't mean that," Sadie had corrected him, "I mean the story about Tabsi."

"A load of bollocks," Merlin replied.

37

"When Mr Stanley returns, please would you ask him to come into the office for a few minutes," Isabella Hall had said to Jackie, as the two women had watched the brown shapes of Caladesi Island and Ranger Station stolidly carrying their companionably conversing riders up the hoof imprinted track behind the house.

Isabella did not work at Sampfield Grange on a Sunday but had turned up unannounced on her bicycle shortly after the departure of the discomfited Australian guest. Noting her arrival from the kitchen window, Lewis and Kelly, uncharitable as usual wherever Isabella Hall was concerned, had assumed that Mr Stanley's presence that day had been the attraction. Seeing Mr Stanley going into the yard office after parting from Mr Sampfield when the two men had returned from their morning ride did nothing to change their assumption, especially when the office door had been shut behind him.

"Good morning, Frank. The flash drive," Isabella began, as soon as Frank Stanley had entered the yard office, where Isabella was sitting behind the desk, still wearing her black and green cycling gear, "I've been thinking. I believe that you've drawn the wrong conclusions."

"You do? How?" asked Frank, immediately interested, sitting down on the wooden kitchen chair placed opposite the tidy desk.

"When we were on Cleeve Hill that day," Isabella continued, "You said that you and George had been incorrect in assuming that Dominik Katz was perpetrating some sort of cybercrime. What was the flash drive for, then? We all agree that it wasn't left in The Charlton Arms by mistake. You suggested originally that Dominik Katz planned to call the people at the inn and get them to plug it in, cause the attack on the Ardua Industrie IT systems and send the encrypted message to London, after which it went on its way, with extra fancy encryption, to a pointless storage facility in Liverpool."

"Yes," said Frank, cautiously, "So…"

"What if he left the flash drive for someone to collect?" asked Isabella, "That would explain why the information on it was in plain text. It was that person who was meant to plug it in somewhere, not the people at The Charlton Arms. So, yes, Dominik Katz would ring up, say that he had left something in his room and that a friend or business associate, or something of the sort, would come in to collect it. He would have given them details of how the person would identify themselves at the reception desk. But none of this happened because he was killed in that freak accident with the Altior's towbar. The person didn't go in to get the flash drive because they never heard from Dominik. They were waiting for an instruction which never came."

"Go on," prompted Frank, as Isabella stopped for a few seconds to organise her thoughts.

"Tegan Colvin stole the flash drive and it sat around somewhere for months until Graham Colvin decided to use it and found the instruction which the other person was meant to get – the location of the things they were supposed to collect, together with the access details, all set out in plain English. That person wouldn't have known anything about the other issues which the flash drive caused. They were just there to pick up the items which Dominik Katz had left there for collection."

"You're being very coy about this 'person'," Frank commented, calmly, "Who was it, do you think?"

"I think it's that woman from Liverpool, Sheryl," Isabella said, "I heard Kye talking in the tack room with Jackie on the day that she called you to come here. Kye said that Sheryl was outside The Charlton Arms on the day after Tabikat won the Gold Cup and that she was making threatening gestures at him, miming cutting his throat, or something. That may well be true, but I think she came here to pick up the flash drive. Kye being nearby at the time was just chance, and she made use of the opportunity to taunt him."

"And Sheryl Mavers had been instructed to pick up everything that she found in the storage unit, including the paper file," Frank finished for her, "Graham Colvin left that behind because he didn't know what it was. He just took away the goods that were with the file."

"What did Graham Colvin take?" asked Isabella, "Do you have any idea?"

"Yes, I do," Frank replied, quickly, "I think we have just found our ghost. Well worked out, Isabella."

"Ghost? You mean Dominik Katz?" queried Isabella, puzzled.

"No, the undetectable horse dope," Frank said, "That's what our Australian friend called it this morning. Ghost."

"The bit I don't get, though," Isabella went on, "Is why Dominik Katz would be involved in racehorse doping."

"He wasn't," Frank replied, "That was just one of the many uses to which the intelligence he was selling could be put. He was selling the process, the process he'd learned about from the APT on the *prizrak* production facility which I told you about when we met in Funchal. You said yourself that the word *prizrak* means ghost in Russian. But it doesn't refer to the nerve agent itself, it refers to the process for disguising it. Racehorse doping is only one usage for such a process. The criminal organisation with which Dominik Katz was in discussion had a more extensive use in mind for it – large scale movement of undetectable cocaine springs to mind."

"But you said the paper file in the storage unit was just a lot of garbled information," Isabella countered.

"It was," said Frank, thoughtfully, "Dominik was keeping his powder dry, playing a devious game, as usual. The real information was sent somewhere else. Somewhere from which he could pass it on to another potential protector if he failed to reach a satisfactory deal on his future with these people."

"The rented data storage in Liverpool," Isabella said quietly.

"Precisely," said Frank, reaching for his mobile phone.

Unaware of the detective work taking place behind the closed door of the yard office, Sam was seated in comparative comfort in his study on the other side of the house. He would have to wait until the evening to call his cousin Teddy in Queensland, which gave him some time to think over what Frank had discussed with him whilst they had been out on their ride. The early part of the conversation had centred on Sam's mother, Raldi. Sam had briefly described the circumstances of her death and the tortuous process of the Queensland Coroner's investigation which had delayed the family's plans for a funeral.

"Then, Frank, there was something unexpected," Sam had told his friend, who had listened in silence to the sad narrative, "As you probably realise, my mother had her own wealth quite independent of that of my father's family. Apart from a number of gifts to staff and friends, she willed it all to a Trust which she had set up after my father died. The Trust was arranged to come into action, as it were, following her death. The odd thing about it, though, is the objects which have been specified for the Trust."

"Which are?' Frank had asked, as the two horses had reached the top gallop.

"The money is to be used for the benefit of education and training for disadvantaged young people in the Charlton and Warnock area, particularly those who have fallen into crime through poverty or lack of opportunity," Sam had replied, "I never knew that my mother gave any thought to local social problems of this sort. She certainly never mentioned her interest to me."

"Your father used to be a magistrate, did he not?" had said Frank, after a pause, "Maybe it is something he spoke to her about. He would have seen plenty of examples of such issues through sitting on the local Bench."

"Yes, that's the conclusion the family eventually reached," Sam had agreed, "My mother certainly knew how to spring surprises. The manner of her death was pretty much of a surprise in itself. Tell me, Frank, do you still blame her for what she did to us? I've thought about it frequently, and I'm quite sure she thought she was doing the right thing by separating us."

"Well, she's no longer here to separate us now," Frank had pointed out, "Which is just as well, because there is something I want to discuss with you. But let's get the horses moving first, so they don't get bored."

The topic which Frank had raised later on the ride had been of his plans for his future.

"I have one last job which I need to see through to completion," he had told Sam, "And then I shall be satisfied with what I have achieved in my career. I have decided that it's time for me to enjoy new achievements in my personal life whilst I am still young and fit enough to do so. I have enjoyed spending time riding horses again, for instance, and would like to do more of it. As you know, Sam, my two ex-wives are both remarried, and I have no children, so I have only myself to consider."

"You are always welcome to ride here at Sampfield Grange, Frank," Sam had replied, cautiously, not sure where the conversation was leading and wondering if Frank was about to announce an intention to move away to another part of the world.

Frank's subsequent description of his ideas for the future had led Sam now to reach for the final DVD of the set which had been created from the collections of old-fashioned video cassette tapes which had been formerly stacked, unwatched, on the dark wooden shelves of the drawing room. Pushing the disk into the slot on the desk top computer, Sam played for the umpteenth time the recording of him and Frank as teenagers, exercising two of the Sampfield Grange pointers on the top gallop whilst his father shouted instructions and his mother called out enthusiastic encouragement from behind the camera. That recording had originally been made in the days when his mother had regarded the boys as nothing more than well-matched schoolfriends. Within a year of that recording, though, the two young men had been destined to be separated for most of the ensuing years of their lives.

Could that sort of comradeship be renewed after so long, Sam wondered? That they could become more than just friends again had not even been hinted at by Frank, whilst Sam was not sure that this was even possible after so much time. Sam knew that the two of them remained reserved and sometimes awkward in each other's company. The plain facts were that the friends had separately immersed themselves in careers designed to absorb all their energy and emotions. As a result, neither of them had family or dependants. They were both alone, except for the buried memory of a powerful teenage bond which had made them both happy long ago. Was that bond still there? Sam did not know.

Succumbing eventually to the effects of the creeping jetlag, Sam's head began to drop onto his chest whilst the recording played itself again, his mother's bright Australian tones confusing themselves with the more recent visions of her funeral and the imagined sight of her lying dead in the dried up stream bed in Queensland, a horse with an empty saddle standing alongside.

Whilst Sam was sleeping with his memories, Merlin's fast car was turning into the entrance of Ffos Las racecourse, its well-defined green Roman circus shape providing a sharp contrast to the patchwork fields and hedgerows of the surrounding Welsh countryside.

Had anyone at Sampfield Grange troubled to think about it, they might have wondered why Merlin and Sadie had given up an entire day of their time for Merlin to take a ride in a single race. They might have thought that the horse he was booked to ride had great potential for the future, which was true, or, more likely, that the reunited lovers simply wanted an excuse for some time to themselves in Merlin's attic love nest in South Wales, far from the listening ears at Sampfield Grange. They would not have connected their absence with a previous half day outing by Sadie and Merlin to view a young horse which it was said Mr Sampfield might be interested in buying. They would therefore not have suspected that Sadie, as an amateur jockey, was about to make her debut ride in a race under Rules. No-one had had any reason to look online at the Ffos Las racecard that day to discover Miss S Shinkins listed amongst the jockeys in the final race, riding an experienced steeplechaser trained in the same yard as the horse which Merlin would ride in the first race.

Merlin had forbidden any discussion of the previous evening's events during the ninety-mile journey from Chepstow to the Welsh racecourse. Intermittent rain had poured onto the speeding car as it had left the M4 at the signs pointing towards Llanelli. The skies, though, had quickly cleared to a bright blue and a cold breeze had made itself felt as Sadie had climbed out of the car.

Merlin's success in coaching Sadie and Indian Rocks to win their point to point race had led him to propose this more ambitious venture on Sadie's part. Selfish to the core, Merlin had not expected that he could harbour ambition for anyone other than himself. Someone with more insight than Sadie would have probably told Merlin that his pleasure was derived from his own perceived achievement as a coach, but Sadie had no such insight where Merlin was concerned. Sadie saw only that Merlin was enabling her to do something that she would not otherwise have attempted. The arrangement therefore suited both of them perfectly, for now, at least.

As the official results were later to show, Merlin's talented novice ride romped home in first place in the opening race. Sadie's race was the last on the card and involved eight horses and riders, none of whom were familiar to Sadie, and some of whom spoke to each other in Welsh. Sadie's mount, which she had ridden only once on morning exercise when she had visited the trainer's yard with Merlin, went by the name of Barchester Chorus.

Sadie had received authoritative riding instructions from Merlin during the journey to the racecourse that morning. It was a novel experience for her to walk out from the weighing room dressed in the unfamiliar light blue silks of the horse's elderly owner. Today, someone else had had the job of turning out and leading up the big bay horse ready for her to ride. Sadie loved it.

"The 'orse 'as been round 'ere a couple of times before," Merlin had told her, firmly, in the car "It's dead flat, so you just 'ave to keep 'im galloping, get a good look at the fences, stay out of trouble. The groun' should be on the soft side but it won't hold 'im up. Keep in the front 'alf, don' try to chase anythin' which goes off quick a'ead of you. Don' anticipate the finish, wait 'til you're sure of getting' a good stride into the last."

Sadie had no difficulty in following these instructions to the letter, tackling the big fences in confident style and eventually bringing Barchester Chorus home in second place, much to the pleasure of the horse's owner, who told Merlin admiringly, "*Mae eich gariad yn jeyi ardderchog*". Even Barchester Chorus, who may or may not have understood Welsh, seemed pleased with his new pairing with the unfamiliar Somerset rider

"We'll make sure you win next time you ride 'im," Merlin announced for the tenth time, as the two of them drove happily back towards the M4 junction, Sadie having recounted in excited detail every stride of the recent race.

"Am I allowed to talk to you about Tabsi now?" asked Sadie, eventually, keen to impart the information she had been forbidden to mention on their outward journey.

"So long as it's not more of this crap about 'im being descended from some bullfighting stallion," Merlin warned her, half-jokingly.

"Well, it might be," Sadie replied, "It's just that Tabsi's really good at dressage."

Merlin was not expecting this observation and, after a few moments' pause, said, "Dressage? 'ow do you know that, *cariad*?"

"You know during all the wet weather, we couldn't use the gallops?" Sadie explained, rather hesitantly, fearing that Merlin might be annoyed, "I couldn't bear putting him in the boring horse walker all the time, so I went out into the schooling area and we did some basic work - transitions, riding circles, serpentine loops, just the usual exercises to keep him supple. He's always so quick on the uptake that I taught him some more difficult stuff, lateral movements, half pass, flying changes, extended paces, that sort of thing. He picked it all up straightaway, Merlin. So, Jackie tried it afterwards with Big Kat too. He was good at it as well."

"Sounds like you all 'ad a good time, then," Merlin replied, flatly, "Look Sadie, Tabikat and Katseye are both three quarters Irish thoroughbred, we know that for a fact. Even if what that Fontes guy said was true, which I don't believe, there are Irish thoroughbred mares in the other bit of Tabikat's ancestry too. If there's any Lusitano in 'im, its well buried now."

"I'm going to talk to Feanna about it, anyway," Sadie informed him, defiantly, "If you won't listen, maybe she will."

38

During the three weeks preceding the start of the Cheltenham Festival, Sam could hardly avoid recognising that Sampfield Grange would come under increasing media scrutiny. Tabikat's bid to win the Triple Crown, with its associated million pound prize, would inevitably attract even more than the usual level of interest in the most fancied prospective runner in this season's Cheltenham Gold Cup race.

In an attempt to manage the media attention, Sam had agreed to participate in a series of vlog pieces with Stevie Stone, which, being readily accessible online, addressed the majority of the general public's requirements for information on the increasingly famous horse's preparation for the Gold Cup race. Stevie came to Sampfield Grange on several occasions over the three-week period to compile several video pieces with a voiceover by Tabby Cat, showing images of the impressive Tabikat and his stablemates in training on the gallops, together with interviews with Sadie, Merlin and even Mr Sampfield himself. The number of users of the Racing Tips for Smart Girls app increased substantially as a result.

Some of the more established racing press, preferring to use their own reporters and photographers, rather than rely on whatever Stevie Stone chose to make available, continued to contact Sampfield Grange directly with repeated requests for personal interviews and pictures. A persistent drone was seen hovering overhead on more than one occasion whilst the horses were working out on the top gallop. It was not clear whether this was operated by some enterprising local resident, hopeful of selling the video footage, or perhaps posting it online under his or her own name, or whether it was associated with the small groups of press representatives who sometimes waited outside the Sampfield Grange gates in the hope of getting a word with Merlin or Sam as they came and went from the rural estate.

Lewis and Kelly rather enjoyed Sampfield Grange being a temporary centre of attention, as a result of which some of the hacks found themselves being offered mugs of hot tea and bacon rolls as they shivered outside in the cold late February air. Lewis was always ready to chat about the yard and its occupants, both equine and human, but it soon became evident to his listeners that Lewis's knowledge of horse training and preparation, planned running tactics on the day of the race, and the threat likely to be posed to Tabikat's chances by the other highly talented competitors to be almost non-existent.

"What are you going to do with the hundred grand, Merlin?" one of the reporters called out as Merlin's black car nosed its way out of the gates past the shivering group. Merlin gave them a cheery wave and did not answer.

In the week following his return home, Sam had initially been looking forward to reverting to his well-established daily routine. He had found, however, that the lingering shock at the death of his mother followed by the unforeseen news given to him by Frank had unsettled his normally single-minded approach to his work. It was as if a new paradigm had been laid out, into which his old routines no longer fitted so neatly as before. There was a buried force struggling to escape from the self-imposed pattern, which, whilst not actually let loose, had now at least been given some air. In addition, the strange story related to Sam by Sadie concerning his stable stars' purported Lusitano stallion ancestor had reminded Sam that he had not yet followed through on his intention to call Eoghan Foley to discuss the plans for Katalyst.

Seated by the window in his comfortable study, watching scattered white clouds scudding across the windswept sky, Sam recalled that he had seen the colt briefly only once, prior to the sale at the Punchestown Festival almost ten months ago, from which the young horse had been withdrawn from sale because Irish trainer Niall Carter's claim to own the animal. Whilst Sam had been given to understand that this dispute had been resolved with the Carter family, the subsequent transfer later in October of title to the horse to Sam, without any further attempt at public sale had left Sam uneasy, all the more so because he had not been asked by Eoghan for any payment. Sam's tacit acceptance of the odd arrangement had been prompted only by his resolve to support the mysterious scheme of Eoghan Foley to find out about the history of his original mare Kat's Gift and hence who has been responsible for the tragic events affecting himself and his family. The recent suggestion from Sadie that the owner of a Lusitano stud in Portugal might also be staking a claim to the disputed colt had revived Sam's determination to speak directly to Eoghan Foley.

When Sam reached for the desk telephone, this time it did not interrupt him with an unwelcome incoming call, and the voice which answered was unmistakably that of Eoghan Foley himself.

"I was sorry to learn of your mother's death," Eoghan said to Sam once the two men had exchanged their customary greetings, "You are glad, I am sure, to be back in your own home and to have the Cheltenham Festival to occupy your thoughts. I have been receiving many calls here about Tabikat and his chance of winning the big prize. Stevie has done a good job for sure with her internet reporting on your Festival runners."

"There is certainly a great deal of media attention," Sam agreed, "Tabikat is the main focus, of course, but, as you know, Katseye is entered in the Novices' Chase on the Thursday and my Champion Hurdle horse Curlew Landings will be defending his title on the opening day. Trying to win races of this calibre is an ambitious target for a small yard such as my own and certainly not something I ever imagined I should experience."

"I am soon to be adding to your ambitions, Sam," Eoghan replied, sounding slightly hesitant, "I am glad that you have called me today."

"In what way?" asked Sam, "Are you wanting to send Katalyst to us now? I am sorry not to have been available to discuss him with you earlier."

"We – that is, Caitlin and I – should like you to enter him in the Champion Bumper on the second day of the Cheltenham Festival," Eoghan stated abruptly and then became silent. Sam got the impression that someone, maybe Caitlin, was standing beside Eoghan as he spoke.

"Does his trainer think he is ready, Genie?" asked Sam, not sure what to make of this information, "I am not aware the colt has had anything other than amateur race experience in Ireland, but I imagine you are about tell me otherwise."

"The trainer, well, that would be yourself, Sam," Eoghan replied, unexpectedly, "Be assured that the colt will meet our requirements at the Festival. Katalyst has been with Brendan Meaghan himself during the time you have owned him, although this is not public knowledge."

"Genie," began Sam, carefully, deciding that he needed to understand the implications of what had been requested of him, "I have been more than happy to support you after what you have done in sending two magnificent horses for me to train. I well know that you and Brendan were kind enough to rely on Frank Stanley's assurances as to my abilities as a trainer, and I believe that I have repaid your confidence in me. But the position with Katalyst is rather different. I am not in fact his trainer and it is I as the owner who would normally be relying on your and Brendan's judgement – neither of which I doubt, of course – but it would help me considerably if I were to understand your thinking concerning the colt. Also, I have been informed by my yard manager, Sadie Shinkins, that another party has now made what sounds like a rather spurious claim to the ownership of a forebear of your mare Kat's Gift and by implication to all three of the present generation of progeny."

"I have had this story also from Feanna," Eoghan responded, answering Sam's final question first, "Sadie has spoken to her too. I do not know if you are aware, Sam, but the Jimenez family from Andalucia is well known to us – or I should say, more correctly, to Caitlin."

"What does the traveller family have to say about this fantastic tale of a horse apparently bred for bullfighting?" Sam asked, curious, in spite of his scepticism as to the credibility of the story Sadie had related to him.

"They say that the story of the creation of the stallion called El Heredero de Sevilla is true," Eoghan replied, to Sam's surprise, "But their telling of the story says that they did not steal either the colt or the mares from the stud in Portugal. They say that they made payment to the stud for the covering of their own mares by the Lusitano stallion. Listen, Sam, they deny most insistently too that El Heredero de Sevilla sired any progeny. They say that, while the stallion was magnificent to behold, he was infertile. So, he was gelded and then performed in the travelling horse shows which the family used to put on in those days. The horse himself is long dead, Sam, and they insist that he had no descendants."

"Then what do you think about Kat's Gift, Genie?" asked Sam, curiously, "What is her ancestry, if not from this stallion?"

"I suspect, though I do not know," Eoghan explained, carefully, "That she was illegally bred from quality thoroughbred stock which was officially recorded as deceased. The Jimenez family, although I and my family have good reason to be grateful to them, did not pursue an honest living in the days gone by."

"I see," Sam said slowly, suddenly remembering the scruffy man who had been trying to attract the attention of Caitlin in the Cheltenham parade ring following Tabikat's victory in the Gold Cup, "So there is no proof that any of these different versions of the story could be the true account. Even a DNA test after all these generations would be useless, I imagine. I suppose it is possible, though, that someone intending to buy Katalyst might insist on one."

"All it would tell them," Eoghan replied, more authoritative now, "Is that the colt is as close to being one hundred percent thoroughbred as to make no difference to his potential as a racehorse and his future progeny if he went to stud. You asked me, Sam, for my plan for Katalyst. Look, whether the horse is descended from El Heredero de Sevilla is not the important factor. The real issue is that someone was promised a mare which was said to be descended from El Heredero himself, and that person has not received what he was promised."

"But if the Jimenez family is telling the truth, there is no such mare," Sam objected, becoming bewildered by the strange story.

"The truth may not have been told to the person concerned," Eoghan said quietly, "This person may have been told that El Heredero de Sevilla sired progeny successfully with the Irish thoroughbred mares. In the same way, the young man from Portugal also believes this to be the truth. But this unknown person, if he wishes to make a claim to the progeny of the mare he has been promised, will need to substantiate his claim. And if he does that, he will need to provide evidence of his purchase or otherwise to give me the reason why he was made such a promise. I believe that he will be both unable and unwilling to do either of those things."

"Are you saying that this man is a criminal?" asked Sam, helplessly trying to grasp the basis of what Eoghan was telling him, "You are suggesting, I think, that a mare descended from this El Heredero de Sevilla was promised as payment for something illegal which he did? And that the mare in question is Kat's Gift, or Maire, who was brought to you by your friend Oisin Cassidy?"

"This is certainly my belief, Sam," confirmed Eoghan, "And I believe also that this is the same man who has caused suffering not only to my family but to the families of many others. This man has seen his opportunity to obtain the reward he was promised many years ago by buying through a public sale a colt who is a direct descendent of El Heredero de Sevilla. We have so far prevented him from doing this."

"You know yourself, Sam," Eoghan went on, his narrative gathering pace "That Katalyst was first entered in, then withdrawn from, the sale at Aintree racecourse last April. Soon after, Caitlin's good friend Niall Carter agreed to help me before the Punchestown sale by claiming the colt was his own property. Niall made out that his own father, Fergal Carter, was swindled over the purchase of a forebear of Katalyst many years ago. The story went that Niall was sent to pick up a horse his father had bought in Monamar but was not given the right animal. That story was all Caitlin's clever invention. Niall could not prove the claim, of course, but it served to prevent the auction of Katalyst at Punchestown. You see now, Sam, that we have twice frustrated the man who wants to own Katalyst. This man now waits for the next sale, only to discover that the colt has been sold privately to you. So, he becomes more frustrated. That is when even the cleverest people make their errors of judgement."

"What kind of errors of judgement?" asked Sam, wondering what Eoghan Foley meant, "Do you mean outright theft, or some kind of outrageous offer to the current owner or perhaps to the trainer, to force them to sell?"

"Just so," said Eoghan, "Which is why you have our gratitude, Sam. Your friend Francis Stanley has assured me that you and your staff will be well supported, even protected, should the situation become difficult. Otherwise I would not have agreed to the plan. Colonel Stanley is of the opinion that this individual will be very cautious about making himself and his intentions known. This man, or more likely those who work for him, have made a serious error already when they attacked the unfortunately inquisitive young jockey at Aintree racecourse. He will not allow that kind of misjudgement to occur twice."

After a moment's silence, during which Sam took in the implications of what Eoghan had told him, not least the confirmation about the direct involvement of Frank Stanley in the scheme, something which he had already suspected, Sam said, "Very well, Genie, I will instruct my office staff to make the entry for Katalyst in the Champion Bumper. When can we expect to receive the horse?"

"Brendan Meaghan will bring him to Cheltenham racecourse on the day of the race itself," Eoghan told him, sounding relieved, "And I will inform Cathal's that you wish the colt to be put up for sale in the following day's auction."

After cutting the phone connection to the faraway Irish farm, Sam remained seated, staring unseeingly out of the window. The bright late February sun flashed and flickered in and out of the wind-driven clouds, sending intermittent grey shadows flitting across the empty sheep paddock. The bare branches of the trees lining the lane outside shook and rattled restlessly against each other.

Sam sat on, deep in thought, whilst the ornate hands of the antique clock in the hall outside the study door crept along their elegant circular route towards noon. The familiar sound of the pleasant musical chimes made no impression on the occupant of the study. Lewis, knocking on the door some time later to ask a question about lunch, received no response, and went away to tell Kelly that Mr Sampfield must have fallen asleep through jetlag again.

At last, Sam stood up, picked up his mobile phone from the desk and pressed a now familiar number into the keypad. Frank Stanley answered almost at once.

"Is something wrong, Sam?" Frank asked.

"Tell me, Frank," said Sam, his tone blunt, "This final job that you need to finish before you retire – is it to find the Fermagarrick bomber and bring him to justice?"

Frank remained silent but Sam knew that his friend was listening.

"Is he the same man who bought, or was promised, one of the illegally bred horses from the line which produced Tabikat, Katseye and Katalyst?" Sam went on, "The same horses which were part of the cover for the illegal arms and drugs trafficking in which Callan Sullivan was involved? Is this man one of the people who were responsible for the death of Niamh Foley's husband and the ending of Genie Foley's career as a jump jockey?"

"I believe you have summed it up very competently, Sam" was all that Frank said in response.

"In that case," replied Sam, "How can I help you with what you are attempting to do?"

"Make sure that your horses win their races, Sam," replied Frank Stanley.

39
The Cheltenham Festival
Tuesday

On the first day of the Cheltenham Festival, a cloying blanket of wet fog lay across the roofs of the yard buildings at Sampfield Grange. A few miles away, at the lower-lying Dicks yard, to which Curlew Landings had been taken on the previous evening, the fog pressed even more heavily. Although the sun had risen shortly before half past six that morning, the thick moisture filling the air seemed to have retained something of the night's darkness, and the awakening yard felt dank and leaden as if under a burden.

Curlew Landings was travelling to Cheltenham racecourse alongside one of Ranulph Dicks's talented handicappers, Nursery Rhyme, who was entered in the third race. The Dicks's taciturn travelling head lad, a weather-hardened individual known only as Reg, was driving the horsebox and would have Travis and Kye for help and company. Having checked the weather forecast, Reg had learned that the foggy conditions prevailed over a large part of the South and West of the country and would therefore affect their journey up the M5 all the way to Cheltenham racecourse itself.

Both of the horses were smartly rugged and protectively dressed for travelling when Travis led them one after the other up the ramp of the red horsebox.

"Bet it's not like this in Melbourne," Kye muttered as the two young men clambered into the cab of the box, pulling off the gloves and hats which had kept them warm in the yard.

"It's still summer there," Travis commented, sounding wistful.

Reg merely grunted in response to these unhelpful observations, turning on the blower to clear the windscreen of the condensation caused by their collective breath and switching on the radio for the traffic news.

The journey to Cheltenham racecourse took almost half an hour longer than usual. The fog showed no sign of lifting as the Dicks horsebox passed GCHQ and approached the busy Benhall roundabout. Creeping traffic populated the Princess Elizabeth Way whilst Swindon Lane became a line of red taillights winking ahead of them as the lorry approached the already congested roundabout at the racecourse entrance. Vehicles containing the many local people who staffed the numerous bars and restaurants at the racecourse were being shepherded into a car park in a field alongside Swindon Lane, their scurrying occupants crossing a temporary bridge which had been newly erected over the Evesham Road. The traffic management arrangements around the racecourse were well-practised but the unshifting fog had provided an additional complication.

Some way behind their lorry on its slow journey were Ranulph and Amelia Dicks who had been collected from their home a little later in the morning by Sam in the green Range Rover. Still further behind, Gilbert and Philippa Peveril, accompanied by a chatty Toby Halstock, were also making their unhurried way through the continuing morning gloom towards Cheltenham. All of them were to be guests of the Garratts in their box at the racecourse, a facility which would be in full and constant use throughout the four days of the Festival.

In a somewhat less luxurious vehicle, in fact the same anonymous white Peugeot in which she had travelled to Wincanton racecourse, sat Tegan Colvin, her brother Graham impatiently negotiating the crawling traffic on the M5. Tegan would not have cared if the two of them had never reached distant Cheltenham, so frightened was she by the role which Graham had forced on her. In vain had she pleaded that Mr Vowles would need her at The Sly Fox during that week, but Graham would hear none of her weakly expressed objections.

"You're such a scuzzy little thing, Plod won't take no notice of you," Gray had told her, cruelly, "You get any money put in that bucket, you make sure you hand it over to me, do you hear?"

Tegan had been less concerned about the police, thinking that being arrested and sent to prison might be preferable to the nightmare which her life at home had now become, than about some of the unpleasant people who would approach her to collect the envelopes which Gray had given to her, secreted inside charity leaflets. The items had already been paid for through a fake online account and Tegan's pose as a charity bucket collector in Pittville Park was simply a means of covert delivery. In the little rucksack fastened on her skinny back, Tegan carried the black and yellow taser gun which Gray had insisted that she look after for him.

"I can't take it in the racecourse, you twat," he had told his nervous sister when she had suggested that he put it into his jacket pocket instead, "They check for stuff like that. They have armed cops and sniffer dogs too. Sheryl says we have to be squeaky clean when we're in there."

Notwithstanding the continuing presence of the unwelcome fog, large crowds were approaching the racecourse, ready to enter as soon as the gates were opened at mid-morning, well before the start time of one thirty for the first race of the afternoon. Laden double-decker buses were beginning to make their noisy way from Cheltenham Spa station whilst others picked up already drunk and mostly male passengers in the crowded town centre. Those racegoers who arrived in cars were being directed into the lower entrance in Southam Lane, currently invisible from the grandstands at the top of the course. Those rich enough to afford helicopter transport were today having to settle for something less luxurious, as the visibility remained too poor for safe operation into the field optimistically called Cheltenham Heliport, where a wet orange windsock hung limply from its white pole.

Curlew Landings and Nursery Rhyme were but two of the dozens of horses being off-loaded alongside the red brick stables at the front of the racecourse buildings. Numerous curious racegoers, reading the names of the trainers emblazoned on the horse transport, hung about on the broad approach to the turnstiles at the Centaur entrance, hoping to catch a glimpse of one of the equine superstars on whom their money would be staked later in the day. Some of the spectators even called out hopefully to the lads and lasses who were leading the valuable horses towards the official standing at the stables entrance and carefully checking their and the horses' names on her day's list.

Travis and Kye were relieved to be settling their two runners at last into their individual stables, whilst Reg went off to find a parking slot for the lorry. Rather to their surprise, the two young men found that Merlin ap Rhys was waiting for them in the stableyard, sporting a zip-up riding jacket with the collar turned up, a dark red scarf wrapped across the lower half of his face. Ludicrously, in view of presence of the fog, the jockey was also wearing dark glasses and an old-fashioned peaked cap.

"Stops the punters from seein' 'oo I am when I walk up 'ere," Merlin explained, in response to Kye's questioning look, "And anyway, it's cold in this bloody murk."

Travis merely nodded, his own black baseball cap having been carefully folded up in his pocket ready to serve the same purpose in the event of Jack Tytherleigh's staff putting in an appearance.

"I've come to 'ave a look at that 'orse Devil Waters that beat Curlew at Wincanton," Merlin explained, as he patted the brown neck of a disinterested Curlew Landings, "The girl at the gate says 'e's not in 'ere yet. I suppose comin' 'ere from up North might be a problem with the weather like it is."

Merlin was not to know that the information which he had been given by the member of the racecourse staff positioned at the yard entrance was not strictly correct. The lorry containing Curlew Landings' nemesis in the Kingwell Hurdle, Devil Waters, had indeed arrived at the racecourse but had been immediately flagged down by two racecourse officials and directed to a cordoned-off section of the parking area, away from the route along which increasing numbers of noisy spectators were now passing. The two Cheshire yard staff who were in the cab of the lorry had both reacted with surprise to the instruction, but had complied with it nonetheless.

It was only when Devil Waters was later included amongst the list of non-runners for the day that Merlin, who had by then returned to the jockeys' changing room, began to wonder if something more fundamental than a simple delay on the road had happened to the horse. Merlin's inability to locate the horse's jockey, Joel Edge, anywhere in the weighing room building served only to increase his interest in finding out what had happened to cause the horse to be taken out of the prestigious race. It was still long enough until racing started for Merlin to be able to use his mobile phone. Thumbing in Kye's number, Merlin soon received some astonishing information.

The racecourse stables were, according to a highly excited Kye, buzzing with the rumour that, acting on an early morning tip-off to the stewards, the lorry containing Devil Waters had been intercepted in the car park. Devi, as the distraught young girl who was one of the two staff accompanying the horse called him, had been taken straight off to the Sampling Unit with a vet in attendance. Meanwhile, a jacket belonging to the other member of the trainer's staff, Kye explained, tumbling over his words, had been found to have a loaded syringe of a drug that someone had said was called RSR13, secreted in an inner pocket. The individual concerned had furiously protested that he had never seen the item before and had insisted that 'some bloke' must have planted it on him, a claim which had been met with scepticism.

"Do yez know what, Merlin?" Kye went on, breathlessly, "The lad who had the stuff - the poor girl that's crying her eyes out over here, she said he was an Aussie. Not been with them long. Travis has gone to look out for him, see if it's one of the people he saw here in January. The horse is back in the stables now but he's not being allowed to race. Dean Parry the trainer's been called down too. I saw him go past just now. And, tell yez what, Merlin, he's the son of the trainer I used to work for, yez know, in Cheshire. I suppose the old boss, Mr Parry, must have retired by now."

Merlin could hardly believe his luck. One of Curlew's main competitors was out of the race. No wonder Joel Edge had disappeared. Devil Waters was the strange jockey's only ride that day, according to the information in the racecard. Perhaps this discovery of a prohibited substance explained Devil Waters' sudden improvement in form at Wincanton. Who had tipped off the stewards about it, Merlin wondered.

"Keep me posted, Kye," Merlin instructed shortly, ending the call and turning to relate to nearby fellow jockeys the information he had just obtained.

"Jammy for you, Merlin," said one of them, "Gives your horse a better shot now."

"Bit weird, though, isn't it?" said another, "The lad just having the stuff in his pocket. No-one would do that. Maybe he really was set up, like he says."

"Why would anyone set the lad up?" asked a third, as Merlin sat listening to the discussion, "Someone who didn't like him. Or someone who wanted the horse out of the race? Not you, was it, Merlin?"

That being as far as their amateur detective skills could take them, Merlin's colleagues left him to the thoughts which were running fast and furious through his sharp mind. Merlin looked the racecard again. It read:

DEVIL WATERS (IRE)
B g Devil's Bridge – Water Lily
Trainer Dean Parry, Warrington
Jockey Joel Edge
Owner Nathan G Lowry Ltd.

Nothing seemed out of the ordinary. Yet, something half-forgotten nagged at his memory, something which someone had once said to him. Or maybe it was more than one person. Merlin could not pin it down. After a few moments of futile effort to prise the elusive information out of his subconscious mind, Merlin resolved to get on with his job and leave the thinking to someone else.

Merlin had no ride in the opening race of the Festival, which went off on time in conditions of still persisting fog. The start was greeted with the usual roar of appreciation from the packed and enthusiastic spectators, notwithstanding the fact that they had had to rely on the racecourse commentator's assurances that the fifteen novices had set off on their extended two mile journey over hurdles on the Old course. Merlin's rides in the second and third races kept him occupied during the remainder of the period leading up to Curlew's Champion Hurdle race, which was the fourth on the card.

As Merlin went to weigh in after the third race, in which Nursery Rhyme had not enjoyed the foggy and damp atmosphere out on the course, Merlin spotted Travis walking smartly along the path leading into the parade ring, Curlew Landings stepping out equally smartly beside him. Mr Sampfield was following silently behind the horse and his loyal groom, Gilbert Peveril and Toby Halstock chatting affably to each other in the trainer's wake.

The race card listed eleven horses in the Champion Hurdle. With Devil Waters now a non-runner, the reason for the withdrawal having been officially recorded as 'vet's certificate', this left nine horses for Curlew Landings to defeat in order to retain his title. A number of these were the usual foes - Southern Cross, Rabbit Punch and The Squire's Tale – but there were a number of tough looking Irish horses also in the field.

Arriving early at the start at the bottom of the hill, the horses milled obediently about, the jockeys trying to keep them moving but without revving them up too soon.

"What 'appened to Joel Edge then?" Merlin asked Southern Cross's jockey, as their two horses stepped alongside each other, "'as he gone 'ome now Devil Waters is out?"

"Couldn' say," replied the other man in a Dorset burr, "I dun' know 'im. Don' think 'e 'ad no more roides today, though. Loikely 'e's well pissed off with what's gone on. Owner too, I sh'd think."

The conversation came to an abrupt end as the starter, standing on his mobile steps, called the riders to bring their mounts forward ready for the off. Sam and Merlin had needed no discussion about riding tactics that day, as both of them knew that Curlew's best option was to make the running, as usual, and to be sure not to get passed. The ground conditions were officially good to soft, which would theoretically present the front-running horse with few problems.

The roar of the distant crowd when the ten horses set off on their extended two mile journey sounded muffled in Merlin's ears. The grandstands at the top of the hill ahead of them were all but hidden in the grey gloom. Curlew reached the first of the eight hurdles at the head of the field, all members of which had set off like a cavalry charge. The hurdle panels rattled and crashed noisily as ten sets of carefully oiled hooves flew across them.

Keeping Curlew Landings at the head of the ambitious group of runners was not going to be an easy task, Merlin well knew. Several of the Irish jockeys were clearly keen to press him for the lead, seemingly in the hope of pushing the previous year's champion into running faster than Merlin wanted. Merlin was too much of an old hand at race tactics to be forced into doing something which he had not planned but he was acutely conscious that Curlew disliked being headed and was quite capable of getting a fit of the sulks if he was not kept at, or very near, the front of the field.

All the horses were flat to the boards as the group motored down the hill in the back straight. The quick pace was telling on a few of them, but most of the runners seemed perfectly capable of handling the speed at which the race was unfolding. Merlin could hear the usual shouts and curses, the clattering of tack, and the snorting breath of the many horses behind them. Curlew could hear it too, and his ears flicked back towards Merlin, his neatly plaited mane rising and falling rhythmically in time with the horse's fast stride.

"Keep it up, *bachgen*," Merlin muttered urgently into Curlew's right ear, "They're on your tail, they are."

Merlin could not properly hear the racecourse commentary coming from the still fogbound grandstand area. Odd words such as 'fast pace .. getting strung out now .. last year's winner' filtered through the strange cut-off world of the racing horses forging their urgent way through the fog.

The field was soon approaching the point at which they were furthest from the spectators, where the track would begin to curve around to the left and descend before finally straightening out over the final two hurdles which would take them uphill again to the finish. Curlew remained ahead, the pack snapping at his heels, Merlin urging his competitive horse forwards.

With two hurdles left to clear, the field had closed up, with the exception of three stragglers who had been tailed off during the hectic journey down the fog-bound back straight. Merlin was aware that Curlew Landings now had the threatening shapes of Rabbit Punch and Southern Cross for close company. Rabbit Punch was being ridden today by his original jockey, his more recent rider Jenna Roberts being an unexpected absentee from the first day of the Festival.

"They're three in line as they come to the second last!" Merlin heard the fragmented voice of the commentator call out, whilst the boom of the rumbling and cheering of the assembled crowd began to make itself heard. The horses progressed furiously up the punishing gradient towards the escalating noise.

Curlew's dark ears flattened themselves angrily against his handsome head as the two unwelcome horses pushed their way upsides.

"Keep goin', Curlew, we can win this," Merlin urged, pushing the horse up the hill with all the mental and physical strength he could muster. He could hear the other two nearby jockeys telling their horses much the same thing.

As Curlew cleared the final hurdle and fought his stubborn way towards the finishing line, the clamour of the massed spectators surrounding the three straining horses each fighting for first place, the adrenalin coursing through Merlin's system suddenly released the elusive information that he had been trying to recall.

"My brother owns a racehorse, Merlin," said a pleasant female voice, with its fake Liverpool accent, in his head, "Trinket Box. He's kept at a yard in Cheshire."

If Merlin had had any breath remaining when he and the even more breathless Curlew Landings finally crossed the finishing line having just retained first place, he would have uttered just one word.

Lara.

40
The Cheltenham Festival
Wednesday

In Sam's dream, the telephone went on ringing. Sam knew that he should answer it but suspected that it would only give him bad news about his mother. He tried to shut out the insistent sound, but it had now changed into a persistent knocking followed by calls of "Mr Sampfield, Mr Sampfield." Sam's eventual recognition of Lewis's familiar voice roused him into wakefulness.

Sam sat up in his over-large bed and reached for his father's old hunter watch which lay open on the bedside table. The luminous green inlay on the gold hands pointed to half past five. The entreaty "Mr Sampfield" sounded once again.

"What is it, Lewis?" Sam called out, not able to fathom who might be wanting to speak to him at this time in the morning, which was early even for the usual routine at Sampfield Grange.

"It's Mr Meaghan," replied Lewis, his voice muffled by the closed door, "He needs to speak to you personally, he says."

"Katalyst!" thought Sam, reaching for the telephone extension by his bed, the bell of which was habitually silenced during the night, "I've taken the call now, Lewis," Sam called out.

As Lewis's feet shuffled sluggishly away down the landing, Sam spoke into the mouthpiece of the elderly telephone handset, "Brendan? James Sampfield here. Has something happened to Katalyst?"

"Good morning to you," Brendan's even voice said into Sam's ear, "Or maybe not so good. Katalyst will not be travelling today. You must withdraw him from the race at Cheltenham."

"Withdraw him?" repeated Sam, "On what grounds?"

"Cast in his box," Brendan stated promptly, "The colt's had a bit of a panic on him in there. He's seems sound but the vet says he'll not be racing today, as a precaution."

Sam, hastily organising his thoughts and remembering his recent conversation with Eoghan Foley, wondered if Brendan's story were true or whether this was just another ploy in the succession of frustration tactics which the Irish friends seemed to think would be successful in drawing out their evasive quarry.

"And the sale tomorrow?" Sam asked, fully awake now.

"We plan to have the horse there," Brendan assured him, "I'll be sure to keep you informed."

The withdrawal of Katalyst from the final race at the Cheltenham Festival that day had little effect on the plans for the Sampfield Grange team. A tired Curlew Landings had been brought back home the previous evening in the Dicks lorry, accompanied by an ecstatic Travis and an only slightly less excited Kye. Sadie had returned with Reg and Travis to the Dickses' and would today travel to Cheltenham with Amelia Dicks and Sadie's former charge, Fan Court, who would be ridden by Merlin in the Queen Mother Champion Chase that afternoon. Katalyst, had he been running, was to have been ridden by Katie Meaghan, Brendan's daughter, after which he would have remained overnight at the racecourse ready for the following day's auction by Cathal's.

Sam belatedly realised that he had not asked Brendan Meaghan whether the young horse would still travel to Cheltenham that day or whether the journey was to be put off until the following day. No doubt he would find out in due course, Sam thought, suddenly tiring of the machinations surrounding the elusive colt. Sam's only role now was to notify the withdrawal, on veterinary advice, of Katalyst from the afternoon's National Hunt Open Flat race, known as the Champion Bumper. Isabella could undertake this task as soon as she arrived for work, he thought, as well as obtaining from Brendan's yard a copy of the Irish vet's certificate. Sam needed to give his full attention to the final preparation of Katseye and Tabikat for their forthcoming races.

The foggy weather of the previous day had been superseded by miserable conditions punctuated by intermittent and spattering cold rain, through which a wet and restless wind blew from the North West. All the work riders participating in the morning's exercise routine were glad to be indoors for breakfast in the welcome warmth of the Sampfield Grange kitchen. Sam had told a yawning Lewis that he would stay behind in the yard to await Isabella's arrival before going as usual through to the breakfast room.

Sam had seen Isabella's bicycle leaning against the wall of the garage and was surprised to find the office empty. Isabella had clearly been in there only recently, as the desktop computer was switched on, a bluish light emanating from the screen. Sam wondered if Stevie Stone and Jayce, who had yesterday advised the Smart Girls to stay loyal to Curlew Landings, had published any useful thoughts on the horses due to race on the second day of the Cheltenham Festival. Sam knew that Stevie's internet tipping service for her followers could be accessed on the office computer by using the mouse to select a little icon showing a picture of the irritating Tabby Cat.

The short series of letters and numbers which constituted the password to access the office computer was one of a very few written items which Sam, in response to former office manager Bethany's prompting, had forced himself to learn to enter onto the computer keyboard. Rather than try to identify the confusedly shifting letters and digits themselves, he had simply memorised the pattern they made on the keyboard. Carefully reproducing the pattern, he was rewarded with a screen of closely ordered information which looked quite different from that which he had been expecting to see. It was a bewildering tabulation of numbers, graphs and accompanying written notation. The one thing which was instantly recognisable, though, even to Sam, at the top of the screen was the word Katalyst.

"Good morning, Mr Sampfield," spoke up Isabella's voice, suddenly, behind him, "I'm sorry, I was just putting my wet things into the tumble dryer. Is there something you need?"

"Katalyst," murmured Sam, hardly realising that he had spoken aloud.

"I have already dealt with Katalyst's withdrawal from the race," Isabella informed him, "Mr Meaghan's secretary called me a little while ago."

"Is that why the horse's name is here on the screen?" Sam asked, seeking to understand the unexpected appearance of the complicated information apparently referring to Katalyst.

"On the screen?" repeated Isabella, sounding surprised. She moved quickly round the desk to stare at the display which glowed in front of them in the dull light.

"I regret I can't see the detail," Sam improvised, quickly, as usual, "I haven't brought my reading glasses with me."

"It's the front page of the record for Katalyst from the training tracker system," Isabella told him, speaking carefully, "You remember, Mr Sampfield, I'm sure, that Travis recommended that you implement it here during the summer?"

"Certainly I remember," Sam replied, puzzled, "Why, though, is a record being kept for Katalyst at Sampfield Grange? I've not been training the horse."

"Mr Meaghan uses the same system," replied Isabella, quickly, "The horse's records have been held for some time at both yards. I was not aware on what date Katalyst would be joining us at Sampfield Grange."

"Very well, I see," said Sam, not noticing the relief with which Isabella received his comment. Leaving Isabella alone with a brief word of thanks, Sam returned to the house and his breakfast.

As soon as her employer had left, Isabella snatched up her mobile phone and pressed in a speed-dial code.

"George," she said, urgently, "It's happened. Katalyst's fake training record self-opened just now. Someone's hacked it."

*

Sam had not been the only person to receive an early summons that day. Frank Stanley had been awakened by a phone call from Australian racing official Craig Wickham, the unsocial hour perhaps selected in revenge for the disruption to the latter's plans for a leisurely tour of UK racecourses.

"That horse, Devil Waters, you sent me to test at Cheltenham racecourse yesterday," Craig Wickham began, without preamble, "You were right on the button, Frank. There wasn't a trace of the stuff which the young groom had in the syringe, but the horse's sample definitely tested positive for Ghost. And, get this, Frank, the groom was an Aussie. Not sure why he had the efaproxiral with him, though. They wouldn't have needed that as well. The boy was hopping, insisted it had been planted on him. You wouldn't know anything about that, would you, Frank?"

"Are you planning to stay at Cheltenham racecourse throughout the Festival?" asked Frank, deflecting the other man's question, "If so, I should keep an eye on the horses from that training establishment, particularly those with the same owner as Devil Waters."

Frank followed up this conversation by making a call of his own. He informed the person who answered that the ruse to ensure the pre-race testing of the horse Devil Waters had produced the result which had been expected.

"What now, Mr Stanley?" asked the female voice, "I can't set up any of the lads at the Parry yard a second time. They're going to be super careful after this. I'm really worried for Jo tomorrow."

"I just want you to stick close to the target now," Frank instructed her, "He'll be at the races tomorrow again, I believe?"

"Yes, he's booked me for the whole day," replied the woman's voice, "I'll be glad when this is over, Mr Stanley. This bastard gives me the creeps."

"You'll be out of there after tomorrow, Lara. Jo too," Frank assured her, and cut the connection.

Almost at once, Frank's phone rang again.

"We're in business," George informed him, "They've hacked Sampfield Grange, as we hoped they would. The hack definitely came from Liverpool."

*

By mid-morning, Tegan Colvin was again shivering in the cold outdoor air near the cafeteria in Pittville Park, holding her blue charity bucket in mitten covered hands. The previous day's business had gone well, at least as far as her brother had been concerned. Tegan had been relieved to find that those who had come to collect the goods they had purchased remotely had been in no hurry to hang around and had simply accepted the folded leaflets she had given them without so much as a word of thanks. A few kindly passers-by had contributed coins to her bucket, for which she had been grateful, surreptitiously removing a few of them to buy herself a hot drink. Gray was not to know how much had been put in there. He had been up at the racecourse with Sheryl.

Tegan did not like Sheryl. Sheryl's contempt for the timid Tegan was obvious. From what little of their conversation Tegan could understand through the other woman's strange accent, Sheryl spoke to Gray about Tegan as if Tegan herself were not present. Mostly though, the two of them ignored her. Tegan could see too that her brother was besotted by the nasty woman. They were welcome to each other, she decided.

Today, before they had left her alone with her collecting bucket, Tegan had heard Sheryl say, "My brother's coming tomorrow. He's driving our boss down here in a dead posh car."

"What sort of car?" had asked Gray, genuinely interested.

"A Roller, I think," Sheryl had responded, vaguely, "It's got a bar in the back, TV and all sorts."

Gray had been less interested in the bar and the TV than in the model of the Rolls Royce itself.

"What is it? A Phantom? A Ghost? A Wraith?" had asked Gray, enviously impressed, "Your brother's a lucky bugger getting to drive one of those, Sheryl. Do you think I could have a look round it, once the boss had gone into the races, that is?"

"Expect so," Sheryl had said, airily, adding, "Now get a shift on, kidda, we need some more orders."

They had walked away, leaving Tegan standing forlornly beneath the bare and dripping trees of the sloping park. The furious resentment burning inside her was the only thing keeping her warm.

*

None of the Sampfield Grange horses was running on the second day of the Festival, but Kye and Jackie, sitting alongside Kelly and Lewis in front of the television screen in the Sampfield Grange kitchen, wanted to look out for Travis and Sadie, who would be with the Dicks party in the fourth race. The small audience was rewarded by the sight of Travis leading out the strutting Fan Court with his lightning-bolt white blaze, whilst Sadie stood with assistant trainer Amelia Dicks in the centre of the busy parade ring, talking to the horse's well-heeled owners. The wife of the couple was wearing a smart outfit which reflected the purple and green of the silks in which Merlin was dressed.

Merlin had initially been frustrated to discover that jockey Joel Edge had no rides at Cheltenham that day. Having spent the previous night alone in his bedroom in the rented house in Prestbury, Merlin had had plenty of time to think. He had become convinced that there was a connection between Lara, the sex worker who had caused him so much anguish last year, and Cheshire trainer, Dean Parry. There were a number of trainers based in Cheshire, and therefore no guarantee that the horse owned by Lara's brother would be trained at the Parry yard, but Merlin's confidence in his theory had been bolstered by the memory of the conversation which he had had in the starkly furnished office at Cardiff Airport with Frank Stanley back in October. Frank had mentioned that Lara was one of his operatives, whatever that meant, and that he may need to involve her in his plans. Had she been the one who had tipped off the Cheltenham stewards about the stable lad with the dope? But why would Mr Stanley instruct her to do that, Merlin wondered. Try as he might, he could not come up with a convincing answer.

As Joel Edge appeared to be the Parry yard's stable jockey, Merlin had decided to turn his attention to him. Joel had lost a promising ride on Devil Waters, who might well have gone off favourite in the Champion Hurdle. Merlin's quick check of Thursday's entries had shown that Joel would be riding the iron grey Altimeter, who would be racing against Katseye in the opening race, the Grade 1 Novices' Chase. Merlin remembered only too well that the gritty Altimeter had beaten Katseye in a race at Ascot before Christmas and then again in the Novices' Chase at Cheltenham at the end of January. He regretted that he had at that time taken little interest in the unfamiliar jockey, assuming him to have been one of a number of Irish jockeys who had made the trip to England to ride on those particular days, and also that he had been unable to capitalise on the opportunity to speak to Joel at Wincanton racecourse. Merlin's online research on Joel Edge using his phone last night had confirmed that Joel was indeed originally from Northern Ireland. His more recent career, though, had been mostly outside the UK - France, Hong Kong, South Africa all featured in the record - until he had joined the Parry yard at the beginning of the current season. Some of the Parry horses had benefited considerably from his presence, judging by their improved results.

Merlin had decided that it would be a good idea to get a bit closer to Joel Edge. Getting a leg up onto Fan Court from Amelia Dicks, Merlin suddenly spotted the burgundy hatted figure of Stevie Stone by the horsewalk speaking animatedly into her iPad, a group of extravagantly dressed young women clustered behind her, pouting into the small screen. Perhaps he would ask Stevie about Joel Edge, Merlin decided.

*

Sam too watched the afternoon's television coverage from Cheltenham racecourse, and was pleased to see Fan Court and Merlin running into third place in the Champion Chase. The Champion Bumper, the last race on the seven race card, was run at breakneck speed, the young horses occasionally bumping and barging into each other as they raced, graphically justifying the nickname given to the short National Hunt flat races. Sam could only guess how Katalyst might have fared. Maybe the training information in Isabella's computer would have given him a clue, he thought, regretfully.

As the day's racing coverage came to an end and was followed by apparently expert speculation about the races due to take place the next day, Sam's mobile phone buzzed suddenly on the coffee table in front of him.

"Good afternoon, Sam, Frank here," the caller announced as soon as Sam answered, "I plan to join you at Cheltenham races tomorrow, if you will have me."

"I should be delighted to have you there, Frank," Sam responded, pleased to hear this news, "Katseye, as I imagine you are aware, is running in the first race. I believe we are in with a chance, although Altimeter, the horse which beat us the last two times out, is in the field again, not to mention a few other good ones, Petit Zazou, Cloud Atlas and Milk Run."

"Did you watch today's final race on television just now?" queried Frank, unexpectedly.

"I did," replied Sam, "It's very disappointing that Katalyst was taken out. Brendan says the colt will go into the sale tomorrow. I should have thought it would have been better to wait now until he has had another chance of a successful run here in England. It would very likely increase his price. But I guess that's not the real objective, if I understand this mysterious business correctly."

There was a short silence at the other end of the line after, which Frank asked, "Sam, do you recall our chemistry lessons at school? You were rather good at chemistry as I recall, especially at memorising all the tables and formulae we had to learn. Do you still remember what a catalyst is?"

"If memory serves me rightly, it's something that speeds up a chemical reaction but isn't itself affected by the reaction" replied Sam, after thinking for a moment, "Why?"

"And, in everyday terms, a catalyst is something that precipitates an event," added Frank.

41
The Cheltenham Festival
Thursday Morning

The empty-handed journey home to Liverpool on Tuesday had provided racehorse owner Nathan G Lowry with ample opportunity to review the latest situation in which he had unexpectedly found himself.

White-faced young trainer Dean Parry, when Gerry had angrily summoned him to the Rolls Royce in the racecourse car park, had been completely adamant that there had been none of the drug which had been found in the possession of his groom anywhere in his yard. The Australian groom himself had been equally adamant that the only substance he had given to Devil Waters had been through a nasogastric tube, now well hidden in the chassis modification under the lorry. It had been the currently undetectable *gui*, sourced originally through the Tytherleigh yard in Melbourne. There would have been absolutely no need for the additional and easily discovered dope which had been in the syringe. The young man had remained completely and furiously insistent that the stuff had been planted on him.

Gerry, notwithstanding his scarcely contained fury at what had happened, had been inclined to believe the protestations of the frightened trainer and his youthful employee, although their carelessness in allowing themselves to be so easily framed was something which he would not readily forgive. He had left them to their mutual recriminations and the task of getting Devil Waters released from the custody of the racecourse stewards and taken back home. That would not be possible, though, until the results of the sample taken from the horse were known. Confident though they had all been that there was no known test available to the BHA for *gui*, Dean Parry would nevertheless face an anxious wait.

As Gerry's black Rolls Royce Silver Ghost had hummed later along the crowded M5 towards the roadworks of Birmingham, Gerry had cradled a comforting cut-glass tumbler of golden Lougheven Irish whiskey in his hands. His silent driver on the other side of the sound-proofed screen had stared straight ahead into the persistent afternoon fog which still swathed the road, the approaching traffic creating distorted haloes of pale light to his right. A dwindling vista of red splashes had predicted the direction of the road ahead.

Someone had planted the syringe on the groom and then tipped off the racecourse stewards, that much was clear to Gerry. Any number of people in the busy yard would have had access to the horsebox carrying Devil Waters and probably also to the lad's jacket, which no doubt had been hung up in the cab or somewhere similarly accessible. Planting the incriminating syringe in the pocket would have been straightforward enough and anyone could have been paid to do it. Gerry would make sure that Dean got onto questioning his staff as soon as he returned home, whenever that was.

More difficult to fathom was why it had been done at all. The most obvious effect had been to prevent Devil Waters from racing that day. The horse would probably, in the light of his performance in the Christmas Hurdle at Kempton Park and the win in the Kingwell Hurdle at Wincanton have started as joint favourite at least. The bookmakers or the other owner would be the obvious beneficiaries from eliminating his horse, but neither of these options seemed truly plausible.

Dean Parry had some time ago researched the background and form of all the horses likely to pose a threat to Devil Waters. Gerry had been irritated to discover that Curlew Landings was both owned and trained by James Sampfield Peveril, the same individual who had for some unfathomable reason been chosen to train the two known descendants of La Herederita de Sevilla, notwithstanding the man's previously obscure status as a rural point to point trainer. The final straw, though, had been to discover the connection with the coveted Katalyst.

Although Katalyst had been withdrawn late in the day from Wednesday's Champion Bumper, Cathal's office had assured Nathan G Lowry's bloodstock agent that the colt would definitely be sold in Thursday's auction sale. Wednesday's racecard had revealed that the colt had evidently been sold privately earlier in the season to James Sampfield Peveril. A hack of the ill-protected Sampfield Grange IT systems by one of Gerry's now more experienced technonerds had shown that the colt had been in training there for some months, no doubt in the hope of demonstrating his future breeding potential to prospective buyers. Having looked at the statistics describing the young horse's prowess in training, it was unclear to Gerry why James Sampfield Peveril would now wish to sell such a clearly talented animal, but Gerry was quite happy to become the beneficiary of that decision.

On Thursday morning, as the Rolls Royce ghosted its way southwards down the M6, Gerry was increasingly confident that the *gui*-assisted Altimeter would defeat Katseye in the Novices' Chase and that by the evening he himself would become the owner of Katalyst, from whom he would be able to produce a line of thoroughbreds which had no need of performance enhancing drugs.

On the comfortable seat beside him sat his hired escort, Lara. Lara had nothing to say for herself, which suited Nathan G Lowry very well.

*

Merlin and Sadie had woken to a cloudy dawn, having pleasurably shared the single bed in Merlin's rented room in Prestbury. The early light outside the thin, striped curtains had been weak and insipid, but, when Sadie had eventually left the warm folds of the duvet to look out of the small window, the clouds had become thin and already showed promise of disappearing. She and Merlin agreed to go to the nearby racecourse on foot, too long before the scheduled opening time to attract attention from anyone other than the early arriving raceday workforce.

Merlin had discussed with Sadie his plan to find out more about Joel Edge, who would be partnering Altimeter in the first race that afternoon. He had decided not to mention to Sadie his conviction that there was a connection between the Parry yard and the woman whom he knew as Lara. Merlin knew that Sadie was aware that he had apparently been a victim of last year's video faking scam involving Lara, but Sadie had also made it very clear that she required no further explanation of Merlin's part in it.

"Does Kye know Joel, maybe?" asked Sadie, as they walked up the slope towards the racecourse, "All the horses he rides are trained in the yard where Kye used to work."

"I think Joel joined Parry's after Kye left," Merlin reminded her, "But you may as well ask Kye anyway."

And I can ask Kye if he knows Lara, Merlin added silently to himself. In the event, however, this was to prove unnecessary.

*

The Sampfield Grange horsebox, driven by Jackie with Kye beside her, also arrived early at Cheltenham racecourse and the imperious black shape of Katseye was already being unloaded in the open area close to the red brick stables by the time Sadie and Merlin were crossing the still deserted bus stop area. By contrast, the lorry park was busy with vehicles of all sizes, either parked for the duration of the Festival or else ferrying one or more horses to the third day's eagerly anticipated races. As usual, a few enthusiastic racegoers had also come especially early to look out for the first appearance of their favourite horses.

"That big black 'orse goin' to win today?" shouted out one of the less savvy racing fans to Jackie, as she led the impressive gelding down the ramp.

"Hope so," Jackie shouted back, "He's called Katseye. You look out for him in the first race."

The shouter's attention was diverted by the arrival of a small horsebox, bearing the name Parry Racing in large black letters on the side. Watching with interest to see who emerged from the cab, Kye had not expected to see the trainer himself, accompanied by the same girl who had shed so many tears over the disqualification of Devil Waters on Tuesday. The bearded young man, a flat cap covering his already thinning ginger hair, did not appear to recognise or even notice Kye standing nearby as he personally oversaw the unloading of the impressive iron grey Altimeter.

Sadie, having parted company with Merlin, who was going for a run around the now sunlit racecourse, stopped to watch Altimeter being brought down the lorry ramp. Sadie and Merlin's online researches on Joel Edge last night had included the owners of the horses which the jockey had ridden for the Parry yard. They had quickly confirmed Merlin's initial recollections. The unfamiliar jockey's most recent rides had not only been confined to Devil Waters, Altimeter, and the beautiful Bees and Mist, but all of these horses shared a common owner, Nathan G Lowry Ltd. The same owner appeared to have numerous other horses, including Tabikat's rival Less Than Ross, at a variety of training establishments, but Joel Edge's rides were the only three trained by Dean Parry. Each of the three Parry-trained horses had recently either beaten, or, in the case of Bees and Mist at Kempton Park, come close to beating, a Sampfield Grange runner.

It was on the tip of Sadie's tongue to ask a few questions of the small red-bearded man who was standing by the ramp, but the angry scowl which distorted his face made her decide against it.

*

The preparations for the collection and distribution of the pre-purchased goods to their recipients would be slightly different today, Tegan had been informed. Gray and Tegan had returned home to their mother's dingy flat the previous evening, having first dropped Sheryl at her temporary billet in the Alstone area of Cheltenham. Gray and Tegan would be staying in the same small brick terraced house with Sheryl that night, as they needed to be up early to service their customers on Gold Cup day itself. Tegan could see that Gray was hoping to get lucky with Sheryl once they were in the house together and had prayed fervently that she would be elsewhere if and when that unthinkable event occurred.

Gray had gone straight into his workshop, ostensibly to make repairs to the small car in which they had been travelling to and from Cheltenham, but in reality to weigh out and package up the contents of the remaining envelopes for distribution the following day. The additional gear to fulfil the Friday orders would be supplied to them at the local M5 service station on their way to Cheltenham on Thursday morning. Constructing a secure hidden compartment in the boot of the Peugeot in which the additional stock could be secretly stored until it was needed had occupied the remainder of Gray's time the previous evening.

Eventually satisfied with his work, Gray had been about to leave the workshop to get some sleep when he had remembered the two bottles which had been gathering dust on his grimy desk since he had found them months ago in the comfortless storage warehouse. Maybe Sheryl would fancy a drink when they were finished tomorrow, he had thought. Gray had put them in the car.

The agreed meeting point with Sheryl near Cheltenham racecourse on Thursday morning had been in the field where the numerous bar and catering staff were either dropped off or left their own cars. There, Tegan had been given her customary charity bucket and folded leaflets and instructed to make her own way down the Evesham Road to her exposed pitch in Pittville Park whilst Gray and Sheryl would go to the Owners carpark to meet Sheryl's brother, Ritch. It had been impressed upon Gray that no vestige of any type of illegal drug should be found on either of them for fear of its being associated with her brother's wealthy employer.

"What's his name then, the bloke with the Roller?" asked Gray, as he and Sheryl climbed the steps to the temporary footbridge over the North side of the Evesham Road.

"Mr Lowry," Sheryl told him, "Nathan G Lowry."

"What, like the name on the lorries?" asked Gray, in surprise.

Sheryl looked at him pityingly. "Yeah, like the name on the lorries," she said.

On his morning run around the racecourse, Merlin was pleased to spot Joel Edge running just ahead of him.

"Mornin' Joel," Merlin called out cheerily as he tried to move up alongside his quarry.

The other jockey appeared not to hear Merlin's call and Merlin soon realised that this was because Joel was listening to music through earphones. Speeding up slightly, Merlin caught the other man up, then reached out and tapped him lightly on the shoulder.

Joel Edge's reaction was instantaneous and shocking. He whipped around to face Merlin, both hands clenched in a threatening gesture, level with Merlin's jaw. Merlin darted quickly to one side, as if to evade a boxer's punch.

"Steady on, Joel *dyn*," Merlin exclaimed, in alarm.

Recognising the man in front of him, Joel lowered his hands. "Sorry, Merlin," he apologised, "You gave me a bloody shock there."

"You bloody gave me one too," Merlin told him, crossly, "I've already 'ad one person thumpin' me, recently. I'm not up for a repeat performance. Let's just finish our run in peace, shall we?"

As the two men picked up their jogging pace again, Joel seemingly intending to continue listening to his portable entertainment, Merlin ventured, "I guess you're lookin' forward to ridin' Altimeter this afternoon. 'e's a good 'orse. Beaten Katseye twice now, 'e 'as. Come on a bit since you started ridin' 'im, goin' by 'is past form."

Joel sighed and pulled the wires from his ears, saying, "Katseye will win this afternoon, Merlin."

"You sound very confident," Merlin said, taken aback by the certainty in Joel's voice.

"I am," Joel replied, "You'll make sure of it, Merlin, won't you?"

Suddenly increasing his running pace to a sprint, Joel left Merlin behind.

*

The Silver Ghost had been neatly parked in a reserved space. There was no further sign of the two passengers whom Gray had seen emerging from the rear doors of the expensive vehicle. One of them had been a grim featured, grey-headed man wearing a dark suit over which he had quickly shrugged a belted coat and then clamped a fedora hat onto his head. A small woman wearing a fur hat on her blonde hair had stepped silently out behind him, smoothing down her tight red dress and fastening up a short coat made of the same fur as the hat. She wore red shoes with tall stiletto heels.

"That's Mr Lowry and his snazzy rented bird," Sheryl whispered, as they watched the couple disappear in the direction of the Centaur entrance to the racecourse, "They're out of the road now, so we can have a word with our Ritch."

The uniformed driver of the Rolls Royce had moved from the front seat and was standing alongside the car, which was attracting admiring glances from the other car park users, even those who were no strangers to pricey transport of their own. Ritch seemed relieved to see Sheryl approaching him, although he looked suspiciously at her companion.

"This is Gray, Ritch luv," Sheryl explained, "Our distributor in this area."

"Shouldn't he be distributing something then?" Ritch growled, directing a hostile glance towards Gray, "The gaffer'll kill me if he finds randoms nosing round his car."

"What's eating you, then?" snapped back Sheryl, equally rudely, "Lost some cash on the horses, have we?"

Ritch ignored the remark and said, "I need to get to an offy, Sher. The bar's out of that Irish stuff he likes. He drank most of it on the way home on Tuesday. Threw a wobbly when he found out I hadn't topped it up before this morning.'

"We can go and get it for yez," Sheryl offered, soothingly, "What sort is it?"

"Lougheven," Ritch answered "Costs a packet. You better try one of those posh supermarkets for it."

"Lougheven?" Gray broke in, suddenly finding his voice, "I've got some of that in my car if you want it."

"What are yez doing with quality booze like that?" asked Ritch, disparagingly, "Sure it's the same stuff?"

"Course I'm sure," replied Gray, becoming annoyed, "You can check the label on the bottle. It was a prize, that's how I got it. I don't like the bloody stuff. You can have it for nothing if you let me have a look round the motor. Don't worry, I won't damage anything. I'm a car mechanic, I know what I'm on about with cars."

After further acrimonious discussion, it was agreed that Sheryl would return to the Peugeot in the field to fetch the bottle of Lougheven whiskey whilst Gray would grudgingly be allowed by the ill-tempered Ritch to admire the engine of the luxurious car.

*

Sam had driven alone in the Audi to Cheltenham following the departure from Sampfield Grange of the small horsebox containing Katseye. The Dicks stable had no runners that day and Sam's cousin Gilbert's interest in the Festival had been confined to the day of Curlew Landings' race.

Sam had enjoyed the peace of his solitary journey. Sam and Frank Stanley had both been invited to join the Garratts in their box, in which Niamh Foley and her daughter Feanna were also to be guests. Arturo Ardizzone and Meredith Crosland, Katseye's present and past owners, would be joining them all in the parade ring prior to the first race. Stevie Stone too would be at the race meeting in her online tipster role. The invisible Essex lad Jayce and the piping Tabby Cat had cautiously tipped Katseye to win the opening race. Notwithstanding this expert feline advice, most of the big bookmakers now had Altimeter as the 3/1 favourite whilst Katseye was shown at the longer odds of 4/1.

Noticing with surprise that a nearby gleaming Rolls Royce apparently required attention to its engine, Sam slid the less flamboyant Audi quietly into the Owners and Trainers carpark. Getting out of the car, the normally phlegmatic trainer found himself suddenly nervous. Frank had told him to make sure that Katseye won his race today.

How the hell, Sam thought, can any trainer do that?

42

The Cheltenham Festival
Thursday Afternoon

"Afternoon, Stevie, fancy doin' an interview with me?" asked Merlin, persuasively, he hoped.

It was midday, and Stevie Stone was standing alone for once alongside the entrance to the parade ring by the weighing room, checking messages on her mobile phone. She had not noticed Merlin coming towards her until he spoke.

"Sure," Stevie answered, sliding the phone into her coat pocket, "What do you want to talk about? Your girlfriend, your taste in clothes, or how you rate the horses you're riding today and tomorrow? The Smart Girls are interested in all these topics."

Merlin had always felt slightly wrong-footed by Stevie Stone's eccentric approach to her role as an online racing tipster. Most of those who followed the calling were interested only in the prospects of the horses and whether any money could be made from betting on them. The personal backstories of the jockeys were usually left untold.

"If I answer some questions about Tabikat's chances of winnin' the Triple Crown tomorrow," he offered, carefully, "Will you do me a favour in return?"

"What's that?" asked Stevie, warily.

"Joel Edge, Altimeter's jockey," Merlin said, "What do you know about 'im? And the Parry yard?"

"Don't go there, Merlin," Stevie told him, firmly, her expression becoming deadly serious, "Mr Stanley's looking after Joel Edge. And the racing authorities will deal with Dean Parry when the time is right. Your job is to do the riding. Just stick to that."

"OK, keep your fancy 'air on," Merlin replied, aggrieved at Stevie's dictatorial tone of voice.

"Don't worry, I will," Stevie told him, "Now then, are you ready to answer some questions about Tabikat before the Smart Girls think you're chatting me up and shop you to Sadie?"

*

Jackie's heart thumped painfully as she started to take a relaxed Katseye down the soft, black surface of the long, downhill path towards the pre-parade area. Ahead of her was the imposing iron grey bulk of Altimeter, being led by Dean Parry, the trainer himself, who was accompanied by a silent girl wearing the numbered armband which identified her right of entry into the saddling area with the horse. Clearly the Parry yard wanted to be sure that no-one would interfere with their runner today. Behind both horses walked Kye, taking care to keep out of Dean Parry's line of sight. Not that the preoccupied Dean would be likely to recognise him, but Kye was not keen to renew their acquaintance just at that moment.

Mr Sampfield was already waiting for his two staff in small pre-parade area with its curved line of stalls fronted by an oval lawn. On the path around the grass, lively rival Petit Zazou was already stepping forward enthusiastically with his handler. Katseye seemed uninterested in the large assembly of spectators gathered on the viewing steps, opposite the saddling boxes, and the Sampfield Grange team were soon happy that their runner was ready to go into the main parade ring.

"Well done, Jackie," Sam told his young groom, "Katseye looks magnificent today. He should win best turned out, at least."

Sam opinion certainly seemed to be shared by many of the spectators, eager for the racing to get under way, who had gathered around the white rails of the parade ring. At the winners' enclosure end, many more people stood in the bright air, some of them even wearing sunglasses as the sun illuminated the busy scene from a now cloudless sky. More spectators watched from the shaded galleries of the Princess Royal Stand whist others thronged along the already noisy terrace above the curved steppings.

Katseye was the third of the nine horses to come into the famous parade ring, Jackie marching briskly forward holding the leather of the lead rein in a black gloved hand. Already she could hear the voices of Katseye's admirers following the horse's progress along the red coloured path, "Wow, that horse is so gorgeous, which one is he... That one looks like the king should be on his back not a bloody jockey... That big black one with the two little stars there, he's Katseye, he's the half-brother of Tabikat, the one that's in the Gold Cup tomorrow..."

Catching sight of the big viewing screen at the North end of the parade ring, Jackie confirmed that Katseye was still second favourite after Altimeter, but Jackie did not care. She knew for sure that her beloved Big Kat was the best horse in the race, whatever the bookies and the betting public thought. Katseye clearly agreed with his diminutive groom, as he stepped proudly forward with his usual regal air, accepting all the admiration as his rightful due.

Mr Sampfield, Jackie saw, was now standing with Mr Ardizzone and Mrs Crosland in the centre of the carefully mown lawn. Mr Ardizzone wore mirror sunglasses but was otherwise soberly dressed in his usual black coat, a green and white pin showing in the lapel being the only concession to his racing colours. Mrs Crosland was today dressed in a long emerald coloured coat decorated with extravagantly large moulded metal buttons. Soon afterwards Niamh and Feanna Foley came to join the group, accompanied onto the lawn, rather to Jackie's surprise, by Colonel Stanley. Kye was now standing with Sadie by the horsewalk exit beneath the viewing screen and gave Jackie a thumbs up signal as she and Katseye walked grandly past.

The knowledgeable TV presenter who was roaming the ring with her microphone and accompanying mobile recording unit had succeeded in telling her viewers about most of the beautifully turned out horses as they gradually turned onto the path around the ring. Trying to get a word out of their nervous owners and trainers had proved more difficult. Arturo Ardizzone had been one of the more forthcoming, stating smilingly that he had every confidence in Katseye running a good race today. Altimeter's owner had been similarly confident. The experienced presenter thanked both men, knowing that they were used to dealing with media questions and would say nothing that would be of any real use to her. At least the viewers had seen at close quarters the owners of their two favourite horses for the race.

Merlin ap Rhys's attention, as he came down the steps of the weighing room, was on joining the connections of Katseye. Merlin had complied, rather grudgingly, with Stevie's fierce instruction not to 'go there' with Joel Edge, who had been the first of the nine jockeys to go outside to meet his own party. Merlin could see Joel walking towards a small group to Merlin's left, which consisted of an older man in a belted grey coat, who Merlin knew now to be Altimeter's owner, the scrappy-bearded trainer Dean Parry, and – Merlin had to suppress a start of recognition – an attractive, slim woman dressed in a fur jacket and red stilettos, standing silently beside them.

"So, I was right about it bein' the Parry yard," thought Merlin, trying not to look directly at the oddly-assorted group, "That bloke's too old to be 'er brother. 'e must have booked 'er for the day."

If Lara had noticed Merlin coming into the parade ring, she gave no sign of it. The man who had paid for her services was too engrossed in his conversation with the trainer to give Lara any attention, but, when Joel Edge joined them, Merlin saw that Lara greeted the jockey by offering him a small and tense smile.

A few minutes later, after Mr Sampfield had legged him up onto Katseye's broad back, Merlin found himself being carried past the Altimeter connections. The trainer and jockey were waiting for their grey horse to approach, the grim-faced owner standing behind them. Lara had taken up a position a little further along the path from the three men, which ensured that Altimeter walked past her immediately after Joel had mounted.

"Be careful, Jo," Merlin was sure he heard her say from behind him, but her voice had been so quiet that he was not sure that he had not simply imagined it.

*

The nine strong field for the race officially known as The Golden Miller, after the prolific chaser of the 1930s, set off promptly at the designated post time of 1.30pm in bright sunshine on the two and a half mile journey along Cheltenham's New course. Had it not been such a serious contest, it might have felt like a schoolboys' reunion, with Katseye, Altimeter, Petit Zazou, Cloud Atlas and Milk Run all settling together in mid field. The remaining four horses surrounded them neatly, two of them companionably racing up ahead, the other two sitting off the pace just behind the main group.

The first fence came up quickly as the runners forged onwards along the section of the track across the centre of Prestbury Park. All the horses cleared the obstacle without incident, although Petit Zazou, travelling keenly next to Katseye, was pulling hard, his jockey having to exert himself to keep the horse from chasing up with the leading pair.

Katseye's connections had remained standing in the parade ring to watch the race as it played out on the large double-sided screen towering above the concourse at the far end of the parade ring. Most of the spectators had surged off to the viewing areas alongside the track as soon as the horses had gone down to the start, each runner having been named in turn by the racecourse commentator as they cantered out. Sam had been relieved to see that Katseye and Merlin had looked well balanced and relaxed. Katseye and Jackie had, as he had predicted, won the prize for the best turned out horse.

The pace continued to be steady as the talented field crossed smartly over the intersection with the other part of the dual course, progressing towards the sweeping left-hand turn into the home straight for the first time. They travelled quickly uphill, crossing four more stiff fences as they climbed higher, the sound of the tightly packed masses in the stands becoming ever louder as the horses drew near.

"McKerrow leads the field as they make the turn, Layamon's Song in close order behind," announced the amplified commentator, somewhat unnecessarily, as the nine horses swept past the Best Mate and Dawn Run stands, a roaring cheer going up as they did so, "Petit Zazou is still running keenly in the centre, Katseye and Altimeter in behind him. There's little between the rest. The pace stays steady as they go out into the country where four fences await them in the back straight."

Katseye's connections in the parade ring were silent as they concentrated on watching what everyone recognised was about to turn into a highly competitive race. Niamh Foley, dressed in a brightly coloured quilted jacket, appeared to be her usual composed self. Feanna was standing thoughtfully by her mother's side, following Katseye's efficient progress over the fences. Sam was keeping a close eye on chief danger Altimeter, who was taking his jockey smoothly over the tough obstacles, the rider himself hardly seeming to move a muscle. Arturo Ardizzone remained quietly impassive behind the mirror glasses.

Stevie Stone, having greeted Meredith Crosland with a cheery wave, was standing alone now in the almost deserted Press area, her iPad temporarily stowed in a leather satchel. Stevie was acutely aware that Jayce and Tabby Cat had tipped Altimeter to win the race and had prudently decided to keep her distance from the Katseye party. She was, though, secretly willing the imposing black horse to run into first place for his connections that day.

As the horses ascended the slope at the far end of the back straight, the pace suddenly lifted and the field started to string out. Clearing the ninth fence, an open ditch, Joel Edge wordlessly pressed the still cruising Altimeter into the lead. Merlin, though, had been ready for the move.

"We're goin' with 'em, *bachgen*," he told Katseye, pushing the big horse forward. Katseye flicked a black ear and silently engaged another gear.

Jackie, positioned with the other grooms at the top of the horsewalk, held her breath as Katseye came up alongside Altimeter. The early leaders started to drop back through the field as the tempo of the race became faster. When the field turned the corner and started to come back down the hill, Jackie heard the commentator call, "Katseye and Altimeter go into the lead together. McKerrow has surrendered tamely and is being passed by Petit Zazou who is on the tails of the leaders."

Although the field continued to separate, the order had not changed when the leaders approached the second last fence up the hill of the home straight. The two horses which had remained in the rear throughout the race had been eased down and pulled up once it had become clear that they could not live with the strong pace now being set by Altimeter and Katseye. The game Petit Zazou chased them hard, his jockey working furiously, with a determinedly galloping Cloud Atlas the only other runner still in realistic contention for a place.

Clearing the second last, Merlin thought he heard Joel Edge alongside him say something to his horse. The roaring of the huge crowd ahead was now loud in Merlin's ears above the snorting of Katseye's breath coming rhythmically through the horse's flared nostrils. Merlin suddenly realised that Joel was speaking to him rather than to Altimeter.

"Merlin, I'll be out at the last," Joel gasped, urgently, "Make sure you win."

The commentator's excited voice rose in pitch as the two horses approached the final fence opposite the tented village.

"Altimeter and Katseye reach the final fence together. And ... Altimeter's fluffed it! The horse put in an extra stride! A misunderstanding between horse and jockey. Joel Edge has gone right to the buckle end. He's done well to stay on board. It's handed Katseye the advantage on the run in!"

A shocked gasp of horror from the assembled spectators echoed into the huge stand roofs and broke like a wave onto the course at the sight of the usually flawless Altimeter crashing through the top of the last obstacle, landing awkwardly and nearly unseating his black and red shirted jockey, who stuck like a limpet to the saddle, quickly gathering up the reins which had been pulled through his gloved hands.

Merlin was quite sure that Altimeter was still close on his heels as he urged Katseye onward up the run in, both horse and rider straining every sinew to ensure they stayed ahead.

"Katseye wins the opening race!" announced the now more formal tones of the commentator, "Altimeter is a close second, third is Petit Zazou. And the fourth placed horse is Cloud Atlas."

Merlin pulled Katseye to a halt and sat back on the tiny saddle, as Joel Edge brought a steaming Altimeter alongside briefly to congratulate him. Merlin could not fathom what had just happened. The incident at the last fence had been no mistake. Joel Edge had let Merlin and Katseye win. But why? Had someone paid him to throw the race?

*

Whilst Merlin was responding to the questions of the excited on-course TV presenter, Altimeter, Petit Zazou and Cloud Atlas were being brought by their jockeys into the winners' enclosure to stand in the places marked with the numbers which indicated their respective placings in the race. Enthusiastic spectators were quickly gathering on the steppings just above them, waiting to welcome the popular victor into the parade ring.

Sam, Arturo and Meredith had hurried away from the others to wait at the entrance from the horsewalk from which Katseye would soon emerge to be greeted by his happy fans. Standing in wait by the winner's position were a strangely composed Niamh and Feanna Foley with an equally undemonstrative Frank Stanley, who had moved slightly apart from them. Stevie Stone had rushed around from the Press area to watch proceedings from the other side of the parade ring rail, locating herself close to the positions allocated to the winner and the second placed horse. Sadie and

Kye had somehow joined the party in the parade ring, ostensibly to offer help to Jackie, should any disturbance arise, as had happened on the last occasion that Katseye had been in the winners' enclosure.

Amidst enthusiastic cheering, Katseye and Merlin paraded triumphantly down the centre of the lawn towards their designated spot, Arturo Ardizzone punching the air, his fedora hat becoming dislodged to one side as he took hold of Katseye's bridle. Sam was calling up his own congratulations to Merlin, his voice hardly audible above the excited cheers of the surrounding supporters.

As the group attending Katseye approached the point at which Merlin could dismount, and the horse would be covered with the winner's sheet and allowed a drink, an out of place movement caught Sam's eye. The owner of Altimeter, looking thunderous, had clearly been berating Joel Edge for the error at the last fence, with the result that the jockey, having unsaddled the horse, had turned away without comment to go towards the weighing room. Evidently remembering that he was in public view, Nathan G Lowry had now composed his angry features into a forced smile and stepped forward to offer his hand to the approaching Arturo Ardizzone.

Niamh Foley also stepped forward and barred Nathan G Lowry's way.

"Do you remember me, Gearoid?" Niamh said, her voice raised as if in challenge.

The man Niamh had addressed by the unfamiliar Irish name stopped where he was, obviously wrong footed by the sudden intrusion.

"Of course, Mrs Foley, you are the owner of Tabikat," he answered, with forced politeness.

"You well know that I am Enda's widow and this is his daughter," Niamh corrected him in a louder tone, her forcefully spoken words beginning to attract the attention of those standing nearby.

"I am glad to meet you both," Nathan G Lowry replied, his body language showing his discomfort in the face of Niamh Foley's confrontational stance, while she continued to block his way, "Perhaps you would kindly allow me now to congratulate the winning owner?"

Niamh did not move. More people were turning to stare in the direction of the unfolding incident. Katseye and Merlin had come to a halt where they were, the position of the two speakers effectively preventing the horse from moving into the winner's place. From his vantage point on the horse's back, Merlin caught sight of Joel Edge standing still, holding his saddle and staring back at his connections. Lara had slipped away from Nathan G Lowry's side and had walked quietly to stand alongside Joel.

The connections of the placed horses were all now looking at the confrontation, as it seemed to have become, between the mild-looking lady with her Southern Irish accent and the stern, grizzle-headed man in whose deeper voice could be heard something of the same intonation. The nearer of the spectators could also see that something unusual was happening and a growing silence began to fall around the couple.

Sam, concerned and puzzled at Niamh's strange behaviour, tried to walk forward to speak to her, but instead found his arm held by Frank Stanley, who, when Sam turned questioningly toward him, shook his head. Arturo Ardizzone stood stock still by Katseye, staring at Nathan G Lowry, Meredith Crosland and the Sampfield Grange staff clustered behind him. Merlin seemed frozen in his saddle above their heads.

"Let the lady 'ave 'er say," Arturo said softly, the mirror glasses and the Italian accent adding an air of menace to his voice which might in other circumstances have seemed theatrical.

"It was I who telephoned the Samaritans that day," Niamh stated in a clear voice, staring the man she had called Gearoid full in the face.

There was a pause before Nathan G Lowry, his face suddenly suffusing with angry colour, replied, under his breath.

"What are you telling me, Niamh Kennelly?" he asked, "That you are a traitor?"

The TV presentation team had soon realised that something more interesting than the usual polite congratulations between owners and trainers was going on in front of them, and had directed their mobile cameraman away from Katseye and his supporters. The camera was now trained on the older couple who stood staring fixedly at each other as if in a spotlight in the packed arena, the big black horse towering above them.

"You are a murderer, Gearoid," Niamh told him, loudly, "Your soul is soaked in the blood of my husband and that of the people who died over thirty years ago in Fermagarrick. Enda was murdered not because of Eoghan's fault but because of what I did that day."

Niamh's voice started to shake. Nathan G Lowry stared at her, his body rigid. No-one moved. It was as if a video player had become stuck at a single frame.

Then Niamh suddenly collapsed, her bright jacket falling to the ground like a dead and bloodied bird, and the world started to move again.

*

The second race of the afternoon had been due to start at 2.10pm but eventually had to be delayed by half an hour. Two green-uniformed paramedics and a doctor who had been already close to the parade ring had quickly attended the prone Niamh Foley as she remained lying completely still on the ground, the compact figure of her daughter crouching by her side. The winners' enclosure and the nearby steppings were cleared of horses and

417

people as soon as could be achieved by the efforts of the nearby stewards working with two armed police officers who arrived promptly to help. Niamh, Feanna and the medical staff were quickly surrounded by the green screens normally used on the racecourse itself. The prizegiving for the Novices' Chase was abandoned and would take place alongside that for the next race,

A quick decision was taken to summon an air ambulance to take the victim, who was later said to have suffered a fatal cardiac arrest, to the nearby Gloucestershire Royal Hospital. A yellow helicopter, manufactured, appropriately enough, by Ardua Industrie S.p.A appeared overhead the racecourse with commendable speed and landed neatly in a clear area in the centre of the racecourse. A young doctor dressed in a flying suit ran from the smart rotorcraft and oversaw the removal of a stretchered figure from the now deserted parade ring, two paramedics carrying it over the crossing point on the home straight of the track. The thousands of spectators who witnessed the unprecedented and dramatic activity were unsure whether to be shocked or fascinated by the vision of the helicopter lifting from the grass with its seriously ill patient on board.

The TV racing presentation team, realising that they had a breaking news story in front them, had hovered as close as possible to the green screens, as the ring based racing reporter had attempted to get a word with Nathan G Lowry.

"Can you tell us what happened, Mr Lowry?" she had asked, shoving the TV racing channel microphone under the silent owner's nose as he had stood waiting to be allowed to leave the parade ring. One of the armed police officers had spoken to him briefly, telling him not to leave the racecourse, as a witness statement would be required from him.

"I have no idea," Nathan G Lowry had told the reporter, politely, knowing that it was important that he remain calm and appear to be being helpful, "I think the lady mistook me for someone else."

"She called you a murderer, Mr Lowry," the interviewer had insisted.

"As I said, she obviously mistook me for someone else," Nathan G Lowry had replied firmly, "Now, please excuse me, I have to check on the welfare of my horse."

After both Gerry and the stretcher accompanied by the heli-med doctor had left the parade ring, the screens had been folded up and taken away and the parade ring had begun to return to normal ready for the next race. No-one had noticed that there had been one additional green uniformed paramedic walking away from the winners' enclosure.

*

Nathan G Lowry sat rigid in the deep seat of the Rolls Royce trying to order his chaotic thoughts. There was no sign of his escort Lara, which was just as well, as he did not want her there. He had sent his puzzled driver away, telling him to return in an hour.

The head of the man once known by the code name Gerry pounded with fury. That the colourless Niamh Foley, or Niamh Kennelly, as he had first known her, had been the source of the warning telephoned to the Fermagarrick Samaritans, was something he had never even considered. The realisation that she had not only recognised him but knew his real name and identity was an even worse shock.

But in truth, he reassured himself, it was just Niamh Kennelly's word against his. His present respectable identity as a businessman and racehorse owner was his real identity now and investigation would show that identity to be watertight. If Niamh Kennelly did not die of her own accord, he would have to make arrangements to have her silenced, that was all.

Gerry reached forward for the cut glass decanter containing the Lougheven whiskey which his now absent driver had earlier topped up, as instructed. Nathan G Lowry needed to be his usual calm self before Cathal's Cheltenham Festival sale started at 6.15pm.

43

The Cheltenham Festival
Thursday Evening

In the light of the reported tragic death of Niamh Foley on the way to hospital in the ambulance helicopter, no-one was surprised when auctioneer Jack Carter announced to Cathal's assembled clientele that Lot 30, Katalyst, had been withdrawn from that evening's sale as a mark of respect to his breeder's family.

The cleverly planted speculation amongst those attending the sale was that the present owner of the colt, James Sampfield Peveril, deeply shocked by the sudden death of the woman who represented the owners of Tabikat, the Sampfield Grange trained horse due to run in the Gold Cup the following day, had taken the colt back to Sampfield Grange in order to consider his future. Some suggested that the colt would be sold back to the Foleys, others that James Sampfield Peveril would now keep the horse himself rather than sell him on, and still others that Katalyst would be put up for sale again once the Foleys had been given due time to mourn their tragic loss. As it was to turn out, however, none of these predicted outcomes was to prove correct.

Cathal's Cheltenham Festival sale otherwise proceeded smoothly, other than that a small number of people left the tiered auction arena on hearing Jack Carter's sad announcement. A scruffy man with long and greying black hair, who had spoken to no-one, and had been regarded with suspicion by other attendees, rose to his feet and walked to the exit without a backward glance. No-one could tell whether he was pleased or annoyed at the news of the withdrawal of the interesting lot. At about the same moment, a young man, accompanied by jump jockey Jenna Roberts, it was noted, threw down his sale catalogue onto his vacated seat and walked, apparently frustrated, from the marquee. Jenna remained in her place for a few minutes before leaving to join her companion, who could be seen waiting impatiently for her on the concourse outside. Sir Andrew Cunningham and his son Luke remained seated alongside their agent, who subsequently secured the purchase of two promising young horses on their behalf.

Those of the prospective buyers who stayed for the entire sale, a highly successful event from Cathal's viewpoint, were surprised to discover when they departed that part of the racecourse parking area had been cordoned off. In the centre of the cordon an opulent Rolls Royce Silver Ghost was visible, its doors standing open, the police and an ambulance in attendance. It did not take long for it to become generally known that the expensive vehicle belonged to Mr Nathan G Lowry, the owner of Altimeter, the man who had been in acrimonious conversation with Niamh Foley at the time she had suffered the ultimately fatal heart attack.

The evening radio news, which many of the same people later heard in their cars on the way home, further informed them that Belfast businessman and prolific racehorse owner, Nathan G Lowry, whose unexpected absence from Cathal's Cheltenham Festival sale had triggered a search for him, had been found dead in his Rolls Royce Silver Ghost at the racecourse. His driver was helping police with their enquiries.

*

Sam had returned alone to Sampfield Grange in the Audi shortly after the horsebox containing Katseye, accompanied by the still subdued Kye and Jackie, had left the racecourse. Sadie too had joined them in the cab, having left Merlin to complete his further two booked rides for the afternoon. Sam had waited at the racecourse just long enough to join Arturo Ardizzone in collecting the prize for Katalyst's win. Both men had refused a post-presentation interview, a decision which had been respected in the light of the earlier dreadful incident, as well as the racecourse management's wish to catch up on the delayed schedule for the afternoon. Frank Stanley had briefly spoken to Sam before he left, telling Sam that he would call at Sampfield Grange later that evening.

Kye and Jackie had arrived home to find Kelly and Lewis agog with scarcely suppressed curiosity at what had happened earlier in the afternoon. Sadie had left her two staff in the yard to look after Katseye and had joined her sister in the warm kitchen. The sun had been beginning to fall behind the house and the bright light of the strange day slowly fading to a damp and hazy glow.

"We saw it all on TV, Mrs Foley saying that man was a murderer," Kelly had exclaimed, her eyes, a lighter blue than Sadie's own, rounded with horror, "Then she fell down, right in front of you all, it looked like."

"It said on the news she'd had a heart attack," Lewis had added, not wanting to be left out, "Good thing that that medical helicopter came for her so quickly. It looked like that one that's up at Old Warnock airfield. It had the same registration letters on its side, G ARDI that is."

The conversation had ranged confusedly over the afternoon's upsetting events until it had been interrupted by the arrival of Mr Sampfield, who had briefly added to the dramatic horror of the discussion by informing his staff that Mrs Foley had died in the helicopter on the way to hospital.

"I shall go out to check on the horses for a while, and then be in my study, Lewis," Sam had said, firmly, "Kelly, Mr Stanley will be arriving later. We will eat together. He may want to stay the night, so I should like you to get a room ready for him. Sadie, join me in the yard now, would you? I know Amelia has been deputising for you this morning with Tabikat, but you and I need to talk about the plan for him tomorrow. Tabikat must continue to be our priority at the moment."

*

Frank Stanley arrived at Sampfield Grange shortly before 9.00pm, by which time the yard had been shut up for the night. Sadie had already gone up to her flat over the garage and had received a call on her mobile phone from Merlin, informing her not only of the death of Mrs Foley but also that of Nathan G Lowry, who had been found lying dead in his expensive car. The rumour now doing the rounds amongst the jockeys, stable staff and assorted racecourse hangers-on was that Mr Lowry had committed suicide by taking a massive dose of cocaine lethally mixed with several glasses of Irish whiskey.

"That's awful," Sadie had exclaimed, in response to this unpleasant news, "I suppose he was rich enough to afford to buy plenty of coke for himself. But, Merlin, who's going to come and see Tabsi run tomorrow now that Mrs Foley is dead?"

While Sadie was engaged in her conversation with Merlin, Frank Stanley was making himself comfortable on one of the large sofas in the drawing room, a large plate of roast beef sandwiches, a decanter of Scotch whisky and a crystal jug of water on the coffee table in front of him.

"I need your advice, Frank," Sam began, "I was wondering whether to contact the Foleys. I don't want to add to their problems. I imagine they'll not be travelling to join us tomorrow. I have already had Helen on the telephone, asking if there is anything she can do to help. Perhaps you have more information on the situation."

"The first thing you should know, Sam, and this information is for you alone," replied Frank, helping himself to a sandwich and a glass of water, "Is that Niamh Foley did not have a heart attack and is not dead. She is on a private flight to Bahrain which left three hours ago from Gloucestershire Airport. The air ambulance took her there and then returned to its base at Old Warnock. It is one of Arturo's experimental fly by wire rotorcraft. It operates by Artificial Intelligence, you know, very clever stuff."

Sam simply looked at his friend with exasperated resignation, waiting for him to go on. After a moment Frank continued, "Everything was going according to plan. Katalyst had been withdrawn from the sale, by you, as it was announced at the auction itself, where our person of interest Nathan G Lowry was expected to be present. Contrary to expectations, however, he did not arrive at the sale and that was because he was discovered to be dead in his car. The word has been put about that it was a suicide, but that's unlikely. The whiskey he was drinking contained a lethal amount of dissolved cocaine, a mouthful of which would have been enough to kill him. This was done deliberately, Sam. His chauffeur, Ritch Mavers, is in custody. He was responsible for keeping the bar stocked. We believe that he must have been paid by someone to fill the decanter in the car with the stuff. Nathan G Lowry had plenty of enemies as well as some vicious rivals for his criminal businesses."

"Lowry's the Fermagarrick bomber, isn't he?" asked Sam, "The one you have been trying to bring to justice all these years."

"He is," confirmed Frank, "And he is also the head of the drugs and arms smuggling operation which grew out of the original operation of which Callan Sullivan was part. The old Army colleagues you saw me with at Aintree racecourse last year helped confirm the identification. The difficulty we had in taking anything further was that most of those who knew who he really was were either dead or too frightened to speak out. That is why the Fermagarrick families got nowhere with their attempts to get justice."

"I guess from what you are saying that Niamh Foley was one of those who knew something but was too frightened to speak up," Sam commented, "I can understand why, considering that her husband had been murdered. What made her change her mind?"

"It was Eoghan Foley's decision to seek out the history of his horses and their association with Enda's murder and the attempt on his own life which made Niamh realise that she needed to tell someone what she knew," Frank replied, "She was afraid that Eoghan's actions would cause the bomber to fear that the security of his present identity was under threat. Eoghan, though, had no idea of Enda's involvement in the supply of materials to make the Fermagarrick bomb. So, Niamh spoke to Meredith Crosland when she was stayng at Enda's Farm."

"Meredith Crosland?" Sam could not help showing his surprise, "She seems a strange choice."

"Not really," Frank replied, "Meredith is Susan Stonehouse's sister, you remember. It was Niamh's way of contacting me without involving Eoghan. When Niamh revealed what she knew, I realised that it was the connection with Eoghan Foley's horses which would provide me with a way in. The plan relied on the help of a lot of other people as well as the Foleys themselves: you, Stevie Stone, Meredith Crosland, Arturo Ardizzone, even Merlin ap Rhys and Sadie Shinkins. And my own operatives of course."

"Jackie," suggested Sam, "And I suppose Isabella Hall. That's why she came back."

"There were a few others," Frank added, not inclined to elaborate, "But, yes."

"What Niamh did today was pretty dangerous," Sam commented.

"Just so, but it was about the least dangerous of our limited number of options," Frank contradicted his friend, "The confrontation took place in a public arena with thousands of witnesses, millions, in fact, if you include those watching the televised coverage. Lowry was unable to retaliate in any physical way to shut Niamh up, and, in the unlikely event that he did, there were armed police nearby. He himself could not be armed, given the security checks at the racecourse. The setbacks with his two horses had upset his normally carefully managed persona and put him off his guard. And, also, he genuinely had no idea that Niamh was the person who had called all those years ago to report the bomb. He just knew her as Enda Foley's wife, under Callan Sullivan's control, someone he had never regarded as any threat to him. And until now, Niamh has not been any threat. She knew that if she had spoken up, there would be reprisals. Remember, Sam, that she had four young children at the time Enda was killed and Eoghan had also been seriously injured. There would have been nothing to gain and everything to lose if she had revealed her knowledge."

"And now she has spoken out, her surest protection is to be dead, which as far as anyone but her family knows, she now is," finished Sam, "I understand that part of it, but what about Katalyst? You said it was announced that he had been brought back here to Sampfield Grange. But, as we both know, that is untrue. I have never owned the horse, whatever the official records may say, so I guess he still belongs to Eoghan Foley."

"Inasmuch as he belongs to anyone, Sam," Frank told him, "I believe that Eoghan Foley discussed with you how we had made use of the stories put about by the Jimenez and de Fontes families. Gerry, Nathan G Lowry, believed that Tabikat and Katseye were descended from this unusually bred stallion. But they are geldings and there will be no progeny from them. That meant that we simply had to invent the colt Katalyst."

"Are you saying that Katalyst does not exist?" Sam exclaimed so loudly that Lewis, hovering in the hallway outside the drawing room door, heard for the first time anything of what the two men had been discussing. Controlling his voice again, Sam continued, "I saw him myself in the barn at the Punchestown sale. Admittedly, that is the only occasion. There was a training record held here for him too which Isabella said came from the Meaghan yard."

"The Punchestown colt was one of Niall Carter's stock," Frank told him, "That's why we had to have his brother pull the animal out from the sale at the last minute. The training record was faked, thanks to some people's expert work both on the equine and technological front."

"So Katalyst vanishes back to Ireland into Eoghan Foley's imagination. You seem to have everything sewn up, Frank," Sam said after a pause.

"Regrettably not," replied Frank, shaking his head, "The person who killed Nathan G Lowry may well have done the world a favour by getting rid of him. His death will enable the police to start mopping up his evil criminal empire, something which has had to be put off until we completed our operation to expose Lowry as the Fermagarrick bomber. But all of us who have worked together to call this monster to account have absolutely no idea who is responsible for bringing about his death."

"Perhaps it's a ghost come back from the dead to haunt him," suggested Sam, wearily, "God knows, there must be enough of them."

Frank looked up.

"You know, Sam, old man," he said, slowly, "I think you're right."

44

The Cheltenham Festival
Friday

By 3.00pm, the mounting tension and excitement associated with the upcoming race for the Cheltenham Gold Cup had drawn thousands of the day's racegoers to the parade ring like iron filings to a magnet.

The mid-March sun had risen into a cloudless sky shortly after seven thirty that morning, casting weak shadows onto Prestbury Park as it had crossed the multiple grassy tracks and felt its tentative way into the empty brown seats of the deserted grandstand. The racecourse buildings and concourses had been already populated by scurrying early morning workers getting ready for the challenge of the venue's busiest and most exciting day of the year. The numerous restaurants and bars had been in efficient preparation for the hectic day's business. Stable staff and jockeys had been exercising some of the temporarily resident horses on the course whilst the inexorably moving sun had warmed their backs and dried the night's dew from the carefully maintained course. A light mist had arisen above the grass, but it was not destined to develop into the fog of a few days earlier.

Grounds staff had been out to check the hurdles and fences and to assess the state of the going. The racecourse marketing team had recorded the early social media video promotions and prepared the day's radio schedules. The TV presentation team had arrived and been in conference, planning for the morning's pre-race broadcast. The extensive car parks around the course had been still mostly empty, their line marked surfaces showing only a neatly laid out grid pattern.

As the gathering light had washed into the cool blue of the coming day's sky, the rumpled face of Cleeve Cloud had emerged golden against the broad green expanse of its hillside background. No wind had moved the curved trees visible on the ridge of one of the most recognisable backdrops to any British racecourse, tall aerial masts standing out like distant black sentries against the pale sky. The sun had continued to shift onward along its daily route, gathering power as it had travelled. A bright and dry late winter's day had soon been created, the perfect stage for the climax of the Cheltenham Festival.

The Cheltenham Gold Cup had always attracted greater interest from the general public than the many other events in the horseracing calendar, with the possible exceptions of the Grand National and the Derby. As a result, the mainstream media normally gave horseracing that day a little more attention than was usual in their sports coverage. Today, though, things were entirely different. The astonishing events of the previous afternoon, involving one of the racehorse owners, later found dead in his Rolls Royce, being publicly outed as the Fermagarrick bomber by the owner of the favourite to win the Cheltenham Gold Cup, who herself had then collapsed and died, had made the front pages of every newspaper in both the UK and Ireland as well as being the biggest trending topic on social media. Even the international press had picked it up, the early working picture desks in Australia and the Far East being the first to source and publish the photographs of the event which had been put up for sale by fortuitously located photographers. The images showed the small and brightly clad figure of Niamh Foley standing face to face with the stern-faced Nathan G Lowry in the smart winners' enclosure at Cheltenham racecourse, the imposing dark frame of a magnificent racehorse behind them with his jockey still on his back, an encircling crowd of nearby people captured with various expressions of puzzlement, astonishment and horror on their faces. The Jockey Club Press Office had been under siege since the story had broken.

Neither the print nor online media had had any difficulty in finding contemporary reports and images from the Fermagarrick bombing of nearly thirty-one years ago. The ghastly scene of the devastated town centre with its wrecked cars, demolished buildings and police officers futilely searching the rubble was recreated endlessly on televisions, computer screens and in breakfast table and commuter newspapers, the traumatic morning story progressing in company with the sun through the European media outlets into those of North America. Niamh's reference to the urgent call made to the Fermagarrick Samaritans in an attempt to give the town warning of the impending explosion was highlighted throughout the world.

The general consensus by the hastily composed and highly judgemental analyses which accompanied these images had been that Nathan G Lowry had committed suicide later that same afternoon in order to avoid being made to answer for his evil crime. **MURDERER!** had shouted many of the bolder tabloid-style headlines, echoing Niamh Foley's words. Others had picked up and highlighted the more harrowingly descriptive phrase **A SOUL SOAKED IN BLOOD**. Images of Nathan G Lowry's Rolls Royce and his two expensive looking homes, the one outside Belfast and the other in Cheshire, were produced as evidence of his vile character.

Had Niamh Foley been available to explain the basis for her frightening accusations, the press pack would no doubt have been already on her doorstep, notwithstanding the relative inaccessibility of the remote farm in South West Ireland. As it had been reported that she too had died, in her case as a result of a cardiac arrest, presumably brought on by the trauma of confronting the terrorist Nathan G Lowry, there was little to be gained by making such an awkward trip. Some of the Irish press did make the effort, only to find that the Foley family themselves knew no more about what had happened than had been reported in the media and wanted to be left alone to come to terms with the death of a much-loved family member. Other representatives of the news media made it their business to try to discover the current whereabouts of Niamh's daughter, Feanna Foley, who was understood to have been with her mother when the older woman had collapsed, whilst still others took themselves to the empty homes, and thence to the unforthcoming business premises, of Nathan G Lowry in Belfast.

There were, though, easier ways of grubbing for information, such as setting up camp at Cheltenham racecourse, or, after the day's racecard had been studied, at Sampfield Grange and the Parry yard. Most of the media chose one or all of those potential sources. Those selecting the Parry yard drew the shortest straw, as it appeared that Nathan G Lowry's horse, Bees and Mist, had been taken to Cheltenham racecourse the previous day and no-one still present at the yard had any knowledge of the affairs of the horse's now infamous owner. The staff at the yard were already under pressure as a result of the midnight flit of two Australian grooms and had been disinclined to be helpful to uninvited enquirers at their gates.

Those hacks choosing to sit outside the gates of Sampfield Grange had been met by a small woman who had arrived at the attractive country estate on a bicycle and had re-appeared a few minutes later to read out a prepared statement. This had unhelpfully said that the staff at Sampfield Grange had been very shocked by the previous day's events, that their thoughts were with Mrs Foley's family, and that they had no knowledge of the events and people to which she had referred. Although an instant barrage of questions had been fired off in response, it had soon been clear that there was no further information on offer.

Cheltenham racecourse had been self-evidently the most likely place for anything useful to be learned. The racecourse was where the action involving the horses and people closest to the principal players in the drama would unfold later in the day. The reporters from the racing press and the teams from the TV racing channels were already at the racecourse and stood ready to exploit their privileged positions to best advantage. Amongst this specialist group, there had been much speculation as to whether either Tabikat or Bees and Mist, or both, would be withdrawn from the Gold Cup in the light of the two recent deaths. Levy Brothers International's PR office, when contacted, had quickly confirmed that they intended Tabikat to run, whilst Dean Parry, the trainer of Bees and Mist, already at the racecourse, had stated that no-one from Nathan G Lowry's company, the officially registered owner of the horse, had instructed him to withdraw the existing declaration.

At Sampfield Grange, Tabikat had been quietly loaded in the early morning sunshine into the small horsebox, well out of sight of the now reduced number of reporters surrounding the closed entrance gates. Tabikat himself had walked, dignified and unruffled, up the short ramp, with Sadie, Jackie and the small songbirds which flitted about the Sampfield Grange yard in attendance. Kye and the teenage work riders had stood nearby, excitedly taking pictures on their mobile phones. The remaining equine residents, looking on from their stables, had viewed Tabikat's departure without interest, their only apparent concern being when they themselves would go out on their morning exercise.

"Wish your brother good luck," Jackie had called to an inscrutable Katseye as she had climbed into the cab of the lorry. Notwithstanding Katseye's silence. Jackie was sure that the clever horse had telepathically fulfilled her request.

Much as she might have liked to run them down, Jackie had managed to steer the lorry past those reporters and photographers still stationed at the yard gates, and the journey to Cheltenham racecourse had been completed without incident. Only when the vehicle had been turning into the racecourse entrance had Sadie realised quite how major a centre of attention Tabikat, and by extension Sampfield Grange, had now become. James Sampfield Peveril and his staff had expected and prepared for an elevated level of interest in their stable star in relation to his bid to win both the Gold Cup and the Triple Crown that day, but dealing with the attentions of the wider press was well outside their experience. Fortunately, the racecourse management had been better prepared, with the result that Jackie found the path of the lorry to the unloading area in front of the red brick stable buildings smoothed by the presence of uniformed security staff. Sadie wondered if Mr Sampfield, following shortly behind them with Mr Stanley in the latter's less recognisable vehicle, would receive the same treatment.

Unloading the unruffled Tabikat and leading him into the stableyard had been a nerveracking affair, characterised by mostly male voices shamelessly yelling unanswerable questions towards the unheeding horse's bemused attendants.

"Hi girls, over here, girls, that's Niamh's horse you've got there, isn't it? Did you get to know Niamh when she came to see her horse? Did she give you a heads up about the bomber? Is her horse going to win this afternoon? Who gets the money then?" were a few of the more comprehensible of the aggressive and ill-framed enquiries.

The subsequent arrival of Mr Sampfield and Mr Stanley had generated a renewed onslaught of similar questions. A nervous Dean Parry, already in the stableyard with Bees and Mist, had been less accessible to the pushy questioners, but it had soon become clear that any movement around the racecourse by anyone associated with the two horses would attract unwanted and disruptive attention. It had therefore been agreed that everyone connected with the Tabikat and Bees and Mist would remain in the stableyard until it was time to set out along the path to the pre-parade ring. The two horses would be taken down together, they and their grooms accompanied by security staff to prevent any unwanted disruption to their important journey.

Merlin and Joel Edge had fared little better than the trainers and their staff. Joel Edge had no rides other than that on Bees and Mist and had been able to stay in the safety of the weighing room building but Merlin had been booked to ride in the first two races, in both cases on horses trained by Justin Venn. Security around the weighing room, including the presence of an armed police officer, had been stepped up, but Merlin had nonetheless found himself subject to loudly shouted questions about Niamh Foley and her family from the nearby Press area on the steppings. Other jockeys had been supportive but there had been little any of them could do to take the pressure off the besieged man who was about to take the famous Tabikat into the most important race of his life.

Everyone involved had heaved a collective sigh of relief when 3.00pm had arrived.

Sam had never before met youthful trainer Dean Parry, but the two men had now found themselves thrown together by the strange circumstances surrounding the owners of their runners in the Gold Cup. Sam remembered that Dean's father, Josh Parry, had provided a reference for Kye when he had joined Sampfield Grange, but that was the only contact Sam had had with the yard. As the oddly assorted group, comprising the two horses and their band of human attendants, made ready to set off from the stableyard, Dean suddenly said, without preamble, to Sam, "Just so you know, Mr Sampfield Peveril, Misty is completely clean and always has been. They checked him last night and again this morning."

"Thank you for telling me," Sam replied, politely, not knowing how to respond. Frank Stanley, standing alongside them, said nothing.

When the little procession eventually reached the pre-parade area, halfway down the hill, spectators were standing several rows deep at the top of the viewing area waiting for the ten high-class Gold Cup runners to arrive in the saddling boxes. The presence of so many ordinary racegoers served as an effective deterrent to the trumpeting of intrusive questions but both Sadie and Sam felt happier once the saddling process was complete and Sadie was able to lead the still unperturbed Tabikat into the main parade ring, where a huge crowd of excited racegoers eagerly awaited them. People lined the rails and the grandstand galleries and squashed themselves together on the concrete steppings. Those few people not interested in the proper business of the next half hour were well outnumbered.

The beautiful light grey Bees and Mist was brought into the parade ring immediately behind the mahogany-coloured Tabikat by an older woman who looked rather unnerved by the frenetic atmosphere which surrounded them all. She nevertheless walked out proudly with the striking fairytale horse, who, fortunately, seemed to share Tabikat's dignified and calm temperament. The warm sun shone cheerfully on the ten gorgeously appointed horses as they walked along the rose-coloured path before their admiring public.

"That's Dean Parry's mother," Kye informed Lewis and Kelly as they watched the unfolding scene on the TV screen in the comfort of the Sampfield Grange drawing room, Lewis having deemed their usual perch in the kitchen, with its smaller television screen, too informal a location for such a momentous occasion, "I thought she'd gone when old Mr Parry retired."

Spectators soon noticed that the Sampfield Grange party comprised the tweed jacketed James Sampfield Peveril, and a tall man wearing a dark fedora hat who was accompanied by two young women. Eoghan Foley had called Sam that morning to say that Feanna was safely home at *Feirm Enda* and that no-one from the Foley family would be at Cheltenham that day. It had been decided that Tabikat's present owners, previously represented by Niamh, would now be represented by previous owner Susan Stonehouse's two daughters, Stevie Stone and Captain TK Stonehouse. Eoghan had made no mention of Niamh, during the discussion, simply thanking Sam for all his help.

"It has been my privilege, Genie. Please tell the owners that we shall do our best for them with Tabikat," was all that Sam had said in response.

The presence of Stevie Stone, the well-known online racing tipster, and the unfamiliar TK in the parade ring caused some questions to be asked amongst the TV presentation team in the parade ring until their relationship to the deceased Susan Stonehouse had been discovered. The story of how Susan Stonehouse's evidence at the Old Bailey had secured the conviction of a vicious gangster over three years ago was soon dug out and dusted off by the print and online media, ready to add to their armoury of sensationalist headline material in the event that Tabikat won the Triple Crown.

Although Stevie Stone was well known to Sam, he had met her sister only once before, when she had arrived unannounced at the racecourse two years ago by helicopter in the company of young Daniel Levy. After greeting Sam today with a formal handshake, TK, her long dark hair tied into a neat ponytail which lay down the back of her tailored dark green coat, now stood chatting quietly to Frank Stanley, whom she seemed to know well, both of them watching the ten athletic horses circling the parade ring. Stevie, meanwhile, suggested to a relieved Sam that she take charge of answering the questions of the determined looking television presenter who was making a beeline for their group.

"Good afternoon, Stevie Stone, racing tipster to the Smart Girls" the smartly attired young man with blond streaked hair began, rather flippantly, as Stevie positioned herself in his path, "It must be a novelty for you to be on the other side of the microphone. What do Jayce and Tabby Cat have to say about Tabikat's chances of landing the Gold Cup and the Triple Crown today?"

"The Smart Girls already have their money on Tabikat today," Stevie told him, promptly, "He's the 4/1 favourite, as you know, so there will be a bit of money to be made when he wins. Jayce's tips are available on our vlog for all the races on the card today."

"Your late mother used to own Tabikat, is that right?" asked the young man, trying to discourage Stevie from handing out more racing tips through the medium of his TV channel, which employed its own pundits.

"My mother and my sister owned him jointly," Stevie corrected him, "And we're all here today to witness Tabby Cat's namesake fulfilling his true potential. The Smart Girls' favourite jockey, Merlin ap Rhys, will be on board as a bonus. You can read all about him on my vlog."

At that moment, the presenter spotted Merlin ap Rhys himself confidently approaching them across the lawn, wearing the blue and gold starred silks of Levy Brothers International. Sensing that any question he asked Stevie would simply turn into a broadcast to Smart Girls, the presenter wished the Tabikat team luck and decided to find an owner who would not use the occasion as a PR opportunity.

Tabikat's increasingly nervy connections had only a few moments to talk amongst themselves before the bell sounded for the ten well-prepared jockeys to mount. With practised efficiency, Sadie brought Tabikat alongside the group, stirrups pulled down ready for Merlin to be legged up into the saddle by Mr Sampfield, who quietly said, "Good luck, Merlin".

As the magnificent horse, Merlin perched high on his back, disappeared along the horsewalk under the golden stone bridge which led to the Princess Royal Stand, the figure of Sadie now hidden by the pressing crowds, Sam, Frank, Stevie and TK, along with the rest of the world, could now do nothing more than watch.

45

The Cheltenham Festival
The Triple Crown

When Sadie later recalled the events of the day that Tabikat made his bid to win the Triple Crown, one of her clearest memories was of the pre-race parade which took place in front of the frenetically crowded stands.

The horses were all carrying the same weight, so their race numbers and corresponding positions in the parade were allocated in alphabetical order. Bees and Mist was at the head of the line, a chance casting of which any movie director would have strongly approved. The grey horse, so light in colour as to pass for white, was led out by the competent Mrs Parry, and looked as if he should have been carrying a legendary knight rather than the more ordinary looking Joel Edge, who was still wearing the black and red colours of Nathan G Lowry. Behind them was Champagne Cork, another grey, but darker in colour, followed by recent Irish success story, a bay horse called Gridlock. Fourth and fifth in the expensive line up were Inkspot, ridden by Jenna Roberts, and Less Than Ross, also owned by Nathan G Lowry. They were followed by Macalantern, who, as usual, had the annoying Aidan Scanlon on board. The remainder of the field was made up of Poseidon's Gold, a newcomer called Shuttlecock Sprint, old adversary Stormlighter, and, finally, the majestic Tabikat.

As Sadie led Tabikat up the grass slope in front of the cheering spectators, she heard the racecourse announcer proclaim, "And last to go out is Tabikat, ridden by Merlin ap Rhys, trained by James Sampfield Peveril. Tabikat is the winner of the Lancashire Chase and the King George VI Chase. Tabikat is ten years old and the current holder of the Cheltenham Gold Cup."

"This is brilliant, Merlin," commented Sadie, excitedly, looking up at the jockey sitting quietly above her, "Tabsi's so famous now."

"We'll see you back 'ere in a few minutes, *cariad*," Merlin replied, as Sadie released the rein to allow him to turn Tabikat to the left to canter down to the start, following in the hoofprints of the other horses, "We're goin' to knock 'em dead out there, aren't we, Tabikat, *bachgen?*"

The Sampfield Grange connections left behind in the parade ring could easily see on the giant viewing screen the large image of Tabikat and Merlin cantering without undue haste down the hill towards the start line for the three mile two and a half furlong race. The rays of the slowly sinking sun were still strong enough to pick out the gold stars scattered over Merlin's cobalt blue racing silks. The screen shot changed to show the alert horses grouping off the track, close to the start, the starter positioned on his steps ahead of them further up the lower part of the hill.

As the superior field was called forward for the start, a murmuring buzz of anticipation could be heard by those still standing in the parade ring. It emanated from the other side of the two large grandstands, where most of the spectators were now situated, standing cheek by jowl in every available space. Even those people occupying the restaurants and hospitality tents stopped what they were doing and paid attention. The racecourse commentator's customary cry of "They're off!" was met with a ringing cheer which could be easily heard by the jockeys and the officials and television support staff grouped by the start at the lower end of the course.

Sam felt as if his heart had jumped up suddenly into his throat as the drop of yellow flag sent the ten runners off towards the first of the twenty-two obstacles. He could feel the tension emanating from his three companions. Stevie Stone, who had watched so many horse races in the course of her work that she probably could have voiced the official commentary herself, seemed to be hanging onto the commentator's every word, her hands pressed together in front of her. Why were there no female race callers, Sam wondered, for no immediate reason. Stevie's sister, the oddly named TK, stood bolt upright and stock still, only her eyes betraying her reaction to what was unfolding on the screen. Sam could sense that even Frank was ready to ride every step of the race with Merlin. It was as if the four of them were to be suspended in limbo together for the next few minutes, powerless to intervene.

The same pictures were being viewed by Isabella Hall and George Harvey, who were sitting on the front edge of the compact sofa in the small living room of the cottage in Warnock. They held their breath as all the horses expertly cleared the first fence and motored confidently towards the second. Far away in South West Ireland, Eoghan, Caitlin, Feanna and young Enda were clustered in their farmhouse sitting room, willing Tabikat and Merlin to be successful. Even further away, occupying a capacious sofa in a large air-conditioned lounge in the Levy home in the modern sprawl of wealthy Manama, Niamh and her eldest daughter, Aiofe, sat transfixed by the same images, sent by satellite from four thousand miles away.

Sadie, standing in state of nervous anticipation with the other equally excited grooms at the top of the horsewalk by the finishing chute, could see the moving horses rapidly approaching them up the hill. On the viewing screen at the other side of the track, the runners could be seen pouring over the second fence, only a few lengths separating the entire field. The noise of the crowd behind her swelled to a roar, rippling to the other side of the track as the runners curved away to the left and passed a second group of equally enthusiastically packed stands. Those watching on screens everywhere were presented with a view of the impressive horses galloping towards the camera mounted on the trackside vehicle which drove along ahead of them, the well populated grandstands providing a panoramic and dramatic backdrop to the action. High up in their box at the top of the main grandstand Sir John Garratt and his wife Helen, with their fortunate guests, were lining the balcony rail to follow the race.

Completing the sweep of the turn, the colours of the jockeys' shirts made a cheerful pattern above the more muted shades of the horses' coats.

"They're approaching the third as they start to run downhill," intoned the commentator, "Gridlock still holds the lead followed by Poseidon's Gold. Tabikat in blue and gold and the light grey

Bees and Mist in black and red are together in behind, Macalantern and Inkspot just after. Then comes Champagne Cork and Less Than Ross, also in black and red colours, with the white hat. Stormlighter and Shuttlecock Spring are the back pair.

"And we've lost Shuttlecock Spring at the third! He's unshipped Mark McConnell. The horse is continuing after the others as they approach the fourth, the water jump, which they all take well, with Stormlighter slightly detached now from the rest. Back at the third, Mark McConnell's up on his feet."

Running down the familiar back straight, Merlin could see the fifth fence, the first open ditch, ahead of him between Tabikat's dark ears which were moving smoothly up and down in time with horse's long and confident stride.

"And Tabikat's stood off a mile from the fifth!" exclaimed the commentator, "Bees and Mist has taken it well too, but Tabikat lands slightly ahead."

Joel Edge and Bees and Mist soon cruised back by Merlin's side.

"You won't shake us off that easy," Joel called out, tauntingly.

"Wait an' see!" shouted back Merlin, adrenalin fuelling his exhilaration in the high profile and competitive race.

Tabikat and Bees and Mist continued to pound along toward the sixth and seventh fences, hot on the scudding heels of Poseidon's Gold just ahead. As the horses reached the top of the hill and began to descend around the turn, the field gradually began to separate. By the time the tenth fence was in Merlin's sight, Tabikat and Bees and Mist, still racing together, had passed the two leaders and were now out in front. Macalantern and Inkspot had also moved forward and were keeping up with them. None of the horses was as yet under any real pressure, although it was clear that those at the rear of the field would be unlikely now to catch the leaders, who were setting a deceptively challenging pace.

Back at the top of the horsewalk, Sadie found that Mrs Parry had come to stand beside her.

"You're Tabikat's lass, aren't you?" Mrs Parry said to Sadie, as the two women watched their respective charges clear the tenth fence, "Yours is the only one as'll see our Misty off."

But Sadie could not reply, all her efforts now concentrated on repeating the mantra "Tabsi, Merlin, Tabsi, Merlin" over and over under her breath, like the hoofbeats of the galloping runners.

The nine horses remaining in the race had now completed a circuit and were back at their starting point, ready to climb the famous hill towards the grandstands once again. Sam could see that Tabikat and Bees and Mist were now slightly ahead of the rest of the field, all of whom still motored along determinedly behind the leaders, not letting them get too far ahead. The runners took the two fences before the grandstand turn without difficulty, most running well within themselves, none having as yet hoisted any distress signals.

"This is a really strong field," Stevie Stone spoke aloud to no-one in particular as the Sampfield Grange group continued to follow the race from the relative calm of the parade ring, "Things are going to get interesting once they've completed the back straight fences."

Sadie was watching the retreating colours of the jockey's backs above the swishing tails of their horses as they tracked away towards the downhill run which marked the first part of the back straight. On the screen, all the horses continued to look full of running, their riders positive on their backs.

"The order remains unchanged as they approach the thirteenth fence," went on the commentator, waiting for something new to happen.

Merlin was conscious that his fellow riders were holding themselves ready to up the pace. Like Stevie Stone, he too expected that this would happen after the remaining field had cleared the final open ditch of the seventeenth fence at the far end

442

of the course. It was not important who made the decision, they would all go together, and some would find it easier than others.

"It's five out, and the pace is lifting," called the commentator, his voice rising slightly, "Merlin ap Rhys takes Tabikat out in front with Bees and Mist in close attendance. Macalantern and Inkspot follow. Early leaders Gridlock and Poseidon's Gold have dropped right back through the field. A good leap keeps Tabikat out ahead."

"Go, Tabikat!" shouted Stevie and TK simultaneously, the sudden sound making Sam jump. Frank stepped forward and stood beside Sam, putting his hand briefly on his friend's shoulder.

"There are four fences still to go in the Cheltenham Gold Cup," cried the commentator, just in case anyone might have forgotten what they were watching, "Tabikat and Bees and Mist have them on the stretch. Some of the runners are feeling the heat, Stormlighter's been pulled up. Champagne Cork too. There are seven still in contention as they approach four out."

"Come ON, Tabsi!" screamed Sadie, unable to contain herself. The other grooms were also becoming more animated as the leaders came into view at the bottom of the hill, the moving image on the screen opposite showing Tabikat still in the lead. The horse had his head a little lower now.

"A mistake at the nineteeth puts Gridlock out of contention," the commentator informed them, "There are three fences still to jump."

A collective groan rose from the stands as one of the horses suddenly pitched forward on landing after the third last fence, rolling onto his side, hooves flailing, his unlucky jockey thrown helplessly onto the ground.

"Less Than Ross has gone at the twentieth," shouted the commentator, "Horse and jockey are both up."

As Merlin and Tabikat straightened to tackle the home straight, Merlin could see the unforgettable scene of the heaving grandstands up the hill ahead of him, the collective noise of thousands of spectators echoing down the slope.

"Come on, Tabikat, *bachgen*," Merlin said quietly into the ear of his still strongly galloping horse, "You an' me, we're goin' to make 'istory now."

Sam held his breath as Tabikat cleared the second last. The tumultuous racket now being made by the spectators seemed to shake the fabric of the buildings to his right. Sam had spent many years carefully keeping his emotions in check, but the presence of Frank Stanley and the two excited young women beside him seemed suddenly to blow away some of his usual inhibitions. Sam could see that, barring accidents, Tabikat would certainly win the race. Bees and Mist was a good horse, but he was not as good as Tabikat.

"Go on, Merlin," Sam exclaimed aloud, "This is yours to win!"

Tabikat had never yet fallen in a race, but the pressure under which he and Merlin were now running as they approached the final fence was obvious to everyone. As Tabikat took off in front of the orange board at the foot of the obstacle, there was a collective intake of breath from the packed stands, as if the oxygen had been sucked from the atmosphere.

The dark shape of Tabikat, the white bulk of Bees and Mist behind, seemed to Sam to be held briefly in suspense over the final fence, two knights on a chessboard. Tabikat landed still ahead.

The run to the finishing line was over in seconds. Tabikat and Merlin, working together like an efficient machine, forged up the final section of the hill. Bees and Mist maintained the short distance between the two leaders but could not get to Tabikat, who crossed the line a length ahead of his nearest rival, Merlin standing in the stirrups and punching the air. Inkspot with Jenna Roberts finished two lengths behind them, followed by Macalantern carrying Aidan Scanlon. Poseidon's Gold and Gridlock were the only other horses to finish. Less Than Ross, having scrambled to his feet, came galloping riderless after them, ready to join in the celebrations.

The noise around the six finishers was deafening. It boomed and thrummed around the concrete of the main grandstand, enveloping the sweating horses and jockeys as they came to a grateful halt together at the top of the hill.

The other jockeys brought up their mounts to offer Merlin the congratulations on his win.

"Brilliant ride, Merlin," Jenna Roberts told him, excitedly, "That horse is something else!"

"None of my doin', then?" asked Merlin, cheekily, forgetting his annoyance with Jenna.

"Definitely not," was all Jenna said, adding, "All down to Sadie and Mr Sampfield."

"Well done, Merlin," said Joel Edge, clapping Merlin on the shoulder, "Never would have got past that horse of yours. Bullfighting horse, that one, isn't he?"

As Merlin looked aghast at the other jockey, Joel laughed and said, "Just kidding," before walking the tired Bees and Mist towards the nearby horsewalk ready to return with a delighted Mrs Parry to the second place spot in the winners' enclosure.

Before Merlin could work out how Joel Edge could know anything about the ridiculous stories surrounding Tabikat, he found a joyful Sadie at Tabikat's side. She had flung her arms around Tabikat's neck saying tearfully, "You clever boy, Tabsi. You've shown them all who's the best horse ever in the world."

"What about me, then?" asked Merlin, grinning down at her, "Don' I get a mention?"

Sadie looked up at him, her face beaming, "I know you're brilliant, Merlin, but Tabsi's the one whose name's going to be on the trophies".

"Can't argue with you there, *cariad*," replied Merlin, laughing, "Can't wait to see Mr Sampfield's face when we bring Tabikat into the winners' enclosure."

Over in the parade ring, Stevie Stone had grabbed hold of the hands of TK and Sam, shouting, "Come on Mr S-P and TK, we're going to meet them. I'm not waiting here. Are you coming, Mr Stanley?"

As the four of them hurried towards the exit towards the horsewalk, shouts of congratulations from the other owners and trainers following their passage, Sam could not believe what was happening to him. Frank Stanley had readily accepted Stevie's invitation and jogged along behind them, his hat in his hand, as Sam and Tabikat's two temporary owners ran together along the horsewalk.

Ahead of them at the top of the hill, almost drowned out by the cheering, the result was being announced.

"First, number 10, Tabikat. Second, number 1, third number 4, and the fourth placed horse, number 6."

Sam's progress along the horsewalk was slow, as many people, recognising him, called out to congratulate him and reached out to try to shake his hand. Stevie, TK and Frank were also included in the greetings, although only Stevie was recognisable to the racegoing public. The defeated horses passed them, walking slowly in the opposite direction down the slope, their jockeys and grooms adding to the congratulations offered to the increasingly overwhelmed trainer.

And finally, the magnificent dark figure of Tabikat, an ecstatic Merlin still on his broad back, a smiling Sadie by his handsome head, came walking steadily towards Sam as he made his way up the horsewalk in the late afternoon sun.

Epilogue

By the middle of April, the Sampfield Grange garden had come full circle once again. The reliable purple and yellow crocuses were nodding gently in the mild air, stretching their elongated petals up towards the sun, whilst the bright yellow of the familiar daffodils congregated in companionable clumps around the still damp lawn. The hedges alongside the flowerbeds were well populated with small and noisy birds which flitted importantly back and forth across the view from the drawing room window. The larger trees above the track glowed fresh green with strengthening early leaves.

The month which had passed since Tabikat had won the jump racing Triple Crown had been a busy time at the rural training yard. The triumphal picture of Tabikat entering the Cheltenham racecourse parade ring, Merlin with his arms raised above his head in victory, Sam, Stevie and TK walking beside the lordly horse, as Sadie led him to the winner's position in front of the steppings, had been featured on the front page of every newspaper and online news outlet. Frank Stanley, who had accompanied the group earlier, had declined the opportunity to be included in the momentous photograph, saying that this was not his achievement.

More extensive information had appeared in both print and online sports coverage, emphasising the extreme difficulty of the unique achievement by the Irish bred horse. Profiles of James Sampfield Peveril had been run in the more equestrian focused publications and, in Ireland in particular, Eoghan Foley's personal story had also been told. Merlin ap Rhys had merited plenty of attention and even Sadie had been the subject of interest, especially when her relationship with the winning jockey had been discovered. Fortunately, there had been no mention of bullfighting or mysteriously hidden ancestry in relation to the information given about Tabikat himself.

The exciting news of Tabikat's achievement had quickly displaced the incident with Niamh Foley and Nathan G Lowry from the news media, although this would certainly have made a re-appearance as the nation's top story had it not been for a new horror which had been considered at least as immediately newsworthy. Two young people had been found unconscious on a bench near Cheltenham racecourse exhibiting symptoms which had caused a Hazardous Area Response Team to be called out by the attending ambulance crew. A third person lying nearby on the ground had proved to have been tasered. Speculation had been rife that a nerve agent, concealed in a half empty bottle of vodka found beneath the bench, had been involved, all the more so when it had been revealed during an appeal for witnesses that the vodka was a hitherto unknown Russian brand by the name of *Prizrak*.

This latest incident would have had no bearing on life at Sampfield Grange had it not been for two things. The first was that Frank Stanley, who had been invited to stay for a few days at Sampfield Grange to join in the celebrations which had been organised at the rambling country house and in the nearby village of Charlton, had been called away and had unfortunately missed out on the partying. The second had been that one of the two Cheltenham park bench casualties had turned out to be a local man, Graham Colvin, the owner of Colvin's Garage in Charlton village.

Tegan Colvin, her employer Barnaby Vowles at The Sly Fox had told his enthralled customers, had returned home after accompanying her brother to the Cheltenham races, claiming that she had been unable to find Gray and his new girlfriend in the chaos which had enveloped Cheltenham on the evening of Gold Cup Day. Tegan had travelled alone on the train, she had said, trusting that her sibling was well able to take care of himself. Unluckily for Tegan, she had been quickly identified as the person who had called the emergency services on the morning following Gold Cup Day, having returned to the spot where she had for the previous few days been impersonating a charity collector whilst in fact dealing drugs. In her attempts to escape the scene that Saturday morning, she had used an illegally held taser on a member of the public who had stopped to help, a weapon which she had then thrown into the boating lake in Pittville Park before fleeing the scene. It had not been long before Tegan had been traced and arrested, the shocked community in Charlton those who knew him.

The second casualty had been identified as a known drug dealer from Liverpool called Sheryl Mavers, whom Lewis and Kelly had recognised as the person Kye had 'shopped to the bizzies' sometime in the past. Lewis and Kelly would have had more gossip than they knew what to do with during the previous month, had it not been for the fact that they themselves had become the centre of their own attention as a result of Kelly finding out that she was pregnant. This personal news had been much more exciting than anything that the scandal-grubbing newspapers could provide and had even threatened to eclipse Tabikat's amazing achievements.

Lady Helen Garratt too had brought news for discussion at Sampfield Grange. Now that the Air Ambulance training operation had been completed at Old Warnock airfield, Helen had asked her solicitor to make an application to the local planning authority with a view to establishing her cherished project to house and retrain retired racehorses on the site. The facility would meet the Council's required criterion of offering training and employment opportunities to young people in the local area, and, if residential facilities could be secured, also from inner city areas. Sam had quickly recognised the project as a chance to make good use of his mother's recent bequest and Helen had in turn suggested that the equestrian enterprise might bear the name of Geraldine Elliot Sampfield, who had been a friend of her mother and well known in the local Charlton and Warnock area.

Sadie had been thrilled to discover that she was to become an aunt and had been already making highly premature plans to secure a suitable pony for her niece or nephew. Merlin had been secretly amused by the news that Kelly and Lewis had clearly had more productive ways of passing their leisure time than raking up damaging gossip about those around them. Both Merlin and Sadie had benefited financially from Tabikat's success to the extent that

Merlin had decided to take a break from riding once the Aintree meeting and the Grand National were over, ostensibly to help Sadie to compete successfully during the final weeks of the point to point season. Indian Rocks was doing well in the points and Sadie was quickly becoming recognised as a competent amateur jockey.

Isabella Hall, having congratulated a smug Lewis and a now glowing Kelly on their news, had announced that she would be leaving the yard to join her partner in running a cycle business in the South of France. At Sam's request, Isabella had agreed to stay until a replacement office manager had been recruited.

The biggest change, however, to affect Sampfield Grange in early April was the announcement by Mr Sampfield that he planned to be absent for at least three months and would be leaving the yard in Sadie's charge. Mr Stanley, it appeared, had decided to retire from whatever job he had been doing and to spend time at his family home in North Yorkshire, to which he had invited his old schoolfriend to join him for a while.

Sam had broken this news to Sadie after she and Merlin had returned from a successful outing to a point to point meeting at Cuffborough. Sadie had had no hesitation in accepting her employer's proposal that she take sole charge of the pointers and hunters which would be living and training at the yard during this period. Tabikat and Katseye had done their season's work now Cheltenham Festival was over and had been turned away for the summer, once again going to Helen's family estate to join their eventers. Curlew Landings, much to Travis's delight, had been sent over to the Dicks yard, where he would be kept fit alongside their resident horses.

Frank Stanley had returned to Sampfield Grange that warm day in mid-April to finalise with Sam their plans to leave for North Yorkshire the following day. The two men had agreed to ride out together, as no horses were currently kept at the Stanley property. Jackie and Kye had tacked up Caladesi Island and Ranger Station that warm April morning and the two hunters were waiting patiently in the yard when Sam and Frank came out of the house together.

Sadie watched from her window as her employer and his companion made their leisurely way on the large bay horses up the familiar track which ran behind her flat. Merlin, having made himself ready to drive to Aintree racecourse, was sitting on the edge of the bed checking the messages on his mobile phone.

"It's nice for Mr Sampfield to have his old friend to ride with him again," Sadie said to Merlin, "My mum told us they were like brothers when they were young."

Merlin came to Sadie's side to peer out of the window after the departing riders. Not for the first time, he wondered at Sadie's, not to mention Lewis's and Kelly's, lack of perception about the people around them. But it was not his business to reveal Mr Sampfield's secrets and he doubted Sadie would have believed him anyway. Mr Sampfield and Mr Stanley would choose their own time to speak out.

"Come on, *cariad*," Merlin suggested instead, "We've just got time for a bit of fun before I go."

Even Merlin, for all his sharpness, could not have imagined the conversation currently taking place between James Sampfield Peveril and Frank Stanley. As the two stolid horses bore their riders easily up to the top gallop, Sam said to his friend, "Now that we are air gapped, to use your jargon, Frank, may I ask you a question?"

"Well, you may certainly ask," replied Frank cautiously.

"Niamh Foley," Sam went on, undeterred, "When she confronted Lowry at Cheltenham, she called him by his own name, something like Gerard, I believe."

"Yes," said Frank.

"And he called her Niamh Kennelly, not Foley," Sam continued, "That means, then, that they must have already known each other before Niamh married Enda Foley."

Frank remained silent.

"Genie and Enda had three more brothers, as I recall from what Brendan Meaghan told me," Sam told him. "Callan Sullivan recruited Enda to his .. er .. illegal activities and tried to draw in Genie too. My question is this. Might he not have recruited at least one of the other brothers as well?"

After a pause, Frank replied, "You're a good listener with an excellent memory, Sam. Gearoid Foley was indeed one of Eoghan Foley's brothers, the one nearest to him in age."

"As you know, Frank, I have no siblings," Sam went on, bringing the patient Caladesi Island to a halt at the top of the track, "But I find it impossible to understand how any man could be party to the murder of one of his brothers and the attempted murder of another."

"Gearoid was less than two years older than Eoghan," Frank said, quietly halting Ranger Station alongside his stablemate, "Gearoid had been in charge of the horses at the farm until Eoghan took his place. Gearoid shared Eoghan's passion for and talent with horses, but he was never allowed to realise it. After their parents died, Enda invested all his efforts in Eoghan's career as a jockey whilst Gearoid, a displaced and resentful young teenager, suddenly had to make his own way in the world. Enda was married and had a farm to his name, Eoghan had the promise of a career. Gearoid had nothing. As such, he was very easy prey for someone like Callan Sullivan."

"Does Genie know that Nathan G Lowry was his brother?" asked Sam, pointedly.

"It is almost forty years since Eoghan last saw Gearoid," responded Frank as the horses began to shift restlessly beneath the two friends, "And they were scarcely older than schoolboys then. So, no, Sam, Eoghan does not know, and Niamh will never tell him. Now Gearoid Foley and Nathan G Lowry are both dead and it is no longer my business to be concerned about either of them. You and I have better ways to occupy our time."

"I could not agree more," replied Sam, "And the first of them is for us to enjoy this morning's ride."